SILVERSWORD

A Medieval Romance

By Kathryn Le Veque

Print Edition

Text by Kathryn Le Veque
Cover by Kathryn Le Veque

Kathryn Le Veque Novels

Medieval Romance:

The de Russe Legacy:
The White Lord of Wellesbourne
The Dark One: Dark Knight
Beast
Lord of War: Black Angel
The Falls of Erith
The Iron Knight

The de Lohr Dynasty:
While Angels Slept (Lords of East Anglia)
Rise of the Defender
Steelheart
Spectre of the Sword
Archangel
Unending Love
Shadowmoor
Silversword

Great Lords of le Bec:
Great Protector
To the Lady Born (House of de Royans)

Lords of Eire:
The Darkland (Master Knights of Connaught)
Black Sword
Echoes of Ancient Dreams (time travel)

De Wolfe Pack Series:
The Wolfe
Serpent
Scorpion (Saxon Lords of Hage – Also related to The Questing)
Walls of Babylon
The Lion of the North
Dark Destroyer

Ancient Kings of Anglecynn:
The Whispering Night
Netherworld

Battle Lords of de Velt:
The Dark Lord
Devil's Dominion

Reign of the House of de Winter:
Lespada
Swords and Shields (also related to The Questing, While Angels Slept)

De Reyne Domination:
Guardian of Darkness
The Fallen One (part of Dragonblade Series)

Unrelated characters or family groups:
The Gorgon (Also related to Lords of Thunder)
The Warrior Poet (St. John and de Gare)
Tender is the Knight (House of d'Vant)
Lord of Light
The Questing (related to The Dark Lord, Scorpion)
The Legend (House of Summerlin)

The Dragonblade Series: (Great Marcher Lords of de Lara)
Dragonblade
Island of Glass (House of St. Hever)
The Savage Curtain (Lords of Pembury)
The Fallen One (De Reyne Domination)
Fragments of Grace (House of St. Hever)
Lord of the Shadows
Queen of Lost Stars (House of St. Hever)

Lords of Thunder: The de Shera Brotherhood Trilogy
The Thunder Lord
The Thunder Warrior
The Thunder Knight

Highland Warriors of Munro
The Red Lion

Time Travel Romance: (Saxon Lords of Hage)
The Crusader
Kingdom Come

Contemporary Romance:

Kathlyn Trent/Marcus Burton Series:
Valley of the Shadow
The Eden Factor
Canyon of the Sphinx

The American Heroes Series:
The Lucius Robe
Fires of Autumn
Evenshade
Sea of Dreams
Purgatory

Other Contemporary Romance:
Lady of Heaven
Darkling, I Listen

Multi-author Collections/Anthologies:
With Dreams Only of You (USA Today bestseller)
Sirens of the Northern Seas (Viking romance)
Ever My Love (sequel to With Dreams Only Of You) July 2016

Note: All Kathryn's novels are designed to be read as stand-alones, although many have cross-over characters or cross-over family groups. Novels that are grouped together have related characters or family groups.

Series are clearly marked. All series contain the same characters or family groups except the American Heroes Series, which is an anthology with unrelated characters.

There is NO particular chronological order for any of the novels because they can all be read as stand-alones, even the series.

For more information, find it in **A Reader's Guide to the Medieval World of Le Veque**.

TABLE OF CONTENTS

Author's Note

This book has a lot of things going on in it! Lots of old friends – Bose de Moray, Gallus de Shera, Maximus de Shera, Tiberius de Shera, Davyss de Winter, Daniel de Lohr… I could go on and on. It's one of those books that hit at the right time, historically, for me to include all of these Le Veque characters. We also meet many new characters, not the least of which is the heroine!

We also meet a new group of knights – men who are called the Guard of Six. They are the private guard for Henry III. Torran de Serreaux is the leader and I am fairly certain that I will do a spin-off series for this group, so keep an eye out for them in months and years to come. This book has quite a bit of politics in it – and the Lords of Thunder figure fairly prominently – so there is a heavy undercurrent subplot with them in it, but most of all, this story is about two people thrown together, unexpectedly, who discover they have feelings for each other.

A few things to note: Newington Priory, where our story begins, actually existed at one point but very little is known about it so I took the liberty of creating a history for it. You'll recognize names in this book (du Bexley from While Angels Slept, de Russe, du Bois, etc.). Remember in my world, there are no coincidences, so any secondary characters are somehow related to major Le Veque houses.

Let's also talk a bit about the cathedral that appears in this story. In my research, I learned quite a bit about the cathedrals of Coventry – the one in this story is St. Mary's Priory, which did exist at the time, but the big one, St. Michael's, wasn't built until about a hundred years after this story takes place. That's the cathedral that the *Luftwaffe* so happily bombed in World War II. Also, much of Coventry hadn't changed much until the twentieth century when infrastructure and other demands had developers bulldozing down Medieval homes to make way for modern structures (GASP!!). There are interesting stories about Coventry's lost Medieval structures that you can find on the web.

Bulldozers and cathedrals aside, I hope you enjoy the fact that Chad is different from other Le Veque knights – he's more apt to let loose, to show emotion, and to profess his opinion. He's not as straight-laced as some of them. He's much like his father, Daniel, who was also a bit of a funster, but at the core, he's a de Lohr, and that makes him a better man than most. At least, I think so. I think you will, too.

Happy Reading!
Kathryn

Many thanks to those that keep me going in this crazy world of publishing – Scott Moreland, Violetta Rand, Suzan Tisdale, Barbara Devlin, Tanya Anne Crosby, and the World of de Wolfe Pack authors, to name a few. What a fantastic network of support we have around us. Truly, much like those in this story, we are blessed with those we love – and are loved in return.

PROLOGUE

August, 1266 A.D.
Newington Priory, Kent

"YOUR FATHER IS dead and those who killed him are now after you."

A very big knight hissed those words in a deep and throaty tone, the same knight who had broken into the abbey with a company of cohorts who had scared the nuns nearly to death. There were dark dealings these days, with the politics of England bleeding into every aspect of life in the country.

No one was safe from the madness of King Henry after the battle at Evesham that saw Simon de Montfort murdered and his supporters scattered. No one was safe from the king and his sense of vengeance against those who stood with Simon, not even a novice nun whose family had sided with Simon against Henry's particular brand of royal incompetence. Therefore, when the knight muttered those horrible words, the young woman's heart leapt into her throat. No more than sixteen or seventeen years of age, her terror was evident.

"What do you mean?" she gasped. "What has happened to my father?"

The knight snatched her by the wrist and began dragging her behind him. He didn't seem inclined to answer her but he did seem intent on yanking her arm out of its socket as he towed her behind him like an unwilling barge.

They were quickly surrounded by the men he'd brought with him, men in well-used armor with weapons secured upon their body that were still caked with blood from recent battles. Not literally, of course, because poorly maintained weapons were more of a hindrance than a help, but the men who now closed ranks around them were men who smelled of death.

The stench filled the nostrils of everyone in the room.

They were in the smaller chapel of Newington Priory, the stark whitewashed walls and well-swept floors where the nuns held their daily prayers. The knights had broken down the door to the priory right after sunset, just when the nuns were beginning their prayers for Matins and would have created chaos had the Mother Prioress not kept her head.

Being that the woman was calm, her charges at least gave the illusion of being calm, and when the knight with the raspy voice demanded Alessandria de Shera, the Mother Prioress tried to question him on his need for the woman. Questions weren't well met and in order to prevent the knights, eight of them – and one with a very big ax – from doing something drastic, the very woman that they asked for stood up hesitantly and identified herself.

And that was where Alessandria found herself now.

"Please," she begged as the knight dragged her from the chapel. "Please tell me about my father. What has happened? Where are you taking me?"

The knight in the lead snapped orders to the knights around them and the men, as a group, bolted for the broken entry door and fled into the night beyond. The chapel of the priory was dimly lit from the spartan use of tallow tapers, creating a glow that was barely above a whisper, but that glow was like the brilliance of the sun once the knight dragged Alessandria out into the moonless night. It was darker than dark but for the two dozen soldiers milling about outside with heavily smoking torches in their hands, sending gray clouds into the blackness of night.

"You must not take her!" the Mother Prioress was shuffling after them, waving her hands. "She is protected by God!"

The knight who had a viselike grip on Alessandria came to a suddenly halt and turned to the old woman in the woolen robes.

"Did you hear what I said?" he asked. "This woman's father has been killed and those same men are after her. Her life is in danger and I have been directed to take her to safety. God would not be able to save her from the king's men who, even at this moment, are riding to claim her. They will be here very soon. What you tell them is your affair, but I would suggest you let them in to search the place. If you do not, they will burn the priory over your head and spit on your ashes."

The Mother Prioress, with her round pink face and browless eyes, appeared stricken with terror at the thought. "But why?" she begged. "Sir Knight, why can you not tell us what has happened? The woman you hold is in my charge. She is God's handmaiden."

The knight, who was clearly in battle mode, must have realized how overbearing he was coming across to these terrified women because his driven manner seemed to soften. His gaze drifted over the little priory, a charity priory that was supported by the local diocese at Rochester, with its centuries-old walls that enclosed a holy haven comprised of women who tended goats and grew herbs for medicinal use. The walls were made of wood, covered with thorny vines, and the door he'd had to break down with an ax was unimpressive to say the least. It had been a simple task to break in.

But it had been necessary, mostly because the nuns had ignored his knocking and he hadn't the time to coax them forth. He hadn't the time to explain why he'd come or the sense of urgency that fed him. But he struggled to calm, just a little, so the Mother Prioress would know he meant what he said.

"Henry's men will be here very soon for the lady," he said. "They want her because of her father's devotion to Simon. Eight days ago on a sultry August day, there was a great battle at Evesham that decided the fate of the nation. Simon de Montfort fell and Henry is now king. He reigns with an iron fist, one that is aimed for those who stood with Simon. The lady's father is one such man and Henry is intent to destroy the entire de Shera family. Even now, he intends to use this woman as a hostage to force de Shera loyalty and that is why I must take her to safety. The de Sheras are family, you see, and the de Lohrs stand with them. If you think Henry's battle with Simon tried to tear this country apart, the de Lohrs standing against the crown will bring about more havoc than you can possibly comprehend. An apocalypse is coming, madam, greater than any we have ever seen."

The Mother Prioress understood a good deal now and rather than ease her mind with the knowledge, she was even more frightened than before. "You are from the House of de Lohr?"

"I am."

"Are the de Lohrs rising in Simon's stead, then?"

The knight shook his head. "That is not the intention," he said. "But neither will we allow Henry to wreak havoc on the House of de Shera."

The Mother Prioress' gaze moved from the knight to the frightened woman in the knight's grasp. "And her?"

The knight glanced at the lady beside him. It was so dark that it was difficult to make out any features on her face although he could see her eyes glittering. "I have been charged with removing Lady Alessandria de Shera from Newington before Henry's men can come for her," he said. "They will not be kind to her if they get their hands on her. Is this in any way unclear?"

By the time he was finished, the Mother Prioress was visibly defeated. The nuns and neophytes who had spilled out after her were weeping softly, frightened at the intrusion into their safe little haven.

"How do I know you speak the truth?" the Mother Prioress asked. "You have violated our sanctuary. You were denied entry yet you still entered by force."

The knight's voice was like ice. "I have a task to complete, madam," he said. "No one stands in the way of my duties, not even God. And if you do not believe what I have told you, you will in about an hour when Henry's men come. They will not be as kind as I have been."

Not only was there fear of what had just occurred but now there was fear of what was coming. The Mother Prioress looked to the women huddled around her, uncertain and afraid. But something told her this knight was telling the truth. She wasn't sure how she knew, but something inside her told her that he was being honest.

"I suppose I have no choice but to believe you," the Mother Prioress finally said. "But God forgive you if you are lying to me."

The knight sighed heavily, returning to full battle mode. "There is not enough forgiveness in the world to forgive me for all of the wrongs I have committed," he said. Then, he gestured to the little priory with the vine-covered walls. "If I were you, I would simply vacate the priory altogether. If Henry's men are angry enough about the lady not being here, they might do something you will regret. Flee into the woods and stay there until they leave."

In spite of the fact that the knight had broken down their entry door, the Mother Prioress sensed that he was trying to help them. Moreover, she didn't have much of a choice in the situation. She simply nodded her head, her anxious gaze on Alessandria, who looked at the Mother Prioress with a good deal of fear of her own. She was terrified.

"I will pray for you, Aless," the old woman murmured. "Go with God, child."

Alessandria didn't have the chance to reply because the knight tugged on her again, yanking her after him as he headed for the tethered horses. As the nuns retreated to the priory to prepare to flee before Henry's men arrived, the big knight let go of Alessandria's hand, grasped her around the waist, and practically threw her onto the back of a fat charger with a wide arse. It made for comfortable riding but it was a very big horse.

As the other men around them mounted their own steeds, the knight who had wrested Alessandria from the priory very nearly leapt onto the saddle, seating himself behind her and putting a big arm around her to steady her as he took the reins of the excited animal. Alessandria clutched the saddle, praying she wouldn't fall off.

"Go," he commanded his men. "Ride east to Canterbury. We will seek shelter at my father's home of Canterbury Castle."

"With a moonless night like this, Henry's men will see our torches like beacons," another knight said. "We will be leading them straight to Canterbury, Chad."

Sir Chadwick de Lohr knew that. As a son of the great House of de Lohr, warfare, as well as politics, was in his blood. This wasn't anything he hadn't thought of himself in their harried flight from London.

"Let them," he said. "They cannot catch us. Let them follow us to Canterbury and discover the wrath of my father's army. Henry depends so deeply on the de Lohr army that I doubt he will want to tangle with it."

With that, he spurred his horse forward, the long, slender spurs digging into the horse's side where it was scarred from repeated punctures. Chad was a man of action, and of battle, and the horse was a reflection of that vocation. He followed in a long line of warriors, generations of knights who fought, and died, for their king.

Only now it was different. The battle between Henry and Simon de Montfort made it different. Now, the de Lohrs were shifting loyalties because of family ties, as evidenced by the woman in Chad's arms. She was his cousin, although by marriage, but she was still an important part of the de Shera family tree, and an important enough heiress that the king himself had declared his want for her.

A hostage to force the House of de Shera to their knees.

It was a foolish move on Henry's part considering the House of de Shera was full of accomplished knights and abducting one small lady would not bring them all to their knees. But it would bring her brother to his knees, potentially, as the man was now in control of the de Shera might and wealth in Chester at the death of his father. Aurelius de Shera was already on his way back to The Paladin, the de Shera fortress in Cheshire that had been home to the heart of the de Shera family for centuries. While Aurelius headed home to reinforce the castle against Henry's vengeance, it was up to the House of de Lohr to protect the sister.

And protect they would.

Into the moonless lands they rode, made dangerous by the fact that there was so very little light to see by. Only a blanket of stars to light their way and torches that hardly burned holes into the blackness, but travel they must. They had to make it to Canterbury Castle before Henry's men caught up with them.

It was a race against time.

Or it would be a battle to the death.

CHAPTER ONE

Two days earlier
The Bloody Head tavern
London

"WE ARE HEROES!"

"We are more than heroes! We are the *saviors*!"

"The king thinks so; otherwise, I would not be so bloody rich. Rich, rich, rich."

"You are already rich, you hag. What are you going to do with more money?"

"I am not a hag. Only women can be hags."

"With your long hair, you look like a woman. Chad, why is your hair so long?"

Sir Chadwick de Lohr grinned at the knight who called him a woman, a gesture that looked very much like his father and grandfather. All of the de Lohr men had that same bright, big-toothed smile that women found irresistible.

"Find me a woman who tells me I do not look like a man," he said, wavering because he was drunk. They all were. Suddenly, he unfastened his breeches and they fell to his knees. "Does this look like a woman? Tell me the truth! Have you seen this on a woman, ever?"

The knights around him were laughing uproariously as Chad took to flashing his bare arse to the patrons in the smoky, smelly tavern.

Most of them cheered his display while a few of the women yelled proposals. Chad encouraged the rowdy group until a couple of the tavern whores approached him and propositioned him in graphic detail. Frowning unhappily, he turned his back on them and pulled up his breeches.

"Great Bleeding Lucifer," he slurred. "It seems that my manhood is a magnet to everything ugly and fetid in this room. Did you see those vermin approach me? What gall! What nerve!"

Standing next to Chad was his younger brother, taller and skinnier, with the de Lohr blond hair and a rather stylish mustache that he was quite proud of. Stefan de Lohr shook his head at his eldest brother.

"If you flash your fishing tackle around like that, you are bound to have some bites," he said, listening to the men around him roar. "I've never seen a man more apt to drop his breeches than you, Chad. Sooner or later, someone is going to cut something off that you may be in need of."

Chad scowled at his younger brother. All of the men had been drinking, all seven of them, but no one could blame them. Having spent the past several months in various skirmishes, culminating in the biggest battle of all at Evesham, these were knights of the highest order, men upon whom the fate of a nation often hung in the balance. Drink was a way of alleviating that pressure, even if it was only for a short time.

Along with Chad and his brothers, Stefan de Lohr and the dark-haired, dark-eyed Perrin de Lohr, they were joined by Jorden de Russe, a mountain of a man with dark hair and a swarthy look about him, and also Rhun du Bois, a stunningly handsome young knight who possessed the bright blue eyes that the du Bois men were so famous for having.

Rhun's father was Maddoc du Bois, a great friend of Chad's father, Daniel, and a knight who had served Canterbury for many years. But Maddoc and his wife had returned to France when Maddoc's father had passed away to oversee the lands and responsibilities of Rhys du Bois, a man who had been a close kin to the Duke of Navarre. But when

Maddoc had departed, he'd left his youngest son with Daniel, and Rhun was every bit the great knight his father had been.

All of these men were descendants of great knights, of men who had shaped England, but that was especially true of the men from the House of de Lohr. It was a name much like de Wolfe or de Russe or de Moray or de Winter or de Lara. These men were giants in the military circles of England during this turbulent time, men of benevolence but also men of power.

They were men who controlled the power of a nation that had just righted itself after Simon de Montfort's defeat at Evesham those weeks ago. Now, these men were heading home with their armies, having done their duty for king and country. As their vast armies camped on the outskirts of London, awaiting orders to head home, those in command of those armies were in the tavern getting drunk and relaxing for the first time in months. It seemed like years and Chad, displeased with his brother's attempts to control his behavior, dropped his breeches again and displayed his tight, white buttocks to the room again. Everyone cheered.

"Bloody Christ," Stefan shook his head; he tended to be a brother without much humor, even when drunk. "We must get you home, Chadwick. Mother and Father will be anxious to see us and if you drop your breeches in front of our mother, she will not hesitate to take a stick to you."

Chad was too drunk to care at the moment, unusual for the man who usually kept himself tightly under control. He found that he liked it when the room cheered for his naked arse.

"Stefan, you've not had enough to drink or you would not be speaking like that," Chad said. "Why so serious, brother?"

Stefan threw a thumb at their youngest brother, Perrin. "Because Perry is drunker than you are," he said. "One of us has to keep a level head or all of us will end up stripped and beaten in an alley somewhere. I should not like for that to happen."

Chad made a face at his brother before looking to Jorden de Russe, who was standing next to him. All of the men were standing around a table near the corner of the room that they could just as easily be sitting at, but it was such a habit with them to be ready to move at a moment's notice that none of them seemed to realize that they could actually sit and relax. They preferred to stand as if surveying the room, presenting their powerful and armored presence for those in the tavern to worship.

"Where do you go now, de Russe?" Chad asked his friend. "You have often spoken of your home at Clearwell Castle. Do you intend to return?"

Jorden was a handsome man with a quiet manner. But he was also more apt than any of them to snap a man's neck at the least provocation. He was into his third cup of ale, his gaze distant as he thought on Chad's question.

"I suppose so," he said. "I have not seen my father in months and I should like to see him again. But then… I was thinking that I might like to travel. After the hell of the past few years, I feel as if I want to get away from everything. I have always wanted to see Rome. Mayhap I shall make the trip there."

Chad cocked his head thoughtfully. "I hear they have full women and delectable food," he said. "But that is provided Henry lets you go. You know that our fight is not over with, Jorden. The younger Simon de Montfort has an army and all sources indicate he will continue his father's fight. I would not yet leave the country if I were you. We may have need of your mighty sword, my friend."

It was a sobering statement that dampened their revelry. They all knew that regardless of Henry's victory, and of their celebration this night, the fight to secure the throne of England was not over. It was wishful thinking on de Russe's part to suggest he could travel out of the country. None of them could. The mood around the knights began to weigh heavily, no longer that of laughter and reflection. Now, their thoughts returned to the battle on that great and terrible day.

"What of Davyss?" Rhun du Bois asked. "Has anyone spoken to de Winter since the battle? With what happened to Simon…."

Oddly enough, Chad didn't seem so drunk as he answered. "Everyone knows that Simon de Montfort was the best friend of Davyss' father," he said, looking into the dregs at the bottom of his cup. "De Montfort was Davyss' godfather, for Christ's sake. Davyss was very fond of the man. And the way he died… I have no love for de Montfort but what Prince Edward's men did to him was dishonorable at best. No man deserves to die the way de Montfort did."

"Roger Mortimer took his head," Perrin de Lohr said quietly, nearly weeping into his cup. He was the sensitive brother. "He took his head and I heard Davyss say he wanted to buy it back. Has anyone even seen Davyss or Hugh? I worry what has happened to them."

Chad grunted unhappily. Draining what was left in his cup. "Our cousins went with Davyss and Hugh," he said. "They are not alone because they would get into trouble with Henry if no one was there to advise them. The House of de Winter serves the crown of England but the heart of the de Winters is with de Montfort. They want his body back and that is not going to happen, I fear. It is a tragic situation, indeed. Therefore, our cousins went with Davyss and Hugh to ensure something terrible does not happen to them."

"Your cousins?" Rhun du Bois clarified. "The sons of Curtis de Lohr?"

Chad nodded. "Aye," he said. "I realize there are a good many de Lohrs that sprang from the mighty Christopher de Lohr's loins, but I speak of the current Earl of Worcester's sons. Chris and Arthur and William have been shadowing Davyss and Hugh to make sure they do not end up in any trouble. In fact, they were to bring Davyss and Hugh to this tavern. I am surprised they have not arrived by now. We were all going to meet here, have a final drink together, and leave for home. I hope they haven't run into any trouble."

That was a very real possibility and the mood of the men plummeted further. Chad went so far as to set his cup down. He just didn't feel like drinking anymore as thoughts of Evesham tumbled upon him. He'd been trying to forget what he saw.

Chad had been there when Roger Mortimer, among others, had cut down Simon de Montfort and he had held Davyss de Winter back when Henry's loyalists went mad and carved up de Montfort's body. Mortimer took the head while the hands and feet were cut off the body as prizes. Worse still, someone castrated the corpse and gave over the bloody trophies to Mortimer, who swore to take it home to his wife.

In all, it had been a horrific scene as Chad had comforted his friend, Davyss, who had been genuinely distraught. But even as he kept de Winter from doing anything foolish, he was very concerned for his de Shera cousins who had been fighting with de Montfort. Gallus de Shera, Maximus de Shera, and Tiberius de Shera had sided with de Montfort, along with several other major barons, and Chad had been told that his cousins, the grandsons of the great Christopher de Lohr, had covered the de Shera rear as the beaten army retreated to Coventry.

In all, it had been a complicated mess and Chad was simply glad it was over for now. Still, a little voice inside of him told him the worst was yet to come. Years of experience in battle gave him that insight.

He prayed he was wrong.

"I have never understood why the House of de Winter served the crown when their dearest friend was de Montfort," de Russe said, rousting him from his thoughts. "That never made any sense to me."

Chad shrugged, his gaze moving out over the crowded, smoky common room of the tavern. "Because much like the House of de Lohr, the House of de Winter has historically supported the crown of England," he said. "I suppose when it came to make that choice, either support de Montfort or Henry, Davyss' father went with the traditional choice for his family's legacy. But let us be truthful – it is never in anyone's best interest to side against the king. That never ends well in most instances. De Winter did what he felt was right for his family."

That was as good a reason as any and de Russe went back to his ale. The whole de Montfort/de Winter relationship was very convoluted and, as some whispered in the inner circles, it had very much to do with Davyss de Winter actually being de Montfort's bastard. But those were just rumors from idle tongues, men who spewed untruths before they had a chance to think about what they were saying. As the knights stood there and mulled over the situation, and Chad ignored more calls from the prostitutes to drop his breeches, the door to the tavern jerked open and men began to pour in.

From the angle of their table, Chad and his knights couldn't see who was coming in the front door until they were already well into the room. They watched that door closely, watching all who entered and left, so when the latest group of armed men entered, Chad recognized them immediately. He called out across the room.

"Chris!"

Sir Christopher de Lohr, named for his famous grandsire, turned in the direction of his shouted name. A big man with shaggy blond hair and a blond beard, he also looked a good deal like the man he was named for. Heir apparent to the Earldom of Worcester, he made his way across the crowded tavern floor, kicking aside anyone who didn't move out his way fast enough. He was followed by four other knights, including two that Chad instantly recognized. He struggled to shake off his drunkenness at the sight.

"Davyss," he hissed.

Davyss de Winter and his brother, Hugh, were being effectively pulled along by the younger brothers of Chris de Lohr. Chad moved swiftly towards the group, grasping at Davyss, who was in the grip of Arthur de Lohr. Only when Arthur saw that someone else had hold of Davyss did he let go.

"Do not release your grip, Chad," Arthur said to his cousin. "He has been trying to escape us for the past several hours. That is why it took us so long to meet you."

Chad fixed on Davyss, who was a pale and angry shadow of himself. "If I truly wanted to escape you, I could," he said. "No man could stop me."

Chad could hear the defiance, the anguish, in the man's voice, which was unlike Davyss. He eyed the man's broadsword strapped to his right leg. *Lespada*, it was called, the hereditary weapon for the firstborn males in the de Winter family. The sword was more famous than the entire family, in fact, an exquisite combination of function and beauty. No one knew how old it really was, only that it was at least one hundred and fifty years old, but it was so well-made, and so well-tended, that it looked nearly new. Chad knew that if *Lespada* were unsheathed, they'd have real trouble. He sought to ease Davyss' agitation.

"No one is trying to stop you," he assured him, hands on the man's shoulders. "We are worried about you, Davyss. You know that."

Davyss glanced at his friend. Davyss, a powerful man with wavy dark hair and flashing dark eyes, was a force of nature with a sword. "I know," Davyss said, wiping a weary hand over his face. "But I must go home to my wife and children, and your foolish cousins cannot stop me."

Chad sighed faintly, glancing at Chris and Arthur and their younger brother, William. All three of them were gazing back at Chad with varied degrees of sorrow and doubt. They could all sense that Davyss wasn't himself, agitated and exhausted. Chad pulled the man over to the table where the other knights were waiting. He was amiably greeted and someone handed him a cup of ale. As Davyss downed the entire thing in three swallows, his younger and more volatile brother, Hugh, came up behind him.

"We may as well have fought for Simon the way Henry is treating us," Hugh said, grabbing a cup of ale from Stefan's hand. He tossed it back in one big swallow. "It does not matter that you and Chad and I saved Henry from certain death by recognizing the fact that Uncle Simon had placed him in enemy armor. We saw through Simon's scheme and we saved Henry's life. You would think that would matter to him!"

Stefan and Perrin shushed Hugh by shoving more ale at him while Chad and Davyss and the rest of the knights seemed to be looking at each other, uncertainty in their expressions now. Hugh spoke of something they were all aware of; Henry had been prisoner of Simon on the day of Evesham and to deceive Henry's forces, Simon had dressed the man in armor that was similar to what Simon himself wore.

They all knew that Simon hoped that Henry would be killed by his own forces but that didn't happen when Chad and Davyss, and finally Hugh, recognized Henry purely from his build. He had very small legs and broad shoulders, and Henry had kept tossing off his gloves, revealing his big-jointed hands.

That was when Chad and Davyss had grown wise to what Henry was trying to tell his men. Being that they were up on the front lines, they had a clear field of vision to the opposing forces. After that, orders went out not to kill the knight who kept tossing off his gloves.

And that's how Henry was saved and de Montfort was defeated.

But it had not been without peril. They'd had to fight off several of de Montfort's men, among them a very big and powerful knight named Luc Summerlin. Chad had managed to knock Summerlin off his horse and give the man a very bad slice to the neck, and he seriously wondered how Summerlin would react to him if ever he saw the man again. But he couldn't worry about that now, nor would he. The battle was over and every man present knew how Henry had been saved without Hugh shouting it out for the world to hear. They were humbler than that. But the fact remained that Hugh had also shouted out something about Henry's attitude. Chad turned to Davyss.

"Has something happened with Henry?" he asked quietly, struggling with his drunkenness. "What is your brother talking about?"

Before Davyss could answer, Chris spoke. "We heard through some of Henry's knights that Henry is grossly displeased that my brothers and I covered the de Shera retreat," he said, his voice low. "He also heard about Davyss trying to buy de Montfort's head and rumor has it that he is now doubting de Winter loyalty. Henry is already going after those who openly supported Simon, Chad. He's rallying his forces and intends to strike at anyone he perceives as an enemy."

Chad listened without much reaction. "He would be a fool to strike out at de Lohr and de Winter," he said. "Your father controls half of the Welsh Marches, my father controls a huge portion of Kent, and de Winter *is* Norfolk and Sussex. Is he really so stupid?"

Chris shrugged. "Be that as it may, those are the rumors," he said. "We would be wise to leave London immediately. This is no place for us if Henry is on a rampage."

"He would not dare strike against Chad," Perrin said hotly. "My brother saved his life. Is this how he would repay him? By accusing him of siding with de Montfort?"

Chad put his hand on Perrin's shoulder to calm the young, excitable knight. "I fear he may not be taking my part in saving his life into consideration," he said. "I suspect that all he sees is that the de Lohr army protected the de Shera army, a known supporter of de Montfort. Chris, what about de Wolfe and de Bohun? They were openly supporting de Montfort as well."

Chris shook his head. "Henry will not touch de Wolfe," he said. "That house is above reproach. Moreover, they've already fled north and Henry isn't about to go into the north where de Wolfe has the support of the House of de Lohr as well as the House of de Llion, kin to the House of du Bois."

Hearing his family name, Rhun nodded when the attention turned to him. "Our houses are friends and allies," he said. "If Henry moves against William de Wolfe, my cousins on the Marches will not hesitate to support him. The Houses of de Titouan and de Llion are very tight with de Wolfe and de Lohr. Besides… they have never liked Henry, anyway."

It was a very complex issue with friendship and family bonds overriding the loyalty to the king. In these trying and dark times, there was no line between loyalties, mostly because de Montfort had many supporters. Henry had been an insufferable king at best but the fact remained that he was, indeed, king. Davyss poured himself more ale.

"I must go home to my family," he repeated. "I want to see my wife and I must consider my loyalties and options. I may be the first de

Winter in the history of our family not to fight for the crown after this."

It was a shocking thought to consider that de Winter might have wavering loyalties towards the king. Chad had his hand on Davyss' broad shoulder.

"You have every right to think that way, my friend," he said quietly. "But what do you intend to do after this? About… de Montfort, I mean. What will you do, Davyss? Whatever it is, you know you can count on us for support."

Davyss looked to his friend; Chadwick de Lohr had every good quality that his grandsire and granduncle had ever possessed. He was blindingly brilliant and an infallible commander. *Silversword*, they called him. It was because of the spectacular sword his grandfather had given him when he'd been awarded his spurs, a weapon that was the perfect blend of gleaming art and powerful functionality.

The nickname had meant to be an insult when Chad was young and brash and aggressive, but as the years went on, it became more of a distinction from the rest of the de Lohr brood. More than that, Chad had wisdom beyond his years, something both friends and family trusted, including Davyss. He could see that Chad was trying to be kind to him, given what had gone on. He smiled weakly.

"I will go home and discuss the situation with my wife," he said. "She will know what to do."

Chad simply nodded, eyeing Hugh, who was into his third cup of ale already. "What about Hugh?"

Davyss turned to look at his younger brother, passionate and rash and foolish at times. But he was a good fighter and loyal to the bone. He sighed.

"He worries me," he said. "Hugh would be the one to run out and get himself killed over this. I must get him home as soon as possible, to his wife, so that she can maintain some control over him."

Chad lifted his eyebrows with regret. "Is that even possible?" he asked. "His wife is a daughter of Roger Mortimer. After what her father has done…."

Davyss held up a hand in both a gesture of understanding and a gesture of silence. "We are allies of Mortimer, are we not?" he said wryly. "What the man did was for the good of England, so I was told. In any case, it is my hope that Hugh's marriage to Isolde will enable me to get back that part of de Montfort which I seek. I have already spoken with the canons at Evesham Abbey and they are determined to collect what is left of Simon and bury it. Once I have his head, I will give it over to them. The man deserves a proper burial at the very least."

Chad clapped him on the shoulder one last time before dropping his hand. "Agreed," he said, feeling the angst in Davyss' words as he spoke of Simon. "But for now, we shall go home and regroup. If you need me, however, all you need do is send word. I, and the Canterbury army, will respond."

Davyss smiled faintly. "You are a true friend, Chad," he said. "Thank you for everything."

Chad simply smiled in return; words weren't needed to reaffirm their bonds. They were strong and true. As Davyss returned to his ale and Chad resumed his drinking, the front door to the tavern opened again, ushering forth more men in armor. The wind blew in behind them, scattering leaves across the hard-packed floor of the tavern. Chad was just bringing his cup to his lips when Stefan grabbed his arm.

"Chad," he hissed. "It's de Moray!"

Chad nearly spilled his drink as Stefan jerked him about, pointing him towards the entry. Chad could clearly see the big, hulking frames of Bose de Moray and his son, Garran, as they entered the establishment. The elder de Moray, Sir Bose, was a legend in the annals of England, a man with a long history with the king. Years ago, he had been the captain of the king's personal guard but the ensuing years saw him leave his post, marry, and become a great warlord with a sizable army.

The man, even at his age, continued to fight for the king even though his daughter had married one of the de Shera brothers, the same brothers who had retreated from Evesham after de Montfort's defeat. The de Moray/de Shera relationship was another one of those alliances where blood ran deeper than loyalty to any one side, and de Moray was greatly respected by Henry and de Montfort allies alike. Chad was too far away to effectively get the man's attention so he had Perrin and Rhun, who were closer to the door, call out to him.

"De Moray was with Henry last I heard," Chad said though clenched teeth, watching as his knights captured Bose's attention. "He left the battlefield with him. What in the hell is he doing here?"

Davyss watched the big knights lumber over in their direction. "I do not know," he muttered. "But I do not think I like it."

"We told him we would be here and invited him to join us, but I did not think he would show himself. He never has before."

Davyss turned back to his drink. "As I said, I do not like that he is here," he said. "Mayhap he has come to take me to Henry so the king himself can punish me for my ties to de Montfort. 'Tis not as if I have ever made them a secret."

Chad didn't say anything. He was more interested in watching Bose and Garran as they approached the table. Both men appeared particularly weary. Truth be told, he was as wary as Davyss was about their appearance and something told him to be on his guard. He wasn't even able to open his mouth to greet de Moray before Bose was on him, his black eyes intense.

"Praise God that you are still here, Chad," Bose said, relief in his expression. "I was not sure I would still find you here."

Chad didn't like the tone of his voice. There was much seriousness there. "And so you have," he said, trying to remain casual. "Will you drink with us, Sir Bose?"

Bose shook his head. "Nay," he said. "It is not for hospitality that I have come. I have just come from Henry and there are dealings afoot that you should be aware of. In fact, all of you should be aware of it."

He was looking at the collection of knights, all of them loyal to Henry. The de Lohrs closed rank, as did de Russe and du Bois and de Winter, all of them curious about what news de Moray had brought them. Already, the mood was quite grim and sobering, and they didn't even know the why. Any alcohol happiness they had been experiencing was summarily quashed.

"What is it?" Chad asked seriously, although it was difficult considering his head was still swimming with drink. "What has happened?"

Bose looked directly at Chad. He wasn't the oldest knight of the group but he was the most respected. He was always the leader, in any situation, and men listened when he spoke. Bose knew this, which is why he directed his words to the man.

"Henry is going after de Shera," Bose said, lowering his voice. "They were the most outspoken in their support of de Montfort and Henry's first order of business is to force Gallus and Maximus and Tiberius into submission. He will threaten to take their lands and titles if they do not support him."

Chad struggled to think clearly at the news, which wasn't all that surprising, considering. "But… Tiberius is married to your daughter," he said. "Will you rally to his defense?"

Bose lifted his dark eyebrows, tinged with gray. "Henry has asked me to ride to Isenhall Castle and present a proposal to the Lords of Thunder that they surely cannot refuse," he said, sounding disgusted. "I have agreed to mediate. But that is not the problem, Chad. The problem lies with Aurelius de Shera, their cousin. I assume you know the man."

Chad nodded. In fact, all of the knights were nodding. "I know him," he said. "He is a cousin to the Lords of Thunder; their fathers, Antoninus and Julius, were brothers."

Bose nodded. "Although Antoninus died years ago, Julius de Shera was still alive until he fell at Evesham."

Chad's grim mood sobered further. "He should have never been there," he said. "My God, the man was in his seventh decade. He should have never ridden to battle."

They all knew that the elderly de Shera had ridden to de Montfort's aid because he felt strongly, as the oldest living de Shera male, that he should be the one to lead the family, even over his very powerful nephews: Gallus, Maximus, and Tiberius. It had been a mistake, for

Henry's archers took him out very early in the battle.

"Julius fell and left it up to Aurelius to lead his troops," Bose said, frustrated. "When the battle concluded and the Lords of Thunder retreated to Isenhall, Aurelius fled north with the de Wolfe army. He retreated back to The Paladin and left his father's body on the battlefield. There wasn't the opportunity to retrieve it."

Chad felt as if he were rehashing the entire battle again, reliving what he was trying hard to drown away with ale. "I know all of this," he said. "My brothers made sure that the canons at Evesham Abbey retrieved and buried Julius' body once de Montfort supporters had retreated. Why are you telling me this again?"

Bose's angular jaw ticked. "Because Aurelius left someone behind, unprotected from Henry's wrath," he said. "Aurelius' sister, Alessandria, is a ward at Newington Priory, west of Rochester. Since you are from Canterbury, I would assume you have heard of it."

Chad nodded. "Of course I have," he said. "I know where it is."

Bose grunted. "So does Henry," he said. "He is sending men to collect the girl as we speak and hold her ransom against the surrender of the Lords of Thunder and their cousin, Aurelius."

Chad frowned. "Holding a ward of the church hostage?" he hissed. "That is madness."

Bose simply nodded. "Mayhap," he said. "But that is Henry's intention, nonetheless. He told me of his plans and assumed I would keep it to myself, but I cannot. This girl is part of the House of de Shera and by virtue of that fact, she is related to you and to me. We cannot let Henry take the girl hostage, Chad."

Of course, they could not. It was terrible news, indeed, and the ale was clouding Chad's mind as he thought on what he'd been told. The implications were even bigger than he could grasp and he put a hand to his head, rubbing already-throbbing temples.

"Would Henry truly do this?" he asked, baffled. "He would hold a de Shera hostage to force the entire House to their knees?"

"That is the sum of it, aye."

"But he knows the House of de Lohr will support de Shera, always. Does he realize what he is doing?"

"I do not believe he is thinking along those terms. He believes the House of de Lohr will support him no matter what. De Lohr *is* the crown."

"Not when he forces us into a choice between the crown and family."

"I agree."

Chad stared at him, his mind working, slugging through the drunkenness to think clearly. After a moment, he shook his head. "I must go and get her," he said. "I will take her to my father. He will know what to do. But one thing is for certain; he will not let Henry get his hands on her."

"I thought you would think so," Bose said. "There is no time to waste. Henry's men were preparing to leave when I departed London so I can only imagine they are already on their way."

Chad realized he had a task ahead of him, now with the burden of a swill-head. He struggled to think clearly, to shake off the wooziness. He turned to his brothers and cousins.

"You heard the man," he said. "Get the horses ready. We must ride for Newington Priory and we must get there before Henry's men do."

Stefan, Chris, Arthur, and William were already moving. Perrin was slower because he was quite drunk, being pulled along by his cousin, William. Jorden and Rhun began to move, also, only being mildly inebriated. There was a sense of determination now and all of the knights were moving with purpose as Chad remained with Bose and Garran. While Garran wandered to the table to steal a cup of ale before he and his father continued on, Bose remained with Chad.

"Henry is bent on vengeance, Chad," Bose said quietly. "You must warn your father. He will not take kindly to your support of the House of de Shera, especially when he discovers you have the hostage he so badly wants."

Chad thought on that a moment. "I cannot believe Henry would actually demand that my father stand against the Lords of Thunder," he said. "Their mother was great-uncle Christopher's youngest daughter. She married Antoninus and, to be truthful, I have only met Julius twice in my life, the second time being at Evesham. A very old man who should not have been there."

Bose couldn't disagree. "How well do you know Aurelius?"

Chad shrugged. "Not well," he said. "I have heard the man has a foolish streak in him, something I've heard from Gallus and Maximus. They do not like him much."

Bose grinned wearily. "And the sister?" he asked. "Have you ever met her?"

Chad shook his head. "Nay," he said. Then, he eyed Bose. "But after what you have just told me, I will soon enough."

Bose clapped the man on the shoulder. "Godspeed, then," he said. "I ride to Isenhall. Send me word when you can about the girl. Gallus and his brothers will want to know."

"Make sure they understand that we will protect the girl with our lives. She will be safe."

Bose nodded. "I know they will be grateful."

The mission was set now; there was no turning back. Chad wouldn't even if he could. He took a last drag on a cup of ale when he knew he shouldn't. He found that he needed it. So much for relaxation; he was heading back into the fray, possibly worse than before, going to save a girl from Henry's clutches. He couldn't believe he found himself in this position. It wasn't something he was looking forward to. Better to get the girl, take her to his father, and then be done with it. She would be his father's problem after that.

Without another word, he and Bose parted ways. Bose and his son headed from the front of the tavern while Chad went through the back, drunkenly weaving his way out into the kitchen yard beyond even though he was trying very hard to pretend he was sober. Across a small avenue was the livery stable where the warhorses had been lodged and he found his men there, cleaning hooves and brushing down the horses, making sure they were prepared for the trip ahead.

They didn't dwell overlong on the preparations, however, knowing it was essential they beat Henry's men to the priory. The horses were hastily groomed and saddled, and while Davyss and Hugh headed for the outskirts of London to Wintercroft Castle, where their wives were in residence, Chad and his brothers and cousins and knights headed southeast towards Kent where the Newington Priory had just become a very popular destination for Henry, as well as for those who opposed him.

Not that the de Lohrs opposed him yet, technically, but with this latest development, every man wondered if that wasn't where the situation was heading.

Would they soon be at odds with the very king they had rescued from de Montfort, a man they were sworn to obey?

That was the question that no one seemed to have an answer to.

CHAPTER TWO

Alessandria hadn't been out of Newington Priory for six years, not since she had been sent there by her father because she had been fairly incorrigible at Orford Castle where she had been fostering. It wasn't so much that she had been incorrigible as it was that she and the lord's wife didn't get along. The woman seemed to hold a grudge against Alessandria, being a beautiful girl, because the Lady of Orford's daughter was plain and homely, with a mean streak in her, and Alessandria and the daughter would get into scrapes constantly. Alessandria didn't take kindly to bullying.

But that wasn't the story that got back to Julius de Shera. The story he heard was that his daughter was terrible and nasty, and in need of discipline, so without even speaking with her to get the truth behind the complaints, he sent her to Newington Priory where the nuns could see to her discipline. Julius had hoped a holy beating or two might help his daughter mend her ways. More than that, he simply didn't want to be bothered with her.

But quite the opposite happened at Newington Priory – without the constant taunting, Alessandria settled into Newington very nicely. She was obedient to the nuns because they treated her with surprising respect and she found that priory life suited her well. She even made new friends there, girls that had been her friends for the past six years. She considered Newington her home and dreaded the day when her father would send word to either recall her back to The Paladin, her family's home, or notify her that she had been betrothed to some lord she'd never even heard of. Either way, Alessandria knew she didn't want to do either. She wanted to remain at Newington and become a nun. They had, in fact, been some of the only people who had ever been kind to her.

Therefore, the appearance of eight hulking knights demanding that she accompany them had come as something of a horrifying shock. She'd never even really been around men, and especially not for the past several years, and the fact that she found herself on the front of a charger as they raced through the black night was utterly terrifying. She understood that there was some threat and hazard afoot, from the king no less, but she still wanted to go home. She didn't want to go wherever these men were taking her.

Yet, they'd made it clear she had no choice. They'd swept her from the priory and out into the blackness, so black that she could hardly see a hand before her face. There were men with torches up ahead, trying to light the path, but it was dangerous going as they tried to keep pace, to stay one step ahead of men they had said were coming for her. What if, in fact, *they* were Henry's men? What if they had lied to the prioress about everything?

Then she was in a good deal of trouble.

Alessandria came from a long line of powerful men and strong women. She wasn't a tall girl, or even very big for that matter, but she was strong in both mind and body. She wasn't afraid to stand up for herself, to defend herself if necessary, as Lady Orford and her stupid daughter had discovered.

Truth be told, she had been shocked and overwhelmed when the knights had come to Newington and she had allowed them to take her without a fight. Now, that shock was wearing off and she was coming to feel quite threatened by these men. As they charged through the dark night, she gripped the saddle and struggled not to fall off.

"Where in Canterbury are you taking me?" she yelled to Chad, seated behind her with his big arm wrapped around her waist to keep her from slipping. "I heard you speak of your father?"

Chad's visor was up as they charged through the night. He couldn't see very well with it down and he was quite concerned with the night traveling they were doing, for many reasons.

"Be silent," he commanded sharply. "Your voice carries."

Alessandria didn't like the tone of his voice. He sounded angry and evil. She was starting to think that perhaps she shouldn't show any resistance, not now when he had seven men and two dozen soldiers at his disposal, men who could easily force her into submission, or worse. Perhaps it would be foolish of her to do anything other than what she was told, at least for the time being. But she would never give up hope that there would be an opportunity for her to escape.

So she shut her mouth, holding fast to the galloping horse and praying she wouldn't fall to her death. If she fell, the horses behind would surely trample her and she wasn't ready yet to die in any case.

At some point in their harried flight, men in torches broke off from the main body of men and disappeared to the north, taking a smaller road and heading into a thick cluster of what seemed to be trees. Truth be told, Alessandria couldn't really tell because it was so dark but she thought she saw the outline of trees against the blanket of stars and she could see the torches flitting in and out of sight, fading away as they went.

After that, the group seemed to ride faster. There was already a sense of urgency but it seemed to increase. They moved as fast as they could along the road, which wasn't very well maintained, and the horses were tripping and struggling on the uneven ground. One horse even pulled up lame at one point, which wasn't unexpected, and the rider of the horse, a soldier, was told to remain behind with his horse and seek shelter until the morning. Another soldier remained with him and they slipped away with the limping horse.

It seemed like an endless journey at this point. Alessandria had no idea how long they had been traveling because she'd lost all track of time. It could have been ten minutes; it could have been forever. It was difficult to gauge. But that sense of uncertainty eased when the moon began to peek up over the horizon and there was a tiny bit of light now for them to see by. It made all of the difference in the world.

Onward they went, now with more confidence, but it was nearing the dead of night as they reached an enormously swollen body of water. Everything before them seemed to be flooded, the sounds of water swirling in the darkness. Behind her, Alessandra could hear Chad sigh.

"Damnation," he hissed. "Boughton Creek is overflowing its banks. This is an unexpected bit of nonsense."

There were knights swarming around him on excited horses. "Is there any way around this?" someone asked.

Chad shook his head. "Nay," he replied. "We must cross this. There is no other way."

That seemed to concern the group a great deal. "Then we have no choice," one very big knight said. He had a crossbow in his right hand, controlling his horse with his left. "You called this creek by name, Chad. How close are we to Canterbury?"

Chad turned to look behind them, concerned with what might be coming up from the rear. "Not far," he said, returning his focus to the dark water. "Another half an hour at the very most. But we must get across this creek."

"You seem worried."

Chad nodded. "This creek comes from the sea," he said. "It is not far to the north of us. It can be deep in places and the mud is like glue. There is, in fact, another road, but it is fairly far to the south. We may not have the time to…."

"Chad!" Someone shouted his name. "Riders!"

The knights all whirled around, weapons at the ready, seeing two lonely torches approach at a distance. Since Chad had sent out two riders, he wasn't particularly concerned with whoever approached, but he was suddenly very concerned when, far in the distance, they began to see more pinpricks of light. They were very faint, but it was clear that they were moving. He pointed.

"Look," he said to his men. "Our scouts are being pursued."

The knights around him began to hiss. The one with the crossbow spoke. "Do we try to go around this watery mess, then?" he asked. "Can we do it in time?"

Chad knew this land. He'd spent many years here as a small boy. It was marshy land at best because of its proximity to the sea. "I fear we may get into more trouble if we act in haste," he said. "There are swamps about here and if we get stuck in one, we will be finished. Unfortunately, our best option is to cross the swollen creek at this point and pray we can make it. I will go first; follow me in a line and do not stray."

The knight with the crossbow rallied the others and, soon, they were crossing in a single-file line across the swollen creek. They were trying to move quickly but not foolishly, so Chad kept a steady pace. On they went, watching the water and mud rise to the knees of the horses, going deeper and deeper, but still Chad went forward. The creek usually wasn't very wide and he, through the darkness, could see dry land on the other side, about a dozen feet away. It gave him something to aim for.

But it would get worse before it got better. The closer they drew to the opposite shore, however, the more the horses seemed to be sinking. A couple of the animals towards the back of the line seemed to be panicking a bit and the knights astride them were struggling to keep them under control. Chad didn't look back to see how close the pursuing riders were; it didn't matter much at that point how close they were so he kept his gaze forward, his manner calm, as he directed his horse further and further into the water.

There was a definite current around them as they drew closer to the dry land, sweeping past them, washing away into the dark night. It was quite unnerving but the men kept their heads, knowing they had no choice if they were going to live through this. Chad, in particular, kept his head. The man had nerves of steel as Alessandria, in his lap, simply closed her eyes and held on. She couldn't swim and the water swirling around them was terrifying her, but she kept her composure. But the eyes stayed closed; it was better for them all if she couldn't see what was going on.

Suddenly, Chad's horse seemed to come into contact with firm ground beneath the water and the horse, eager to be free of the muck, jumped to get out of it and onto the firmer soil ahead. Chad was semi-prepared for the horse's movements but Alessandria, only holding on by the horn of the saddle, lost her grip. Chad was trying to keep his seat as his horse jumped not once, but twice, and on the second jump, he lost his grip on Alessandria and she went flying off of the horse and into the dark, swirling water around them.

Immediately, she was swept downstream and she screamed in terror, her head barely above the water. Without a second thought, Chad jumped in after her.

Unfortunately, he was in all of his heavy clothing – chain mail, leather breeches, boots, and at least three tunics. It was weighty, worse still with the water, and even as strong as he was, he couldn't swim very well in all of that gear. He also couldn't take the time to remove it because he saw Alessandria's head go under the water and then bob back up again. She was screaming at the top of her lungs.

So he struggled after her, realizing that the water wasn't all that deep but it was moving swiftly. Therefore, he began to half-run and half-swim, using the current to his advantage, closing the gap between him and the lady who was being swept just out of his reach. He reached out, almost managed to grab her, when her head went under again. Blindly, he began grabbing at anything he could in the water, hoping to come across an arm or a head. He ended up grabbing her hair and with a big yank, pulled her up to the surface.

Alessandria was sputtering and weeping, absolutely terrified, as Chad literally reeled her against him using her hair. When she came close, a big arm went around her.

"I have you, lass," he assured her in a steady, calm voice. "Do not fear. I have you now."

She didn't really answer him other than to throw her arms around his neck, sputtering and gasping for air. She had him so tightly that he was starting to gasp for air so he was forced to shift her arms as he struggled to make his way out of the churning water.

Fortunately, it was only at his knees at this point and he was able to climb up on the bank, carrying the lady. But his men were far away, over on the road to the northeast, and the pinprick torches were getting closer. He didn't want his men to be caught in a skirmish. With Alessandria still in his arms, he bellowed to his men and hoped they could hear him.

"Go on!" he yelled. "Get to Canterbury!"

He hoped they would listen. He didn't want them to try and make their way to him in this swampy land where a misstep would break a horse's leg or sink them into mud they couldn't get out of. When one of the knights, Stefan he thought, tried to do just that – make his way over to him – Chad yelled at him again and de Russe blocked Stefan off from going after his brother. They would have to trust Chad to take care of the lady while they would lead the men pursuing them away from her, which was presumably the target. They could only assume that Henry's men had somehow caught up to them.

As Chad's knights took off towards Canterbury, which at this point was a very short distance away, Chad carried Alessandria back towards a heavy grove of trees, silhouetted black against the night sky. There, they would hide.

He prayed it would be enough shelter to keep Henry's men away from them.

☙

SWEET JESUS… SHE'D never been so cold.

Wet and muddy, Alessandria was wrapped in very heavy wool, soaked through with the sludge from the swollen creek. She was shivering uncontrollably, huddled down in a heavy thicket of bushes, while Chad lingered over near the edge of the trees, watching the road in the distance. The pinpricks of light were torches, growing closer and closer, but she didn't much care. The only thing she was aware of at that point was her misery.

So she rolled herself into a ball, her face against her knees, trying desperately to warm herself even though it was impossible with her soaking clothing. It was August and although the temperatures were relatively mild, the nights could be cool and they'd had rather cool weather over the past several days which included the rain storms that had caused the creek to overflow.

Alessandria could hear the knight in the bushes, watching the road in the distance. *Chad*, they had called him. He had admitted to being from the House of de Lohr, so she could only assume that was his full name – Chad de Lohr. She hadn't gotten a good look at the man as he'd pulled her from the priory but what she could see had been intense – eyes the color of a hot summer sky had gazed back at her, scorching, and she could see blond tufts of hair peeking out from beneath his helm. Beyond that, she could see nothing else and the truth was that she didn't care one way or the other.

She wasn't the least bit curious about him, this man who had extracted her from her home under the guise of trying to save her from the king. She didn't care for him or his alleged mission. She simply wanted to be warm again, and without fear, because, at the moment, she was fairly wretched. But she kept her face buried in her cold clothing because it was all she had, keeping her eyes closed and hoping she might be able to fall asleep that way. At least she wouldn't be aware of the cold if she could sleep a little. But the problem was that she was far too on edge for sleep and, ears at attention, she could hear the ground give when he took a step or two, moving about in their hiding place. She was aware of his every movement, like the prey aware of the hunter.

She felt very much like prey.

"Did you hurt yourself when you fell?"

His deep voice, quite raspy, was very quiet in the darkness. Still, the sound startled her. Alessandria shook her head.

"I did not," she muttered against the cold clothing.

He fell silent for a moment but he was moving and it was too late when Alessandria realized he had moved close to her. In fact, his big body was right next to her by the time she realized it and she startled, trying to move away from him but tipping over in the process. He reached out, politely, to keep her from falling into a bush with thorns in it but Alessandria didn't realize that. She didn't take kindly to being grabbed and, resisting him, fell into the thorny bush in spite of his efforts to prevent it. She yelped.

"I was trying to prevent you from poking holes in yourself," he told her in that low, hoarse tone. "There are sharp things on that bush beside you."

Alessandria rubbed her left arm, trying not to appear too foolish. "You… you startled me," she said. It was the truth. "Did those men who were following us go away?"

He turned his head in the darkness, looking in the direction of the road. "They continued on after my men," he said, "but not without two of them becoming stuck in the mud. They are still out there, trying to pull one of the horses free."

That had Alessandria's interest somewhat. She craned her neck, trying to see what he was looking at. "So we must stay here?"

He nodded. Then, he turned to look at her. "For a short time, at least until I can figure out what those two fools are doing," he said. He studied her for a moment in the darkness. "Forgive me for my bad manners, but we were not formally introduced because there was not time. I am Sir Chadwick de Lohr. I am the eldest son of the Earl of Canterbury."

For some reason, the formal introduction made her feel a bit better, as if she hadn't been abducted by some nameless, terrible ruffian. At least the man had the trappings of nobility.

"De Lohr," she repeated. "I have heard the name."

He shrugged, turning his attention to the road once more. He was quite interested in what Henry's men were doing in the distance. "Most people in England have," he said without arrogance. It was simply the truth. "And you are Lady Alessandria de Shera, sister of Aurelius de Shera."

"I am."

"You and I are distantly related. Did you know that?"

She shook her head, intrigued. "How?"

He turned to look at her again. "It is only by marriage, but we are related nonetheless," he said. "Your cousins are Gallus, Maximus, and Tiberius de Shera."

"Aye."

He continued. "Their mother, Honey de Shera, was the youngest daughter of my grand-uncle, Christopher de Lohr," he explained. "I realize family trees can be quite confusing, but Honey married Antoninus de Shera, who…."

She cut him off. "Uncle Antoninus," she said. "He was my father's brother."

"Exactly."

Indeed, she felt more than a little better about their association now. But she also wanted answers to the situation. "I heard what you told the Mother Prioress," she said. "Henry would really hold me hostage against my cousins and my brother's surrender? But I do not understand. I am nothing of importance to anyone, not even my brother. He will not care if Henry holds me hostage or not."

He pulled his helm off, revealing shoulder-length hair, wet and dirty. He ran his fingers through it, scratching his scalp. "Why would you say that?" he asked. "He is your brother. He should care very much if Henry gets his hands on you."

Alessandria shrugged. "You would think so, but you would be wrong," she said. "I have not seen my brother in years and the last we saw each other, he hardly gave me a glance. Aurelius is only concerned with himself and no one else. Or did you not realize that about him?"

Chad knew that about Aurelius. Indeed, most everyone did. He was a petty man without the de Shera command ability that seemed to be a trait within all of them. All of them but Aurelius. Chad wasn't sure what to say to that and uncertainty caused him to change the subject somewhat. "He was at Evesham along with your father," he said. "Please accept my condolences on the passing of your father. Although I did not know him well, he fought bravely."

Alessandria snorted, a rude sound. "If there is anyone I care less for than my brother, it is my father," she said. "I do not mean to sound cruel, but my father was my sire in name only. He never cared much for his only girl-child. My mother died when I was five years of age and when she passed, I was immediately sent away to foster. I do not much know Julius de Shera and I do not much wish to, so his death to me means nothing."

Chad listened with some interest. It seemed as if Lady Alessandria wasn't much attached to her family or them to her from what she was saying. "Am I to assume that your entire family doesn't much care for each other?"

She nodded. "That is a fair statement," she said. "They have no use for me, or I for them, which is why Newington has been my home these last six years. I intend to take my vows. I like it there. *They* are my family."

Chad scratched his head, thoughtfully. "Then if Henry were to hold you hostage…."

"It would not mean a thing to my brother, I assure you. He would bid the king welcome to me."

Chad had to think on that situation. Henry wanted the girl to force the House of de Shera into submission, but clearly, that would not work with the brother, or at least it wouldn't from what Alessandria said. It would be something interesting to tell his father. He was eager to get to Canterbury and dump the girl off so she would no longer be his problem, but in speaking with her, the situation had him the least bit intrigued.

"But your cousins would not let the king take you with glee," he said. "I know Gallus and Maximus and Tiberius personally. They are good friends. If Henry held you hostage, they would take it most seriously."

She sighed, hugging her knees again because she was so cold. "I have never met my cousins," she said truthfully. "They do not know me and I do not know them. I only know they are great warlords. Why would they bother with me?"

"Because you are their family."

"I am insignificant."

Chad scratched his head. "You do understand that if Henry is able to capture you, your future is uncertain," he pointed out. "He will take you back to London, more than likely to the Tower of London where political prisoners are held, and keep you there. If your family refuses to surrender to his will, he would not be beyond sending you back to them in pieces. He did worse to Simon de Montfort and I would not put it past Henry to do the same thing to you. Does this not concern you?"

She looked at him, her delicate features haunting in the darkness. "I could not stop him if he decided that was to be done," she said. "I know where my soul is going, Sir Knight. I am not afraid of death."

She was a stoic little thing. Rather surprised by her attitude, Chad was determined more than ever to sweep her into the safety of Canterbury where his father could take charge of the situation. Still, there was a small part of him that wanted to stay, too, just to see how everything turned out. This small, wet, and brave young woman was rather intriguing.

"Mayhap you are not afraid of death, but I do not intend to meet mine anytime soon," he said, once again turning his attention to the road off to the northeast. "It looks as if those soldiers have managed to remove the horse from the mud and they are heading back in the direction they have come. That being the case, I think we can slip through these trees and join up with the road further to the south. Are you up to it, my lady?"

Alessandria nodded even though her legs were frozen solid. It was difficult for her to move and try to stand up.

"I am," she assured him. Then, she paused in her quest to stand on her feet. "I… I did not have the chance to thank you for saving my life, Sir Knight. I did not mean to be rude and not convey my gratitude, but you must understand that I am in a rather strange predicament."

Chad smiled faintly, taking her by the elbow to help her to her feet. This time, she didn't try to pull away. "And I am not?"

She grinned, her white teeth flashing in the dim light. "I suppose we both are," she said. "But you… you extracted me from Newington with all of the grace of a surgeon yanking a rotten tooth. You broke down the door, told the Mother Prioress that men were coming to kill me, and then you forced me to go with you. In an odd chain of events, you saved my life when I fell into the water. As you can see, I am not sure I should thank you for saving my life or slap you for abducting me. How do I know you are telling me the truth about any of this?"

Chad snorted quietly. "Quite a dilemma, I should say."

"Indeed, it is. But will you answer my question?"

"What question?"

"How do I know you are telling me the truth?"

He had her by the elbow, looking down at her in the darkness. He could just see the outline of her heart-shaped face. "You do not," he said quietly. "You are going to have to go on something called faith. I believe you have heard of it."

It was a clever statement. She was studying him, too, in the darkness. She didn't know why she should trust him, or have faith in him, but, at the moment, she had little choice. "I could run away, you know."

He nodded. "You could," he agreed. "But we are surrounded by swamps and if by some miracle you made it through them, where are you going to go? Back to Newington? It would be a simple thing to go back and get you."

He was right. She really had nowhere else to go. That realization gave her a sinking feeling in her stomach, already quivering with the cold. She felt rather sick about the entire situation and she supposed there really wasn't anything she could do about it. Feeling cornered, and somewhat resigned, she sighed heavily.

"So I must have faith that you are telling me the truth?" she asked.

He nodded. "I swear upon my oath as a knight that I am," he said. "I will protect you with my life until such time as it is no longer necessary. Do you believe me?"

She didn't want to insult him. "I suppose I must."

He simply nodded his head and pulled her along, out of the bramble and back into the cold, damp trees. "You will not regret it," he said quietly, still watching the road even as he pulled her along. "I shall take you safely to Canterbury and once I deliver you to my mother, all will be well again. My mother will make you warm again and feed you until you are bursting."

It sounded rather wonderful, to be honest. She was so cold and miserable that, at this point, she was willing to go with him without a fight, the lure of warmth and food too much to resist. Moreover, it was as she had said – she had little choice in the matter. It was time to put that faith he spoke about to the test.

"Very well," she said reluctantly. "I will go peacefully."

Chad didn't say another word. Soon, they were both rushing through the trees, heading off to the south and away from the swollen creek and Henry's two men. But the rest of Henry's men had made it through and Chad stuck to the trees, paralleling the road, until the sun began to peer over the eastern horizon.

By that time, the mist was laying low and heavy in the fields, and everything was covered with dew. More than that, Alessandria was seriously dragging, exhausted and cold in her damp clothing, lack of sleep and lack of food. Chad offered to carry her but she staunchly refused, struggling to keep pace with him as he left the shield of the forest and raced across a field, heading for the outskirts of the village that surrounded Canterbury.

Once inside the town, he had to stay to the alleyways and side streets, crossing through gardens that were heavy with growth and, at one point, through a blacksmith's stall. He wasn't sure where Henry's men were, for he hadn't seen them leave Canterbury once they'd followed his men down the road leading into the town, so he suspected they were somewhere about. He didn't want to run into them.

Finally, the great castle of Canterbury loomed ahead and Chad suspected, if Henry's men were anywhere in this town, that they'd be camped out watching the gatehouse, keeping an eye on people coming and going. It also occurred to him that they wouldn't know Alessandria on sight but they would know him. Most of Henry's men did, especially with a battle so recent. With that in mind, he came to a halt.

Alessandria, dead on her feet, crashed into the back of him. He turned to tell her that he was going to have her remain behind in the alleyway while he approached the castle but one look at her ashen face and he changed his mind. She was so pale that her lips were nearly blue and in the light of the new morning, he got his first real look at her.

Even with the white face and blue lips, he could see that she was absolutely stunning in beauty. Her hair was a rich, dark red, more brown than red, and dark brows arched intelligently over eyes the color of the sea. She had a long column of neck, graceful even with the unflattering, damp, and smelly clothing she was wearing, and he looked down at her arms, realizing he had such a grip on her wrist that her small, calloused hand was turning an odd shade of purple.

The woman looked absolutely miserable but she'd never said a word about it. To Chad, that said something about her character as well as her strength. He was coming to feel very badly for her and he knew he had to deliver her into his mother's hands as quickly as possible. She looked as if she were ready to collapse. Therefore, without a word, he scooped her into his big arms and made haste towards the castle.

"Keep your head down," he whispered loudly to her. "Lay it down and keep it down. Hold on to my neck. That's right; hold tight. We shall be to safety in no time."

Alessandria was beyond arguing with him at that point. She was so exhausted that she was close to swooning and when he picked her up, she didn't even have the strength to refuse him. She was so cold that she honestly couldn't remember what it felt like to be warm and she simply wanted to sleep. She didn't even care where; they could shove her into a corner by the hearth and she would be happy. At Newington, they slept on the floor, anyway, so she wasn't used to a bed. But she didn't tell him that; she didn't say a word. She simply kept her head down as she'd been directed, cradled in his rather big and strong arms. That part, she rather liked.

Chad rather liked holding her as well but he pushed those thoughts aside, more concerned that Henry's men were on to him as he came around the corner of the castle, heading for the gatehouse. There was a wide berth around the castle made up of dirt, keeping the village several dozen yards away even though the village surrounded the castle. No one was allowed to build any closer to the castle for fear that structures could be used by the enemy in times of siege, but that didn't mean that there weren't many small houses and businesses crowded as close as they could get.

It was from one of these structures that Chad feared he was being watched. In fact, there was a popular inn nearby, in clear view of the castle, where Henry's men could have been easily watching him. Moving as swiftly as he could, he made his way to the gatehouse without incident, bellowing to the soldiers standing guard to open the gates. Recognizing the earl's son, they did without hesitation and the cry that Chad had returned was taken up. Chad could hear it echoing all along the wall and into the bailey beyond.

The big, iron portcullis lifted and he slipped under it, quickly, and was immediately surrounded by soldiers who offered to help him with the lady but he shrugged them off. He was struggling at this point, exhausted from travel, exhausted from the run across the swamps. It had nothing to do with the fact that he was carrying the lady, who was a featherweight in his arms. He was, simply, weary.

But he was also relieved. Finally, he felt as if they had made it to safety but he still didn't feel as if he could relax. He had to get the lady to the keep where his mother would tend her. Slogging through the mud of the bailey, water still puddled from the recent rains, he made his way to the big, squat keep. As he approached, men were coming at him from the direction of the newly-built knight quarters. He could see Jorden de Russe and Rhun du Bois heading in his direction and as he neared the keep, they broke into a run and intercepted him.

"Nay," de Russe said, blocking his path to the keep and reaching out his big arms to take the lady. "Henry's men are in there. Your father opened the gates to them and they are all in there. I will take the lady, Chad. You go inside and see what is transpiring."

Chad let Jorden take Alessandria without a fight. In truth, the news that Henry's men were actually inside the castle came as something of a shock.

"He let them in?" he said in disbelief. "Did you tell him that they had chased us all the way from Newington?"

Jorden nodded. "I did," he said, glancing at the pale, frozen lady. "Let Rhun tell you. Let me get the lady to a fire."

Chad watched Jorden whisk Alessandria away but his view of the man's retreat back to the knight quarters was blocked by Rhun' face.

"Your father is loyal to Henry," Rhun said simply. "That is why he let the men in. He did not want them to return to London to tell the king that Canterbury denied them entrance. Moreover, he wants to know why they have come. He wants to hear Henry's directive from their own lips."

Chad sighed heavily. "Did he?"

Rhun shook his head. "I do not know," he said. "Your brothers and cousins are all inside, gathered in your father's solar. They have been there since dawn. I do not know what has been said so you must go to your father immediately."

Chad had every intention of doing that. In fact, he found that his temper was rather piqued at this point. He didn't like that his father had opened the gates to men they had been running from. Men who wanted

Alessandria. He took the first step into the keep, pointing in the direction of the knight quarters as he went.

"You and Jorden stay with the lady," he said. "She is cold and hungry and wet. Make sure she is dried and fed, and protect her with your life. Keep her out of sight until we can settle this. Is that clear?"

Rhun nodded. "It is, Chad."

He turned and made haste to the knight quarters as Chad continued up the wide stone steps, having recently replaced the retractable wooden stairs. More and more modern conveniences and comforts were coming to Canterbury Castle these days, but Chad wasn't thinking about any of that. He was thinking of Henry's men, now possibly filling his father full of the king's venom, and he wasn't pleased in the least. They weren't going to get their hands on the lady and if they did, it wouldn't be without a fight.

He'd give then a good one.

His fists were balled by the time he entered the keep.

CHAPTER THREE

ALESSANDRIA HAD NO idea who the enormous knight was who had taken her into a fairly new structure that had been built against the outer wall of Canterbury, but at this point, she was beyond caring. Her hands and feet were so cold that she could no longer feel them and when the knight set her down, carefully, on a stool in the middle of the structure's common room, she nearly fell over. The cold, and her exhaustion, gave her little by way of balance.

But she managed to stay upright. She just sat there and shivered as the big knight stood over her, looking at her with a great deal of concern. Finally, she heard him sigh.

"Lady," he said in a soft, deep tone, "you are clearly in distress. Would you permit me to be of service?"

Alessandria lifted her head to look at him. He had a big head and a big, square jaw, and his long, dark hair was tied at the nape of his neck. He didn't look particularly wicked and even if he did, she couldn't summon the strength to fight him off.

"W-what did you have in mind?" she stammered through chilled lips.

The big knight took a knee next to her. "Firstly, I believe proper introductions are in order," he said. "I am Sir Jorden de Russe. I serve the House of de Lohr. Believe me when I tell you that it is my earnest desire to be of service to you and nothing more."

Alessandria looked at him, her teeth chattering. "I-if you truly wish to be of service, I could use a fire to dry my clothes."

"And food?"

"I could eat."

De Russe swung into action. The first thing he did was reach out to touch her clothing. He simply touched her right sleeve and he could feel that it was still damp. Her wrist was exposed and he brushed her skin, feeling that it was like ice. Quickly, he stood up and disappeared into another room. He was banging around when the entry door opened and the other knight entered. He looked at Alessandria curiously and, lured by the banging in the other chamber, went to see what the commotion was about.

Shivering and twitching, Alessandria could hear the knights in the other room, discussing her situation, and she heard more banging about and doors opening. They were evidently moving from one chamber to another. She couldn't see them but she could hear them. As she listened with some interest, a small male servant suddenly appeared from the chamber where the knights had been and fled from the structure.

Surprised, Alessandria watched the entry door slam as the man bolted into the bailey. Curious why the man should run like that, she turned in time to see de Russe emerge from the chamber.

"My lady," he said. "I have moved a bathing tub into the far chamber. I have sent a servant for hot water and something dry for you to wear. If you would come with me, I shall show you where you can rest."

Alessandria stood up, unsteadily, and moved stiffly in the direction he indicated. The chambers of the knight quarters were all connected, with no corridors linking them, so she passed through one chamber with two beds in it into another chamber with three beds in it, and finally to the last chamber where there was only one big bed and a small window that overlooked the keep and bailey.

Inside this chamber, she found the other knight on his knees in front of a hearth, loading it with wood and kindling. He noticed her when she came in and he smiled politely, but Alessandria was rather wary of the man's appearance. He had bright blue eyes, rounded big at her approach, which were disturbing. It gave him a rather mad appearance. De Russe, coming in behind her, indicated the knight on his knees.

"This is Sir Rhun du Bois, my lady," he said. "He is also at your service."

Alessandria simply nodded, looking around for the nearest stool because she was convinced her legs wouldn't support her for any length of time. Everything about her hurt. As she went to plant herself on the edge of the bed because there was no chair or stool that she could see, they heard the entry door open and a female voice called for Jorden.

He responded immediately. "In here, Lady de Lohr."

Swift footfalls approached and, suddenly, there was a tall woman standing in the doorway, her bronze-colored hair pulled back and pinned at the nape of her neck. She was quite lovely and directly behind her came a young woman about Alessandria's age. The younger girl had the older woman's hair color but not nearly the woman's height. She, too, was very beautiful. Before anything could be said, the older woman went straight to Alessandria as she sat on the end of the bed.

"Sweet Mary, look at her state," she breathed, appearing greatly concerned as she looked over Alessandria's condition. Then, she turned quickly to the young woman behind her. "Gather something from your sister's chest. They look to be about the same size. Bring her something warm and bring combs and soaps. And have the cook send food right away."

The young woman fled but the older woman wasn't satisfied with the speed in which things were happening. She snapped her fingers at de Russe, although it was not an impolite gesture. It was simply a gesture of haste.

"You have sent for hot water, Jorden?" she asked.

"Aye, Lady de Lohr."

"I require a blanket or a large measure of linen."

Jorden disappeared into the next chamber as Rhun, still on his knees, managed to strike the flint on the first try and coax forth a rather healthy blaze. With the knights in motion, the older woman smiled kindly at Alessandria.

"Forgive my haste, my dear," she said gently. "I am Liselotte de Lohr. This is my home. I will take great care of you."

Alessandria sensed kindness from the woman. It was in her eyes and expression more than her manner. Her manner suggested that she was no one to trifle with.

"M-my lady," she greeted through quivering lips. "I am Alessandria de Shera."

Liselotte put her hand on Alessandria's shoulder, meant to be a gesture of comfort, but the moment she touched the rank, damp wool, she drew her hand back with a look of horror.

"*Sweet Mary,*" she hissed again. "We must remove you from your clothing *now*. Jorden?"

She very nearly bellowed to the big knight, who immediately returned to the chamber, holding a big coverlet in his hands.

"Here, my lady," he said. "This was all I could find that would be acceptable."

Liselotte took it from him. "Thank you," she said. "Now, go inside and find Veronica. I fear she will be overwhelmed with what she must find for the lady. Make sure she brings female servants with her and make sure they bring everything I need to tend the lady."

De Russe hesitated. "Chad told me not to leave her, my lady," he said. "Henry's men are here and they want to take her."

"Why?"

"Because Henry wants her, my lady."

"*Why?*"

De Russe scratched his head, seeing that she wanted an answer. "It is a political move, my lady," he said. "If you want to know more about it, then you must ask your husband. Meanwhile, I have been ordered to guard the lady and guard I shall. Henry's men will not take her unless I am told otherwise by Lord Daniel or Chad."

Liselotte's eyes flashed. "Ridiculous," she said. "What on earth could Henry want with this child? Go, now, and do as I say. Rhun will guard the door for now. We will be perfectly safe until you return."

De Russe turned to do as he was told but he wasn't happy about it. Chad had told him to remain with the de Shera girl and Lady de Lohr, Chad's mother, was sending him out on errands. His choice was to either have Chad upset with him or Lady de Lohr. Those being his choices, he chose Chad. Better not to rouse the anger of the formidable Lady de Lohr.

When the door shut behind the big knight, Liselotte returned her attention to Alessandria. She smiled timidly at the girl, knowing that there was something of a mess brewing that involved her and feeling rather sorry for the child. But first things first; the lady needed to be tended and Liselotte indicated the fire.

"If you will, my lady, please stand by the fire and remove your damp clothing," she said kindly. "I will hold up this blanket to protect your modesty."

Alessandria was already on her feet, nearly toppling, but managing to keep her balance. The lure of the fire was great. Still, something that Lady de Lohr had said made her pause.

"*All* of my clothing, my lady?" she clarified.

Liselotte nodded. "Everything," she said. "I do not know how long you have been in damp clothing, but the sooner we remove it, the better. How did you come to be so wet? Was it raining whilst you traveled?"

Alessandria shook her head, uncertain about removing her clothing in general much less in the presence of a woman she did not know. It was all very awkward for her and she was fearful that she might offend Lady de Lohr with her reluctance.

"It was not raining," she said hesitantly. "I fell from a horse and into the water. Sir Chadwick jumped in to save me. I do not know how to swim, you see, so if it weren't for him, I am sure I would have perished.

Then there were men chasing us so we hid from them."

Liselotte listened with concern. "Forgive me, my lady, but I am ignorant of why or how you have come to Canterbury," she said. "All I was told was that there was a young woman who required my assistance. My son told me that, but it was all he told me. Why are Henry's men after you?"

She was persistent. She didn't receive a suitable answer from the knight so she was seeking clarification to her confusion. Unfortunately, Alessandria didn't know much more than Lady de Lohr did. She lifted her slender shoulders.

"I was told it was because Henry wishes to hold me hostage to ensure the loyalty of my brother and cousins," she said. "I have been at Newington Priory for the past six years, you see, and have been far removed from whatever the rest of the House of de Shera has been involved in. Sir Chadwick and his men came to Newington last night and said that I was to come with them, otherwise, Henry's men would take me and I might find myself in the vault."

Liselotte was shocked. Shock gave way to outrage. "Henry would hold you *hostage*?" she repeated, aghast. "I know that the House of de Shera supported Simon de Montfort, but to take a young woman hostage to enforce their loyalty to Henry is disgraceful. What a horrible man!"

Not strangely, Alessandria felt better hearing the woman's outrage. It made her feel comforted, as if she had a defender in the tall and elegant Lady de Lohr. Though the nuns at Newington had always been kind to her, they had never shown quite as much concern as Lady de Lohr was showing. That kind of attention was all quite new to her.

As Alessandria stood there, uncertain about stripping off her clothes, Liselotte began to help her, unfastening ties and encouraging her to pull off the damp, smelly clothing. Knowing she had no choice, Alessandria began to pull off her clothing, which didn't amount to more than a rough woolen overdress, a damp shift beneath, and shoes that had been passed down to her from another ward at Newington.

There was a hole in the left toe. But she dutifully pulled off the outer dress, laying it carefully before the hearth as Liselotte held up the coverlet to shield her from the room. The shift quickly came off then, as did the shoes, and as soon as she was completely nude, Liselotte wrapped her up in the warm, dry coverlet.

"There," Liselotte said with some satisfaction. "Sit by the fire and you will warm up quickly now."

Alessandria was in heaven wrapped in the heavy coverlet. She didn't even care that she was nude beneath it, her modesty shot to pieces by the comfort of the thick blanket. Nay, she didn't care in the least. The dry coverlet won out over any foolish protests of stripping off her clothing and she sank to the floor where the fire was warming up the stones of the hearth, wrapping the coverlet tightly around her and getting as close to the fire as she could without setting herself ablaze.

Heat blasted Alessandria in the face as she huddled close to the fire while Liselotte picked up her damp clothing and held it up, inspecting it. It was durable and well-made, but hardly the dress of a noble young lady. Liselotte eyed the clothing and the young lady seated by the hearth. All of this was quite curious to her because it was most definitely clothing worn by the clergy. The fabric was horrifically coarse and the shift underneath wasn't much better. Liselotte cringed when she thought about such things close to a delicate lady's tender skin.

"Are you a nun, Alessandria?" she finally asked.

Alessandria shook her head. "A ward, my lady," she replied. "I have been considering taking my vows, however."

"Why?"

Alessandria had to grin; Lady de Lohr was very curious about things and not afraid to ask questions. She rather liked that kind of direct honesty. "Because I consider Newington my home," she said. "Truthfully, it is the only home I have ever known. My mother died when I was young and my father immediately sent me away to foster."

Liselotte was looking at her with some sympathy. "How old were you when your mother died?"

"I had seen five summers, my lady."

Liselotte shook her head, clucking with sympathy. "So young," she said. "I am sorry to hear that. I have five children and it was difficult to send each one of them away to foster. With my youngest, I could not bear it, so she simply went to Rochester, which is not far away and the stewards of Rochester are related to the House of de Lohr. They are family. I went to visit my youngest every week until my husband put an end to it."

Alessandria wondered what it would be like to have a mother that was so attentive. "How long did your youngest stay away?"

Liselotte turned away, busying herself with Alessandria's damp clothing. "When my husband told me I could no longer visit her, I simply brought her home," she said, eyeing Alessandria and seeing that the woman was fighting off a grin. She broke down into a smile. "Do not think me so smothering, my lady. Veronica wanted to come home. At least, that is what I told her to tell her father. Wait until you have children of your own; you will understand."

Alessandria's smile faded. "I will not marry, my lady," she said. "I plan to…."

She was cut off by a knock on the door and Liselotte went to answer it, producing a parade of people when she opened the panel. Servants with buckets of hot water rushed into the room and to the copper tub, filling it. A female servant had brought linens and other things to bathe with, while Liselotte's youngest child, Veronica, brought up the rear with her arms full of garments.

Alessandria pulled the big coverlet tightly around her, covering herself completely as the crowd of people filled the chamber. She could smell fresh bread and her stomach growled, but she didn't move, rooted to the spot and afraid to move lest the coverlet fall away and some measure of skin was exposed. So she remained huddled by the fire, out of the way, as people went in and out, and Liselotte held up the garments her daughter had brought to see which ones would be the best option for a small and rather skinny young lady.

Alessandria watched the hustle closely, very warm and comfortable in her blanket. In fact, she was becoming rather drowsy with the heat and more than once her eyelids had started to droop, but she shook it off, struggling to remain awake because the lure of a bath and food was just too strong. It had been a long time since she'd had either.

Eventually, the servants took their buckets and left, leaving Liselotte and her daughter behind. Alessandria could still see Rhun lingering just outside of her door, watching all who entered and exited, and she had to admit that she was starting to feel rather important. She had a guard and the lady of the castle was tending her personally. It was such an odd realization for she'd never had any reason to feel more important than anyone else. It wasn't a wholly unlikable sensation.

"My lady, are you ready for your bath?" Liselotte asked when everyone was gone. "Please allow my daughter and me to help you."

Alessandria looked at the lovely young woman standing next to Liselotte. "Your youngest, my lady?"

Liselotte laughed softly. "My darling daughter, Veronica Emilie de Lohr," she said. "This is the child I could not do without. Ronnie, this is Lady Alessandria de Shera. We are going to take care of her and make her feel most welcome."

Veronica smiled at Alessandria. "W-welcome, m-my lady," she said, a heavy stammer evident. "I-I have p-picked out some garments t-that I hope are t-to your liking."

Alessandria smiled timidly at the young woman with a noticeable stammer. "I am sure whatever you have chosen will be fine."

Veronica grinned and went to her, pulling her to her feet. Much like her mother, she wasn't shy or timid. "Come with m-me," she said, pulling her away from the hearth. "I b-brought some bathing oil m-my father bought me in P-Paris. It smells of exotic f-flowers."

Lured by the idea of bathing oil, something Alessandria had never seen or used in the sparse setting of Newington, she didn't notice that the corner of the coverlet flopped into the fire and, as she moved towards the tub, a small blaze cropped up on the fabric. She only realized it when Liselotte yelped and tried to yank the blanket off of her, but Alessandria wasn't apt to let the only thing go that was protecting her modesty. She had no idea what was going on with Lady de Lohr trying to wrest the blanket from her body and she held on to it for dear life until she saw the smoke.

"Fire!" she screamed.

Alessandria let go of the blanket just as Liselotte and Veronica gave a good yank, pulling it off of her body. Completely naked, Alessandria did the only thing she could do; she jumped into the copper tub, trying to conceal her nakedness, hardly caring about the fire that was consuming the blanket. She didn't even care that it could quite possibly spread; all she cared about was the fact that she was nude and vulnerable.

With the burning blanket over by the chamber door, blocking the exit, Liselotte and Veronica backed up next to the tub, screaming for help. Instantly, the chamber door flew open and de Russe and du Bois were standing there, startled to see all of that fire. When more bodies appeared behind them, Alessandria panicked and plunged her head beneath the water, trying to hide. It was her worst nightmare come to life; not the fire, but the hordes of strange men seeing her naked.

Dear God, could this get any worse?

That being the case, she'd rather burn to death.

A hand grabbing her hair and pulling her head out of the water told her that someone else had a different idea about it.

had been chasing him all night, men who wanted to take that small woman hostage. Bracing himself, Chad entered the chamber.

It was a low-ceilinged room that had a layer of smoke hanging next to the ceiling beams. Two big Irish Wolfhounds were sleeping in front of the fire, their heads popping up when Chad entered the room. In fact, every man in the chamber turned to look at him when he entered, including his father.

"Chad," Daniel de Lohr, Earl of Canterbury, sounded very happy and relieved to see his son. He came out from behind the table he'd been standing behind, a table that was cluttered with parchment and quill, maps and a couple of very precious books. "Come in, lad. Do come in and embrace me."

Chad went to his father, eyeing the six knights who were standing in a cluster over near his father's table. He recognized all of them; they were men known in the military ranks as Henry's Guard of Six.

So it was the Six who followed me….

Chad didn't say what he was thinking. In fact, at that moment, he was prepared to feign ignorance of the fact that he'd been followed and see where that took him. Therefore, he forced a smile at the group, projecting as much congeniality as he could.

"Greetings, Father," he said as Daniel came to him and embraced him. "It is good to be home."

Daniel squeezed his eldest son tightly. "Praise God you have made it," he said, his voice tight with emotion. He released Chad long enough to look the man in the eye. "You are without injury?"

"Without, Papa," he smiled wearily at the man. "You needn't worry."

Daniel's tired gaze lingered on him a moment and in that expression, Chad could instantly see that not all was well. Something had his father on edge; he could see it in the man's eyes. Therefore, his pledge to be congenial fled.

Stefan and Perrin were in the room along with Chris, Arthur, and William. Chad glanced over at his brothers and cousins, acknowledging them, before returning his attention to his father.

"Henry was victorious at Evesham," he said to Daniel, "but I am sure you already know that. It looks as if Henry sent his Six to inform you personally."

Daniel nodded. Nearing his sixth decade, he was still a handsome and healthy man, more than most. His arm was still around his son's shoulders as he turned to Henry's knights.

"Aye," he said. "They have come to tell me a good deal. You know these men, do you not? Greet them properly, Chad."

Chad knew them, indeed. Everyone did. They were some of Henry's most trusted men, all of them knights of the highest order; Aidric St. John, Dirk d'Vant, Jareth de Leybourne, Torran de Serreaux, Britt de Garr, and Kent de Poyer. Chad knew de Serreaux and d'Vant particularly well, and he'd fought side by side with de Poyer at Evesham. They were good men, but their loyalties and their relationship to the king were complicated.

"Good knights," Chad said evenly. "Didn't I just see you a few weeks ago on those bloody fields at Evesham? Did you miss me so much that you had to come to Canterbury?"

The knights grinned to varying degrees. The leader of the Guard of Six was Torran de Serreaux; a big man with dark hair and dark eyes, he was as handsome as he was cunning and strong. His family was very old and his relations, both blood and political, ran deep. He and Chad had a long history and a pleasant one, and he would do his best to keep it that way.

"Chad," he greeted politely. "My friend, as much as seeing you brings me pleasure, I am afraid that my visit here is on business for the king."

Chad looked at the five other knights. "He usually does not send you in a group like this," he said. "Moreover, one or more of you usually remains with him. At least, that is how it was before Simon de Montfort managed to capture him. What is so important that you are all here?"

It was a direct question following a statement that could have been construed as an insult against the Six. They were Henry's personal guard, men who both protected him and did his bidding, and it was common knowledge that when Simon de Montfort had overwhelmed and captured Henry, Simon had stripped the Six of their weapons. He had allowed them to remain with their liege, but it was in a purely captive role. They'd remained with Henry for more than a year in captivity until Evesham, when Henry had been freed by Chad, among others, and the Six, who had been with Henry, had been subsequently armed. They had fought like madmen for Prince Edward and had been instrumental in bringing down de Montfort. Chad had even seen de Leybourne and de Garr participate in mutilating the man. It had been gruesome, but from their standpoint, understandable. Warfare had made it so.

De Serreaux didn't seem to take Chad's statement as an insult, fortunately. He smiled wryly. "Much has changed in this past year, has it not?" he said. "I can hardly believe that we have our freedom once more and a debt of gratitude goes to you. Had you not recognized Henry in de Montfort's armor, the battle could have been quite different."

Chad lifted his eyebrows expectantly. "So you have come to thank me?"

De Serreaux nodded. "Indeed," he said. "From Henry's own lips. He is very grateful for your loyalty. For the loyalty of the entire House of de Lohr. Surely Henry could not survive without your support."

Chad sensed something more to that statement. He wasn't sure what more, but he didn't like it. It was almost as if de Serreaux were being too complimentary, too thankful. It seemed odd. Chad glanced at his father to see the man's reaction to all of this before responding.

"The House of de Lohr always stands with the crown," he said. "I was glad to be of assistance. Now, with Simon gone, Henry shall once again enjoy his right upon the throne. He no longer has to worry about de Montfort the Elder. Now, the young Simon is still flirting with rebellion, but with the father gone, I believe the son's rebel tendencies shall fade with time."

De Serreaux shrugged. "I was just speaking to your father about that this morning, in fact," he said. "Simon de Montfort the Younger can still lead a substantial rebellion. Even with Simon the Elder gone, Henry does not feel that the situation will be calm. Simon the Younger can still stir up trouble for him."

Chad was starting to see where this conversation might be going and what had his father edgy. "How?" he asked. "He does not command nearly the men his father did."

De Serreaux nodded. "That is true, but there are those that still support de Montfort and the rebellion."

Now it comes, Chad thought. "There will always be those that support rebellion, Torran," he said, a smirk on his lips. He was trying to make light of the situation before the real reason behind their visit came to light. "You will never have a country that is completely free of rebellion. If it is not de Montfort, it is the Welsh. If it not the Welsh, it is the Scots. You cannot possibly believe that we can wipe out every bit of rebellion."

De Serreaux shook his head. "Not every bit," he said. "But at least within England, all men should be supportive of the king, don't you think?"

"I think men have a free will to support whomever they please."

De Serreaux's dark eyes were fixed on Chad as if realizing that Chad knew everything he was going to say. It was in Chad's expression and de Serreaux, being a man of respect as well as of tact, lowered his gaze and moved to the nearest chair. When he sat, it was heavily.

"Mayhap," he finally said. "But there are men that Henry very badly wants to court, Chad. I have been discussing the situation with your father. Henry wants the support of the House of de Shera. They have supported de Montfort for many years and with the man dead, Henry is hoping to entice them back into supporting the crown. I was asking your father how he thought we should go about such a thing."

Chad looked at his father now, understanding why the man had been disturbed. "You could have gone to Lioncross Abbey and discussed all of this with Curtis de Lohr," Chad said. "His army is bigger than my father's and he controls the Marches. Why come to Canterbury?"

De Serreaux shrugged. "That was not my intention," he said. "My intention was only to go to Newington Priory but I was told that you got there before me. Therefore, I came to Canterbury to explain the situation in the hopes that you will give me what Henry seeks."

He said it most politely. In fact, it was very non-threatening and because de Serreaux was calm, Chad remained calm. He sighed heavily, crossing his big arms.

"The de Shera girl?"

"The de Shera girl."

Chad shook his head. "Torran," he said reproachfully. "She is a small lady who is absolutely terrified of what is happening. She does not even like her father or brother, for Christ's sake, and they have much the same feeling for her. There is no love between these family members and Henry holding her hostage to force the House of de Shera into supporting him will be a waste of time. Do you truly think Gallus and Maximus and Tiberius will surrender because you hold a cousin? Of course they will not. They will not surrender their convictions for one little woman."

De Serreaux was listening with interest. Or, at least he pretended to. "May I speak with her at least?"

Chad turned to look at his brothers and cousins behind him, noting that all of them were posturing with hostility one way or another. "I don't see why not," he said. "But she will have a heavy escort. I am sure you understand."

De Serreaux's dark eyes glimmered, as if finding humor in this tense situation. He threw a thumb over his shoulder, back at the men behind him. "I come with a heavy escort, too," he said. "It will be a crowded interrogation."

Chad grinned because de Serreaux was starting to. They ended up snorting at each other, the determination and stubbornness of each man. Neither one wanted to offend the other, but they both knew the truth of the situation. It was serious, indeed.

"I am going to take a wild guess and say that de Moray told you of Henry's plans for the girl," de Serreaux finally said. "It does not take a genius to figure out that de Moray put you up to this. His daughter is married to Tiberius de Shera and it is well known that de Moray, de Shera, and de Lohr are as thick as thieves, even if you do not all fight on the same side. De Moray was there when Henry spoke of his intentions. No one else in that room would have run to you *but* de Moray."

Chad wouldn't give away his source. He chuckled, waving the man off. "It does not matter what I know or how I know it," he said. "Besides, de Moray is so loyal to Henry that the man practically bleeds crimson and gold. He would not betray his king."

De Serreaux threw up a casual hand. "Who said anything about betraying Henry?" he said. "It is only natural that he would be concerned for his daughter's husband and the man's family. I hear he is quite fond of Tiberius. So when he heard of Henry's plans for Aurelius de Shera's sister, it is only natural that he would whisper in your ear about it. The de Lohrs are also related to the House of de Shera, are they not? Mayhap he told you so that you could slip in and save the girl from Henry's clutches. And just so you know, Henry doesn't want to hold her as a hostage. He actually has an advantageous marriage planned for her."

Chad frowned. "Since when does Henry burden himself with the marital arrangements of lesser nobility?"

"Since the lady no longer has a father. Henry thought a marriage to a warlord would be to her advantage. Create an alliance and all that."

"An alliance for Henry."

De Serreaux cocked his head knowingly. "What else?"

Chad looked at his father full on now, coming to understand that what he'd been told was not what was actually transpiring. Daniel gazed back at his son, rather caught up in the political dealings going on in his solar. Now, a good deal was starting to come clear to Chad and he turned back to de Serreaux, confusion evident on his features.

"So Henry wants to marry the girl off?" he clarified. "He does not wish to keep her hostage?"

De Serreaux nodded. "Let us be honest, Chad," he said. "No amount of pleading or coercion or hostage-taking will force the Lords of Thunder to do something they do not wish to do. So Henry thought that by marrying one of his loyal barons to the girl, it would create an alliance that would weaken the House of de Shera's loyalty to de Montfort. Tiberius is already married to de Moray's daughter and if another member of the house were to marry another of Henry's barons…."

"Then it would strengthen the de Shera ties to the crown."

"Exactly."

Chad was rather surprised by the entire suggestion. He was trying to come up with something more to say about the scheme when Daniel spoke.

"You heard my son," he said. "The girl does not have a relationship with her brother or father. How would her marriage to one of Henry's loyalists weaken the House of de Shera?"

De Serreaux pointed to Chad. "As your son said, it would strength the de Shera ties to the crown," he said. "It would also breed a host of half-de Shera sons who would be loyal to the king. Do you really think the Lords of Thunder would fight against their own blood?"

Daniel frowned. "But you are talking years down the line," he said. "And you are speaking in theory. This girl is being used as a pawn but she means little in the grand scheme of things. I must say it is a foolish plot."

De Serreaux lifted his hands, indicating the situation was out of his control. "It is not my plot," he said frankly. "It is Henry's. He is hoping a marriage might help the Lords of Thunder see the light. Now, may I please speak to the girl?"

Chad's brow furrowed. "Why are you so anxious to see her?"

"Because I am the warlord Henry would have her marry."

Chad's eyes widened and he looked at de Serreaux as if the man had lost his mind. "*You*?" he repeated. "Are you serious?"

De Serreaux didn't seem too happy about it. "I wish I wasn't," he said. "But Henry wants me to marry the girl. He has promised me lands in Devonshire if I do."

As Chad stared at de Serreaux, something odd happened. He actually felt… jealous. Aye, it was jealousy, something he hadn't experienced in years. He almost didn't recognize the emotion but as he looked at tall, dark, and handsome Torran de Serreaux, he wasn't at all apt to produce Alessandria for the man's perusal. To the devil with that thought. Nay, he wasn't going to do it in the least.

"But…," he said, "but you clearly do not sound as if you want her or this marriage. Why did you not refuse?"

De Serreaux shrugged. "Because I must have heirs some time," he said, sounding resigned. "I suppose this is as good a time as any. Plus, she is a de Shera. They breed strong sons. Just look at the Lords of Thunder – how many sons between them now?"

Chad had no idea how to answer that. "I do not know," he said, disinterested. "A half dozen, at least. So… this is all about using her as breeding stock?"

De Serreaux simply lifted his hand, a helpless gesture. "If I am being forced into marriage, how else can I view it?" he said, although he wasn't trying to be cruel. Simply factual. "Will you let me see her or not?"

Not! Chad thought, but he immediately bit his tongue. He had no idea why he was reacting so oddly to the suggestion of a betrothal between Alessandria and de Serreaux. All he knew was that he didn't like it. But he stilled himself, embarrassed that he should feel so strongly about it.

"She is with my mother," he said, realizing that he very much wanted to wrap his hands around de Serreaux's neck and squeeze the life from him. "She has had a difficult night, so at least let my mother tend to her before you speak with her."

De Serreaux scratched his dark head. "We have had a difficult night as well," he said, glancing back to the knights behind him, all of them in various stages of exhaustion. "I believe we could use a meal and some sleep. I was chasing some fool all night long, you know."

"I would not call if him a fool if he managed to evade you. It would seem *you* were made the fool."

De Serreaux grinned wearily. "I would agree with that."

With that, he stood up, exhausted. It was clear that the subject at hand was finished for the moment and looked at Daniel.

"May we have use of your guest accommodations, my lord?" he asked. "I would beg upon de Lohr hospitality this day. The troop house or knight quarters would do just as well."

Daniel started to nod until he saw Chad's expression, which suggested his father would do no such thing. Confused by his son's agree-and-die expression, he tried not to look too confused.

"There is a small hall next to the entry," he said. "Go there and I will have food brought to you while we... um... work out sleeping arrangements."

If de Serreaux sensed something odd, he didn't acknowledge it. He simply nodded gratefully and motioned to his knights, and the six of them headed over to the indicated hall. As they moved, Chad turned to his brothers and cousins, silently indicating they follow, which they did. The Six were not to be left unattended. The entire group lumbered over to the smaller hall, leaving Chad alone with his father.

When the solar had cleared, Daniel turned to his son. "Now," he said quietly. "What is going on? What has you so on edge?"

Chad shook his head. "I do not believe de Serreaux in the least," he said. "I think he just wants to get his hands on the girl to take her as a hostage. I do not truly believe there is any marriage involved here."

Daniel lifted his eyebrows, scratching his head, as if he were perplexed by the entire situation. "Even if there is, I cannot, in good conscience, permit a wedding to take place without the consent of Aurelius de Shera at the very least," he said. "Stefan told me that Julius fell at Evesham."

"He did."

"Which means his son is now in command of that branch of the family."

Chad nodded. "He is," he said, looking at his father and finally realizing, for the first time since entering the solar, that he was really and truly home. Reaching out, he put a hand on the man's shoulder. "It was a nightmare, Papa. The brutality and the complexity of the battle at Evesham is something I hope I never see again."

Daniel put a hand on his son's face. "But you triumphed," he said quietly. "You survived and you triumphed. That makes it a good day, indeed. Stefan and Perrin also told me what happened with Henry, how de Montfort put him in enemy armor and how you recognized him. You saved the king, lad."

There was such pride in his tone, something that embarrassed Chad. When he was drunk, it was fine to boast of his role in saving Henry, but when sober, he found that praise made him uncomfortable. To him, incidents like saving the king or winning a battle were simply things that needed to be done. He didn't consider them achievements to be boasted about, in sharp contrast to a father who would make sure everyone praised him for the smallest accomplishment. Daniel savored praise while Chad shrank from it.

"I saved the man so he could go mad with vengeance against everyone who supported de Montfort," Chad said, "including Gallus and Max and Ty. Now, I've got their cousin holed up in the knight quarters with Jorden and Rhun guarding her. That is why I did not want you to send de Serreaux and his men in there yet. Let me remove her from the knight quarters while they are eating and put her someplace safe."

Now, Daniel understood that expression Chad had given him when de Serreaux had requested accommodations. It would have been usual to direct the man to the knight quarters which, at this moment, held the young lady Chad was trying to keep from them. He nodded his head.

"Ah, I see," he said. "Go and remove her, then. Put her in Ronnie's chamber for the time being, but I suspect de Serreaux will not leave without her. We may have a fight on our hands."

Chad shrugged. "We outnumber them," he said frankly. "They can return to Henry and tell the man that we are now her protectors and have no intention of giving her up."

Daniel sighed faintly, thinking on that subject. He'd been thinking on it ever since Stefan and Perrin had told him about Evesham and Henry's determination to punish everyone who supported de Montfort. He particularly thought about it when they further told him that they'd wrested Aurelius de Shera's sister from Newington so that Henry could not get to her, with the intention of using the woman as a hostage against the House of de Shera. That was, of course, shortly before Henry's Guard of Six showed up at the gatehouse and Daniel had been told that they had come to take the girl to Henry.

It was all quite complex, and all quite dangerous. Daniel did not want to make the wrong move, especially with the king involved. Therefore, he had to think of what was best, not only for the de Shera girl, but for Canterbury as a whole. He turned for his table, lost in thought.

"I do not disagree with you, lad," he said. "But we must be practical – if Henry is out for vengeance as you say he is then he could see our refusal to deliver the de Shera girl to him as a declaration of loyalties. He may see us as his enemy. He may even bring his army here to Canterbury to lay siege. I must say that I am not entirely willing to see that happen with your mother and sister here. Would you see them face Henry's wrath?"

Truthfully, Chad hadn't looked at the situation from that perspective and it gave him pause in his determination not to deliver Alessandria to Henry. Now, he was starting to see what his father was suggesting and he didn't like it, not in the least. He'd only meant to take the girl to safety, to keep her from being used as a pawn out of respect

CHAPTER FOUR

THE MAIN LEVEL of Canterbury's keep housed a smaller family hall, the earl's private bedchamber, along with a small receiving room for Lady de Lohr and a solar for the earl. As far as keeps went, it was a very large one and had generous-sized rooms.

Chad knew the keep as well as he knew the grooves and contours of his own face. He'd spent much time here as a child before going to foster far to the north at Sommerhill Castle and then moving to Lioncross Abbey Castle, the seat of his famous grand-uncle. He'd spent about twelve years away from Canterbury before finally returning after he'd receive his spurs, and the place was still home for him. It had a certain smell to it that he found comforting – smoke, dogs, and freshly baked bread. His mother liked to bake bread herself, in fact, and she always seemed to be baking loaves with currants or herbs or cheese in them. So much bread. Even now, as he entered the keep, he could smell that bread. It gave him comfort like nothing else in the world.

But he could also hear voices in his father's solar off to the right. It was a room that had been used by two generations of de Lohrs and before that, several generations of the Hampton family. Chad's grandfather, David, had married the Hampton heiress, which is how Canterbury became a de Lohr property. But to him, it was simply home.

And he drew strength from his home, strength to face the men that to the House of de Shera. But the truth was that in doing that, he realized now that he'd put his family in jeopardy.

Perhaps it had been a mistake to bring her here in the first place, especially with Henry bent on vengeance against all things de Montfort. Perhaps he'd brought danger home when that had not been his intention.

"Of course I would not see them face Henry's anger," he said, torn. "What he did to de Montfort… Papa, the man was as brutally murdered as I have ever seen. It was anger that turned to madness. Do I wish to see that madness brought here? Of course not. But the more I think on it, the more frightened I am that Henry would tear through Canterbury and cut you to pieces just as he did de Montfort. If he thinks you are siding against him, there is no knowing what he will do."

Daniel nodded with some sadness. "I agree," he said. "You know that I have no problem fighting off Henry and would gladly do so for the right cause, but it is your mother and sister that I fear for. I fear he would punish them for our stance and no offense to the House of de Shera, but risking everyone for their cousin does not seem like a fair and just cause."

Chad had a sinking feeling in the pit of his stomach. "I have to remove Alessandria."

"Aye, you do."

"But where?"

Daniel threw his thumb in the general northerly direction. "Take her back to The Paladin," he said. "Or take her to Isenhall. In fact, Isenhall is closer. You have done your duty; you have kept her from Henry's clutches. Deliver her to the Lords of Thunder and let them protect her."

"She is our cousin, too, you know."

Daniel waved him off. "Distantly only," he said. "Very distantly. She is much closer to Gallus and Max and Ty. Chad, if she has nowhere to go, that would be one thing. I would keep her here and dare Henry to take her. But she belongs with her close kin. You must take her there."

"You mean let her become their problem."

"A harsh way of putting it."

Chad would have liked to have scolded his father for his unchivalric attitude but he knew the man was correct in this case. "Henry will still be furious that we interfered in his plans," he said.

Daniel shrugged. "Mayhap he will, but if we do not hold the girl here, he really has no reason to attack us or harass us," he said. "Chad, you must take her while the Six sleep. When they awaken, I will tell them you have taken the girl to Isenhall and they can find her there. If they wish to search Canterbury for her, they are welcome to do it, but they will find nothing. I think this is the wisest course of action."

Chad mulled over the plan, thinking that it was all probably for the best. He didn't want to create trouble for his entire family over the de Shera girl.

... the beautiful de Shera girl.

"Very well," he said, turning for the solar entry. "I will go to her now and tell her of her immediate future. Your job will be to keep the Six occupied while I slip away with her."

Daniel grinned. "I have been known to be sly and cunning when the situation called for it," he said. "Just ask your mother."

Chad snorted. "What would she know about your dirty dealings?"

"How do you think I got her to marry me?"

Chad laughed at his father, who was truly a humorous and, at times, devilish man. He went to hug him one last time before quitting the solar, slipping by the smaller hall where the knights were gathered, before fleeing the keep.

The day had dawned sunny, a far cry from the storms they had been suffering as of late, as Chad moved swiftly across the bailey towards the knight quarters. He was lost in thought, thinking of the journey to Isenhall Castle and realizing he was reluctant to take Alessandria there. He might never see her again and that thought didn't sit well with him. He wasn't sure what it was about the lass that intrigued him so, but there was something about her that had his attention. Something in those beautiful, wide eyes that had his interest.

Mulling over that sweet little face, he caught a whiff of smoke and looked up to see black smoke billowing from one of the narrow windows that lined the knight quarters. He thought he heard screams, too. *Female* screams.

He took off at a run.

CHAPTER FIVE

SOMEONE HAD HER by the hair, pulling her up into the smoky air above. As Alessandria sputtered and tried to beat away the hand that held her, she could hear Chad's voice.

"Are you well?" he demanded. "My lady, are you injured?"

He sounded panicked. Alessandria's eyes were closed, water rushing in her face. "I am fine!" she shouted. "Let go of my hair!"

Chad instantly let her go and rushed to help Rhun and Jorden, who were pulling the burning blanket away from the door so Liselotte and Veronica could escape. He ushered his mother and sister out of the room, quickly, pausing in the chamber beyond to grab a bucket that was usually used to piss in. It still had some urine in the bottom of it but he didn't give it a second thought. Rushing back into the chamber where thick, black smoke was gathering near the ceiling, he went straight to the copper tub where Alessandria was trying desperately to cover herself.

"Sorry, my lady."

He said it swiftly, apologetically, as he dunked the bucket into her bathwater. Alessandria shrieked as some of the urine backwashed into the tub, watching as he threw the bucket onto the burning blanket, creating clouds of white steam and smoke from the doused flame. Meanwhile, Jorden had grasped a second bucket and also apologized to Alessandria before dropping the bucket into the bath and tossing the water onto the burning blanket.

Horrified at the fact that her bathwater was being depleted and her nakedness would be all that more apparent, Alessandria looked around with desperation for something to cover herself with and spied the stack of garments that Veronica had brought for her to wear. The closest thing she could get her hands on was red, and silk, and she yanked it into the tub with her, trying to cover herself up from the eyes of the men in the room.

But the attempt to cover herself made the situation go from bad to worse. With the water splashing and the silk in the tub with her, the dye ran and began to turn the water pink. Holding it up against her body as she was, the dye also ran onto her skin, turning it a lovely, blotchy shade of red.

Unfortunately, Alessandria didn't notice any of this right away; she was too involved watching the knights put out the fire on the blanket. More than half of it had burned. Jorden and Rhun were still stamping on it as Chad stood over them, watching the situation with a critical eye.

"For a blanket, that put out a hell of a lot of smoke," he muttered. "I thought the entire building was burning down."

Jorden stamped down the last of the embers, coughing as he did so. He tried to keep his head down, out of the fog of smoke overhead. "We are fortunate the entire room isn't ablaze," he said. "I have seen that before."

"So have I," Rhun said, pulling at the blanket to make sure all of the embers were out. "I have seen something smaller than this burn out entire keeps."

Chad, too, coughed as the smoke swirled around his head. "Now to get the smoke out of here," he said. Then, he turned to Alessandria. "My lady, if you…."

Startled that the attention was back on her, and struggling to cover her naked breasts, Alessandria cut him off, screaming.

"Cover your eyes!"

Startled, Chad did as he was told. Jorden and Rhun, also startled by the lady's scream, naturally turned to see why she had shouted and she screamed at them as well.

"Cover your eyes, all of you!"

The knights immediately complied, now the three of them standing in the middle of a smoke-filled room with their hands over their eyes. Covered from her neck to her pelvic region with silk that was bleeding red dye all over her, Alessandria had never been more mortified in her entire life.

"Now," she cried, "get out of here!"

The knights weren't sure what to do. They couldn't very well leave without seeing where they were going but when Rhun attempted to remove his hand so he could see, Alessandria screamed again.

"I told you to cover your eyes!" she yelled. "Get out of here, all of you!"

"My lady," Chad said, struggling not to laugh at the ridiculousness of the situation. "We cannot leave with our eyes shut. We have to see where we are going."

"You do not have to see anything," Alessandria snapped fearfully. "Turn around and walk out."

Chad sighed heavily and did just that, turning around with his hand still over his eyes and then when his back was turned, peeping through his fingers so he could see where he was going. Rhun was doing the same thing but Jorden was too far away to do it and not be seen. Still, he tried to turn away and walk, tripping over the blanket and crashing into Chad. Chad grabbed the man to steady him, pushing him through the chamber door. But he stopped short of going through himself when he suddenly heard soft sobs behind him.

He pretended to shut the door but he couldn't help but look and see what had Alessandria so distressed. She was looking down at herself now, still seated in the tub, which at this point was barely half-full. She was holding a red garment of some kind over her chest that had leaked red dye all over everything. He could see her hard nipples through the fabric, which was very alluring, but the water was red and so was Alessandria. He could see the dye on her skin.

As the woman sat there and looked at the mess, she was weeping. Chad felt just as bad as he possibly could. He was about to say something to her when he heard his mother and sister behind him.

"Is it safe to go back in now?" Liselotte asked. "The fire is out?"

Chad nodded. "The fire is out," he said. "Mother, it looks as if her tub needs to be refilled and she needs more clothing. Whatever you brought her has been ruined."

Liselotte started to move into the chamber to assess the situation but Chad stopped her. "Go and get her something else," he said in a low voice. "Make it warm and durable. Father has instructed me to take her to Isenhall so she will need something that will travel well."

Liselotte looked at him with some surprise. "Isenhall?" she repeated. "Why are you taking her there?"

Chad couldn't explain the entire thing. It would only upset her. "It is a long story," he said. "Please do as I ask, Mother. And if you would be so kind as to give her a few more things, ladies clothing and mayhap a comb, I would be grateful. She has absolutely nothing."

The lure of packing a bag for the lady's travel had Liselotte suitably distracted. "Of course," she said. "Your sister, Angelica, left some things behind when she was married. I believe there is something serviceable for the lady to take with her."

Chad grinned. "You mean that she had so many possessions her husband would not let her take them all."

It was a dig at his mother for spoiling her girl children, and Liselotte swatted her son on the buttocks as she turned to leave. Veronica, standing behind her mother, also turned around when her mother did.

"We will see what we can find," Liselotte said, escorting Veronica from the chamber. "I will send servants with more water for the tub. We will return shortly."

Chad watched his mother and sister leave before returning his attention to Alessandria. She wasn't weeping as loudly as she had been but he could hear her sniffling. He knocked on the door softly.

"My lady?" he called gently. "If I promise to cover my eyes, may I speak with you? It is important."

He could hear more sniffling. "I need something to dry myself with," she said. "I cannot reach it."

"I can."

"How will you see what it is I need with your eyes covered?"

He grinned because it sounded like a rather snippy question. He didn't blame her, considering what the woman had suffered through since the moment he took her from the priory. He imagined she was becoming quite sick of him and the chaos he had put her through.

"If you tell me what it is you need and where it is in the room, I can find it," he said.

Alessandria didn't say anything. Then, Chad heard the water sloshing and what sounded like footfalls against the floor. Unlike most single-story structures, the floor was not dirt. When the knight quarters had been built, Daniel had the floor lined with stone to keep it better insulated. Chad could hear her moving around inside the room.

"My lady?" he called again, politely. "May I please come in? I promise I will not…."

The door suddenly yanked open and Alessandria was standing there, wrapped in a big section of drying linen that had been left behind by Liselotte and Veronica, along with the clothing. Alessandria stepped away from the door and wandered back over to the tub, and Chad couldn't help but notice the red silk dress on the floor. At least it used to be red. The dye had run out of it and it was streaked and faded, from white to pink to red. Alessandria stood over the dress.

"I am afraid I ruined it," she said, sorrow in her voice. "I did not mean to but… you were in the room and those knights, and I was in the tub with no clothing on and I… I had to cover myself."

Chad knew that. His gaze on her was soft. "I am sorry we upset your delicate balance so," he replied, "but there was no time for proprieties. We had to put the fire out and I am sorry that in our haste, we made you uncomfortable."

Alessandria stuck a hand out from the drying linen and reached down, gingerly picking the dress up and draping it over the tub in a futile gesture to somehow hang it to dry.

"It was my fault for setting the blanket ablaze in the first place," she said. "I must have gotten too close to the fire. You did what needed to be done so I did not burn the entire place down."

She was calm, much calmer than she had been only moments before, but Chad thought she sounded rather sorry for herself. Not that he blamed her. "My mother and sister have gone to bring you more clothing," he said gently, trying to comfort her because he felt as if, ultimately, he was the root of her problems. "They will return shortly but before they do, I must speak with you. The men that were chasing us – Henry's men – are here at Canterbury. They are in the keep. As I told you, they have come to take you on Henry's orders but not for the reasons we believed. I am told that Henry does not wish to take you hostage."

Alessandria looked at him, her eyes widening with surprise. "He doesn't?"

"Nay."

He thought he saw some outrage flash across her face. "Then you were wrong?" she said. "You took me from Newington for no reason at all?"

He held up a hand to soothe her rising anger. "It was still the right thing to do, my lady," he said. "Henry does not want you as a hostage but he has another purpose for you. He wants you as a wife for one of his knights."

Her outrage turned to confusion. "A wife for –?" she couldn't even finish the sentence, so great was her bewilderment. "Why would he want me as a wife for one of his knights? I am of no political value to anyone. It makes no sense."

Chad wondered just how much to tell her, thinking to spare her fear, but he opted for all of it. It was her life and she had a right to know what was happening.

"With your cousin, Tiberius, married to the daughter of one of Henry's greatest supporters, marrying you to another of Henry's knights would only strengthen his ties to the House of de Shera," he said quietly. "It is a political move, my lady. Nothing more, nothing less."

Alessandria had to digest that. It was shocking to say the least. "But… but I am a ward of the church," she said, baffled. "I have spent the past six years at Newington, living a simple life. I am not a fine lady with fine skills. I know how to sew and weave and harvest vegetables and mix herbs for healing, hardly the skills the wife of a fine knight needs. Does Henry even realize this? Does he even know anything about me or does he see the name and assume I am a fine and cultured lady?"

Chad folded his big arms across his chest, leaning back against the doorjamb. "I am sure that he sees only the name," he said honestly. "That name means something to him. The knights that were chasing us… one of them is the man slated to be your husband. He was coming to the priory to marry you, so he says."

She cocked her head curiously. "You sound as if you do not believe him."

Chad shrugged, averting his gaze. "I do not," he said frankly. "I do not really believe that Henry wants a marriage. I believe that the knight told me that to lead me astray from Henry's true goal with you."

Alessandria wasn't a fool. She was, in fact, rather astute. She could see where he was leading. "You mean as a hostage?"

Chad simply nodded. "I have been discussing your situation with my father and he believes it would be safer for you if I took you to Isenhall Castle to be with your family," he said. "I must agree with him. Better to take you to your cousins and let them protect you. My mission was to remove you from the priory and I have done that. Now, I must take you to Isenhall so that your family may protect you."

Alessandria deliberated on what she'd been told. It was unpleasant to say the least. Even if Henry didn't want her as a hostage but rather a bartered bride, she wanted no part of a marriage contract. She wanted no part of politics or intrigue or whatever else her cousins were involved in. It was a big and frightening world.

"When you found me at the priory, your first words to me were that the men who had killed my father were now coming for me," she said quietly. "Do you remember the words you spoke to me?"

Chad nodded faintly. "I do."

"Is Henry one of those men?"

Chad sighed faintly. "I do not know if he truly wants you dead," he said. "In fact, I do not know what he really wants of you. All I know is that men who want you for Henry's purposes, whatever they may be, are here and I cannot give you over to them. I will take you to Isenhall where you will be safe."

"And I am not safe here?"

Chad reflected on the conversation he'd had with his father about putting his mother and sister at risk should Henry decide to ride on Canterbury. "My father believes you will be safer with your kin," he said, avoiding telling her that she was creating danger for his entire family. He didn't want to hurt her for something that wasn't really her fault. "They are the Lords of Thunder, after all. They will make the right decisions for you and they will protect you from Henry."

Alessandria studied him a moment. He seemed rather sedate but with an edge of frustration about him. It was difficult to put her finger on but she got the distinct impression he was sorry that he had involved himself. He wouldn't look her in the eye, which seemed strange for him. She'd never seen that side of him before.

"I did not ask for any of this," she said, feeling defensive for reasons she did not understand. "You can just as easily return me to Newington and no one would be the wiser. I want to go home, Sir Knight, and my home is not Isenhall. I want to go back to the priory."

Chad looked up at her, hearing the anger in her voice. "Chad," he finally said. "Please call me Chad. Sir Knight sounds so… formal and stiff. I would hope after experiencing the raging river together and sneaking across miles of forest and swamp to reach Canterbury that you and I would have formed a bond, like brothers in sorrow and all that."

Her defensiveness eased somewhat. Plus, he had the hint of a smile on his lips, which told her he was jesting with her a bit, trying to lighten the mood. She gave in to his attempt, smiling weakly.

"I have never called a man by his Christian name before," she admitted. "I have not known enough men to become comfortable enough to do that."

"I would hope you are comfortable with me."

She shrugged. "Obviously, I am somewhat, if I am standing here with only a drying towel to protect my modesty.

She watched him grin to that statement. She rather liked his smile and as she watched the curve of his lips, she felt some curiosity about him. So they were brothers in sorrow, were they? Odd that he should say that. Although she had friends at the priory, she'd never truly been through the tribulations with them that she'd experienced with Chad. He was right – it had bonded them somehow. They were now linked in a way she'd never before experienced. It made her want to know a little something more about the handsome knight with the long blond hair.

"Chad is an unusual name," she finally said. "I have never heard that name before. What is your birth name?"

His smile broke through. "Chadwick," he said. "It is a very old name meaning the warrior's city."

"Oh."

"Alessandria is an unusual name, too."

"I know. The Mother Prioress didn't like it and only called me Aless. She said that was a proper, humble name."

"I like it very much. May I call you Aless, too?"

She flushed; he could see it. "If you wish."

The mood between them had eased, growing more comfortable now. They were speaking of something other than Henry and marriages and hostages, now coming to know one another on a more personal level. Chad thought me might have even felt a spark of something between them, of warmth perhaps, but he quickly chased that thought away. She wasn't meant for marriage. That was very clear.

Unlike his brothers, who had no interest in marrying, Chad had some interest in it. But finding a suitable candidate had been something of a challenge. In looking at Alessandria, it crossed his mind that had the circumstances been different, she might have been a worthy candidate, indeed.

But that was impossible and he had a mission to complete. The woman needed to be cleaned up, fed, and properly dressed so that they could flee Canterbury as soon as possible. The longer they lingered, the more chance there would be of being unable to escape de Serreaux and his men unseen. That was his priority and he forced himself away from the feelings of attraction and back to the situation at hand.

"My mother and sister will return shortly and I am sure my mother can help you with the red color that leeched onto your skin from the dress," he said, indicating her skin. "I wish you had all of the time in the world to bathe and be comfortable, but unfortunately, we do not have the time. You must bathe and dress as quickly as you can. We must leave for Isenhall while Henry's men are eating and resting. It will buy us time."

Alessandria looked down at her red hands, embarrassed that she was such a mess. "I grabbed the garment in haste," she said. "I was afraid… I am so ashamed that I acted in such haste. I hope your mother is not too harsh with me."

Chad eyed her. "She will not be harsh at all," he said. "It was an accident. You had men in this room while you were in a rather compromised position. Anyone will understand that."

Alessandria continued to look at her red-stained hands, her gaze inevitably trailing to the bathwater, now lukewarm, that was a faint shade of red. She sighed.

"I feel as if I have made a mess out of everything," she said. "I burned the blanket then ruined the garment. It would be well within your mother's right to beat me."

It was the second time she had mentioned harsh treatment from the lady of the house. "My lady, I promise that no one will beat you or become harsh with you for an accident," he insisted. "I am not sure why you think that she would, but you are a guest. Most certainly we do not punish guests."

Alessandria pulled her gaze away from the tub, looking at him. She seemed confused by the concept of an unpunished transgression. "I did not mean to intimate that your mother was cruel," she said quickly, hoping she had not offended him. " 'Tis simply that… well, I fostered at Orford Castle prior to my tenure at Newington and the lady of the keep had little patience with accidents. Or with me, in fact. That is why I was sent to Newington – because Lady Orford's daughter and I did not get on well."

"I cannot imagine that you did not get along well with anyone," he said. "You are not a disagreeable creature."

She shrugged. "It was not me who was disagreeable," she said. "Lady Orford's daughter was disagreeable enough for the both of us. She invented new ways to bring her mother's wrath upon me and Lady Orford was not hesitant to take a willow switch to my backside. The beatings were fairly regular."

Chad didn't particularly like the sound of that. "The woman beat you?"

"Whenever she could."

He was appalled. "Did you write your father, then, and ask to be removed?"

She shook her head. "Lady Orford wrote to my father and told him how terrible I was," she said. "My father had me quickly removed and sent to Newington. I told you that I had no love for my father… he took Lady Orford's side against me. He never even asked me what had happened. He simply sent a man to Orford Castle who escorted me all the way to Newington, nearly as far away from my father, and home, as

I could go. The man drank heavily on our trip south and he told me, more than once, that my father wanted no hint of the sight of me. Then my father's man made advances against me and… forgive me. That is more than you need to know."

Chad frowned deeply. "He tried to molest you?"

Alessandria was somewhat embarrassed that she had prattled on so, but Chad was easy to speak to. It had all come out before she could stop it.

"He tried," she said, sheepish. "But he did not succeed. Because of my resistance, he only took me as far as Rochester and then told me to find my own way on to Newington. A kindly merchant took pity upon me and escorted me the rest of the way."

It was quite a story, one that had Chad genuinely outraged. This petite, beautiful woman seemed to have a bitter and cold past, something he found difficult to accept. She was intelligent and kind; he had spoken to her enough to see that. He believed she had a good heart. But it seemed she had been treated abominably in the past, only finding peace at Newington until he came along to brutally yank her from her haven. Now, she found herself an unwilling pawn in Henry's political game.

That understanding, of her sorrowful past, lit a fire in Chad. The de Lohr men, historically, were do-gooders, men hoping to change the world and protect the weak, and Chad was no exception. He had that innate sense in him. What he saw before him was a woman who needed protection, but it was more than simply protection against Henry. It was as if she needed to know that there were genuinely kind people in the world, people that would treat her with respect. He wanted to be one of those people. He wanted her to know that not everyone was lecherous, or careless, or mean. There were men of honor still left in the world.

She needed someone to be kind to her and he wanted that kindness to come from him.

Pondering the situation, he was distracted when servants began heading back into the knight quarters with buckets of hot water and also empty buckets to remove the red-tinged water from the tub. He started to stay something to Alessandria but she heard the servants, too, and her easy manner fled. She grew nervous again and pulled the linen cloth around her as tightly as it would go, covering everything but her feet and head from the servants, several of whom were male.

Chad watched her back away from them, standing over by the wall as they moved around the chamber quickly and efficiently. He thought about going to stand with her, simply to make her feel less nervous about the strangers in the room, when he heard his mother entering the knight quarters.

Liselotte came bustling in through the entry door, speaking to Veronica, who was coming in behind her. Both women had linens and other items in their arms and Veronica raced past her brother, arms full, and on into the room where Alessandria was practically cowering over against the wall. Chad watched as his sister went to Alessandria, making the woman feel comfortable again, but he was distracted from further observation as his mother tugged on his arm.

"We will take good care of the lady now," she said, her gaze moving over her eldest son. "You look tired, Chad. Go inside and have a meal and rest, and I will send for you when the lady is ready to go."

Chad cocked a serious eyebrow at her. "It must be very soon, Mother," he said. "I must remove her while Henry's knights sleep from their long night."

Liselotte smiled knowingly. "Not to worry about them," she said, lowering her voice. "I had the servants slip a poppy draught into the wine they are drinking. It will put them to sleep until tomorrow, at least. You have time."

Chad looked at his mother in shock. Then, he chuckled. "*You* did that?"

"I did."

"You *drugged* them?"

She shrugged, almost defiantly. "Your father suggested it," she said.

"It will not hurt them, but it will buy you time. Now, go inside and eat and rest. I will send for you as soon as the lady is ready."

Chad continued to chuckle at his parents' devious ways as he put his arms around his mother and kissed her on the head.

"I adore you," he said before releasing her. Then, he sighed as if suddenly feeling his exhaustion. Now that his mother had worked her poppy magic with de Serreaux and the others, he did, indeed, have time to rest a bit. And, God only knew, he was desperately tired. "If I do not hear from you in an hour, I shall be back."

Liselotte pushed him towards the exit of the knight quarters. "Two hours."

He kept walking, nearly stumbling as his exhaustion caught up to him. "One."

"Three!"

He simply grinned at his mother, waving her off, as he quit the structure. The opportunity to rest was entirely unexpected and the closer he drew to the keep, the more weary he felt. By the time he hit his chamber on the third floor next to the stairwell, he was dragging horribly. Stefan was on another bed in the chamber, snoring away, but Chad didn't give his noisy brother a second thought. All he could see was the bed before him. He remembered throwing himself onto it, but little after that.

Two hours later, a servant awoke him from a heavy sleep with a message from his mother and he bolted back for the knight quarters.

CHAPTER SIX

THE ONLY REASON Torran had awoken was because he needed to piss, badly. It was all of the wine he had consumed, lavished upon him by Lord Daniel and his servants. He had consumed a good amount of it and then he found himself waking up because he had to piss so badly.

Truthfully, he wasn't even sure where he was. He remembered being in a small hall inside the keep of Canterbury but at this moment, it was quiet, the sounds of snoring men around him, and he didn't recognize where he was. It took him a moment to realize he was looking at the horizontal view of a tabletop. He had fallen asleep on the table.

His bladder was killing him, preventing him from falling back asleep. He tried to lift his head but it felt as if it weighed one hundred pounds. It was swimming and heavy and throbbing, all at the same time. He could hardly keep his eyes open. He looked around; he was still in the smaller hall only now it was empty except for his men.

Torran rubbed his eyes; he could see de Garr sleeping on the table next to him and the others – de Leybourne, d'Vant, de Poyer, and St. John were in various positions around the room. De Leybourne was actually lying on the floor next to the hearth, surrounded by sleeping dogs, while d'Vant was in an upright position against the wall, seated on the floor near the hearth, and snoring his head off. St. John and de Poyer were sleeping on the benches next to the feasting table, arms hanging onto the ground.

All of them, sleeping like the dead. Torran had never seen his men sleep so heavily. Struggling against the urge to ignore his bladder and go back to sleep, he pushed himself off of the tabletop and, seeing the spot on the wood where he had drooled, he wiped at his face as he stumbled over to the hearth.

The fire was still blazing, still quite healthy, and he fumbled with his breeches, pulling them low enough so that he could expose his manhood. So he stood there, pissing into the fire, feeling a huge amount of release and struggling to keep his eyes from rolling back into his head. He actually had to reach out and support himself against the mantel, positive he needed the support to stand. Never in his life had he been so tired. All he wanted to do was go back to sleep.

But he wanted a proper bed. He was sure that de Lohr had spare beds for them, somewhere, so he pulled his breeches back up, fastened them, and stumbled over to the hall entry. The solar was just across the foyer and the keep entry was to his right. The door was open, in fact. As Torran staggered across the foyer, heading for the solar in the hope of finding Lord Daniel there, he caught movement in the bailey beyond the open door.

The movement brought him to a halt. It was still light outside, so he hadn't been asleep too long, and in the bailey beyond the keep entry, he could see several men standing outside, including Chad de Lohr. The man was dressed in armor and his horse was with him, a big white thing with a fat arse, fully loaded with tack and saddlebags. Torran had seen that horse enough during Evesham and previous battles, enough to know it on sight.

It was a curious sight down in the bailey but not a concerning one. Torran had no reason to be concerned at all, but he did think that, perhaps, Lord Daniel was in the bailey because so many of his sons and men were, so he staggered over to the door, leaning against the stone, trying to shake off the extreme grogginess as he searched for Lord Daniel.

Finally, he spied the man as he emerged from a single-storied structure that was situated across from the keep, built up against the outer wall of Canterbury. Daniel was pointing to Chad, or at least beyond the man, and Torran noticed the younger de Lohr brother, Perrin, walking up with a long-legged mare. That horse, too, was fully tacked with a saddle and bridle and what looked like a traveling satchel strapped to it.

Still, Torran wasn't concerned with anything. He had no idea what was going on out there and, frankly, because of his overwhelming exhaustion, he didn't particularly care. All he wanted was a bed to sleep on and not a table. But that all quickly changed when he saw Lady de Lohr and her daughter emerge from the one-storied building with a small, feminine figure between them. Daniel went to take the figure's arm, leading her towards the long-legged mare that had been brought to stand beside Chad's horse. It was clear that the woman was meant to ride the horse and, already, Chad was mounting his.

In that instant, Torran knew what he was seeing and instead of rushing out to prevent Chad from taking the de Shera woman out of Canterbury, which was clearly the plan, he rushed back into the small hall as fast as his wobbly legs would take him. Shouts and shoves began to rouse his men, who were even slower to stir than he had been. Only d'Vant seemed able to get to his feet; everyone else was fumbling about, useless.

Snatching his sword, Torran barked at his men to follow him out into the bailey of Canterbury.

ଓ

THE HORSES WERE prepared and so was Alessandria.

At least, that's what Chad had been told. His mother had sent him word to make sure the horses were ready and that was exactly what he had done. His brothers had helped, however, giving him time to don his mail and prepare his equipment, but that hadn't taken much time considering he hadn't even unpacked since his arrival. In fact, his possessions were still in the stables, having been removed from his horse by the grooms, and they were still in a neat bundle just inside the door. That also included his precious broadsword.

Therefore, it had been a simple thing for Chad to pack his belongings back onto his horse and prepare himself for the ride to Isenhall. He finished securing the broadsword, the silver sword that David de Lohr had given to him right before he passed away, looking at the craftsmanship of the hilt.

He smiled faintly, running a finger over it, remembering that David had commissioned it from a local Canterbury blacksmith and had practically hovered over the man during the process of creating it. At least, that was how Chad's grandmother, Emilie, told the story. David had insisted he'd done nothing of the kind but Chad tended to believe his grandmother. David de Lohr, if nothing else, had been a determined and exacting man, especially when it came to the production of a weapon for his eldest grandson.

Chad's memories lingered on his grandfather. There wasn't a day that went by that he didn't think of the man somehow. David had lived to Chad's twenty-second year, but he hadn't been particularly healthy for the last twenty years of his life. He'd had breathing problems, and finally heart problems, and the physic had instructed him to rest frequently but David never would. He was under the belief that any show of weakness or illness in front of his wife upset her, so he pretended he felt fine until one morning, he simply didn't wake up at all.

David's wife, Emilie, had found him cold in his bed with a faint smile on his lips, having passed peacefully away sometime during the night. The great David de Lohr who, in his prime, had inarguably been the finest swordsman in all of England hadn't died on the field of battle in a flurry of blood and glory. He had died in his bed, a very old and very happy man.

To his wife, that had been a fitting end to his magnificent legacy and Emilie was quite positive that the smile was because, the moment he passed from life, David had been welcomed by his brother. David had never emotionally recovered from Christopher's death eleven years earlier so she had comforted herself with the knowledge that he was with his brother once again. It was a thought that brought comfort to the entire family.

The de Lohr brothers were together once more.

Chad remembered the day his father had come to Lioncross Abbey, where he had been serving, bearing the unhappy news. Daniel had escorted his father's casket all the way to Lioncross Abbey so that David could be buried next to his brother's crypt in the abbey's small chapel. Emilie had accompanied her husband's body, also, and one of the saddest sights Chad had ever seen was watching his grandmother and his Uncle Christopher's wife, Dustin, kneel at the foot of the crypts of the great men they loved and hold hands as they prayed.

The two women who had married two of the most powerful knights in the realm looked small and old and fragile, but the truth was that they were stronger than any of the men in that entire room. It was their love for Christopher and David that had made them strong, something that continued on until two years ago when they lost first Dustin and then Emilie within three months of each other. It had been a terrible blow to the family but the women had each been buried in their husband's respective crypts, finally with the men they loved for all eternity.

Their beautiful love stories had passed into legend.

Chad's smile faded as he remembered the tears he'd shed for his grandfather and grandmother. He hadn't been ready to let them go yet, still seeing them through the eyes of a child who believed they would live forever. But the tears he shed had been in private, for he had to be strong for his father, who was truly devastated by his father's passing. Something about missing "the Daniel veins" that would pop out on David's temples, but Chad never fully understood that joke, which seemed to be something only David and Daniel understood. All Chad knew was that the entire family had been devastated by the passing of Christopher and David de Lohr, and then Dustin and Emilie, but the sword that David had given Chad was a link to his grandfather like nothing else ever could have been.

The silver sword.

Chad had forced himself from those reflections when Daniel had entered the stable, eager for his son to collect the lady and get started on the road to Isenhall. Perrin accompanied his father and when Daniel and Chad left the stable, Perrin was in charge of preparing a suitable mare for the lady.

As Daniel and Chad had headed across the bailey towards the knight quarters, Daniel had given Chad some last minute instructions.

"It will take you at least seven days to reach Coventry and Isenhall," he had said, "six days if you move swiftly. The rains have been heavy to the north, so I have heard, so your travel may not be as quick as we had hoped."

Chad understood. "Evesham came between storms, fortunately," he'd said. "But riding to Coventry and the Marches may be different. The lady and I will do well enough."

Daniel's brother, Stefan, and his cousins had been gathering in the bailey near the knight quarters, waiting to see Chad and the lady off. De Russe and du Bois were not there, instead, they were inside the knight quarters, still providing the lady with protection should Henry's men decide to make a break for the structure and try to drag the lady away.

But that was impossible in any case because Henry's Six were passed out like drunkards all over the small hall. The poppy potion had worked wonders so no one felt a huge sense of urgency, but there was no leisure mood, either. It was time to see the task well on its way.

As they neared the knight quarters, Daniel broke away from his son and moved swiftly into the structure to ensure that the lady was ready for her trip. Chad watched his father go before coming to a halt beside Chris and Stefan, engaging in small talk while Daniel went to fetch the lady.

For some odd reason, Chad was coming to feel edgy now and he wasn't entirely sure why. Henry's Six would sleep for a day, his mother had said. It wasn't that he didn't believe her, for he did, but he knew from experience that even the best laid plans could be thwarted by something unexpected. He glanced at the keep once, twice, as Stefan spoke beside him.

"Father is going to be truthful with de Serreaux when the man awakens," he said. "If they want the lady, they'll have to move on to Coventry, but Father intends to keep Henry's Six here as long as he can. That should buy you at least a day and a half, if not more."

Chad couldn't explain his sense of uneasiness now. He found that he was quite eager for his father to emerge from the knight quarters with the lady. "Providing the weather and the roads hold," he said. "I will certainly make every effort to reach Isenhall before the Six catch up with me."

"What do you plan to do once you have delivered the lady over to Gallus and his brothers?" Chris wanted to know. He had been standing close enough to hear. "I told Uncle Daniel that we should ride with you to Isenhall but he seems to think you will travel faster with just the two of you. What are you going to do once you reach Isenhall?"

Chad shrugged. "Make sure the Lords of Thunder are not in need of me, I suppose," he said. "I would expect they will not require my services so it is my sense that I will be heading for home fairly quickly. When are you and your brothers leaving for Lioncross?"

Daniel emerged from the knight quarters at that point, shouting out to Perrin, who was just coming around with the lady's mare. Chris watched his uncle and cousin a moment before returning his focus to Chad.

"Right after you leave, I am sure," he said. "I think Uncle Daniel wants us to remain here to see what the Six will do when they are told that you and the lady have left for Isenhall. I do not know if Uncle Daniel is expecting trouble, but we will wait and see."

Chad was satisfied with the plan. In fact, he was glad his cousins were remaining to ensure that de Serreaux and his men didn't turn violent when they were told the lady had slipped through their fingers yet again. When obedient knights were carrying out the orders of the king, there was no telling how they would react, which only increased Chad's sense of unease. He very much wanted to depart as quickly as possible now. The sooner they were away from Canterbury, the better. Impatient, he struggled not to appear so.

But his impatience didn't last long. His mother, his sister, and Alessandria suddenly emerged from the knight quarters with de Russe and du Bois behind them, and Chad felt a sense of relief at the sight of her. That, and a distinct sense of pleasure; she was wearing a traveling outfit of dark green wool, durable and well made, clinging to a figure he didn't know she had. Though petite, she had a narrow waist and flaring hips, quite alluring and shapely. In fact, he was rather shocked to realize she not only had an exquisite face but a body to match. Through the wet wool and darkness of their travels, he'd never had the chance to notice.

But he wasn't the only one who noticed; his brothers as well as his cousins were riveted to the lady, seeing an enchantress emerge into their midst. The dark auburn hair was braided, draping over one shoulder, and she had a kerchief wrapped around her head, tucked behind her ears and tied at the nape of her neck to keep her hair from blowing about or becoming unruly. Veronica was trying to fix the billowing cloak, a cloak that was streaming behind Alessandria like a banner and allowing every man there a view of that marvelous figure.

The goddess was revealed.

"Finally!" Daniel exclaimed softly, holding out a hand to Alessandria as she approached. "Come along, my lady. There is no time to waste. You and my son must be along your way."

Alessandria looked at Chad, standing by his horse, and Chad swore he could feel a jolt of warmth from her sea-colored eyes. The sensation startled him and he wasn't sure if he should smile, or say something, or simply mount his horse and ignore her. He'd never spent a muddled day in his life but, at this moment, her warmth and charm and beauty had him muddled. It truly did. As his father reached out to take the lady's arm, he seemed to break from his bewilderment.

"My lady," he greeted. "I see that my mother and sister have taken great care of you."

Alessandria smiled shyly. "They have," she agreed, looking at Liselotte. "My lady, I must thank you again for your kindness and generosity. I will take very good care of the items that you have loaned me and return them to you."

Liselotte reached out to take Alessandria's hand. "I would be hurt if you returned them," she said. "They are a gift."

Alessandria looked down at the beautiful traveling ensemble she was wearing. "I… I do not know if I will be able to wear this when I return to Newington," she said. "I do not know if the nuns will allow it."

Liselotte glanced up at her husband and son and, seeing their hesitant expressions, understood that the lady might never make it back to Newington, not with Henry after her. But it was clear the young woman didn't understand that yet. Forcing a smile, Liselotte squeezed Alessandria's hand.

"You can keep it until such time as you no longer need it," she said. "Then, you may send it back to me if you wish."

Alessandria smiled at the woman with the slight Germanic accent, a lady who had been kinder to her than any lady she had ever known. In fact, the two hours she had spent with Lady de Lohr and her daughter had been quite eye opening. She never knew women, at least outside of Newington, to be kind and pleasant to speak with. That had been a strange experience but one she quickly grew to like.

Lady de Lohr and her daughter had been attentive and polite, and they'd worked very hard to scrub her skin of the red dye from the silk garment. Lady de Lohr hadn't been angry about the ruined silk in the least, which was surprising enough, and went out of her way to clean off the red stains with, of all things, buttermilk and a horsehair brush. However she did it, it worked, leaving Alessandria's skin a little sensitive but clean and very smooth. In fact, Alessandria was quite sure she'd never been so clean in her entire life.

And she smelled good, too. After scrubbing the red splotches away, Veronica had rubbed her skin with oil that smelled of roses. It was attention and treatment that Alessandria had never experienced and she found that when it was over, she didn't want to leave. She very much liked to be fussed over and treated as if she were something special, as if she mattered. It was a glimpse of a world she wanted to be part of and in that realization, it was her first awareness that perhaps she didn't want to join the cloister, after all. She liked the comforts and pleasure of a kind family.

Of Chad's family.

It was the unfortunate part of never being exposed to men, for her to be attracted to the first man who had truly been kind to her. Since Chad had left her with his mother and sister, truthfully, all Alessandria had been able to do was think of him. Being around Lady de Lohr, the woman who gave birth to him, only made her think on him more.

In spite of the fact that he had brutally wrested her from Newington, she had come to believe that he had only been trying to help her. Henry's men in the keep proved that. He'd been truthful about her situation all along. There were wards at Newington that whispered of courtly love, a concept that had intrigued Alessandria, and now she believed she was seeing an example of true chivalry in Chad de Lohr. The man was preparing to risk his life to take her to safety… how could she not be attracted to him?

With all of these thoughts on her mind, Alessandria's attention turned to Chad, still standing next to his big white horse, and she couldn't help but smile at him. He was looking at her rather strangely, a sort of wide-eyed expression, but she didn't have a chance to consider the fact he hadn't returned her smile because Chris and Arthur, who had been standing several feet away, suddenly let out a shout. Startled, Chad and the rest of the family looked over to see de Serreaux and d'Vant rushing from the keep, weapons drawn.

After that, chaos reigned.

The de Lohr men were, if nothing else, bred for battle. The sight of flashing swords only seemed to feed that innate sense in them of what needed to be done in order to survive. Already, Chad and Daniel began to move – Daniel to his wife and daughter and Chad to Alessandria. De Russe and du Bois, who were, in fact, the only men armed out of the group, unsheathed their broadswords and charged at de Serreaux and d'Vant as the men rushed the group. As the four of them immediately engaged in a nasty sword fight, Daniel motioned to Stefan and Perrin.

"Get your mother and sister back inside the knight quarters!" he snapped. With his younger sons on the move, he turned to his eldest. "Get the lady on her horse and get out of here. We'll hold the Six as long as we can!"

Chad already had hold of Alessandria, practically throwing the woman onto the leggy mare. He was cool but swift in his actions and he leapt onto his steed, gathering the reins, as de Poyer and de Leybourne came staggering out of the keep, weapons drawn. The Six were outnumbered but they were seasoned knights, and very skilled, so this was a deadly fight from the onset.

Chad knew that very well; he'd seen what these men were capable of upon the fields of Evesham. Now, his sense of urgency was starting to make some sense. There was something in him that told him he'd needed to leave, immediately, so perhaps he had a sixth sense when it came to danger in this instance. Whatever little voice had told him to leave had been right.

But he didn't have a chance to leave. As he was grabbing at the reins of the leggy mare to encourage the horse to move, St. John and de Garr came pouring from the keep and a dagger suddenly sailed past his head, straight past the lady and nicking her on the arm. Alessandria screamed in fright and pain, so startled that she lost her balance and fell backwards off the horse.

Chad flew off of his steed and was at her side in a minute, picking her up and rushing towards the knight quarters. Putting her on her feet, he saw that the wound to her arm was not life-threatening so he shoved her inside, where his mother and sister would tend her, and slammed the door.

"Bolt this!" he shouted. "Do you hear me? Bolt it!"

He heard the bolt thrown on the other side and that was all he needed to shift into full battle mode. Knowing the women were safe, that Alessandria was safe, allowed him to think the way he was born to think. Rushing back to his horse that was trained for battle, he unsheathed his sword, the silver sword, and plunged into the fray.

He knew that de Garr was the one who threw the dagger, mostly because that was what the man was known for. Some men used crossbows but de Garr used daggers. He was an intellect of a man that Chad genuinely liked but, at this moment, he felt nothing but hatred for him. He knew that if de Garr had meant to kill, he would have, so the dagger had only been a warning. But it was a warning that had targeted the lady and Chad would not tolerate that. The man had injured Alessandria and everything protective that Chad had ever held inside of him suddenly came out, all of it seeking revenge against de Garr.

He would beat the man within an inch of his life.

So he shoved through the ruckus that was going on, not paying attention to the de Lohr soldiers who were rushing from the troop house and the wall to break up the fight. He could hear his father shouting and the clash of swords upon swords as his brothers and cousins went head-to-head with the Six, but still, all he cared about was finding de Garr.

He didn't have far to look. Britt de Garr was engaged in a sword battle with William de Lohr, both men grunting and shoving and swinging the swords when the situation permitted. Chad could see the back of de Garr's red head as he approached from behind, not at all concerned that he would be attacking the man from the rear, considered bad form in a sword fight among honorable knights. One always faced the enemy.

But in this case, Chad was so angry, and so bent on avenging what de Garr did to Alessandria, that he came up behind de Garr and used the hilt of his sword to smack him on the head, hard enough to send de Garr to the ground in a daze. Then, he pounced.

Being dazed as he was, de Garr was barely able to defend himself as Chad pummeled him. He went for the head, beating de Garr so badly with his big fists that in little time, the man was unconscious and bleeding. In fact, Chad was so unrestrained in his beating that his cousin, William, whom de Garr had been fighting, went to fetch Daniel. When Daniel, who had been supervising his soldiers as they restrained de Poyer, came around and saw the beating his son was dealing de Garr, he immediately reached down to pull his son off of the downed knight.

"Chad," he grunted, trying to pull him away. "Enough, lad. You are going to kill him."

Chad resisted his father. "The son of a whore deserves it," he snarled. "For that dagger he threw at Alessandria, he is going to pay."

Daniel hadn't seen the dagger. Concerned, he looked around to see if there was an injured lady on the ground but seeing nothing, he continued to try and pull Chad away from de Garr. But his son wouldn't move and Daniel turned to William, standing behind him.

"Help me," he commanded.

William jumped in and between the two of them, they managed to pull Chad away from de Garr, who was a bloodied mess on the ground. They dragged Chad several feet away, turning him around so he no longer had visual contact with his victim.

"Where is the lady, Chad?" Daniel demanded. "What happened to her?"

Chad, his face splattered with de Garr's blood, bobbed his head in the direction of the knight quarters. "I put her inside with Mother and Ronnie," he said. "That bastard threw a dagger that clipped her in the arm."

Daniel understood a great deal now. He let go of his son but his focus was on William, a young and strong man. "Do not let him go," he instructed firmly. "Go and see to the lady. If she is well enough to travel, send them both on their way."

William nodded, pulling Chad over to the entry to the knight quarters as Daniel went to see about de Garr. William rapped on the door, loudly, and called to Liselotte. Chad, still in his cousin's grip, was struggling to push aside his rage. He still wanted to go back and bash de Garr's brains in, but the moment the door opened and he could look inside the common room of the knight quarters and see his mother tending Alessandria's arm, the rage faded away. He became more concerned with the lady's wound.

"Mother?" he asked, stepping inside. "How is she?"

Liselotte was tying a bandage around the arm, bandages torn from a coverlet on one of the beds. "It is not bad," she said. "It is not too deep, not deep enough to stitch it. She will be fine."

Chad watched his mother as she tied off the bandage before looking at Alessandria. She was gazing back at him, pale and frightened, but the moment their eyes met, she smiled. It was a timid smile, but a smile nonetheless. Chad took a deep breath, shaking off his rage.

"I am so sorry," he said, his voice hoarse with emotion. "Ever since I took you from Newington, it has been one tribulation after another. I have not done a very good job of protecting you, which has been my mission all along. I have allowed harm to befall you twice and for that, I must beg your forgiveness."

The tone of his voice caused Liselotte to look at her son. She'd never heard that level of emotion in his voice and she was surprised by it. Nay; *pleased* by it. Then she looked at Alessandria, who seemed to be gazing at her son in a most besotted way.

Besotted!

"You have done all you could to protect me, Sir Chad," Alessandria said quietly. "You have been chivalrous and brave, and I am grateful that you would risk yourself so for someone you do not even know."

Chad smiled weakly, looking at Alessandria as if she were the only one in the room. He didn't even notice his mother or sister any longer. "It is a pleasure, my lady, I assure you," he said with soft sincerity. "Are you well enough to travel, then?"

Alessandria nodded, looking at the bandage wrapped around her upper arm. "I am," she said, looking to Liselotte gratefully. "Your mother says it is merely a scratch."

Chad reached out to grasp her, politely, for the purpose of escorting her back outside but he ended up taking her hand rather than her elbow, a much more personal gesture and not one missed by his gleeful mother.

"Then we must leave," he said. "Henry's men are contained, at least for the moment, so let us be gone."

Alessandria went with him, willingly, leaving Liselotte and Veronica still in the common room, watching them head out into the bailey where the skirmish was essentially over. The Six were contained, at least for the moment, and de Garr was brought into the knight quarters, unconscious and badly beaten, as Chad and Alessandria mounted their horses and headed out of Canterbury.

But the last vision of them had a lingering effect, at least to Liselotte. Even as she tended de Garr, who was beaten so badly she wasn't sure he would ever recover, her thoughts were of her son as he had spoken to the woman he was trying very hard to save from Henry's clutches. She thought, perhaps, that it was only duty he was feeling but she hoped it was more than that.

Chad was a virtuous man of great character and she wanted very much for him to find love, to know the joy and triumph that she had known with his father. Every mother wanted what was best for her son and Liselotte was no exception. She truly hoped he could find love with the beautiful Lady Alessandria, and even as she prayed for the recovery of the knight her son had badly beaten, she also said a prayer for Chad's heart. She prayed that love found its way into it. It was a big and giving heart.

From what she had seen of the interaction between Chad and the lady, perhaps love already had found its way inside.

Call it Mother's Intuition, but she suspected as much.

CHAPTER SEVEN

Isenhall Castle
Coventry

"It is my sense, at this point, that Henry is not beyond anything distasteful. Holding Alessandria as a hostage simply proves that."

Gallus de Shera, the Earl of Coventry, sat in a small room on the entry level of Isenhall's big, squat keep. It was a low-ceilinged room, vaulted, with heavy beams supporting the ceiling and smoke that gathered up at the apex.

The room was usually used for family meals, much smaller and cozier than the massive hall in Isenhall Castle's compact complex, but it was also used for conferences. Men could sit more closely to one another around the heavy oak table that could seat fifteen to twenty people at a time and conversations could be heard. On this day, Gallus and his brothers, Maximus and Tiberius, sat around the table, unmistakably hearing what Bose de Moray was telling them.

It was sobering news, indeed.

"Chad de Lohr and his men have gone to take Aurelius' sister from Newington Priory before Henry's men can get to her," Bose said. "I trust Chad and I know you do also. If it is at all possible for him to take the lady to safety, he will."

"And Henry has one less bargaining chip," Maximus, the big, gruff middle brother spoke. Green-eyed and dark-haired, much like his older and younger brothers, his voice was ominous. "For Christ's sake, why would he seek out Aurelius' sister as a hostage? Doesn't he know we cannot stand the man?"

Tiberius, the youngest brother, grinned even though the situation as quite serious. He was grinning because Maximus was the brother who never had any tact.

"I have only met the sister once," Tiberius said. "Honestly, I do not even remember her, but she is a de Shera. Henry is as wise as he is devious in using her against us."

Gallus shook his head. "It will not work," he said. "Although I am saddened to know she is his target, surely he knows that I must look at the bigger picture. I cannot surrender the entire House of de Shera for a cousin I hardly know. Her single life is not worth all of ours, as harsh as that sounds."

Bose, seated across the well-used table from Gallus, sighed faintly. He was exhausted from his ride to Isenhall to deliver Henry's ultimatum to three men the king very badly wanted. Henry was desperate for the support of the Earl of Coventry and his brothers but, as the conversation over the past hour had proven, the earl and his brothers, men known as the Lords of Thunder, were not eager or even remotely inclined to support the king at this point. Not after what Henry and his supporters had done to Simon de Montfort. That, in truth, was abundantly clear.

"As I said, Henry wanted me to make it clear to you that you could retain your lands and titles and fortune if you were to recant your support for de Montfort and give Henry your fealty," Bose said. "If you do not, Henry has also made it clear that he intends to destroy you. Gallus, the man is bent on vengeance and you are at the top of his list. How can I make this any plainer to you?"

Gallus, the handsome eldest brother, eyed his youngest brother's father-in-law. "You have made it very plain, Bose," he said. "You know that we adore and respect you. But our path was set from the beginning of de Montfort's rebellion. We have always, and only, supported him and his ideals of a government that should be run by the people and for the people. Henry may be the rightful king but he has no business administering this country. He has proven himself incompetent time and time again. I know you are friends with him and that you admire him, but I must differ with you on that opinion. There is nothing of the man to admire or support as far as we are concerned."

Bose didn't like where the conversation was heading. "Is that stance worth the life of your wife and children?" he asked, hitting Gallus where it would hurt him the most – his family. "For that is what it will come to, my friend. Henry can raise a bigger army than you can and he will come to Isenhall and he will destroy her. He will then take you and your wife and children to London where he will more than likely send you to the ax and keep your family locked up for the remainder of his reign. You will not see your children grow up; you will not see your son attain his rightful title of Earl of Coventry. Is that what you wish, Gallus? Is your stubborn stance worth everything you have?"

Gallus was listening to Bose carefully. After a moment, he scratched his chin in a pensive gesture. "Do you truly believe it will come to that?"

"Unfortunately, I do."

Gallus glanced at Maximus and Tiberius, who met his gaze without emotion. Gallus held his brothers' gazes for a moment longer before looking away. "Then we will send the women and children away," he said. "I will send them to Lioncross Abbey where they will be safe until this blows over. Bose, I know you mean well and I appreciate that you have come to Isenhall to discuss this, but I cannot and will not surrender to Henry. I do not like the man and I do not like his politics. I must continue to stand for what I believe in, in what Simon believed in."

Bose sighed faintly, fearful that he truly wasn't getting through to Gallus. "What purpose will your stance serve when you are dead?" he asked quietly. "Henry has that power and I do not want to see you or your brothers die, Gallus. I know that Ty's death would destroy my daughter. England needs the three of you and your patriotic, progressive ideals. Please do not let that end now. Swear fealty to Henry yet keep your ideals. There is a time and place for every fight and, for now, you have lost this fight with Simon's death. Do not lose your life, too."

Gallus could see that Bose was distressed. He felt badly for the old man, put in such a position as he was. Bose was loyal to Henry and always had been, ever since his days as captain of the guard for the young king. Rumor had it that Henry even saved Bose's life once, so there was a very strong bond there that Gallus would never diminish. He admired such loyalty. But the fact remained that Bose was in a precarious, and emotional, position trying to negotiate for the king with the Lords of Thunder.

The immovable object had met the mountain. No one was budging.

Slowly, Gallus stood up, making his way around the table to where Bose was sitting. He didn't want the table between them for what he had to say. Sitting beside the old knight, he looked into the man's black eyes.

"Simon de Montfort the Younger has asked us to continue his father's rebellion at his side," he said quietly. "At Evesham, when we saw the turn the battle was taking, the young Simon came to me and begged me not to let his father's ideals die with him. He is mounting a counterattack to Henry and has asked me to lead it."

Bose stared at him for a moment before closing his eyes and shaking his head in a painful gesture of disbelief. "Nay, Gallus," he hissed, opening his eyes to look at the man. "You must not do this. Simon the Younger doesn't have the command capability that his father had. He is not the leader his father was."

Gallus grasped the old man on the arm. "Nay, he is not," he said quietly. "But *I* am. It is my intention to assume Simon's mantle now that he is gone. Bose, I do not want my children growing up, commanded by a king who is inept at best. I want them to have a say in their country and in their world, in the things that affect them, and I want their voices heard when it comes to the governing good of England. It is every man's right to have a say in the world that he lives in. We do not follow the king blindly, like sheep. It is my intention to provide my children with the opportunity to help the king rule his kingdom in a fair and just manner."

Bose could only stare at the man, feeling sick to his stomach. "You… you cannot be serious, Gallus," he finally said. "Henry will do to you what he did to Simon – he will kill you. He is the king, for Christ's sake… do you not understand that his resources and armies are greater than yours? He will crush you if you rebel."

Gallus didn't seem particularly worried. "I could not live with myself if I did not do what my heart tells me to do," he said. "It is something I must do."

Bose's gaze lingered on Gallus before turning to Maximus and Tiberius, across the table from him. He could see the brothers were united in this and it scared him to death; especially Tiberius. His daughter's husband was a great and noble man, and he didn't want to see his head on the top of a pike, cut off by Henry in his vengeance. The mere thought made him feel ill. He couldn't even look at them anymore.

"This is what it will come to," he muttered. "I will return to Henry and tell him that you refuse his offer and then he will order me to lead an army against you. I will refuse, in such case he will send another commander – Davyss de Winter mayhap – to march on you. If given the choice, you know that de Winter will refuse and, in that case, Henry will order Curtis de Lohr to march on you. Curtis will refuse him as well. That means that me and Davyss and Curtis will all be considered enemies of the crown and we will be forced, by virtue of having refused the king, to side with you in this matter whether or not we believe the rightness of what you are doing. Do you understand what you are creating here? This situation isn't only about you, Gallus. It is about all of us who love you. Do you understand what you will be doing to all of us?"

Gallus' expression was tense and he stood up, moving away from Bose, his manner edgy as well as pensive. "I do not ask you to refuse the king when he orders you to lead an army against me," he said. "That is your choice, Bose. If you chose to refuse him, it will not be because I asked you to."

Bose sighed heavily, feeling his age, his exhaustion. "We would refuse because we love you," he said simply. "We would refuse because we could not lift a sword to kill you as much as you could not lift a sword to kill me. But it will come to that. God help me, it will come to that if you insist on pursuing Simon's quest. There is little more I can say about it, I fear."

Gallus looked at the lowered head of the old man, his friend for a great may years because Bose's son, Garran, had served Gallus and was a close friend. Garran had gone on home to Bose's seat in Dorset, taking the de Moray army with him, whilst Bose rode north to Coventry. Frankly, Gallus was glad that Garran hadn't come. He wasn't entirely sure he could have refused both Garran and Bose in their pleas to side with Henry.

"You understand a man's conviction, Bose," Gallus finally said. "You are a true and honorable friend for what you have said, and for what you have done for my brothers and me, and please know that it pains me greatly to say what I must. But in this case my brothers and I intend to continue de Montfort's dreams, up to and including sacrificing our own lives. It is something I feel very strongly about. I hope you can understand that."

Bose was feeling defeated and hollow. "What of your cousin?" he asked, his voice dull with sorrow. "What of Aurelius' sister? If Henry holds her hostage, what do you intend to do?"

Gallus seemed uncomfortable with the question. He looked at Maximus and Tiberius. It was Maximus who finally shook his head and averted his gaze. Gallus exhaled a long, slow breath, one of great regret.

"Nothing," he said. "I cannot and will not let Henry coerce our loyalty by holding a family member hostage. I will lose all credibility if I agree to any kind of exchange or change of loyalties. As much as I regret saying this, I cannot let the life of one person determine the lives of so many, Bose. I am truly sorry. I pray that Chad has been able to save the woman from Henry's clutches and we do not have to worry about this scenario, for if, in fact, Henry has her, then the situation will not go well in her favor."

Bose understood. God help him, he understood all too well. There was honor at stake here and, as Gallus said, his credibility. What man would allow himself to be manipulated with a hostage? A weak man, indeed. Wearily, Bose stood up from the table.

"You understand that I had to try," he said, looking at the three brothers. "I could not live with myself if I did not do everything in my power to prevent your fall, or worse – your death. Ty, let me take Douglass back with me to Ravendark Castle. She will be safe at the home where she was born in case Henry decides to raze Isenhall."

Tiberius looked at his father-in-law. "She will not go and you know it," he said quietly. "She is heavily pregnant now, too, and will not travel well. Nay, Bose, she remains here. She is my wife and her place is with me."

Bose's expression tightened. "Are you so selfish that you would see her killed because of your foolish ideals?" he snapped in an uncharacteristic burst. As soon as it left his mouth, he put up his hands to beg forgiveness. "I apologize. I did not mean it. I am simply… weary. It has been a very long few weeks since Evesham and I am simply weary."

Tiberius stood up and rounded the table, going to put his arm around Bose's broad shoulders. "No harm done," he said, the characteristic twinkle in his eyes. "Come with me. Let us go and see my wife and then you can rest. She is anxious to see you, anyway. I told her to stay away from our conference and she was quite unhappy with me."

Bose smiled weakly, making sure to reach out and touch Gallus on the arm as Tiberius led him from the room. It was a gesture of affection, not lost on Gallus. He watched the old knight go, hearing his boot falls, slow and heavy, as the man took the stairs. When the sounds faded, Gallus turned to Maximus.

"Are we being stubborn, Max?" he asked. "Are we simply poor

losers that refuse to give up the fight because we did not triumph at Evesham? I am having difficulty separating myself from the reality of the situation and the convictions we have fought so long and hard for."

Maximus leaned forward on the table, pondering his brother's question. "I don't know," he said honestly. "All I know is that I feel like vomiting every time I think of serving Henry. But if we did, it would save our lives and the lives of our children. We have a great many children to think of, Gallus. I do not want our sons punished for the sins of the fathers."

Gallus looked at his brother, long and hard. "Nor do I," he agreed. "But neither do I wish to serve an incompetent king."

"Then this matter is not settled as far as I am concerned."

Gallus nodded; what Maximus said was the truth. It wasn't settled in the least. "Let de Moray sleep and we will speak with him more when he is rested," he said. "Mayhap… mayhap I am simply being too stubborn in all of this. Mayhap Bose has been right all along."

Maximus lifted his eyebrows. "It is certainly something to consider," he said. "But what he said about Aurelius' sister – do we really allow the girl to come to harm as Henry's hostage? That is not like you, Gallus. You are concerned for everyone in our family so to consign the girl to her fate as you did sounded cruel."

Gallus shrugged. "I will not surrender to Henry because he threatens me with a de Shera hostage," he said. "But do not fear; we have enough people who side with Henry who could free the girl if it came to that."

Maximus was interested. "De Winter?"

Gallus nodded. "De Winter, de Moray, and even de Lohr," he said. "The girl will not suffer a terrible fate, of that I am certain. I will rescue her myself if it comes to it. But I will not surrender to Henry based on a bribe. He would never respect me if I did."

It was the truth. Perhaps the Lords of Thunder would, indeed, swear fealty to Henry at some point; perhaps they wouldn't. But if they did, it wouldn't be because they were forced to.

It would be of their own doing.

The de Sheras were stubborn that way.

"What now, then?" Maximus asked. "Bose said that Henry would send his army after us if we do not agree to swear fealty to him. We lost a good portion of our army at Evesham and if Henry lays siege, I doubt we have enough men and material to fight him off. We need time and reinforcements."

Gallus knew that. "I have been thinking of just that fact," he said. "All thoughts of Aurelius' sister aside, we do, indeed, need reinforcements and the only person I can think to ask is the same one who covered our rear when we fled Evesham."

Maximus lifted his eyebrows. "De Lohr?"

Gallus nodded. "His father is our grandfather," he said. "Mayhap if Henry sees the de Lohr army camped around Isenhall, he will think twice before attacking us."

Maximus wasn't so sure. "But Curtis de Lohr is loyal to Henry," he said. "Covering our retreat from battle is one thing but coming to Isenhall and preparing to fight against Henry is entirely another. Henry will think that the de Lohrs have abandoned him. It is as Bose said; he will think Curtis to be his enemy."

Gallus scratched his head. "It is possible," he said. "But one thing is for certain – if we do not have reinforcements, and Henry truly means to attack us, then what Bose said is correct – he will raze Isenhall and we will all die. I do not wish to see that."

"Nor I."

They had a massive dilemma on their hands and each brother knew it. It was difficult to realize that they either had to swear fealty to a king they did not respect or face death. They'd known it all along but this was the closest they'd come to admitting it.

"Bose was right about something else," Gallus said quietly. "We do have our families to consider."

"We do."

"Is it our pride standing in the way, then?"

Gallus shook his head. "I do not know if it is my pride or my conviction that the beliefs Simon held were right and true, above my life and the lives of my family."

Maximus raked his fingers through his dark hair. He had come to a conclusion even if his brother had not. "I am willing to risk my own life for my beliefs but not the lives of my wife and children," he said, standing up from the table. "Send de Lohr a missive and ask if he will reinforce our ranks should Henry come. If he will not, then I send my family to Lioncross for protection. I will not have them here if Henry comes."

Gallus understood. "Jeniver and my children will go with them," he said, sounding defeated for the first time during their conversation. Like it or not, they had to face what was coming. "I am sure Ty will send Douglass and his children as well. That way, when Henry comes, *if* he comes, it will only be the three of us facing him."

Maximus didn't say anything more. He didn't have to. Without another word, he quit the chamber, heading upstairs to see to his wife and children. He had a sudden urge to hug them all and never let them go. Gallus let his brother go, the brooding middle brother, as he was lost to thoughts of his own.

The Coventry earldom had been in his family for two generations; only two. He didn't want to see it end with him. He had a son to pass it along to, Bhrodi, and he wanted to make sure that happened. His conviction to stand for what he believed in was dwindling with the idea of preserving his lands and titles and fortune for his son and coming generations.

He prayed to God that he would make the correct choice.

Chapter Eight

Bexley Manor
Northwest of Rochester

IT WAS VERY dark on this night, so dark that Alessandria could hardly see her hand in front of her face. It had been the same way the night before, with the moon rising more towards morning so that the entire night was as black as ink. Not even the blanket of stars above could pierce the veil of darkness very much. It was quiet, dark, and eerie.

The land smelled of compost, too, that moldering smell when there is heat and moisture, with the leaves rotting on ground. Although Alessandria couldn't see the tree groves except for black masses against the moonless night, she could certainly smell them. She could imagine the creatures and even spirits out in the darkness that she couldn't see. The Mother Prioress had told her charges that there were no such things as spirits or phantoms, but Alessandria had seen a ghost, once while she was fostering at Orford, so she believed in such things. She was rather frightened by them.

But riding with Chad made her feel safe. Having left Canterbury earlier that day at a dead run, there hadn't been the opportunity for much conversation but Alessandria didn't much care. She was comforted by his mere presence. As they'd cantered across the land, heading northwest, she'd stolen glances at him now and again. He was such a fine-looking man with an effortless posture as he rode his big, fat-arsed horse. Effortless in that he rode the horse with such ease, holding the reins but seemingly guiding the horse only with pressure from his thighs. That was true horsemanship.

As they rode along, Alessandria kept reliving their last conversation in which he'd asked to call her Aless. It made her heart thump simply to think on it again. In fact, everything about the man made her heart thump as of late – she had to only look at him to feel her heart begin to race. It was a feeling like she couldn't even describe – something to do with a lightness of heart and soul, of joy, because the mere thought of him made her smile. No one had made her feel the way Chad did but she was quite certain the feelings were one-sided. A man as great and prestigious as Chad de Lohr could never feel the same way about her; of that, she was certain. But it didn't stop her from dreaming.

Dreams that kept her occupied until Chad slowed their pace. They entered a small village called Bexleyheath, a sleepy town that, at the late hour, was all bottled up for the night. Alessandria looked around the village with interest, for having been stuck in Newington for all of those years made her very interested in new places. She wanted to ask what Chad's plans were for the night but it seemed ill-advised to speak since he had been so silent. Perhaps there was a reason he'd not said a word, remaining quiet as they moved through the town.

Therefore, Alessandria simply followed without saying a word even though she was dying to. It wasn't so much out of curiosity than it was simply because she wanted to hear the sound of his voice. She did so love the sound of his voice.

"There is a manor home at the end of this village," he said, his deep, raspy voice filling the damp night air. "That is where I intend to seek shelter for the night. However, the lord of Bexley Manor is loyal to Henry and I have been wracking my brain trying to determine how I should introduce you. The de Shera name is not welcome amongst Henry's loyalists these days."

Alessandria shrugged. "You certainly do not have to be truthful about my identity, do you?"

Chad shook his head. "Nay," he said. "But that brings us to another issue – you are an unmarried woman and I am an unmarried man, and we are riding together without a chaperone. That factor alone will probably give you a worse reputation than if I tell them you are a de Shera."

"So what will you do?"

Chad looked over his shoulder, glancing at her. "You may not like it."

"You will not know unless you tell me."

A flicker of a smile crossed his lips. "It would be far easier if I simply introduce you as my wife," he said. "There will be no questions and certainly no judgment. In the morning, we shall leave and they will be none the wiser."

My wife. Alessandria looked at him in shock at the impropriety of what he was suggesting when she suddenly realized that nothing on earth would be more pleasurable. The wife of Chad de Lohr, a strong and virtuous and talented man, chivalrous to a fault. Nay, nothing on earth would please her more than to be the man's wife and she began to feel some sorrow at the fact that something that gave her such pleasure could never be.

Oh, what a dagger to her foolish heart was that awareness.

Chad could never be hers.

"I have no objections," she said, feeling depressed even as she said it. "Whatever you feel is best."

She didn't seem enthused about it. "Are you sure?" he asked. "I could come up with another excuse, but it would not be nearly as neat."

"I am sure. You may tell them I am your wife."

Chad turned to look at her, wondering why she sounded so moody. Was it possible that such a suggestion, even the mere mention of it, was so distasteful to her? His heart sank for reasons he could not begin to understand. Surely she believed him to be a heartless and cruel individual considering the misfortune and discomfort she'd met with since he wrested her from Newington. She certainly couldn't think otherwise. Chad realized he would have given his right arm to be able to court the woman, to show her a side of him that wasn't brutal and reasonable and warlike. All he'd ever shown her was hardship. God, he wished he could show her so much more.

But he kept his mouth shut, feeling her morose mood, trying not to feel too badly for the way things had gone for her from the moment of their association. Instead, he focused on ahead, through the miserable little pimple of a village to the other side where a large manor house was situated.

Even in the dark of night, he could see it outlined against the dusting of stars in the sky. The structure of Bexley Manor was rather tall and oddly shaped, with the bulk of the structure being on the second and third floors, which made it project out from the ground floor below. It was quite lit up, lights in the windows acting like beacons in the darkness, and as Chad and Alessandria drew near, they could see a massive moat encircling the structure and then an enormous wall on the other side of the moat. There was a bridge, which had been removed for the night, and Chad drew his horse to a halt on the banks of the moat and yelled across to the sentries, identifying himself.

At first, the sentries didn't seem apt to believe he was who he said he was. They yelled back at him, ridiculed him a bit, but Chad seemed to know how to deal with it. Mention of the threat from the House of de Lohr seemed to force the sentries to take him seriously. When Chad also mentioned Evesham and news from someone who had been in the battle, it prompted them to order some men to produce the bridge over the moat. Several men emerged from the protection of the manor, carrying the narrow bridge between them, and they pushed it across the moat until it reached the other side and came to a rest on firm ground.

More men bearing torches came out to greet them as they crossed the skinny bridge. The wood creaked and groaned under the weight of the horses and Alessandria was a bit nervous about it, relieved when the horses finally returned to solid ground on the other side. She directed her horse behind Chad and listened to him as he spoke with a bald-headed man, one of the men who had come from the manor bearing torches.

Evidently, the lady of the house was having some kind of feast and there were other guests inside, crowded into the odd-looking manor house. Chad, however, didn't care about any other guests. He only cared about himself and Alessandria, and made sure to throw the de Lohr name around a few times before the man he had been speaking with offered to usher him inside. It was the answer Chad had been seeking.

So they followed the men with torches into a large, rounded doorway that Alessandria took to be the entrance, only she was puzzled that the horses were allowed in. She soon saw why; the entry door led to an inner courtyard of sorts and as soon as they entered the spacious courtyard, Chad dismounted his steed and made his way to Alessandria, removing her from the leggy mare. He then took her satchel, his saddlebags and sword, and followed the bald-headed man into an arched entryway, which led directly into a two-storied hall.

The heat and stench of the hall hit both Chad and Alessandria in the face like a slap. The smell of dogs was nearly overwhelming, as was the smell of roasting meat. Smoke lay across the ceiling in a haze from the blazing hearth, filling their nostrils with the acrid scent. It was noisy inside, with musicians in the corner playing and about a dozen people seated at a heavily-laden table.

Food and wine scattered all across the table and the bald man approached an older woman with wild gray hair seated at the end, bending over to whisper in her ear. When he was finished, the woman immediately looked to Chad and Alessandria, practically shoving away the bald man.

"You two!" she cried rather happily. "Come closer! Let me get a good look at a de Lohr!"

The entire table turned to them at that point, looking to Chad and Alessandria, standing several feet away and mostly in the shadows. When the lady with the wild hair waved them over, Chad simply took

Alessandria's hand and obeyed. He gently pulled Alessandria with him, their bags in one big hand and her in the other, until he came to within a few feet of the older woman. He dipped his head at her in greeting.

"My lady," he said. "I apologize for the intrusion, but I am Sir Chad de Lohr. My father is the Earl of Canterbury and a friend of Lord du Bexley. Is he not at home?"

The woman shook her head, causing her wild gray hair to whip about. Her hair was so curly that it was literally standing on end, frizzy and unkempt. "My husband died last winter of a fever," she said. "We miss Merlin, God rest his soul, but life must go on, mustn't it? I am Felicia, Lady du Bexley, and you and your wife are welcome in my home."

Chad forced a smile. "You are very kind, my lady," he said. "We have had a rather long journey and are grateful for shelter this night."

Lady du Bexley waved him to the table. "Please," she said. "Sit by me. I would hear all about your travels and your family, Sir Chad. My husband spoke often of your father. He was quite fond of him."

She was shoving the couple immediately to her left down the table, pushing at them to make room for Chad and Alessandria. The couple, a well-dressed man and woman, moved reluctantly, clearing space on the bench. Chad helped Alessandria to sit before taking the space next to her.

"Thank you," Chad said as servants immediately appeared, placing food and drink in front of them. "My father often spoke of Sir Barnabas as well. I believe your husband knew my grandfather as well."

Lady du Bexley was zeroed in on Alessandria and Chad as if there weren't a dozen other guests at her table. Her small eyes were quite intense.

"My husband knew everyone," she said frankly. "Barnabas was in his eightieth year when he died. He knew Moses himself, I believe."

She laughed at her joke, bringing a smile from Chad as Alessandria dug into her food. Literally, she plunged her hands into it and shoved meat in her mouth, absolutely starving. Chad couldn't help but notice that she was eating with an urgent edge and neither could Lady du Bexley. The old woman put her hand out, touching Alessandria on the wrist.

"Slow yourself, Lady de Lohr," she said, "or you will choke. You will not want to choke because if you die, I fear I will have to match my daughter with your handsome husband. You'll not want to die if you know a woman is waiting to take your place!"

She meant it as a joke and those who had heard her laughed, including a rather giddy and homely looking young woman across the table. As Alessandria sat in embarrassed silence, the young woman's silly, high-pitched laughter was above everyone else's.

"Mama, you are so right," she said, eyeing Chad. "He is, indeed, a comely boy, is he not? Why did you not have Papa send for the de Lohr sons when you were seeking a husband for me?"

Lady du Bexley and her daughter seemed quite pleased with themselves in a giddy, silly way. Lady du Bexley pointed to the young woman.

"Sir Chad, meet my daughter, Eloise," she said proudly. "A pity that you did not know her before you married your wife. Oh, I mean no disrespect to your wife, of course, but a fine marriage between the House of de Lohr and the House of du Bexley would have been a grand thing, indeed. Eloise is the heiress to her father's estate, in fact. She will inherit more land than the House of de Lohr holds, of that I am sure. You do not have any brothers, do you?"

Chad was trying very hard not to be rude. The mere thought of being married to that bug-eyed, frizzy-haired creature horrified him and he could hardly believe that Lady du Bexley had brought about such a personal subject so quickly. Perhaps the woman was rich, but she clearly had the manners of a boor. He took a very long drink of his wine before answering.

"I have two brothers, my lady," he said, thinking on Stefan and Perrin and realizing he had a prime opportunity to play a very nasty joke on them. Not that his father would ever agree to a marriage with the du Bexley heiress for either of them, but it was great fun to think of the lengths his brothers would go through to avoid the woman if she was on their scent. "Neither of them is married."

Lady du Bexley was intrigued. "Is that so?" she said, very interested. "Are they as comely as you, my boy?"

Chad shook his head. "Of course not," he said. "I am the beauty in the family. Just ask my wife."

Lady du Bexley turned her attention to Alessandria, who was taking a long and satisfying drink of her wine. After the choking rebuke, Alessandria had hoped to stay out of the woman's conversation but evidently that was not to be.

"Is this true, Lady de Lohr?" Lady du Bexley asked. "Is your husband the only handsome son in the family?"

Alessandria swallowed her drink, wiping her mouth with the back of her hand as she looked at Chad. "Aye," she said after a moment. "He is the only handsome son. He is kind beyond measure. Therefore, you may not wish to waste your time with the other two sons. I have the only one worth having."

Chad grinned at her. God, he'd give anything for her words to actually mean something. As he looked at her, he thought that there was something in her eyes that suggested she did, indeed, mean every word. But there was also something twinkling in the sea-colored eyes that spoke of mirth. Perhaps she was simply playing the game or perhaps she, too, was coming to think that Lady du Bexley was quite bold and without tact. It was quite ridiculous, really, to show such behavior towards people she had just met.

"A pity," Lady du Bexley said, unaware of the fact that her two newest guests were inwardly laughing at her. "Imagine – my daughter marrying into the House of de Lohr. What a magnificent thing that would be. Nonetheless, I shall write to your father about a betrothal, Sir Chad. If he has two unattached sons, no matter how homely they are, they are still de Lohrs. Either one will make a fine match with my daughter."

Chad could see that there was no discouraging the woman. Like a dog with a meaty bone, she wasn't going to let go of the fact that she had a de Lohr in her midst with two eligible brothers. He couldn't keep the smile off his lips when he thought of Stefan and Perrin hiding from the obnoxious Lady du Bexley and her equally-obnoxious daughter. He hoped he was around to see it.

Someone down the table was telling a joke and Eloise shrilly called to her mother to listen. Lady du Bexley turned her attention from Chad, listening to one of the men tell a joke about the king, in fact. It was something ribald, not even mildly appropriate for women, but Eloise laughed her cackling laugh and Lady du Bexley admonished the man to watch his tongue even though she, too, was laughing.

Lady du Bexley was also eating, having pulled a leg from a roasted swan, and bits of food were flying out of her mouth as she chewed. Some of it sprayed into Alessandria's trencher and Alessandria looked at the mess in front of her, bits of half-chewed bird flesh, rather sadly.

Chad, seeing what had happened and suspecting she wouldn't eat from her trencher now that Lady du Bexley had blown her spittle all over it, tore some beef off the hunk before him and placed the un-spit upon meat on the corner of her trencher.

"Here," he said quietly. "I will share with you."

Alessandria looked at him gratefully, accepting the beef and pushing it into her mouth. "Thank you," she said quietly, chewing politely, "but I am not quite sure how I am going to tell our hostess that I have no intention of eating where she has spit."

Chad grinned as he cut more meat for her, off the bone. "I am not entirely sure she will notice," he said softly. "She seems to have the attention span of a sparrow."

Alessandria giggled. "She *was* very kind to allow us into her home."

"Very kind."

"But her manners…."

"I know."

Alessandria grinned, taking another bite. "Where will we stay tomorrow night?"

Chad thought on that as he handed her more meat. "We should be well north of London tomorrow," he said. "There are many inns or taverns where we can find lodgings."

She pictured what adventures in accommodations tomorrow night might bring for them. "It has been a long time since I have stayed in an inn," she said. "In fact, it has been a long time since I have slept in a bed. We slept on the floor at Newington. The Mother Prioress believed it made us strong to sleep in discomfort."

Chad shook his head. "I am not entirely sure I agree with that," he said. "I have spent my share of nights sleeping on the ground, but it did not make me stronger. It made my back hurt."

Alessandria laughed softly. "Mine, too," she said. "I have had an aching back for six years. I cannot imagine what it would feel like not to sleep on the hard earth."

"You will find out tonight."

Alessandria started to say something but Lady du Bexley suddenly let out a cry of delight as several servants flooded into the hall, bringing with them trays of sweets and other delights to conclude the meal. Alessandria watched, wide-eyed, as many delicacies were placed on the table – marzipan, which was an almond paste, shaped like a little castle with little cloth banners flying from the turrets while a tray of fried dough balls coated in honey and cinnamon sat nearby. A pudding of mashed apples and raisins was displayed in a lovely painted bowl while an entire tray of baked pears sat near the middle of the table.

It was more food than Alessandria had ever seen in one sitting, decadence on a grand scale. Lady du Bexley was wealthy and not afraid to show it. The servants were dishing out the sweets to the diners and Chad made sure to get his trencher in there so they could serve him up some treats as well. When he drew his trencher back and set it between him and Alessandria, they both inspected the marzipan and the fried dough balls and the pudding. Chad cut the sweets into pieces so Alessandria could eat them more easily and she ended up gorging herself on nearly everything that was there.

In truth, Chad was deriving a good deal of pleasure simply watching her eat, even if she was eating some of the things meant for him. He really didn't care. It was clear that she was very hungry so he let her eat whatever she wished. He was happy to take her leavings. In fact, the more he sat with her and watched her, tossing around light conversation, the more enchanted he was becoming with her. She was sweet and beautiful and he liked to watch her laugh – she had a silly little giggle. She ate, they both drank, and the evening passed pleasantly and quickly.

In fact, Chad had no idea how late it was by the time Lady du Bexley's guests began to excuse themselves. All he knew was that he had enjoyed one of the more pleasurable evenings of his life, made far more pleasurable after the hell of the past several weeks. He and his army had been deployed a very long time before Evesham, and then after that horrific event, the days following had been full of trying to grasp the political situation in the wake of Simon's death. It had all been so complex and unpleasant. But sitting here with Alessandria, in this warm and fragrant hall as the wine flowed freely, he felt truly at peace for the first time in months.

More guests left the table but Chad remained, still drinking wine and sitting beside Alessandria, who was so full of sweets and food that she could barely move. But the wine was delicious and warming, and soon enough they were having their own giggling conversation over how Stefan and Perrin would react to Eloise du Bexley showing up at Canterbury Castle. Mostly, it was Chad making faces when he imagined what his brothers would do to him and Alessandria was laughing uncontrollably. He must have been quite entertaining because Lady du Bexley soon realized that her new friends were having a marvelous time and she sought to capture Chad's attention.

"What are you and your wife laughing about?" she demanded to know. "You must tell the rest of us so that we may laugh with you!"

Chad's eyes widened. He had been making great sport of Lady du Bexley's daughter and knew he couldn't tell his hostess that, so quickly, he scrambled for an excuse.

"I...I was singing a song, my lady," he lied. "It is a very humorous song."

"Then you must tell us!"

Chad shook his head. "Nay, my lady," he said, trying not to sound as if he were lying. "It... well, it is not meant for ladies' ears."

Lady du Bexley was incensed. "But you told your wife!"

Chad looked at Alessandria, who was silently laughing at the fact that he'd wedged himself into a corner. She'd had far too much to drink and soon couldn't hold back her laughter at all.

"Tell her," she said impishly. "Oh, do tell her what we have been laughing at."

His eyes narrowed at her threateningly, although it was in jest. "Cheeky wench," he muttered. "You shall not have the last laugh."

"Is that so?"

"It is!"

Taking a deep breath, Chad stood up and set his wine cup down, which was empty. It had been his fifth or sixth cup; he wasn't entirely sure, but he did know that he was quite drunk. He was up to having some fun, now with too much alcohol flowing through his veins.

"Very well, Lady du Bexley," he said with some exaggeration. "If you wish to hear my song, here it is."

With that, he climbed right up onto the cluttered table, much to the delight of the diners, and began belting out the first naughty song that came to mind.

"A young man came to Tilly Nodden,
His heart so full and pure.
Upon the step of Tilly Nodden,
His wants would find no cure."

Chad had a remarkable baritone singing voice, quite lovely, and the women at the table sighed with delight while the men, who recognized the song, cheered for the bawdy tune. Encouraged, Chad began to dance across the table, kicking dishes out of the way and listening to everyone laugh at him. He was being quite dramatic and entertaining as he continued.

"Aye! Tilly, Tilly, my goddess near,
Can ye spare me a glance from those eyes?
My Tilly, sweet Tilly, be my lover so dear,
I'm a-wantin' a slap of those thighs!
Then our young man, his life less grand,
Since the day he met our Tilly.
His love for her nearly drove him daft,
When he discovered not a puss, but a shaft!"

With that, he untied his breeches and exposed his bare buttocks to the diners as they screamed in laughter. Lady du Bexley nearly fainted because she was laughing so hard and as everyone else screamed and cheered, Alessandria sat there with her eyes wide at the sight of Chad's white, naked arse. The man was stripping down before her very eyes and her mouth popped open in shock when she heard Lady du Bexley beside her.

"Now we see what you see in your young man, my dear," she laughed. "His buttocks are as plump and perfect as two unbaked loaves of bread. Your husband has a bread-dough arse and I want to sink my teeth into it!"

The few people that heard her comment roared with laughter as Chad pulled up his pants, tied them off, and then took a tremendous bow for the room. Every movement had flourish. Even the minstrels in the corner, who had been playing quite beautifully all evening, cheered and clapped for him.

Quite pleased with his drunken display, Chad leapt off the table and staggered his way over to Alessandria, who was sitting there with her mouth still hanging open. Reaching down, he pulled her to her feet and dragged her over towards the musicians.

“Play!” he commanded the quartet. “Play something that my lady and I can dance to!”

Before Alessandria could utter a word of protest, Chad pulled her into his arms, her body pressed against his, and the music began to play. His mouth was on her temple as he spoke, their bodies indecently close.

“I want to feel you against me,” he murmured. “I have been struggling for the better part of the day with thoughts of you and I cannot deny them any longer. Let me feel your breasts against my body, even though the damnable clothing stands between us.”

Chills raced up Alessandria’s spine as his heated voice filled her brain. The music was playing but they weren’t really dancing; they were simply standing there as Chad held her close, running his hands up and down her back, up into her hair, cupping her head as his lips nibbled on her forehead.

Alessandria was so startled and consumed by his actions that her knees were growing weak. Her breath began to come in pants, her body rubbing against his in a manner that was both terribly inappropriate and overwhelmingly alluring.

“Chad…,” she whispered, trying to pull away. “What… what are you doing?”

“What I have wanted to do from nearly the beginning of our association.”

She gasped as a roaming hand found her buttocks, caressing them lewdly through the traveling dress. “Please… there are people watching….”

Chad had her pulled so tightly against him that she was bent backwards as he held her. “Let them watch,” he said, nuzzling her. “We are married, are we not? I can do whatever I wish. I am your husband, Aless. God help me, I wish I really was. I would take you upstairs and ravage you until you could no longer walk.”

They were shocking, bold words that he spoke, words that should have sent Alessandria cowering. She should have run from him at the very least. But no amount of righteousness could force her to pull away from him now. *God help me, I wish we were really married.* Was it possible he really said that? Did he really speak of the hope that was in her heart?

Clearly, he was drunk – there was no denying that. And if she was to be truthful, she was drunk as well. It was the drink that was preventing her from running away. It was the drink that was begging her to give in to the sins of the flesh, to know the touch of a man. It was as wicked as it could possibly be, but Alessandria didn't care. She was deeply enamored with Chad; nay, it was *more* than that. Was it possible to love someone after only knowing them for no more than a day? Alessandria couldn't imagine that what she was feeling for Chad wasn't love and she couldn't imagine that she would ever feel any other way about him. He said that he wished they could be married. She wished the same thing, as well.

Surely, that meant the man loved her.

Chad was still nuzzling her face, simply standing there as the music played around them. Alessandria could feel his seeking lips moving across her cheek and she turned her head so that his path would bring him to her mouth. When he claimed her lips with his own, it was as if everything else in the world suddenly faded away and it was only the two of them, becoming acquainted on a level that was beyond Alessandria's comprehension.

The only stories of sexual contact she had ever heard had been from foolish servants at Orford or from the frigid sisters at the priory. What they had described was not what Alessandria was experiencing. She was experiencing the taste and scent and feel of a man that was causing her heart to race and her head to swim. She could taste him and she loved it. It was the most exciting thing she had ever experienced.

"Sir Chad!" Lady du Bexley's admonishing voice filled their ears and Chad pulled away from Alessandria to see that the frizzy-haired old woman was heading in his direction. "Such a lusty display, my fine lad.

You have given every woman in this hall something to dream about tonight. For now, take your wife to your chamber and I will see you come the morning. Sleep well… that is, if you sleep at all."

With that, she giggled knowingly and turned back for the table, leaving the bald-headed man in her wake, who was evidently the majordomo of Bexley Manor. He seemed to have some measure of authority for Lady du Bexley. Silently, he motioned for the panting pair to follow him.

Dazed from his kiss with Alessandria, Chad quickly moved back to the feasting table to collect their possessions before returning to Alessandria's side and following the bald man to a staircase that led to the upper floor.

It was darker in the house now that they were away from the hall and the hard-packed earth floors were covered with straw, not rushes. As the bald man led them up the mural stairs, neither one of them seemed to be too observant of their surroundings; Alessandria was looking rather dreamily at Chad and Chad was struggling to keep his balance as he moved up the stairs. Had they looked around, they would have noticed a beautiful two-storied window of precious glass overlooking the stairwell and a large and expensive tapestry hanging on the wall.

Once they reached the second floor, the bald man took them to another smaller staircase that led to the top floor. On this level, there were several chambers that had a central corridor connecting them, which was an unusual architectural feature. Usually, rooms connected to each other, but with a central corridor, every room had only one entry and exit for maximum privacy.

This level was low-ceilinged and as the bald man opened the door to their chamber, Chad nearly hit his head crossing over the threshold. He staggered in, pulling Alessandria in behind him, as the bald-headed man stood at the door.

"Lady du Bexley will have a morning meal served three hours after dawn," he said. "She should like all of her guests to attend."

Chad dropped the baggage near the door. "We shall be gone before dawn," he informed the man, rubbing at his eyes because everything in the room was swimming. "We should like to have our morning meal brought to us an hour before dawn and I should also request food to take with us, if that will not be too much trouble."

The bald-headed man shook his head. "No trouble, my lord," he said. "I shall ensure that you are fed accordingly. Is there anything else you require this night?"

Chad looked at Alessandria. "Is there anything you wish?"

Alessandria nodded. "Water to wash with."

Chad turned to the bald man, who had heard her request and was already nodding. "I shall have warmed water sent up," he said. "I shall also send wine for you. Good eve, my lord."

He shut the door softly and Chad rubbed at his eyes again. "Great Lucifer's Ghost," he hissed. "Just what we need. More wine. I can hardly stand as it is."

Alessandria felt much the same way, only with her, she was particularly fatigued. Too much wine always made her terribly sleepy. She looked over at the bed in the chamber, which was a lavish piece of work, well off the floor, with a silk coverlet and curtains that attached to an overhead canopy.

"I am so weary that I could sleep for a week," she muttered, still eyeing the bed. "Well, what are the sleeping arrangements to be tonight? Will you take the floor or will I?"

Chad looked at her, standing there in her dark green traveling garment that clung to her so indecently. His heated gaze moved to her breasts, lovely perky things. He had very much liked the feel of her in his arms and the taste of her upon his lips. He hadn't forgotten any of that. In fact, his lust for her, fed by the wine, was stronger than he was. He couldn't resist his attraction to her, like the moth to the flame. He couldn't even think that being alone with her, being as drunk as he was, wasn't an entirely good idea.

All he knew was that he needed to have her.

Without a word, he moved to her, swiftly, and took her in his arms, pulling her against him as his lips slanted over hers. He could hear her gasp and, for a split second, feel her stiffen in surprise. But just as quickly that stiffness turned to pliability and she became a soft, warm mass in his arms. He could taste the wine on her just as he knew she could taste the wine on him, but neither one of them cared.

Now, the alcohol was in charge.

Chad had to have her. It was blinding, this lust he felt, and as he undid the fastens on her dress, Alessandria didn't resist. She was too busy being overwhelmed with her first serious kiss, her first experience with a man that was already bleeding her dry of her sanity and reason. Everything about it was wrong, so very wrong, but they had no choice in the matter. No one was resisting or begging for pause. Chad, already aroused, yanked the green traveling dress off of her shoulders, tore it down her body, and dumped it on the floor.

Clad only in a shift, hose, and shoes, Alessandria gasped as he picked her up and carried her over to the bed. His mouth had left her lips and was now forging a blazing trail down her neck, to the soft cleavage of her chest, as he lay her down upon the feather-stuffed mattress.

She sank down into it, unable to effectively move; it was like lying in mud. There was nowhere for her to go and although a little voice in her head screamed at the impropriety of the situation, the drunken part of her pretended not to hear it. Chad loved her, of that she was certain, and she had come to the conclusion that she loved him as well. It was a sin to demonstrate that love outside of marriage but she didn't care. Everything he was doing to her was making her body tingle and her heart jump. She wanted to experience all of it, whatever Chad wanted to show her, and propriety be damned.

Aye… *damned.*

The shoes and hose came off, yanked off by Chad in his lust. His hands slithered up her shift, coming into contact with her hot, silken flesh, and Alessandria shivered violently as he touched her. Her nipples grew hard, like pebbles, and Chad ripped the shift over her head, his heated mouth descending on her peaked nipples. He suckled powerfully as she writhed and bucked, groaning, uncertain and unfamiliar with his touch but loving it all the same.

She was too drunk to be frightened.

And Chad was too drunk to realize he was about to deflower the woman. All he knew was that his attraction to her was stronger than anything he had ever known. He was numb to his sense of reason and as he suckled on her breasts, he began to fumble with his breeches. He was still in a mail coat, which made things difficult, and when the thing got in the way of him cleanly removing his breeches, he rolled off the bed with a grunt of frustration and bent over at the waist, pulling the mail off as fast as he could.

Fortunately, he was an expert at pulling on and removing mail, so it came off with some ease, as did the padded tunic beneath it. But he still had his breeches and boots on, and he leapt back onto the bed where Alessandria was still pressed down into the mattress, and wedged himself between her legs.

His mouth came down on hers, kissing her with passion that left him breathless, as his fingers gently stroked the dark curls between her legs. She gasped at his touch, unaccustomed to it, but her hands were entwined in his hair, holding his mouth to hers. She was rapidly becoming adept at matching him kiss for kiss, his tongue snaking into her mouth as she mimicked his actions. She liked it very much and her heated body was responding to his touch as if she'd been doing it all her life. When he inserted a finger into her wet sheath, gently, she groaned and lifted her hips. It was as if her body knew what her mind did not. Crazed with lust, Chad shoved his breeches down to his knees and thrust into her.

The pain of his entry was unexpected and Alessandria bit off a cry, biting her hand, as he took two more thrusts to fully embed himself in her tight body. Pressed down into the mattress with his weight on top of her, she felt smothered and fearful, but the moment he began to move, measured thrusts in and out of her body, she began to feel the thrill of his body buried in hers.

Something magical was happening.

Alessandria groaned as he moved in and out of her, his mouth to her neck and his hand to her breast, kneading and pulling at the nipple, exciting her beyond reason. The feelings he was stirring within her made her want to open her legs wider for him, and she did. Chad must have felt her relax beneath him because he fell atop her, shifting so he was mostly lying next to her as his hands grasped her tender buttocks, thrusting into her with measured power. There was something so natural and beautiful about this coupling, as wrong as it was, all of it conducted in a drunken haze, but there was no mistaking the true emotion and attraction that drew them together.

As if it was always meant to be.

Wine gave Chad tremendous stamina and he was able to maintain an erection for several long minutes, using that heated manhood to thrust so hard that he rattled Alessandria's teeth. Alessandria, in turn, clung to him, her hands in his hair, on his shoulders, touching his face as if to convince herself of what was happening between them. It never even occurred to her that they shouldn't be doing this; that their actions were so very wrong in the eyes of God and of society, but nothing this wonderful could ever be wrong. Chad was touching her as only he could, making her feel things she never imagined he could.

The moment was pure magic.

The beauty of her first climax came upon Alessandria swiftly, unfurling through her body and causing her legs to tremble. Feeling her tremors start, Chad thrust hard and released himself deep into her tender body. Even after his release, he continued to move and continued to thrust, grinding his hips against hers, causing her to climax again. That only made him lusty again and in little time, he was hard once more and continued making love to her.

That went on three more times into the night until Alessandria fell into a heavy sleep and Chad passed out on top of her.

CHAPTER NINE

"HE SHOULD NOT be riding," Daniel said. "The man is barely able to remain conscious. Leave him here, Torran. We will take good care of him."

Torran sat atop his big black rouncey in the bailey of Canterbury, listening to Daniel's pleas. He turned around to look at de Garr, who was sitting on his horse unsteadily. De Poyer and d'Vant were on either side of the man, making sure he didn't fall, but this was with the horse not even moving. Torran wasn't entirely sure what was going to happen when the beast actually started to move.

"We will see to him," he said to Daniel. "Once we reach London, Henry's physics will tend him."

Daniel could see that Torran was being standoffish, as well he should be. Daniel had permitted his son to depart from Canterbury with the lady the day before and wouldn't tell Torran where Chad had gone. More than that, he'd kept Torran and his men locked up for the entire night, only releasing them in the morning when Chad was too far away to track. It was natural for Torran to be annoyed, and worse, for being denied his quarry, but Daniel had no regrets. He'd done what was necessary to give his son the best chance of escaping Henry's men.

"De Garr is too ill to ride," Daniel stressed. "If he falls off that horse, he could do worse damage and you know it. Stop being so stubborn about this. Leave him here until he is at least well enough to ride by himself."

Torran wasn't budging. "No need," he said. He'd long since stopped addressing Daniel as "my lord". "We will be in London in a day or two."

"You are being foolish about this."

"And you should not be so concerned for someone your son nearly killed."

Daniel sighed heavily. "You were the one who drew your weapon first, Torran. It was not I," he reminded him. "What my sons and I did was to defend ourselves and well you know it. We have been through this conversation before. Did you really think we would not meet violence with violence? Did you really think we would simply let you hold us captive and not react?"

Torran's jaw ticked. "We were acting on order from Henry, a man that I thought you also supported," he said. "I can see that I was mistaken. Be assured that Henry will know of the mistake as well."

Daniel wasn't going to be intimidated. "Do as you must," he said. "But you know as well as I do that telling Henry the House of de Lohr is no longer loyal to him will create more chaos than he can adequately handle. How do you think Henry will react if he thinks my entire family has turned on him? Do you think that will help him? Of course it will not. Therefore, when you tell him of this incident, tell him the truth – that you tried to take the lady by force and were summarily beaten back. The House of de Lohr always protects family, and that innocent woman you tried to abduct is family. It has nothing to do with failing to support Henry."

Torran was growing increasingly upset. "Paint this situation any way you please, but the truth is obvious," he said. "The Earl of Canterbury is siding with the Lords of Thunder, and the Lords of Thunder side with de Montfort."

Daniel shook his head in disgust. "If that is all you see, then you are a fool," he said. "Get off my property. Go back to Henry and tell him your lies. If he wants the truth, I will be more than happy to discuss it with him."

With that, he turned away from Torran and headed over to the group that had gathered near the entrance to the keep to watch him deal with Henry's unhappy men. Stefan, Perrin, Chris, Arthur, and William were there as well as de Russe and du Bois, all of them watching Daniel as he dismissed Henry's Six from Canterbury.

As the group thundered from the gatehouse, trying to keep de Garr in the saddle, Daniel approached the host of young and talented knights. He was feeling some disappointment in the situation in general but mostly for the sake of the young knights. If Henry attacked, they would be on the front lines. It was a sad thought, indeed.

"He will tell Henry that we have betrayed him," he said, scratching his head in a resigned gesture. "I am not entirely sure what will happen now, but we may find ourselves on the wrong end of Henry's sword."

That was a sobering thought for the young knights. They all looked at each other, various stages of concern on their faces at Daniel's words.

"Henry would not do that to you, Papa," Perrin said, ever the optimist. "He needs you too much."

Daniel smiled thinly. "Mayhap," he said. "Remind me to tell you of the time I openly defied Henry. It was when I was courting your mother, well before you were born. Henry issued a direct order that I ignored. For years, I ignored it until one day I happened to come across Henry and that very situation came up through conversation."

Daniel's sons had never heard of this instance, which was unusual. Daniel often spoke of his past great deeds which, they suspected, were told in a much more grandiose fashion by their father than what actually happened. Therefore, for him to mention disobeying the king – and not having told them about it before – was something of a surprise. It would have been much more like Daniel to have gloated about it.

"What was this order, Papa?" Stefan asked, curious. "What happened?"

Daniel thought back to that time, thirty years ago, when he had been a young man very much in love. His thin smile turned genuine. "Henry wanted your mother to marry someone else," he said. "I killed the man and ignored the order. Of course, there is more to it than that and mayhap someday I will tell you all of it, but know that I loved your mother so much that I was not unwilling to kill for her. Years later, when Henry asked me about the man who had been betrothed to your mother, I feigned ignorance of the entire situation. What good would it do to tell him that I killed his nephew?"

That drew a strong reaction from the young knights. "You *killed* Henry's nephew?" Stefan said, aghast. "Papa, why are we just hearing about this now?"

Daniel snorted. "Because I meant that you should," he said. "What happened with Henry's nephew happened a long time ago. Bramley was his name but you will never repeat that, do you hear? It was all in the course of a very bitter struggle. Mayhap I am simply not ready to relive those days yet. Someday, but not yet. Still… I always suspected that Henry knew what had happened. I am not sure how he knew, but I think he did. Therefore, as far as him needing me… it is possible that he needs me simply because I am part of the de Lohr war machine. It would not do for him to punish me and weaken the House of de Lohr. He needs us, especially now."

He effectively put an end to their questioning about his past, but they were awed by the revelation. It was clear they wanted the details of this great and terrible deed but no one would push him. Daniel had told them all he would, for the time being. But there was more in his message, something that they were coming to understand. It wasn't merely about his behavior; it was how Henry had reacted to it.

And, to him.

"And that is how you look upon this situation?" Stefan asked. "That Henry will not punish you for what happened here because he needs you?"

"I am counting on that."

It made sense to all of them but still, Stefan continued. "It is not the king I worry about, truthfully, but Edward," he said. "Henry's son is the battle lord. He may very well bring his army down on us to punish us and Henry would look the other way."

Daniel shrugged. "It is possible," he said. "But I have to believe that with everything Henry is dealing with at this moment, he may find some doubt in Torran's assessment that the House of de Lohr has turned against him. I would expect a missive from Henry before I'd expect his army. Still, the seed of doubt may be planted and that could be problematic."

It was troubling to think that the future for the House of de Lohr had become particularly uncertain. It was bad enough that Henry was bent on vengeance against those who supported de Montfort, but now the potential of the House of de Lohr being targeted as well brought great unease within the young de Lohr men. In spite of what Daniel said about Henry being unwilling to punish him, still, there was always the possibility that Daniel could be wrong.

"Edward is a friend," Chris said. "I fought with him at Evesham. I have known him for years. I cannot believe he would know de Serreaux's words to be true. He could not believe that we have all turned against the crown."

Daniel shrugged. "Time will tell," he said, looking at his nephews. "If I were you, I would return home to your father. Tell him what has happened so he knows. Tell him that I will send him word if I hear anything more, or if anything happens."

The three sons of Curtis de Lohr nodded, hugged their cousins farewell, and headed off to the keep to bid farewell to Liselotte and Veronica. Daniel stood with his remaining sons and two knights, watching his cousin's sons as they went about their business. The mood that had settled was somber and uneasy, for all of them.

"I fear the situation may be worse for Curtis," Daniel finally said. "He has done nothing wrong yet he will suffer by our actions. He has the bigger army and greater holdings. He has more to lose."

Stefan looked at his father. "Do you believe it will really come to that?"

Daniel shrugged. "As I said, it is difficult to know," he replied.

Then, he cocked his head thoughtfully. "Unless, of course, I am able to get word to Henry before Torran can speak with him. Mayhap if I explain the situation and reaffirm that the House of de Lohr stands behind the crown, he will dismiss Torran's assessment of the situation."

Stefan and Perrin liked that idea very much. "Our messenger will be able to move faster than Torran and his men since they are traveling with de Garr," Perrin said eagerly. "The man will not be able to travel very well or very fast, and our man could easily bypass them. Shall I send for a messenger, Papa?"

Daniel thought on that a moment longer before nodding his head. "Aye," he replied. "The more I think on it, the more I think I should. At least this way, Henry will hear what has happened from my own lips. I will go and write the missive immediately. Send the messenger to me."

With that, the five of them separated. Daniel headed into the keep while Stefan and Perrin moved to the troop house to hunt down a messenger. De Russe and du Bois went on their way to the gatehouse, as they had duties to attend to.

From the somber mood of only moments earlier, the simple fact that Daniel intended to send a missive to the king about the circumstances surrounding Chad's escape with the de Shera girl made the men feel as if the situation weren't entirely hopeless. Perhaps Henry wouldn't declare them enemies, after all.

But that remained to be seen.

CB

HE'D AWOKEN WITH his breeches around his knees, his boots on, and no memory of how he got that way.

Chad had awoken with a splitting headache, lying in this very odd position in a bed he didn't recognize. It was dark, telling him that it was still at some point in the night, but he could also hear birds outside of his window. Birds usually awoke before dawn. Now, he had a better sense of time but still no idea where he was or how he had gotten there.

Very concerned, not to mention puzzled, he moved his head slightly to get a better idea of where, exactly, he was, and he caught sight of a sleeping figure on the other side of the bed. Turning his head a little more, he could see the back of Alessandria's dark red head as she faced away from him, sleeping soundly. She had a coverlet wrapped up around the lower portion of her body where she had pulled it up from the sides, but her back and naked buttocks were facing him.

The sight of her nude flesh caused him a good deal of shock. Coupled with the fact that he was lying in bed with his breeches half-off, he could only come to one conclusion no matter how hard he tried to think of another explanation. Wracking his brain, he tried to recall the previous night but memories were slow to come. He remembered arriving at Bexley Manor and he remembered telling Lady du Bexley that his brothers weren't married. There was a good deal of food and even sweets. Did someone ask him to sing a song? He had a recollection of perhaps singing a tune, but after that, he didn't remember a bloody thing until this very moment.

He turned his head all the way to his right so he could get a full view of Alessandria as she softly snored next to him. Even though it was still dark outside, the fire in the hearth provided some light in the room, easily enough to see by. He could see the gentle curve of Alessandria's back in the firelight and a hint of her pale buttocks. He simply lay there a moment, feeling himself grow hard simply looking at her, and he knew that he'd taken the woman even though he couldn't remember it. His body was reacting to her nudity. Even if he did not remember, his body clearly did.

He wasn't sure how he felt about it even though he knew he had feelings for her; he'd known that for some time. There was an attraction between them that he couldn't deny and somehow, someway, the wine had gotten to him last night and his inhibitions had been lifted. He could only pray that she had been receptive to whatever it was he'd done because if she hadn't been, that would be an entirely new set of problems. He could only pray he hadn't been horrid and beastly.

He already felt ashamed and uncertain, even as he rolled out of bed, carefully, and used the chamber pot. He was ashamed and uncertain of his actions, of his behavior, knowing he should have been more careful with his wine intake because he was well aware that he became drunk easily. Drunkenness led to uninhibited behavior. His tunic and mail were in a pile on the floor, undoubtedly where he'd ripped them off in his lust, and he pulled them back on in silence. All the while, he kept his gaze on the bed where Alessandria lay.

She was sleeping like an angel, her luscious hair draped over her shoulders, breathing the deep, easy breaths of contentment. Chad stood there a moment and watched her, feeling his heart swell with emotions that were difficult to grasp. He'd known many women in his life and he'd been fond of a few, but not like this. Never like this. He remembered thinking that he'd not married because he hadn't found a worthy candidate yet, wishing Alessandria could be that candidate. After what he'd done last night, he suspected he wouldn't have a choice in marrying the girl now.

And he didn't regret a thing.

She was intelligent and lively, beautiful to a fault, and he would be very proud to announce to the world that she was his wife. More than that, if Henry wanted to marry the girl to de Serreaux, as he had been told, then he was fairly certain that Torran wouldn't want his leavings. He had marked her. Perhaps it had been a drunken haze, but there was a very old saying… in wine, there is truth. Maybe the truth was, deep down, he had wanted to mark her.

He wanted her for his own.

Chad sincerely wished he could have remembered what went on last night as his gaze lingered on Alessandria's naked back. It was such a beautiful, slender back. His gaze moved over the bed itself, noting that the coverlet was still on it and everything was askew. Whatever had happened, they hadn't even bothered to pull the covers away to get to the soft linens beneath. But as his gaze moved over the red silk coverlet, he noticed a stain somewhere towards the middle of the bed. Curious, he peered at it closely, realizing that it looked very much like blood.

The mark of virginity.

His eyebrows lifted as proof of his dirty deeds were presented. Digesting the reality of his actions, he still didn't feel the least amount of regret. Well, except if she did. In that case, he wasn't sure how he was going to handle the situation.

If he could only remember!

"Chad?"

Alessandria's soft, sleepy voice filled the air and he was momentarily startled by it. He had thought she'd been asleep this entire time. The moment was upon him to face her, to face what he had done, so he squared his shoulders and faced it head-on. There was nothing else he could do.

"Good morn, my lady," he said quietly. "Did you sleep well?"

Alessandria rolled over onto her back, taking the coverlet with her so she was still cozy-warm and covered from his lustful gaze. Sleepy, she gazed up at him, smiling and yawning. That was Chad's first indication that, whatever had happened, hadn't been one-sided. Alessandria didn't look like a woman who'd be ravaged against her will.

"I think so," she said, yawning again. "Is it time to leave?"

Chad nodded. "I think so," he said. "I was just going to find a servant and find out what time it was. I'd also like food for our journey."

Alessandria rubbed her eyes. "You already asked for that last night," she said. "Remember? You asked the majordomo to bring us food in the morning and also food for our trip. He said that he would."

Chad thought very hard on a request he couldn't remember. "Ah," he simply said, covering up his lack of memory. "I am much more efficient than I thought."

Alessandria's grin broadened. "You think of everything," she said, somewhat sweetly. "You have been most thoughtful since wresting me from Newington. I can hardly believe it has only been two days that I have known you. It feels like I have known you my entire life."

He smiled faintly. "Is that a good thing?"

She laughed softly. "It is a very good thing," she said. Then, she sobered, the sea-colored eyes glimmering in the weak light. "What will happen now?"

"We will skirt London today and find lodgings to the north."

She pulled the coverlet up to her neck. "I did not mean that," she said. "I mean what will happen *now.*"

She lifted her eyebrows as she spoke the last word and Chad gradually realized what she meant. It was clear as day. *What happens now that you have taken my virginity?* His uncertainty returned and, perhaps, his chagrin. He cleared his throat softly.

"Aless, I will be honest," he said. "When I drink, I have a tendency to lose my self-control and I am, unfortunately, one of those men who becomes easily sotted. I am very sorry if I forced myself upon you last night. Please know I would never intentionally harm or offend you. I cannot apologize enough or convey my sorrows enough. It should not have happened."

Her smile faded. "Do… do you mean you regret your actions?"

He could see, right there, that if he said the wrong thing, it could easily destroy the fragile relationship building between them and he knew that he needed to be completely honest with her. Gentle, but honest. He wasn't a man who laid his emotions or thoughts open to women but in this case, he suspected that it was necessary. She needed to know what was in his heart.

He wanted her to know.

"I do not regret them," he said, sitting on the edge of the bed. "But I never meant to force myself upon you. My lady, I am not sure if you are aware or not, but I have been attracted to you from the start of our association. You spoke of joining the cloister, and never marrying, and I accepted your choices, but it did not stop my attraction. Last night… I am so very sorry the drink caused me to lose my self-control. That is the only thing I am sorry over. But based on the evidence of our activities last night in this bed, it would seem that you and I have a few things to discuss. I never meant to treat you so callously."

It was a polite, kind answer and Alessandria's heart swelled with joy. He feels something for me! "You did not treat me callously," she said. "I… I will admit that I do not remember everything we did but I do know this – I wanted you to do what you did. As you have found attraction to me, so have I found it to you. You are a handsome and kind and chivalrous man. There is a great deal to be attracted to, so please do not apologize for what happened. I do not regret it in the least. But you are correct – we have a few things to discuss, not the least of which is the fact that I am no longer… well, you know…."

Chad did, indeed, know. *No longer a virgin.* He scratched his neck in a rather nervous gesture but when he looked at Alessandria and saw that she was grinning rather slyly, he burst out into reluctant laughter.

"This is very serious," he said, trying to control his laughter. "We should not be treating this situation so casually. The fact of the matter is that I *must* marry you now and you told me that you did not intend to marry. What should I do?"

She reached out from beneath the covers, touching his hand that was resting on the coverlet. Her fingers wrapped around his as he lifted her hand, bringing it to his lips for a sweet kiss.

"I said that I did not wish to marry before I came to know you," she said softly. "That opinion has now changed."

He lifted his eyebrows, surprised. "It has?"

She nodded, coyly. "It has," she confirmed. "Moreover, what is done… is done. We cannot take it back. I would not want to. But I do not want you to feel as if you are forced into marriage, Chad. That would not be good for either of us."

He shook his head, still holding her hand. "I do not feel forced into anything," he said. "As the heir of Canterbury, I will be the earl upon my father's death and it is my duty to provide a son to perpetuate the family. I had to marry sometime. I have never found a worthy candidate until I found you."

"Are you sure?"

"Never more sure about anything in my life."

"You are not saying it simply because… because of what happened last night? Do you feel obligated now?"

"I do not feel any sense of obligation. What I do is of my own free will."

Alessandria was certain that if her heart swelled any more from sheer delight that it would burst. She squeezed his hand and he kissed her fingers again, their warm gazes locked in the dim light of the room. Everything was so wonderful and serene, happiness such as they had never known cloaking them like a mist, penetrating. They were giddy with it.

It was happiness they were sharing together at this very special moment, unexpected yet welcome. The situation could have been so much worse and in that relief, there was elation. There was the understanding that the feelings between them were plain and that last night's passion had only been a prelude to a lifetime of it. But soon, Alessandria's smile faded.

"What of Henry?" she asked. "You said that he wants to marry me to one of his knights. What shall you do?"

Chad shrugged. "I will marry you and that will take care of the situation," he said. "Henry cannot do anything to dissolve our marriage."

"But he will be angry."

"That cannot be helped."

Alessandria wasn't sure she felt better about that particular part of the situation but he seemed fairly resolute. "Shouldn't you ask your father first?" she said. "He may not want you to marry me, after all. He did not want me to stay at Canterbury because of the king and if you wish to marry me, he may not approve. He may not want anything to do with me."

Chad frowned. "Are you trying to discourage me?"

She shook her head quickly. "Of course not," she said, trying to be logical and reasonable about the situation. "I have never dreamt of having a husband or being married. Truthfully, I never thought I would have the opportunity which is why my intention was to join the cloister.

All of this is happening so quickly… we are being impetuous, you know. Everyone will think so, including your father."

Chad knew that. He squeezed her hand and stood up from the bed. "Whether or not we are being impetuous, all of that was decided last night when we'd both had too much to drink and our feelings became evident," he said. "All I can tell you is that this feels like the right thing to do, whether I know you two days or two years. I will not turn you over to Henry and when we arrive at Isenhall, the first thing I shall do is ask Gallus for your hand. No one else is worthy of you, Aless, and it is my intention to make you my wife. I swear I will do all that I can to be a good husband."

So much for trying to keep a level head about the situation. Alessandria was swept up in his words, in the utter delight of knowing he wanted her and that she wanted him. Was it love? She was fairly certain it was, for her at least. She wasn't sure what he was feeling, perhaps only great affection, but in any case she was overjoyed at what had become of a drunken night. Instead of ruining her future, it had cemented it.

"It is all happening so fast," she repeated, her voice a soft murmur. "When you took me from Newington, all I wanted to do was go back. I wanted to go home. Now… I want to stay with you. Do you think that is love?"

He shrugged, averting his gaze. "Only you can determine if it is."

"Do *you* love me?"

He looked at her, then, his gaze guarded. "I do not know," he said honestly. "Clearly, I hope that I will someday if I am going to marry you. I do not know what I am feeling, only that I cannot let you go. I must have you for my own, Aless. I cannot explain it any better than that." He paused. "Why would you ask such a question? Did… did I *tell* you I loved you last night?"

Her eyes twinkled. "You do not remember if you did or not?"

He shook his head, trying not to look too terribly ashamed. "If I told you that to try and coerce you into bed, then I am very sorry. It would have been a terribly manipulative thing to do."

She bit her lip, trying not to laugh at him. "Rest assured, you did not tell me that you loved me," she said. "But you did show me your buttocks."

He clapped a hand to his forehead. "Great Bleeding Lucifer," he groaned. "Did I drop my breeches again?"

Alessandria couldn't help but laugh at him now. "Again?" she repeated. "That was not the first time?"

He turned his head, unable to look at her. "I have been known to do that when I have had too much to drink," he said. "You may as well know that half of England has seen my lily-white arse."

She laughed uncontrollably. "Lady du Bexley said that your buttocks looked like two unbaked bread loaves that she wanted to sink her teeth into."

She was off in a fit of giggles while he cringed. "That woman?" he said, disgusted. "Christ, I hope I can leave this place without her saying something about it. The mere thought makes me shudder."

"Then mayhap you should not drink so much in the future so your breeches will remain where they belong."

He looked at her, then, giving her a half-grin. "I will try, I promise," he said. "I would not want to embarrass you by displaying body parts only meant for my wife to see."

She flushed deeply and the conversation died, but it was not unpleasant. In fact, the mood was still quite warm and she gazed at him rather coyly, smiling up at him as if she had a very shocking secret. He had much the same expression. They had said all that they needed to say and there wasn't anything left now except to move forward, to proceed with the plans they had made.

Marriage.

Alessandria couldn't believe it even as she thought on the word, over and over. She never thought she would have the opportunity and with the whirlwind that had enveloped her in the past two days, she was still overwhelmed by all of it. Her world had been the simplicity of the priority for so long, but for the past two days, it was as if she were living on another planet. Perhaps a moonbeam had swept down to earth, taking her with it when it returned to the cold and bright moon. A dream state, to be sure.

It was the most marvelous feeling on earth.

"Then we must be on our way," she said. "If you can find a servant to bring me warmed water, I can quickly dress and be ready to depart in little time."

Chad kissed her hand one last time and climbed off the bed. He thought she sounded eager to be on their way; truth was, he was eager, too. The sooner he could speak with Gallus about marrying her, the better. He didn't want to wait. He wondered if, deep down, his sense of determination was fed by Henry's resolve to take hold of Alessandria. He didn't want the king to get his hands on her. But the more he thought on it, the more convinced he was that it had nothing to do with Henry and everything to do with him. He, quite simply, wanted the woman. Nothing more, nothing less.

"I will find someone to send you water," he said, moving for the door. But he paused before opening it and looked at her, embarrassed. "You said that I asked someone to bring us food last night?"

Alessandria nodded. "The majordomo."

Chad pursed his lips, embarrassed to ask the next question. "What does he look like?"

Alessandria grinned. "He is a bald man."

Chad blew out his cheeks, relieved. "That should make it a bit easier, then. I will return as soon as I can."

Alessandria simply nodded and he winked at her before opening the door. But instead of proceeding outside, he came to an abrupt halt, evidently looking at something in the doorway. Curious, Alessandria sat up to see what he was looking at, just in time to see him picking something up from the floor.

The first thing he brought up was a bowl of cool water that smelled like roses. It even had rose petals floating in it and he put it on a small table in the chamber. The next thing he picked up was a tray that was covered with a cloth; when the cloth was pulled away, it revealed cheese and bread and the remainder of last night's baked pears. He set that on the table, too, as Alessandria gasped in delight. The very last thing he picked up was a sack made of roughly woven hemp that contained more bread, more cheese, whole ripe pears, apricots, and a big hunk of cold beef that was wrapped tightly in leaves and tied off with twine.

"I do believe the majordomo remembered what I had asked of him even if I did not," Chad said with some mirth, setting the bag of food down on the small table, which by now was very crowded. "I will have to thank him and Lady du Bexley for their generosity. Now, I will go down to the stables to make sure the horses are prepared. Please be ready to leave when I return."

Alessandria nodded. "I will."

His smile returned, his gaze upon her warm, as he quit the room and shut the door quietly behind him. No sooner was the door shut than Alessandria was leaping out of the bed, completely nude, and gasping because the chamber was cold. Even the weak fire in the hearth wasn't enough to stave off the cold morning dew. Hopping over to her satchel, which was still next to the door where Chad had placed it the night before, she went about preparing herself for the day to come.

It was odd, really. She had fine dresses, food to eat, and even soap to wash with, which was far more than she'd ever had at Newington. There, mornings had been very simple with icy water to wash with and soap that was very rough on the skin, and rough woolen garments to wear to for both the day and the night. It had been a plain and uncomfortable existence at that time, one that, until yesterday, she had been determined to return to.

Strange how her mind could be changed so swiftly.

Now, she had possessions and enough food to eat and a man who clearly adored her. The old life in the priory seemed like years ago. It wasn't unusual that she should prefer comfort and affection to the austere existence in the priory. She'd only wanted to stay there because she didn't realize such luxuries and emotional comforts existed. Now, she knew. God would not have presented this new life for her had he not wanted her to accept it.

It was the life she wanted. She would never go back to the priory again.

A new world was dawning and she intended to embrace all of it.

CHAPTER TEN

One week later
Westminster Palace, London

"DANIEL DE LOHR sent me a missive, Torran," Henry said as the knight stood in front of him. "He has explained what happened and assured me that the House of de Lohr stands behind me. But what you are telling me is something completely different."

Torran was caught off guard by the news that the Earl of Canterbury had sent a message to the king that had reached him before the Guard of Six made it back to London after leaving Canterbury a week ago. It was true that it had been very slow travel with de Garr, who wasn't much improved from his beating even after a week, but to know that de Lohr had sent a messenger to make it to Henry before the Six did was something of a shock to Torran. It was also a very shrewd move by the earl. Already, he could see that Henry wasn't pleased by anything that was happening.

"Your Grace," he said, exhausted and impatient. "I do not know what the Earl of Canterbury told you, but the truth is this – his son, Chad, was informed of your intention to take the de Shera woman from Newington Priory and pledge her in marriage to me. Chad and his men made it to Newington before we arrived and spirited the girl off to Canterbury Castle. We followed them to Canterbury and when we arrived, the earl was informed of your orders and he told me that he had no intention of relinquishing the girl. Then, he drugged us with some kind of… of *sleeping* potion while allowing his son to escape Canterbury. Fortunately, we awoke just as Chad was leaving and tried to prevent him from escaping with the de Shera woman, but we were overwhelmed by Canterbury knights."

Henry of Winchester, King of England, Lord of Ireland, and Duke of Aquitaine, was clearly displeased with the news. Tall, with fair hair, a receding hairline, and one droopy eyelid so common to the Plantagenet line, he pondered what his trusted knight told him. He pondered it with irritation.

"And you did not follow Chad?" he asked.

De Serreaux shook his head. "Nay, Your Grace."

"Why not?"

"Because the earl kept us locked up for the rest of the day until Chad was well away from Canterbury, Your Grace," he said. "After that, there was no point in trying to follow him and the earl would not tell us where he had gone. That is why we returned to London to inform you of the situation."

Henry simply stared at de Serreaux, his frustration building. Finally, he turned away from the man and wandered over to one of the two massive hearths in the room. It was an audience chamber of sorts, more informal, and the place where Henry had done most of his planning and scheming since his return from Evesham. The walls were paneled with wood carvings, exquisitely crafty by Savoyard artisans engaged by Henry's wife, Eleanor. Scratching his ear, Henry stood next to the fire, watching the flames dance.

"Why is nothing ever easy?" he sighed, heavily. "Do you know what I hear, de Serreaux? I hear not only incompetence, but betrayal."

De Serreaux was prepared for the lashing he was about to receive, but the mention of betrayal was unexpected. "We did not betray you, Your Grace," he said. "Your guard has never, at any time, betrayed you."

Henry shook his head. "I did not mean you," he said. "I meant you as the incompetent. The betrayal, it seems, comes from those I believed close to me."

De Serreaux didn't like being called incompetent. He wasn't, in fact. He was very competent. But he'd walked into a no-win situation with Canterbury and he knew that Henry wouldn't see it that way. Because of the insult, he didn't ask Henry what he'd meant by the betrayal statement. He simply waited for the king to continue talking.

"Did you hear me?" Henry said. "I fear that men who have fought for me may not, in fact, be completely loyal to me. That is an unfortunate thing."

De Serreaux responded neutrally. "Indeed, Your Grace."

Henry looked pointedly at him. "Aye, *indeed.* How did Chad de Lohr know of my plans for the de Shera woman?" he asked. Then, he pointed an angry finger at Torran. "I will tell you how he knew – when I spoke of those plans, I was surrounded by men I believed to be loyal to me but there was one man in attendance who has a relationship to the de Sheras. Bose de Moray, as much as I love the man, is related to Tiberius de Shera. Bose's daughter married de Shera. It would be natural for Bose to feel some loyalty to the House of de Shera even though he fought flawlessly for me. He always has. The man is beyond reproach, but in this case, it is clear that he thwarted my plans for the de Shera woman. He should not have done that."

De Serreaux lifted his eyebrows, questioningly. "De Moray is more loyal to you than almost anyone else, Your Grace," he said. "He would not betray you."

Henry scratched his ear again. "Not when it came to my life or crown, he would not," he agreed. "I have trusted my life to Bose many times over. But when it comes to the House of de Shera, his loyalties are torn."

De Serreaux wasn't sure what to say to that. "But you sent the man to negotiate a surrender with the Lords of Thunder, Your Grace," he said. "You must have trusted him enough to do that."

Henry sighed heavily yet again. He was feeling his age this night, unhappy with the way things were changing. Men had changed during his captivity with Simon de Montfort; the whole world had changed. De Moray and de Lohr had changed. Nay, he was not a happy man. He had returned to a world in turmoil.

"The Lords of Thunder will not surrender," he said. "They will never support me. It goes against the natural order of things for them to support me. Bose can no more convince them to side with me than I can convince the sun to give way to the moon."

"Then why did you send him, Your Grace?"

Henry shrugged; it was a very good question. "Mayhap I still hold out hope," he said, less anger in his tone. "If anyone can sway the Lords of Thunder, Bose can. And I very badly want Gallus and Maximus and Tiberius under my wing. They are great knights and noble men, and I respect them. But the only person who could have told Chad de Lohr about my plans for the de Shera girl is, in fact, Bose de Moray. In that move, he has shown me that his loyalties are in question. Whether or not he convinces the Lords of Thunder to swear fealty to me is no longer the issue. Bose has proven to me that he cannot be trusted. Blood, as they say, is the strongest bond of all and he is linked, by blood, to the House of de Shera."

De Serreaux didn't have much more to say to that, fearful that any more discussion might make it seem as if he were defending de Moray if, in fact, it was really Bose who had told Chad about Henry's plans for Alessandria de Shera.

"What would you have me do, Your Grace?" he asked. "Will you have me seek Chad de Lohr and discover where he has taken the girl?"

Henry shook his head. "Nay," he replied. "Logic dictates that he would only take her one of two places – either to Isenhall Castle or to The Paladin. I cannot imagine he would take her anywhere else. Why would he? She belongs with her kin. If I were Chad, that is where I would take her. It makes the most sense."

De Serreaux mulled over the situation for a moment. "Why not ask the Earl of Canterbury?" he said. "Surely the man would not refuse to tell you."

Henry shrugged, turning away from the fire that was spitting sparks out into the room. "I do not wish to push the House of de Lohr too much," he said. "If I push them too hard, it is possible they will side with de Shera as well. They are all related, you know – the House of de Lohr and the House of de Shera. I cannot risk that Canterbury would grow annoyed with my demands and throw his support behind de Shera. If he does, then Curtis de Lohr will, too, and I cannot lose Worcester. It would be devastating."

It was a surprising position to take; at least, de Serreaux thought so. "And Chad?" he asked. "He is the one who abducted the girl and refused to turn her over. Will you punish him?"

Henry shook his head, thinking on the brilliant young knight who had saved his life at Evesham. "*Silversword*," he muttered. Then, he chuckled, an ironic sound. "I will not punish him. In this instance, he is absolved from my wrath for were it not for him, I would have met my death on the field at Evesham. For now, Chad is untouchable. I do not believe the man is disloyal to me for it would be a strange man who would save my life and then overtly disobey my orders. But I do think he believed he was doing what he felt was right in order to be loyal to his family. In that instance, Chad has much the same confusion over loyalty to me that Bose has. These men are both tied up with the House of de Shera."

"Then what would you have me do, Your Grace?" de Serreaux asked again. "Tell me and I shall do it."

Henry's gaze lingered on the man; de Serreaux was one of his finest men, of that there was no doubt. But he didn't have a massive army behind him like some of Henry's other supporters did. Right now, Henry needed an army for what he planned to do. He had been planning this move since receiving Canterbury's missive. He strolled, leisurely, towards de Serreaux.

"I have sent a missive to Davyss de Winter," he said. "He and his brother are at their castle of Wintercroft, outside of London. I have told him to bring his army to me and once he arrives, his orders will be to march to Isenhall and raze her. I am finished with the Lords of Thunder and their disloyalty. I am finished with the fact that they have turned de Moray into a traitor and de Lohr into a weak-willed man. This entire situation starts, and ends, with them. De Moray will never convince them to swear fealty and, I am quite sure, Chad de Lohr has delivered their cousin to them, safely, to put her under their protection. Therefore, now is the time to strike. They suffered heavy casualties at Evesham and I will not wait for them to regain strength. If I am going to destroy them, then I must do it now. De Winter will have orders to raze Isenhall to the ground."

De Serreaux had to admit that he wasn't surprised by the orders. He was, however, wary of them. "De Winter has a connection to the House of de Shera, too, Your Grace," he reminded the king. "You know that de Montfort was Davyss' godfather and Davyss and Gallus de Shera are the best of friends. Why would you send de Winter to destroy his dear friend? He could very well turn on you, pull de Lohr and de Moray into the rebellion, and then you would be facing your worst nightmare – the armies of de Moray, de Lohr, de Winter, and de Shera as they move against you. It is a battle you could not win, Your Grace. I beg you to reconsider."

Henry moved away from de Serreaux, back over to a large oak table in the center of the chamber that was cluttered with the remnants of a meal. Several maps were scattered about as Henry's courtiers and advisors lingered in the shadows, listening to everything that was being said. They'd learned long ago not to speak unless spoken to, so at this point, the conversation was purely between Henry and de Serreaux, but others were listening, preparing to give their opinion when the king asked.

But Henry would not ask them, at least not yet. Their edgy patience would have to endure. Henry pulled up a chair, sitting heavily at the table.

"My son, Edward, has gone to summon Davyss," he said as if he hadn't heard de Serreaux's plea. "My son agrees with me. We must wipe out de Shera once and for all. Once they are broken, whatever hold they have over de Lohr and de Moray and de Winter will also be broken. Moreover, this is a test for de Winter – I know he has been extremely unhappy about what happened to Simon at Evesham. He has made no secret of it. He even tried to buy de Montfort's head from Roger Mortimer. Therefore, if Davyss expects my favor at this point, then he is going to have to prove himself."

De Serreaux knew Davyss; he liked the man and considered him a friend. He'd fought with him many times. Now, he was starting to feel the torn sense of loyalties that Henry had been speaking about all along. He was feeling it about Davyss. Hearing Henry speak of Davyss in such an ominous fashion was disheartening as well as frightening.

"So that is what the situation has come down to, Your Grace?" he asked. "A test of de Winter's loyalty?"

"Mayhap."

"But what about de Lohr and de Moray. Will you test their loyalty, also?"

Henry looked at de Serreaux, a glimmer in his dark eyes. "This will be a test for all of them," he said. "I intend to be with de Winter when he marches on Isenhall. It will be much more difficult to disobey me if I am present, watching his every move. But once we reach Isenhall, who will de Lohr and de Moray stand with? Will they side with de Winter to raze Isenhall or will they stand against their dear friend? Either way, I break their bond and destroy what loyalties they have to each other. This is not only a battle against the Lords of Thunder, Torran – this is a battle to break their love for each other."

It was a sad and pathetic goal, one de Serreaux didn't agree with in the least. He didn't agree with what de Lohr had done as far as disobeying Henry's order about the de Shera girl, but what Henry was planning for those four Houses was astonishingly wicked. It was also dishonorable as far as he was concerned. It was something that caused his respect for his king to waver.

"What happens if de Lohr and de Moray refuse to side with de Winter, Your Grace?" he asked, feeling sick even as he asked it. "Worse yet, what if de Winter refuses to raze Isenhall? What then?"

Henry's dark eyes took on something deep and evil, something that suggested the vengeance he had felt since Evesham had somehow poisoned everything about him. Now, it was a matter of weeding out those who weren't completely loyal to him and to hell with the bonds of brothers-in-arms, or even the strength of families. In this instance, the only loyalty Henry wanted to see was loyalty to the crown.

Loyal to him and him alone.

"If de Winter refuses to raze Isenhall and de Lohr and de Moray are with him, then I will raise such an army as England has never seen," Henry hissed. "I will march on Canterbury and Isenhall, Lioncross Abbey and Ravendark, and finally to Norwich and Thetford where the de Winters have their seat. I will confiscate everything and destroy those who oppose me. Is this in any way unclear, Torran?"

Torran could only see death and destruction on a vast scale, a horribly demoralizing thing. But his answer was the only answer he could give. He had little choice.

"It is clear, Your Grace."

Henry smiled thinly. "Do not worry about your incompetence, Torran," he said, turning back to the table and the myriad of things strewn across it. It was obvious that he was dismissing the knight. "Mayhap your ineptness at gaining the de Shera girl will have a greater good. Mayhap it will finally be the catalyst to the destruction of the Lords of Thunder."

By that time, Henry had turned away from him completely and Torran knew he was dismissed. He'd been through countless audiences with the king and knew when their time was finished.

Without another word, he turned on his heel and quit the chamber, which was a massive meeting room in the maze that constituted Westminster Palace. He could smell the stench from the River Thames as he walked, putting as much distance as he could between himself and the man who was out to destroy the lives of countless people. There didn't even seem to be any logic to it; it was, pure and simple, vengeance.

All Henry cared about was punishment.

The man is mad, Torran thought. Perhaps that's what captivity had done to him. Perhaps it had made him mad. Even as Torran headed out of the palace, to the stables where his horse was tethered, he could only think of one thing – this situation was far bigger than simply abducting the de Shera girl. That was a very tiny part of the larger picture. It was a massive honeycomb of vengeance versus anger, of good versus evil, and all of it was bleeding out from Henry's warped mind. That such a man had power over men of honor like de Lohr and de Moray and de Winter simply wasn't right.

None of it was right.

Later that night, de Serreaux, leader of Henry's Guard of Six, had a flash of conscience and sent a missive of his own back to the very man who had caused him to fail at his mission with the de Shera girl. He knew where Chad de Lohr had gone; there was no great mystery as far as he was concerned, but the situation was so much more complex than Torran had believed it to be. He and Chad were friends; at least, they had been before the incident at Canterbury. But even that slugfest wasn't enough to turn Torran sour against Chad. He had done what he had to do, and so had Chad. It was purely duty.

Now, the situation was no longer a matter of holding the de Shera girl hostage. It was a matter of vengeance against the entire de Shera family and all those associated with them, including men who had proven themselves loyal to Henry time and time again.

Now, Henry's desire to punish everyone associated with Simon was taking on shape and form that went well beyond the scope of something as simple as revenge. There was a hint of madness there but if not madness, surely, there was something wicked behind it. It wouldn't be right not to warn Chad of what was happening.

The missive was heading to Isenhall before dawn.

CHAPTER ELEVEN

Isenhall Castle
Coventry

ISENHALL CASTLE WAS a circle. Literally it was circular walls surrounded by a moat with the only access in or out being a heavy drawbridge of iron and oak. The dark-stoned walls were very tall, and somewhat foreboding. As Chad and Alessandria crossed the drawbridge and passed through a narrow tunnel, the bailey opened up on the other side to expose the underbelly of the castle.

It was a tight fit, all of it. The keep, at least three stories, was attached to a one-storied hall, and other buildings crowded up around them. There were tunnels leading between buildings to a courtyard on the other side where the stables were kept. One could smell the stench of animals when the wind shifted.

Everything was closed in and boxed up, with the tall keep and walls towering over everything. As Chad and Alessandria came to a halt in the middle of the bailey, soldiers were rushing up to collect their horses. As Chad dismounted and moved to Alessandria's horse to help her down, he could see people emerging from the keep. Upon close inspection, he could see all three of the Lords of Thunder heading out to greet them and Bose de Moray was with them.

Lifting up his arms for Alessandria, she slid easily, and gratefully, into his arms. He smiled at her, warmly, as he set her to her feet.

"Welcome to Isenhall," he said, eyeing the collection of knights heading in her direction. "We are about to be set upon by your cousins. I may not see you very much after this."

Her smile vanished as she looked at him with fear. "Why not?"

He kept his eyes on Gallus and the others as they drew near. "I told you yesterday," he said patiently. "If Gallus knows I wish to marry you, he will keep us separated for propriety's sake until a betrothal agreement can be reached. Do not be discouraged, however. I will find a way to see you."

"Promise?"

"I do."

Alessandria had heard this before, as he'd indicated, but that didn't mean she liked or accepted it. The past seven days traveling with Chad had been utter heaven. They'd come to know each other in ways she never imagined possible to know someone. After their drunken encounter at Bexley Manor, Chad made sure not to drink in excess again so other than a kiss now and again, he'd not touched her. They had stayed at inns along the way and he always paid for two rooms, one for her and one for him, but on more than one occasion, she'd discovered him stationed outside of her door, making sure she was safe as she slept.

As a result, Chad had been rather weary on their ride north but he'd never let it affect his mood. He'd remained warm and charming, and if she hadn't been completely certain of her love for him before, she was completely certain of it now. She had fallen in love with the bright, witty man who happened to be the heir to a powerful legacy. Truth be told, she really didn't care about the legacy part; all she cared about was him. He could have been a pauper and she couldn't have loved him anymore than she did now.

"I hope so," she finally said, eyeing the men that were coming close. "When do you plan to speak to Gallus about our marriage?"

He looked at her, a smile playing on his lips. "Sweetheart, we discussed this already," he said. "Several times. I will wait until we have greeted one another and our business regarding Henry is settled before introducing the subject of our betrothal."

She was nodding her head even as he spoke. "I know we have discussed this," she said quickly. "I am sorry. I am just nervous."

"Why?"

She looked at him with her big, sea-colored eyes. "What if Gallus denies us?"

Chad shook his head. "He has no reason to," he said, but was prevented from saying anything more because Gallus, Maximus, and Tiberius were upon him. He grinned broadly at the brothers. "I have not had enough of your ugly faces as of late so here I am. Embrace me!"

The brothers laughed. Gallus was the first one to embrace him, followed by Maximus, the gruff brother, who squeezed so hard he nearly broke Chad's ribs. Then Tiberius got a hold of him and joyfully embraced him as one would a long-lost brother.

"We thought you might come to pay us a visit," Tiberius said, throwing a thumb back in de Moray's direction. "Bose told us what happened with Henry and Aurelius' sister. I see you were able to keep her from Henry. Well done, Chad."

All attention turned to Alessandria, still standing where Chad had left her. She was dressed in a woolen garment the color of wine, durable and made for travel. When she saw all eyes upon her, she smiled timidly and dipped into a polite curtsy.

"My lords," she greeted the general group.

Gallus made his way over to her with Chad by his side. "Lady Alessandria," Gallus greeted, inspecting her closely. "The last I saw you was about ten or twelve years ago. You were quite young at the time. Praise God that you have not grown up to resemble your brother."

He meant it as a joke and Alessandria's smile turned genuine. "I would not know, my lord," she said. "I have not seen him in years."

Gallus shook his head with some disgust in his manner. "He is as ugly and foolish as ever," he said. "And you need not address me so formally. You may call me Gallus."

Alessandria nodded, grateful that he was making her feel welcome. He took her elbow and pulled her in the direction of his brothers. "You remember Max, of course," he said, indicating the dark middle brother, "and Ty. We are very glad to see that you are safe."

Alessandria politely acknowledged the other two brothers just as they politely acknowledged her. She had no idea who the big older knight was standing behind them, a man with black hair, black eyes, and scars on his face, but when their eyes met, the man introduced himself.

"Bose de Moray, my lady," he said. "I am pleased to see that Chad was able to get to you before Henry's men did. Was it a bad fight?"

His attention turned to Chad, who was standing on Alessandria's other side. Gallus still had hold of her and Chad had been thinking that he didn't much like seeing another man touch her, even if it was her cousin. He was stewing about it when de Moray's question caught his attention.

"That depends on how you look at it," Chad said, throwing a hand in the direction of the keep. "We have been traveling long days so take us inside, feed us, and I will tell you all about Henry's men and Newington Priory. I swear to you that I haven't stopped moving since before Evesham. I will admit my exhaustion has the better of me."

Gallus was already leading the way. "I know the feeling," he said, politely escorting Alessandria up the stairs that led into the keep. "I have been home for nearly two weeks and I still do not feel as if I have the ability to relax, especially with de Moray's presence. He makes me nervous."

Maximus and Tiberius snorted. "My wife's father has that effect on people," Tiberius said, eyeing the big knight as he followed behind the group. "I have known him for years and he still makes me nervous."

De Moray cocked a black eyebrow. "That is because you bear watching," he said. "I have no idea what my daughter ever saw in you."

Tiberius flashed an impish grin. "Shall I tell you?"

"Nay!"

They had just entered the cool confines of the keep and everyone laughed at Bose's sharp reply. The small feasting chamber was immediately to the right, low-ceilinged and smoky as usual, and Gallus took Alessandria and Chad into the room.

Already, servants were scurrying about, bringing forth wine and bread and cheese. One servant produced a big bowl of strawberries, setting them next to the cheese, and Alessandria zeroed in on the fruit. It was the tail end of the summer berry harvest and she was quite fond of strawberries. As Gallus helped her to sit, and Chad claimed a seat beside her, she plucked a strawberry from the bowl and bit into it. She simply couldn't wait.

Wine was poured and small talk bounced around the table. Gallus sent a servant for his wife as everyone began to partake of the fruit and bread and cheese. It was early afternoon and not having eaten since dawn, Alessandria was quite hungry. Gallus was near the end of the table, the last man to pour himself some wine.

"How long have you been traveling, Chad?" he asked. "I can only imagine what you must have had to do in order to evade Henry's men. Do they know you have my cousin, then?"

Chad was hungry, too. He swallowed the bite in his mouth before speaking. "They know," he said. "Let me brief you on what happened since de Moray told me of Henry's plan for Lady Alessandria. I was able to make it to Newington Priory, where she was located, before Henry's men did, but they were close behind. We did not know exactly how close but that became evident once I took the lady from the priory. Henry sent his Guard of Six after us and they very nearly caught us. They tracked us from Newington to Canterbury and my father admitted them to the castle, whereupon de Serreaux informed my father that Henry wanted the girl for a marriage."

De Moray, across the table, lifted his eyebrows. "I was there when Henry spoke of the girl, Chad," he said. "He never made mention of a marriage, not ever."

Chad nodded. "I suspected as much and so did my father," he said.

"I think de Serreaux was trying to gently coerce us into turning the lady over to him. Telling us she was wanted for a marriage is less terrible then telling us that Henry wants her for a hostage. In any case, my father had no intention of turning the lady over and told me to bring her to Isenhall so that she could be under your protection. He felt this was a safer place for her."

Gallus nodded. "It is, indeed," he said, his gaze moving to the lady chewing happily on the strawberries. "She is part of our family and therefore entitled to our protection. She is welcome here."

Alessandria sensed the attention was back on her and she smiled hesitantly, sipping at her wine to wash down the berries. But she also sensed that the men wanted to say much more than what they were saying, only refraining because she was present. She couldn't imagine these great warriors, with the weight of a vengeful king upon their shoulders, should only want to speak of travel and protection.

"Thank you for your hospitality," she said. "I fear I have brought a great burden down upon you. I have told Sir Chad that I cannot imagine why the king should want to take me hostage, for I am of no value to anyone. I am not an heiress and I do not hold a high social position. I am a ward of Newington Priory, so this entire adventure has been a bit bewildering to me."

She was well-spoken, with a soft and sweet voice. Gallus smiled faintly. "You are a de Shera," he said. "That makes you a great commodity, indeed. We owe Chad a debt of gratitude for risking himself to bring you here. In fact, we are indebted to all of Canterbury for rising to your defense."

Chad was modest, unusual for him. "I could not let a relation of yours fall into Henry's hands," he said. "Moreover, she is distantly related to the House of de Lohr as well, so she is family. It was my duty. My thanks to de Moray, however, for risking himself to come and tell me of Henry's plans. All of us owe him a great deal."

Everyone nodded as attention turned to de Moray, who was sitting silently at the far end of the table. When Bose saw the eyes upon him, he simply shrugged.

"I could not, in good conscience, allow Henry to use the lady against her own family," he said. "When I discovered Henry's plan, I knew Chad was in London still and it was no small matter to find him. He was drunk at an inn we have frequented in the past. How many times did you drop your breeches that I did not see, Chad?"

The serious mood instantly lightened and the entire table erupted into laughter, but Chad simply lifted his shoulders. "I am sure it was too many times," he said somewhat sheepishly. "I lost count."

Across the table, Maximus poured himself more wine. "I have never in my life seen someone more apt to take his clothing off when drunk," he said. "You have done that on other occasions, too, have you not?"

Chad cocked an eyebrow at Maximus. "Is this truly appropriate conversation in front of a lady?" he asked. "One does not usually discuss naked men in front of a lady."

Maximus pointed down the table. "De Moray started it."

"And I shall end it," Gallus said, eyeing the lady in the hopes that they had not offended her too much. "My apologies, my lady. My wife will soon be here to take you away so you will not have to suffer through this crude behavior much longer."

Alessandria smiled at him. "I am not offended, my lord," she said. Then, she cast Chad a sidelong glance. "He did the same thing at Lady du Bexley's home about a week ago. He jumped up on the table and unfastened his breeches. Lady du Bexley said that Chad's backside looked like two unbaked loaves of bread that she wanted to sink her teeth into."

Tiberius and Maximus roared with laughter while Gallus simply shook his head. "It is unseemly for you to speak of such things, my lady," he admonished as he struggled not to laugh. He looked at Chad. "Did you really do that in front of my cousin?"

Chad was surprised she had brought that up, now struggling not to appear embarrassed. "I cannot recall," he said honestly. "She says that I did but she could be lying."

"Now you call her a liar?"

Chad broke down into snorts. "I do," he insisted, although he was jesting. Everyone could see it. "She is making up stories about me. I would never drop my breeches in front of ladies."

Alessandria pretended to be outraged. "I would never lie about such things, my lord," she insisted. "You jumped on the table and sang a song called *Tilly Nodden* as you showed your buttocks to everyone. It is true!"

Chad put his hands over his face as everyone at the table now laughed at him, including de Moray. "I am ashamed," he said, mumbling through his fingers. "I can never show my face again."

Alessandria, giggling, reached out to pat him on the shoulder. "It was quite entertaining," she said. "I enjoyed the song very much."

Chad kept his hands over his face. "I am humiliated!"

Gallus was grinning. "I rather like this lady," he said. "She is not afraid to humiliate you in every possible way."

Everyone continued to chuckle as Chad continued to pretend he was deeply ashamed. But his hands came away from his face when servants appeared with boiled beef and carrots, and he and Alessandria were served first. Very hungry, they plowed into the food as Gallus and the others spoke of trivial things.

Alessandria stuffed herself on the beef and more strawberries, observing her cousins as they idly chatted. She remembered them from her childhood as brash young men, men she was afraid of even, but now as adults, there was nothing frightening about them. They all seemed quite congenial and pleasant.

Especially Gallus, the head of the family. Alessandria remained quiet, eating as Gallus and Chad spoke of various things. They spoke mostly about the big battle at Evesham but, even then, their conversation was fairly tame and Alessandria knew it was because of her. With the lady present, they weren't going to get in to anything serious or distasteful. So the conversation flowed, with much variation, until a woman appeared in the entry to the chamber.

A very lovely woman with hair the color of a raven's wing and pale brown eyes came into the room, her gaze riveted to Alessandria. Gallus reached out to the woman, drawing her to him, and grasping her hand when she came near. Gallus kissed the woman's hand.

"This is my wife, the Lady Jeniver," he said to Alessandria. "If you are finished eating, please go with her and she will make you comfortable."

The Lady Jeniver ferch Gaerwen de Shera smiled at Alessandria. "Welcome to Isenhall," she said in a heavy Welsh accent. "It is a pleasure to meet you. You must be exhausted from your journey."

Alessandria returned the woman's smile. "It was very long, my lady."

Jeniver looked at Chad. "I am sure Gallus has thanked you for what you have done, but I will thank you for bringing the lady to us," she said. "You are very brave."

Chad was about to put a piece of beef in his mouth but stopped so that he could speak. "Your husband told you?" he asked her.

Jeniver nodded. "He told me what Bose told him, about Henry's plans for the lady," she said "Bose said that you had been asked to bring the lady to safety. There is not much my husband does not tell me."

Chad wondered if that was really true. He wondered if she knew about Henry's determination to wipe her husband and his entire family from the earth. Jeniver was the heiress to the kingdom of Anglesey, a very old kingdom, and she was, perhaps, more astute in the ways of politics and warfare than most women. Her father had made sure to school her on such things. Still, there was so much that Chad wanted to know from Gallus, and wanted to tell Gallus, but nothing would be spoken in front of the women. Therefore, he forced a smile to Lady de Shera's statement.

"And I am sure you are one of your husband's most trusted advisors," he said. "My task is now finished. I deliver Lady Alessandria into your care, my lady."

Jeniver went to Alessandria, holding out a hand. "We are very happy to have her," she said. "If you will come with me, my lady?"

Alessandria looked at Jeniver's outstretched fingers, remembering Chad's words – *I may not see you very much after this.* So this was the moment when she would be separated from him. She had no idea when she would see him again and the mere thought brought on anxiety. She didn't want to be separated from the man, not for a day or an hour or a minute. She wanted to remain here, at his side, because that's what felt natural and right to her. But Lady de Shera was smiling at her encouragingly and she knew she had little choice. Swept with sadness, she brushed her hands off of crumbs and stood up.

"I am honored, my lady," she said.

The sadness was evident in her voice, not missed by Chad. His heart was twisting, just a little, as he watched Alessandria walk out of the chamber with Jeniver, who had her by the hand and was speaking to her on the bath that was being prepared for her. It all sounded quite comfortable and cozy, but Chad was already missing her the moment she left his sight. He wondered if it was evident in his expression as he covered his longing with a long drink of wine.

"Now," he said before anyone else could speak, trying not to think of the angst in his heart. "Let me tell you the details of what happened when Henry's Guard of Six came to Canterbury. My father did not want Lady Alessandria at Canterbury, for obvious reasons. He wanted her out and he directed me to bring her to Isenhall so she could be under your protection, but in order to keep Henry's Six incapacitated so we could leave, he had my mother drug their wine. They were sleeping well enough until someone awoke and saw me leaving with the lady. Then, they tried to wrest the lady from me but were summarily beat back by my father's knights and my brothers. That is the only way Lady Alessandria and I were able to escape but I will tell you this; I am more than certain de Serreaux has gone back to Henry to tell him what happened and I am furthermore certain that Henry is most displeased with the fact that the House of de Lohr denied him his wants when it came to holding the lady as a hostage. I fear that makes my father and the entire House of de Lohr a target for Henry's anger."

The four men were listening seriously. "Henry's Six did not follow you here, did they?" Gallus asked.

Chad shook his head. "I never saw any hint that they did," he said. "I do not know how long my father kept them at Canterbury but I am sure it was long enough that they would not be able to track me. That leads me to assume that when they left Canterbury, they simply headed back to London and to Henry."

Gallus and the others seemed to agree with that assessment, especially if Chad saw no hint of a tail. "Even when they do return and tell Henry what has happened, I cannot imagine Henry would strike out at your father," Gallus said. "Right now, he seems to be saving all of that anger for me. De Moray was sent here to negotiate our surrender to Henry."

Chad nodded; he already knew that. "I would assume you will not be complying."

Gallus smiled without humor. "We will not," he said. "Which puts de Moray, and now the House of de Lohr, in Henry's sights. You are all close to our family and that will not sit well with Henry."

Chad looked down the table at de Moray. "It puts de Moray in a worse position than my father," he said. "De Moray is related by marriage to you."

"You are related by blood."

Chad shrugged. "That is true," he said, "but de Moray is closer still."

The conversation ebbed as each man pondered the situation. The mood was gloomy but there was also a sense of determination – determination that Henry should not win this battle. Family was thicker than any loyalty to the king and they all knew that. But Gallus felt the need to make something abundantly clear.

"I want you to listen to me and listen carefully," he said, addressing himself to Chad and Bose. "My refusal to support Henry is not your fight. It is mine. You have both gone out of your way to assist my family in any way you can, including risking your lives, and you will never know how grateful I am. The bonds of love and family run deep. But I will tell you this – my problems with Henry are my own and when it comes down to the choice of supporting Henry or supporting me, and you know it will come down to that, it is my insistence – nay, my plea – that you support Henry. Do not let my battle become your fall. I could not live with myself if that happened and I know that Max and Ty feel the same way. We will stand, or we will fall, but whatever happens must be our fight and ours alone. I could not stomach the House of de Lohr falling because of me or, worse, de Moray losing his life because of our refusal to support the crown. I love you both more than I can say, but I cannot have your deaths on my hands. I am begging you both in this matter."

Chad looked at Bose, who was gazing steadily at Gallus. "While I appreciate your selflessness in this matter, Gallus, I would be a poor father indeed if I allowed my daughter to stand alone with her husband in this matter," he said. "Therefore, I will tell you this – if you go to war against Henry, by Henry's choice no less, it will be my unhappy duty to oppose the man. My daughter's happiness means more to me than the king does. Having daughters of your own, I am sure you understand my position."

Gallus sighed heavily. He wasn't happy with Bose's response, but he understood. "I do," he said reluctantly. "But I had to make that statement, Bose. You know I did."

"I know."

With that matter settled, everyone's attention turned to Chad. The man was sitting there, one booted foot upon the table, nursing his second cup of wine. He was being very careful not to imbibe too much, for obvious reasons. When he met Gallus' gaze, he lifted his eyebrows because he knew Gallus wanted an answer from him. He was defiant.

"What do you want me to say?" he asked. "My opinion is much the same as Bose's. If Henry forces me to make a choice, then my loyalty is with you and I'm sure my father feels the same way. Besides… I have a stake in all of this."

Gallus was puzzled. "What stake is that?"

Chad took a long, deep breath, to bolster his courage. He had been pondering how, and when, to approach the subject of marriage to Alessandria and it seemed that this was a good time. They were speaking of relation to the House of de Shera by marriage, after all. Therefore, it was as good a time as any.

"Henry wants to use Lady Alessandria as a hostage," he finally said. "But I want to marry her, Gallus. That makes me just as involved as any of you in this situation."

Across the table, Tiberius snorted with giddy laughter at Chad's declaration while Gallus looked at Chad with a great deal of surprise. "What's this you say?" he repeated. "You want to *marry* her?"

"I do."

"It is not true!"

"It is."

Shocked, Gallus looked at his brothers for support in this surprising situation. Tiberius was still snorting while Maximus, much less giddy than his younger brother, simply shrugged his shoulders.

"Why so shocked, Gallus?" Maximus asked. "You took a wife. Now Chad wants to take one. Why should that surprise you?"

Gallus still wasn't over his amazement. "But… but it's Chad. *Chad*. Since when does de Lohr speak of marriage?"

"I am over here," Chad pointed out. "I can hear your conversation quite plainly, Gallus. Please direct your shock at me and I will explain."

Gallus did. "Tell me, then," he demanded. "How did this happen?"

Gallus had gone from shocked to edgy quite quickly. Chad tried not to appear too contrite or embarrassed about the fact that he was admitting that he wanted to marry. Surely, only women showed such sappy emotions and silly dreams, but Chad knew he was on the verge of doing just that. There was no holding back now.

"I cannot tell you how it happened, only that it has," he said quietly. "I… I adore the woman, Gallus, and she adores me. I told her that I would ask your permission to marry her."

Gallus' eyebrows lifted. "Great Gods," he hissed. Then, he shook his head, trying to come to terms with what he'd been told. "You *adore* her?"

"I do."

"Are you in love with her?"

Chad shifted uncomfortably. "I have never been in love before so it is difficult to know, but… but I think so."

"Enough to marry her?"

"More than enough."

Gallus scratched his head, his shock fading as he realized that Chad was completely serious. He'd known the man for many years and liked him a great deal, so the more he thought on it, the more pleased he became. Was it really possible that the shining star of Canterbury, the man known as Silversword, was finally ready to settle down and marry, with Aurelius' sister no less?

Certainly, some of this made sense. Chad and Alessandria had been abruptly thrown together and Chad had spent the last several days protecting, clothing, and feeding the woman. He was a virile man and she was a beautiful woman. There was no reason why they should not adore one another.

Find love with one another.

"Does your father know?" Gallus finally asked.

Chad shook his head. "All of this came to light after we left Canterbury, but I am sure he will not have any objections."

As Gallus digested what he'd been told, a grin came to his lips. "Nor do I," he said. "Congratulations, Chad. But permission for her hand must really come from her brother. I have no authority to give you my blessing. Aurelius might have other plans for his sister, in fact."

Chad's expression tightened. "It does not matter if he does," he said. "Aless belongs to me and I will have her with or without her brother's permission."

This was the Chad that Gallus and the others were much more familiar with – determined, stubborn, and deadly. The man always got what he wanted and woe to the man who denied him. Gallus held up a soothing hand.

"I am sure he will give his consent, but you must seek him and ask," he said. "With Uncle Julius killed at Evesham, Lady Alessandria is now under her brother's control. He will have the final say in any marriage contract."

Chad rolled his eyes. "Aurelius the Idiot," he muttered. "Oh, I know what men say of him. I heard of his cowardice at Evesham. The moment his father was killed, he withdrew all of his troops and sat on the outskirts as Simon's forces were trampled on, including you. That is the kind of man who has a say in my happiness?"

Gallus shrugged. "It is a formality," he said. "At least ask him. At least do your diligence. If he denies you, then marry her anyway. Aurelius will not be able to do anything about it once you are wed."

"I would rather marry her now and just sent him a wedding announcement."

"Then if that is the case, why did you even ask me?"

Chad frowned. "Because you are her current benefactor," he said. "She is under your protection, not her brother's, and that makes her your ward. *You* make decisions for her."

He was correct for the most part and Gallus considered that. He scratched at his chin, eyeing Maximus and Tiberius, who were clearly on Chad's side. He pursed his lips wryly at his brothers' willingness to support Chad over him.

"At least send word to the man, Chad," Gallus said. "At least ask him. If he denies you, marry her anyway. I suppose I will simply tell Aurelius that I told you to. But I want to hear what he has to say first before you do anything. Is that fair?"

Chad wasn't happy about it but he nodded his head. "I suppose," he said. "Will you give me a messenger to send north to The Paladin, then?"

Gallus nodded. "I already have one waiting to depart, in fact," he said. "The man is to carry news to Aurelius of what is happening at

Isenhall. I thought my cousin should know because, sooner or later, Henry will turn on him. He needs to know what is happening."

Chad had to be satisfied with that. He was frustrated at Gallus' attitude, frankly, but he had to respect it. But his frustration turned into a lack of self-control.

So much for limiting his wine consumption; Chad poured himself a third cup and drank it straight down before borrowing Gallus' solar to write a missive to Aurelius regarding his sister's hand in marriage. He had another cup or two of wine as he wrote because he couldn't seem to get the words right, asking permission to marry the sister of a man he had no respect for. When he was finished, Gallus took a look at the message but wouldn't let him send it because it was an emotional mess. Too much wine had made it that way.

When Gallus denied Chad permission to send the missive that night, hoping the morrow would bring a much more evenly written request, Chad's frustration reached an epic level. The breeches came off and Gallus sat in his solar, trying to avoid looking at the buttocks that were continually flashed at him as Chad punished him for not permitting him to send a missive to Aurelius. The more Gallus tried to reason with him, the more the white buttocks flashed.

Tiberius and Maximus eventually joined them in the solar and much to Gallus' displeasure, Tiberius, the most liberated and glib of the brothers, joined Chad in flashing his naked arse. It was all great fun until Maximus grew sick of the sight and took the fire poker leaning next to the hearth, swatting Chad across the buttocks so hard that it left a red mark. Then, he lunged for Tiberius, who was wise enough to cover up his arse and run away from his middle brother. But Chad, furious over the spanking, went after Maximus and a full-scale brawl resulted as Gallus stood by and shook his head over the antics. Men who loved each other could be quite foolish sometimes.

Gallus thought on the matter of Chad baring himself before the world when drunk. He remembered vividly when he, Max and Ty were children and would light their Uncle Quintus' farts on fire. It was an amusing and childish sport. But now, as a respected man who had matured over the years, he found such behavior unbecoming. Chad's propensity for dropping his breeches in front of anyone and everyone was quite troubling. So he completely understood Maximus' frustration and actions.

Later on at the evening meal, Alessandria found herself wondering why Chad had a black eye.

CHAPTER TWELVE

Lioncross Abbey Castle
The Welsh Marches

IF EVER A man looked and acted like his father, it was Curtis de Lohr.

The eldest son of Christopher de Lohr, Curtis was in his sixth decade but one wouldn't know it by looking at him. He had an agelessness about him. He was a big man, like his father had been. He also had his father's hair color, blond that had now mostly turned to gray, and had it gathered on his neck in a long ponytail. He also wore the beard his father had always worn but in Curtis' case, he wore it because his skin had been marred by eruptions in his youth so the beard covered the scars. Many people who had known Christopher de Lohr thought they were seeing a phantom when laying eyes upon his eldest son.

He also had his father's temperament, fortunately. His mother had been a spitfire but Curtis had his father's customary cool, which is why he wasn't cursing like a lunatic at the moment. He had just finished reading a missive from Gallus de Shera. In fact, he'd read it three times. In the message, Gallus told him that Bose de Moray, whom Curtis knew very well, had informed Gallus that Henry required his fealty or very bad things would happen. Henry threatened to send an army to Isenhall and raze it. Curtis knew that Gallus would die before surrendering in any fashion to a king he did not respect, so the news was ominous at best.

It was frightening.

This information, of course, was coupled with news that Curtis' sons, recently returned from Canterbury, had told him. Chris, Arthur, and William had returned from Canterbury the night before with a wild story of Henry's Guard of Six against Daniel and his knights. It all had to do with a de Shera cousin, who was a ward of a convent. Henry wanted to take her as a hostage to force the House of de Shera into swearing fealty to him. It was all incredibly complex and growing worse, but one thing was for certain – Henry was determined to seek vengeance against anyone and everyone who had supported de Montfort. Not that Curtis blamed the man, for Henry had been dealing with Simon's rebellion for many years, but to seek the kind of vengeance that Henry was aiming for bespoke of madness.

Curtis read the missive from Gallus one more time before setting it on the desk once used by his father. It was in the solar of Lioncross Abbey Castle, a castle that was as legendary as it was powerful. It was a massive place with a separate annex complex for troops. Lioncross was able to hold three thousand men at one time and Curtis, being Warden of the Southern Marches, held nearly that now. Even after Evesham, he still held well over two thousand men in a standing army, making him the biggest military might on the Marches, if not in western England.

De Lohr was a name to be feared.

As Curtis leaned on the table, pondering the contents of the missive, he could hear his wife as she spoke to their adult daughter. The woman had lost her husband recently and had brought her children back to Lioncross to stay with her parents because her husband's home was overrun by his brother's family. Curtis and his wife, Avrielle, had seven children of their own. Avrielle had three from a previous marriage and Curtis had two from a previous marriage, so Lioncross was, at any given time, full of family. But Curtis didn't mind; he liked it that way.

As Curtis' attention turned to the hearth, still pondering Gallus' request for assistance, he could hear Avrielle close by, scolding one of the grandchildren for bringing a muddy dog into the keep, or it might have even been a muddy goat. Avrielle was angry about something. When she drew close to the solar door, he called out to her.

"Avie?" he called. "Please come to me."

He could hear his wife fussing with the grandchild a moment longer before, soon, she was standing in the solar doorway. A still-beautiful woman at her age, with curly chestnut hair piled on her head and eyes of a clear green, she looked rushed.

"What is it, my love?" she asked impatiently. "Edward has gotten into a mess in the kitchen yard."

"Let his mother clean him up. I need to speak with you a moment."

"But Stella is not feeling well today," Avrielle insisted. "Can this wait?"

Curtis shook his head. "Nay," he said flatly. "Tell Eddie to run back into his mud puddle for the moment. I need to speak with you."

Frustrated, Avrielle turned to say something to her grandson, who had evidently heard his grandfather and was already running back outside. Avrielle stood in the doorway and pointed to the disappearing child.

"There he goes," she said, resignation and frustration in her voice. "He will come back covered head to toe in mud, just like his foolish dog."

Curtis grinned. "Let him be a boy, Mother," he said. "You have raised eight sons altogether. Why are you so surprised that Eddie wants to be dirty?"

Avrielle waved him off, irritated with his humor as he taunted her. "What is so important, Curt?"

She was coming into the room now, heading for him, and he picked up Gallus' missive on the table. "I have some serious business to discuss with you," he said. "Please be seated."

There was a fine chair nearby, carved oak with a cushion, and she planted her slender body in it. It wasn't unusual for Curtis to discuss business with her because she was the voice of reason when he needed it. She was, if nothing else, pragmatic, and he relied on that side of her. Sometimes, she was too pragmatic for her own good, but he adored that about her.

"Where are Chris and Arthur and William?" she asked. "I have hardly seen them today."

Curtis was preoccupied with the missive, looking at it yet again instead of looking at his wife. "They are in the stables overseeing the new stock I received," he said. "Arthur wants a new steed, as his current horse suffered some injury in battle."

Avrielle grunted. "I have not seen them for months," she sniffed. "I would think they would spend today with me. I want to see how they are and hear of their adventures."

Curtis shook his head. "You do not want to hear of this adventure," he said quietly. "From what Chris told me, Evesham was a disaster for de Montfort. The man lost his life in a hideous fashion and now Henry, once again in control, is out for vengeance."

Avrielle knew all about the politics that were sweeping the country. She was astute that way. Much like her husband, she had heard of de Montfort's defeat at Evesham. News like that traveled fast.

"So he is upon the throne once again," she said. "I was wondering when you were going to tell me what happened at Evesham."

Curtis shrugged. "We have heard that Henry was victorious but I wanted to hear it from my sons' own lips," he said. "Henry is, indeed, upon the throne again and de Montfort is dead."

Avrielle nodded her head as she absorbed that information. "I never believed that de Montfort's death would bring instant peace," she said quietly. "Henry would not allow it."

"You have said that before. You were correct."

She had no pride to feed. She wished she hadn't been correct, in fact. "What did you wish to speak with me about?" she asked. "You received a missive earlier today because I saw the messenger. Is Henry asking you to be party to his vengeance against those who did not support him against de Montfort?"

Curtis shook his head, his manner pensive. "Nay," he said. "The missive was from Gallus de Shera."

Avrielle smiled. "And how is Gallus and his lovely wife?" she asked. Then, her smile abruptly faded. "*Sweet Jesus…* he and his brothers all fought for de Montfort. Curt, did they all survive?"

Curtis nodded his head. "They did," he reassured her. "But the vengeance I spoke of… it would seem that Henry has turned it against the House of de Shera for their support of de Montfort. Gallus and his army are torn to shreds and he has asked if I would consider sending men to reinforce his ranks at this time. It would seem that Henry is demanding their surrender and has threatened to destroy Isenhall and the House of de Shera if Gallus and his brothers do not comply."

Avrielle stared at him a moment. "Will you grant his request?"

"I am thinking on it."

She continued to stare at him for a moment, pondering what he had said. Then she abruptly stood up, wringing her hands as she thought on what her husband had told her. Having grown up in a warring household, and then having married a great warlord as the Earl of Worcester and Hereford, Avrielle knew the seriousness of warfare as well as, or even better than, some men.

"Curt," she finally said, "if you send men to reinforce him and Henry catches wind of it, he might think you have thrown your support behind de Shera."

Curtis nodded. "That is exactly how I see it, too," he said. "But Gallus and his brothers are family. Their mother was my youngest sister. I cannot refuse support to family."

Avrielle looked at him. "And risk Henry's wrath?"

Curtis shook his head. "If Henry expects I will stay out of something like this, he is mad," he said. "Let us look at the overall picture of the situation. I send troops to Isenhall and Henry attacks. My troops fend off Henry. Henry believes I have withdrawn support from the crown. That makes me a bigger problem far more than de Montfort ever was. Between Daniel and myself, we hold a good deal of the Marches and Southern England. Henry cannot muster enough strength to destroy us and I sincerely do not believe he would. We are far too valuable to him. Therefore, it is my feeling that if Henry sees my troops at Isenhall, he would avoid tangling with me for fear of losing me. He would leave Gallus alone."

Avrielle mulled over his assessment. "Mayhap," she said quietly. "But the fact remains that Gallus and his brothers are major landholders and oppose Henry's rules. Curt, they cannot continue on like this. Send troops if you must but go with them and tell Gallus it is time to put aside their grand ideals of a government for the people. They must support Henry if they are to survive. If they do not, they will be the enemy in their own country and you will be forced to station permanent troops at Isenhall simply to protect them. Is that really how they want to live? Is it how *you* want to live? Without de Montfort leading this fight, Gallus and his brothers are simply rebels."

It was the brutal truth and the pragmatic nature of his wife was coming out. She made good sense. Curtis, however, wasn't entirely convinced.

"Avie, I cannot tell a man what his convictions should be," he said. "Each man has to decide that for himself."

She cocked a stern eyebrow. "If he expects you to protect him, then he had better listen to you," she said. "I know what de Montfort stood for and to a large degree, I agree with his ideals. He wanted a body of nobles to help rule the country, to make it fair for all. But de Montfort is dead now and the fire behind those ideals has died with him. Gallus and Maximus and Tiberius must realize that. It is time to lay down their arms if they want to live to fight another day. Whether or not they approve of Henry, the fact remains that he is the king and, by virtue of that fact, he deserves their fealty. Their battle is over and they have lost."

Curtis couldn't disagree. "What you say is true," he said. "But I am not entirely sure I can convince Gallus to swear fealty to Henry. There is no reason why he should listen to me."

"No reason except that if he does not, the House of de Shera will be crushed. It is only a matter of time."

Curtis mulled over her words, knowing them to be true. "You are correct," he finally acknowledged. "Then mayhap I should go to Isenhall with some men and try to talk some sense into Gallus. For his own good, he may have to consider swearing fealty to a man he hates. Not that I have any love for Henry, either, but it would be a matter of Gallus not only discounting his convictions, but also swallowing his pride."

"Better swallowing his pride than losing his life."

Curtis nodded. "Indeed," he agreed. Then, he eyed his wife, standing several feet away. "As always, your counsel is welcome and true. Plus, you are beautiful to look at, so it is a double pleasure for me."

Avrielle grinned. "You are a silken-tongued devil, Curtis de Lohr," she said. "But… but if you do go with your men, please be careful. You are too old to be traveling about."

He waved her off. "It will be an easy ride to Coventry," he assured her. "Not far at all."

"Not far?" she sniffed. "It will take you four or five days."

He shrugged. "It will be a simple thing."

She sighed, unhappy with his dismissive attitude. "And you will speak with Gallus and come right home?"

"I will come right home."

She was satisfied. "Good," she said, making her way over to her husband and depositing a sweet kiss on his head. "I love you, you old fool. But you always meddle in other people's affairs."

He snorted, patting her affectionately on the buttocks as she turned away. "I am *not* meddling," he said, "and if I am, I was asked to. There is a difference."

Avrielle laughed as she headed for the exit. "If I see our sons, shall I send them in to you?"

He watched her go, a full view of her still-lovely figure. "You may as well," he said. "Where are you going now?"

She reached the door. "Out to find Eddie, our little mud hen," she said. "I should make you clean him up since you were the one who told him to go play in the mud."

Curtis laughed, hearing his wife as she left the keep. But his smile soon faded as his focus returned to the missive on his desk. Avrielle had been right; if Gallus and his brothers continued their resistance to Henry, then they would be enemies in their own country. With the death of Simon, there wasn't much left to fight for. Perhaps it was time someone convinced Gallus that for the sake of his family and legacy, he needed to give Henry his due. Curtis knew that whatever Gallus decided, Maximus and Tiberius would go along with. At least, he hoped so. The last thing he wanted to deal with was a rogue de Shera.

When Chris, Arthur and William arrived in their father's solar some time later, Curtis had their orders cut out for them.

The de Lohr army began to mobilize once again.

Chapter Thirteen

Isenhall Castle

FOUR DAYS INTO her stay at Isenhall Castle, Alessandria had barely seen Chad. He had warned her that they would be kept apart, especially after he declared his interest in her, and four days later she was coming to find out he had been correct.

Therefore, her days had been reduced to hoping for a glimpse of him, which mostly came around the evening meal, so her entire day was spent looking forward to that one meal where he would be present and she would be permitted to speak to him.

There were times, however, when she would see him walking about the castle, passing from the structure that housed the troops and on towards the stables, or even the gatehouse, and that brief glimpse would give her a dream to dream for the rest of the day.

It was a strange existence, really, in a castle where she didn't know her hosts very well, although the ladies of the castle, Lady Jeniver and Lady Courtly and Lady Douglass, had been quite kind to her. Even the children had been curious and kind, and there was an entire gaggle of them. They had accepted her quite quickly and she had spent a great deal of time with them, playing with them or even telling them stories. She did love to tell stories, reciting tales she had heard from the nuns at Newington.

Even so, Isenhall was still new and different, and she felt very separated from Chad, leaving her feeling rather lost at times.

On this fine summer day, with a soft breeze blowing and the temperature quite warm, she sat on the steps of the keep because it gave her the widest view of the ward and the best hope for seeing Chad at some point. Because the clothing she had come with had been heavier, meant for travel, Lady Jeniver had supplied her with a bolt of fine, soft linen so that she could sew herself a garment that would be better suited to the warmth of the month.

Alessandria and Jeniver had carefully cut the material into sections that even now, Alessandria was sewing together with fine and sturdy hemp thread. It would hold the fabric better than silk would. She already had the skirt basted together and today she was working on the bodice, sewing the sleeves to it.

It was something to pass the time with and Alessandria was actually looking forward to wearing the garment, the first pretty thing she had ever sewn together. There wasn't much call for anything other than constructing durable garments at the priory, so this was something of a new adventure for her.

It was late morning as she sat on the stairs, alternately watching her work and the activity in the ward. Maximus and Tiberius had a new Belgian charger they were trying to work with, a massive beast that would snap at Tiberius yet nuzzle Maximus, much to Tiberius' outrage. It was evidently his horse but it liked Maximus better, and Alessandria sat on the steps and grinned as Tiberius ranted at Maximus for bewitching his horse. She was greatly entertained watching the interaction between them. But as the brothers had her distracted, someone managed to sneak up behind her and whisper in her ear.

"Good morn, my lady."

Alessandria jumped, startled at the sound of Chad's voice. When she whirled around to him, she was met by his handsome, grinning face. She grinned in return.

"Good morn," she said. "What are you doing so close to me without an escort?"

Chad looked around. "I somehow managed to lose Gallus," he said. "But that is a good thing. Are you willing to do something quite scandalous?"

Alessandria shook her head at him reproachfully, although she was still smiling. "I am afraid to ask what that would be."

"You will not know unless you come with me."

She cocked an eyebrow. "With you? Alone?"

He pursed his lips with some irony. "Aless, you spent an entire week alone with me."

"And you know what happened."

He just looked at her, surprised she should bring that up. But his manner inevitably softened. "Regrets?"

Alessandria shook her head. "None at all," she whispered. "In fact… In fact, I miss our time alone together. It seems as if we have had no time together at all since we arrived at Isenhall."

"I told you that would be the case."

"I know. But it is still difficult to stomach."

He smiled, an impish gleam in his eye. "Take heart, fair lady," he said. "I am about to change that."

"How?"

He held out a hand to her. "Come with me."

Alessandria did. There was no question. But she still had her sewing in hand as Chad quickly took her around the side of the keep where there was a small tunnel leading between the wall and the keep, dumping out into the stables. The entire area smelled of animals and hay, made stronger by the warm weather. When Chad finally came to a pause and saw that she was dragging her sewing about, he removed it from her hand and draped it over a stable ventilation window.

"The town of Coventry is not far from here," he said, his voice low so no one would hear. "Since the only possessions you have are those that others have given you, I thought to take you into the town and buy you a few things so you will not walk about feeling like a charity case. Would you like that?"

He was pointing at the garment she was wearing, the dark green wool that his mother had given her. It didn't fit her quite right, as it had been made for his shorter and somewhat smaller sister. Alessandria looked down at herself, between being insulted by his observations and excited at the prospect of actually having some possessions of her own. More than that, she was excited by the prospect of going to town with him, just the two of them. Her excitement won out.

"Aye," she said, somewhat eagerly. "But won't Gallus and Jeniver wonder where I have gone? What will happen when they cannot find me?"

Chad snorted. "When they cannot find me as well, they will know where you have gone," he said. "Not to worry. Now, you will leave through the postern gate in the kitchen yard. Do not wander; wait by the gate. I will ride from the gatehouse and come for you."

With an enthusiastic grin, Alessandria ran off, back into the kitchen yards, while Chad went to casually collect his horse, whistling all the way, pretending like he wasn't about to do something rather scandalous with a de Shera relative.

Chad's fat stud was munching away on a bucket of grains in his stall and Chad removed the unhappy animal from his feed, taking him out into the yard where skinny stable grooms saddled the beast. Chad ended up helping them because they were taking too long and he wanted to be on his way before someone stopped him, a fear that grew stronger when Maximus and Tiberius came back into the stable yard with Tiberius' new Belgian charger. The horse kept trying to bite Tiberius while Maximus petted and stroked the beast, who obviously favored Maximus. Chad grinned to see Tiberius so upset over his horse's favoritism towards his brother.

"Is that your new stud from Antwerp?" Chad asked Tiberius. "He does not seem to like you very much."

Tiberius' features were molded into a permanent frown. "Max has no shame in seducing animals," he said loudly. "He has bewitched my horse so that it will obey only him. I cannot do a thing with him."

Chad was trying not to laugh as Tiberius came close to a tantrum. "The solution is simple," he said. "Give Max the horse and have him buy you another one. You will not want a horse that is in love with your brother."

Tiberius nodded his head. "You are very correct," he said. He pointed at his brother. "You owe me a new horse."

Maximus merely laughed and led the horse away, putting it in the section of the stable where his two other horses were kept. It was a statement to Tiberius that he was claiming the horse for good and Tiberius waved his brother off, disgusted.

"He always steals things from me," he muttered. "Had he not already been married, he might have stolen my wife from me as well. He even tries to coerce my children in to liking him better."

Chad laughed as he finished up with his own horse. "I am sorry for you, lad," he said, swinging himself up easily into the saddle. "But you must know that you are the smartest and most likeable brother of all. Maximus is a sour bear of a man most of the time."

Tiberius nodded, conceding the point. "That is true," he replied. Then, it was like he was only just noticing that Chad was preparing to leave. "Where are you going?"

Chad gathered his reins. "To Coventry."

"Why?"

Chad cocked an eyebrow at him. "To purchase a gift for a certain young lady, if you must know."

Tiberius grinned. "Ah," he said. "She is a lovely girl, Chad. You are a fortunate man."

"Aye, I am. Now, let me be on my way or I will not make it back in time for supper. That is the only time I am allowed to speak with Aless and I do not want to miss it."

"Frustrated?"

"Unbelievably so."

Tiberius snorted, waving him off, and Chad cantered from the stable yard and out into the ward where men were going about their business. He made his way to the gatehouse, pausing while they lifted the double portcullises in a great symphony of groans and creaks, before spurring his horse out onto the road beyond.

Chad knew that men were watching from the battlements so he continued out along the road until he disappeared into a grove of trees. Then, he swung into the trees and carved a wide path around the perimeter of Isenhall, about a quarter of a mile out, until he came to the rear of the fortress.

Then, he swung inward, through more trees, until he met with the clearing on the other side. He could see Alessandria standing against the wall near the postern gate, patiently waiting, but he had to pause until the few men manning the back side of the fortress moved out of range. Quickly, he thundered across the clearing, pulled Alessandria on behind him, and tore off back into the shield of the trees before anyone was the wiser.

It had been a slick and clever plan that now saw them quite alone. Nestled in behind Chad, Alessandria clung to him as they rode through the bramble, her cheek against his back and the cold feel of mail between her and his muscular, warm body. But it didn't matter; they were together, her arms were wrapped around him, and it was just like it had been for that blissful week when they fled Canterbury for Isenhall. It was as if nothing else in the word existed.

For now, it was only them.

But their solitude couldn't last forever, unfortunately. The town of Coventry was quite close and they arrived on the outskirts of the burg within a half-hour of leaving Isenhall. With the warm, bright day and few clouds overhead, the town was bustling with merchants and farmers, people moving about to conduct their business.

They came up from the southeast, up to the very large wall that surrounded the city, and passed through the New Gate that opened up into a residential part of the city. As the Earl of Coventry, Gallus had men stationed at the city gates, along with soldiers from the Catesby family, who were major landowners in the city itself.

Lord Catesby was a merchant by trade and had amassed a vast fortune that required many soldiers to help protect it. He wasn't a political man and he therefore worked well with Gallus, regardless of the de Shera support of de Montfort. As Chad passed through the gate and into the town proper he saw very few de Shera soldiers; and many more Catesby soldiers. After Evesham, that Gallus shouldn't assign soldiers from his depleted army to guard the city gates wasn't surprising.

"Where are we going?" Alessandria asked from behind him. "Did you have a plan in mind?"

Chad nodded as they plodded down the avenue. Children were playing in the streets and dogs were barking as they moved along. It was a glorious, sunny day and he shielded his eyes from the bright rays as he looked on ahead.

"Indeed, I do," he replied. "Past the cathedral on the north side of the city is the Street of the Cooks and Merchants. We shall go there to see if we can find suitable material in which to clothe you."

Alessandria watched the people as they passed by; one child stuck his tongue out at her and she stuck her tongue out at him in return. As the boy went wailing to his mother, she fought off a grin.

"You truly do not have to purchase anything for me," she said. "Simply to be with you is more than enough. That is truly the only reason I came."

Chad's big, gloved hand found her small hands, clasped around his waist as she held on. "I have missed not seeing you more frequently," he said. "I was going out of my mind with longing even though I know very well that you are in good hands."

Alessandria lay her cheek against his back again, so very content. "Jeniver and Courtly and Douglass have been very kind to me," she said. "I never knew women could be so kind."

Chad patted her hands. "Not every woman is like your Lady Orford and her horrible daughter," he said. "There are kind people in the world."

Alessandria watched a little girl carry around a puppy, with the puppy's legs dangling. "I know," she said. "I discovered that the day I went to Newington, although the kindness from the nuns is much different than the kindness of the ladies at Isenhall. The nuns were kind out of duty, I suppose, but Jeniver and Courtly and Douglass seem to be kind because they want to be."

Chad could see the cathedral up ahead and, beyond that, would be the Street of the Cooks and Merchants. "Of course they do," he said. "It is unfortunate that you've not known much kindness in your life, but take heart that it will no longer be true. I intend to be kind to you and spoil you until you grow sick of it. You deserve nothing less."

Alessandria grinned, now also catching sight of the cathedral up ahead. It was a large complex with a spire, rising into the sky and seen well across the land, constructed from red stone that had turned brown and dingy with age. It was the same stone that the walls of the town had been built with.

"Look," she said, pointing to the cathedral. "Is that the cathedral?"

Chad's gaze was on the cathedral as well. "It is," he said. "That is St. Mary's Priory and Cathedral. Newington did not have a cathedral attached to it, did it?"

Alessandria shook her head. "Nay," she replied. "It was part of the bishopric of Rochester. We went to Matins at Rochester every Sunday regardless of the weather. We would walk the entire way."

He craned his head back to look at her with some surprise. "That is a distance to walk," he said. "How long did it take you?"

She shrugged. "An hour or less," she said. "I did not mind. The cathedral at Rochester is so beautiful. No offense intended for St. Mary's, but Rochester's is far more grand."

Chad simply grinned at her. They passed St. Mary's and its dingy stones, and Alessandria inspected the structure with interest. Just as she had done the entire ride from Canterbury to Isenhall, she inspected her surroundings and the towns they passed through with great interest.

Alessandria had spent so much time bottled up, away from the world, that everything was bright and new to her now, seeing sights she had never seen before. But they soon left the cathedral behind as they passed by the town's center, heading to the Street of the Cooks and Merchants. Alessandria was enamored with everything around her.

"I have been wondering something," she said.

Chad could see their destination up ahead. "What is that?"

"After we are married, where shall we live?"

Chad thought on his reply. "From my father, I inherited the title Lord Thorndon," he said. "The title comes with two small castles that my father staffs with Canterbury soldiers as outposts. One is Denstroude Castle and the other is Whitehill Castle, both of them on the north perimeter of Canterbury lands. I suppose we could live in one of those if you wish."

"Lord Thorndon," Alessandria murmured, rolling the title over her tongue. "It is a prestigious title."

Chad grinned, turning to look at her. "And you will be Lady Thorndon," he said. "When I inherit my father's earldom, you will be the Countess of Canterbury. What a magnificent countess you will make."

Alessandria returned his grin, humbled. "It seems like a dream to even entertain the thought," she said, struggling to explain her feelings on the matter. "I am a simple woman, after all. I did not grow up in a fine home and learn fine things. To be a countess… I must say that I feel wholly unworthy, Chad."

His smile faded. "You are the worthiest woman in the world," he said quietly, firmly. "You are not polluted by politics or poisoned from those fine homes you speak of. You, and only you, are worthy of such a post. You will honor the name of Canterbury and the House of de Lohr."

"Are you certain?"

He pulled the horse to a halt, still looking at her over his shoulder. "I would not say it if I did not believe it," he said. "Aless, do you not have any concept of how beautiful and honest you are? You are a treasure, over any so-called fine woman I could ever find."

His flattery was true and sincere. Alessandria flushed and lowered her head, basking in his compliments. She was unused to such things but Chad was certain to make her accustomed to them with his gentle flattery. He had been like that the entire ride to Isenhall, dropping gentle compliments now and again, introducing her to the world of courtship. It was something she was rapidly becoming accustomed to.

"You are very kind to say so," she said. "The way we are… the way things have been since we have come to know one another… I so hope it will always be like this. I hope we will always say kind things to one another. I see the way Jeniver and Gallus are with each other, and the way Maximus and Courtly speak to one another, and it is clear that there is respect as well as adoration with them. I did not know marriage was supposed to be so warm or pleasant, but I feel… I feel as if we will be the same way. I will do my best to make it so."

He squeezed the hands at his waist. "As will I," he said. "Have no fear; we will be kind and sickeningly sweet to one another until we die. My mother and father are like that. As children, we would watch them kiss and touch affectionately, and we would groan our displeasure. But now I have come to appreciate what my parents have between them."

Alessandria smiled at the thought. "Your mother is a wonderful woman," she agreed. "I do not know your father much, but I am sure he is just as wonderful as his son."

Chad shook his head. "I am by far more wonderful and talented than my father is," he said arrogantly. "You must believe that."

He said it rather dramatically and she fought off a grin. "I do, I swear it."

"Excellent."

They came to a crossroads where their avenue intersected with the Street of the Cooks and Merchants and Chad began looking for a livery or a place to secure his horse. He didn't worry about anyone stealing the animal because it wouldn't respond to anyone but him, but the horse was rather snappish so it was safer to put him away in a livery where he wouldn't try to take someone's arm off.

Moving down the street, Chad soon caught sight of a small livery with a bevy of heavy wagons stationed around it, men off-loading them and moving sacks of grain into the small barn-like structure. Chad made his way to the livery and, finding the man in charge, paid him handsomely to have the horse put back in a stall and fed. With the horse tended, he took his saddlebags and his sword with him as he led Alessandria from the livery yard and into the busy street beyond.

"Now," he said. "It has been a long time since I have been here, but I do believe there are merchants down the avenue towards the Cook's Gate. It is that big gate down there at the end of the street."

Alessandria peered down the bustling avenue, shielding her eyes from the sun. "That big gatehouse down there?"

"That is the one."

"Did they name it for the street, then?"

"I believe so."

She was curious about everything and he liked that about her. Having spent so much of her life in a cloister, Alessandria was a bright woman and wanted to learn about everything now that she'd had a taste of life outside of the priory. Chad loved that he was the one who had the privilege of showing her the joys of life, educating her about the world around them.

They embarked down the street, seeking a merchant who would have fabric for new garments, but since it was the Street of Cooks as well, they immediately came across three food stalls, all of them sharing a common beehive-style oven, which produced variations of bread and other delights. The smells of baking bread and yeast filled the air and, like invisible fingers, reeled customers in with enticing scents. Chad and Alessandria were no exception.

The first cook stall was more of a baker with a vast variety of bread. He had sweet and dense flat cakes which, Alessandria discovered, were heavenly. Made from flour, honey, cloves and saffron, they were delicious and decadent, and Chad ended up purchasing a half-dozen of them. As Alessandria pushed them eagerly into her mouth, one after the other, the next cook stall lured them in with a cake made of honey and ginger and cinnamon, that was actually more bread than cake. Alessandria loved the smell and Chad ended up buying some of that as well.

On and on it went, down the avenue, stopping at each stall to see what wares or delicacies were offered. A man had a trained black bird, a raven he said, that would pick almonds up from a bowl and walk them over to drop them in Alessandria's palm, which thrilled her. Further down the lane they came across a woman who used a loom to knit colorful woolen shawls, and Chad bought Alessandria one. It was warm, and lovely, and she draped it around her shoulders as they continued on their way.

In fact, the journey on the Street of the Cooks and Merchants turned into less of a hunt for fabric and more of a general inspection of the street and its vendors in general. There was a man who imported scented oils and incense, and Chad bought her several items simply because she had liked the smells. They stopped to watch a silversmith work a small piece of silver against his metal anvil, watching as he formed it into the shape of an earbob and then added a yellow stone to it. It was all quite fascinating.

The sights and sounds and smells of everything had them enchanted, transported far away from a world of battles and wicked kings. As they lost themselves in a carefree world, Chad held Alessandria by the elbow or the arm, sometimes even the hand, stealing kisses from her when he thought no one was looking.

At first, she pretended to reject his advances, perhaps embarrassed that he was trying to kiss her in public, but soon enough she gave in to his flirtation and allowed him a kiss or two. Perhaps even more than that. All Chad knew was that he was swept up in something he couldn't control, something that made him as giddy as a young squire. Everything about Alessandria had him enraptured and happily so. He couldn't focus on anything else. In fact, they were near the Cook's Gate, playing another round of kiss-stealing, when he happened to glance up at a group of men coming through the gate.

Then, the games stopped.

Chad recognized the men, unfortunately, and he recognized one in particular – Luc Summerlin, the very man he had slashed whilst freeing Henry from de Montfort's captivity. Summerlin had been Henry's primary jailor, a powerful knight from a fine Norfolk family. Chad had hardly given the man any thought since that day, but here Summerlin was, as big as life, and heading into Coventry with a host of other seasoned knights with him.

And Chad was quite alone.

He flew into self-protection mode. Grasping Alessandria by the arm, he quickly pulled her out of the avenue and back behind a heavily-laden merchant stall. When she looked at him, alarmed at his actions, he simply held a finger to his lips to indicate silence. Frightened, she obeyed, allowing him to push her back against the wall of the merchant stall and into the shadows while he kept out of sight, watching Summerlin and his group move down the avenue.

Chad kept his eye on the big, red-haired knight astride the battle-scarred roan steed. He wouldn't have minded running in to the man had he not been with Alessandria, but the fact was that he was far more concerned for her than he was for himself. He didn't want to find himself overwhelmed by Summerlin and his men, leaving Alessandria alone and vulnerable. There was no knowing what they would do to her.

Now was not the time to face Luc Summerlin. Being that the man had served de Montfort, Chad seriously wondered if he were heading to Isenhall to visit the Lords of Thunder, and it seemed to Chad that departing from Coventry immediately would be the better part of valor for both him and Alessandria. He didn't want to chance running in to Summerlin again. He had to return to Isenhall to take the lady to safety, and also to relay to Gallus and his brothers what he had seen. They would want to know if Summerlin was around. The man had an aura about him, fiercer and more powerful than most.

Chad knew the Lords of Thunder would want to know.

Therefore, he kept Alessandria close at hand as he watched Summerlin move down the Street of the Cooks and Merchants, disappearing off to the northwest. When the man was gone, Chad took that as his opportunity to race back to the livery for his horse. He had packages in one arm and Alessandria in the other as they moved very swiftly back to the livery where his fat horse was, once again, pulled away from a meal of grains.

Lifting Alessandria up into the saddle, Chad settled his saddlebags and packages before swinging himself up into the saddle behind. Alessandria held on tightly as he spurred the animal out into the avenue beyond, fleeing Coventry the way they had come.

Fortunately, they never saw Summerlin as they galloped from the town, making their way back to Isenhall in excellent time. Thundering through the gatehouse, Chad was relieved to see Gallus and Maximus and Tiberius in the ward, all three men saddled up and preparing to depart.

Chad had no idea where the men were going until Gallus dismounted his horse, went straight to Chad's animal, and pulled Alessandria off. He led her back to the keep and Chad could see that he was mildly scolding her. Her head was down and she seemed to be cowering. Leaving Alessandria off at the steps leading into the keep, her head bowed contritely as she made her way inside, Gallus then proceeded back to Chad. And he did not look pleased.

Gallus wasn't nearly as concerned about the news of Luc Summerlin's appearance in Coventry as he was about Chad sneaking Alessandria out of Isenhall without an escort. Chad tried to explain himself but the truth was that there was nothing he could say to explain what he'd done. Finally, he simply gave up and let Gallus berate him. Not surprisingly, Alessandria was much more closely watched after that.

And so was Chad.

CHAPTER FOURTEEN

Isenhall Castle
Two Weeks Later

CHAD COULD HARDLY believe what he was reading.

The missive had been addressed to him, having been delivered to Isenhall by a messenger bearing Henry's colors, which made the soldiers at the gatehouse rather edgy that a king's messenger boy had delivered a missive addressed to Chad de Lohr.

Men whispered, rumors flew, and by the time Chad actually reached the gatehouse where the missive was waiting for him, nearly all of Isenhall knew of the missive, Gallus and Maximus and Tiberius included. Bad news traveled fast.

What did the king have to say to Chad?

No one, of course, wondered that more than Chad did. The edginess from the men was settling heavy, making it a palpable thing, and he accepted the missive from the sergeant in charge of the gatehouse, as if he really didn't want it to begin with. Something about the weight in his hand made him want to drop it and run. The messenger had already retreated, not surprisingly, because no man loyal to Henry wanted to be within the confines of Isenhall, so Chad had no one to ask about the contents.

He would have to open it to find out.

Chad wasn't entirely sure he wanted to do that and his denial had the better of him. It would have been very easy not to read this missive, to simply pretend he'd never seen it. It couldn't be good, any of it, but curiosity soon overcame his shock and by the time he walked from the gatehouse, he'd broken the seal on the vellum and he was reading it intently. He had walked to the middle of the bailey when he finally came to a halt, still reading the missive or re-reading it; no one was quite sure. Whatever the contents were had his full attention.

Gallus and Maximus and Tiberius, having been informed of Henry's messenger by a nervous servant, were already coming to find Chad, emerging from the keep to see him standing in the middle of the dusty bailey, focused on the yellowed piece of vellum. A gentle breeze blew about and chaff brushed by him from the stables, but he didn't notice. He stood there reading. The de Shera brothers didn't waste any time in finding out why Henry should be sending a missive to Isenhall.

"Chad?" Gallus called as he approached. "What is it?"

Chad heard the shout but wasn't going to shout in return. He remained silent, still fixated on the missive, until the brothers were grouped around him. Tiberius was even looking over his shoulder, but Chad handed the missive over to Gallus before Tiberius could get a good look at the contents.

"It is from de Serreaux," Chad said, his voice low. "Henry has ordered the de Winter army, led by Davyss, to march on Isenhall. They left London over a week ago."

Gallus stared at him a moment, startled by the news, before looking to the vellum to read the information for himself. It was clear that he wasn't sure how to react to the news but as he read, his features screwed up to reflect his astonishment. The carefully-scribed words impacted him.

"Henry is riding with Davyss," he said, trying not to sound as if the very thought had him reeling. "De Serreaux says that Henry is coming to determine loyalties."

The crux of the missive was revealed to those who hadn't yet read it; *the king is coming to determine loyalties.* In disbelief, Maximus snatched the vellum from his brother, reading it intently as Gallus and Chad focused on one another. As Maximus read and Tiberius tried to read over his shoulder, Chad spoke in a low voice.

"So it has come to this," Chad said, foreboding in his tone. "He is riding to see just how much support you have."

Gallus was bewildered. "He already knows," he said. "There has never been any secret about the fact that the House of de Lohr and the House of de Winter are both family and friends. More than that, de Moray's daughter is married to my brother. Why should Henry come all the way with Davyss' army to see for himself?"

Chad shook his head as if Gallus were missing the point. "Can you not see what de Serreaux is really saying?"

"Evidently not."

Chad grunted his displeasure in the situation; he could see it as clear as day. Everything in the days from Evesham leading up to this very moment were coming to make sense to him and de Serreaux's unexpected missive was the catalyst. He grasped Gallus by the arm.

"I told you that Henry's mindset has been one of vengeance against anyone who supported de Montfort," he said. "You know this. Now Henry's madness has turned into paranoia; he is coming to test all of us, to see who is truly loyal to him. Of course he knows that de Lohr and de Winter are your friends and family, but his sense of vengeance against you is making him suspicious of us all. He knows that I took Alessandria from the convent to keep her from being his hostage and he further knows that my father not only sanctioned my actions, but did all he could to prevent the Six from carrying out Henry's orders. Now the king believes the House of de Lohr to be against him. I would wager to say that he is expecting to see Canterbury troops here or, at the very least, Lioncross troops. He wants to see if we have all joined you in your rebellion."

Gallus was shaking his head, still puzzled by the entire circumstance. "Based on the fact that you did not allow the Six to get their hands on Lady Alessandria?"

"That is only part of it, I am sure. Henry's lust for vengeance started well before that."

Gallus still wasn't convinced. "But how can you be so sure of this?" he asked. "And what is puzzling me the most is why de Serreaux should send this missive? *How* did he know you were here?"

Chad lifted his big shoulders. "De Serreaux and I have known each other for many years," he said simply. "We have fought side by side in many battles and in spite of what happened at Canterbury with Alessandria, I would hope that camaraderie is still strong between us. It must be. De Serreaux must be as disgusted with Henry's quest for vengeance as we are, 'else he would not have risked himself to send me a missive on Henry's intentions. He is one of Henry's Six, for Christ's sake – a man that Henry trusts above all else."

"Yet he sends you a missive informing you of the king's plans."

Chad nodded. "He would not have done it had he not believed Henry's intentions go beyond de Shera submission," he said, thinking on Torran and feeling guilty for having tricked the man the way they had back at Canterbury. "Think on it, Gallus; Henry is forcing Davyss to march to Isenhall. Clearly, the intention is a threat against you but it also shows a lack in faith towards de Moray. He does not believe the man will be able to convince you to swear fealty to him. So he orders Davyss and his army to march on Isenhall, presumably to destroy you. If Davyss refuses, Henry will see that de Winter's loyalties are more to you than to the crown. If he sees de Lohr troops here, what will he think? That the House of de Lohr has chosen to side with their family. And de Moray... you know that Henry loves and depends on him. What will happen when Henry forces Bose to choose between his daughter's husband and the crown? Don't you see, Gallus? Henry is testing *all* of us."

Gallus rubbed at his chin, deep in thought. By this time, Maximus had finished reading the missive and had handed it off to Tiberius.

"Chad is right," he said grimly. "There is no other reason for Henry to ride with de Winter. This has nothing to do with our swearing fealty to the king, Gallus. Henry is coming to see the situation for himself, and to see if blood and friendship is stronger than fealty to the crown. His appearance will be about de Lohr, de Winter, and de Moray loyalties, and little else. At this point, the House of de Shera is secondary."

Gallus listened seriously to his middle brother. Maximus was usually the doom-and-gloom member of the group but he was also, more often than not, correct in assessing a situation. He had that grasp. The more Gallus thought on the situation, the more he was coming to dislike it.

"Have we pulled these houses down with us already?" he asked softly. "Is that what this amounts to? We destroy our friends and family because of our loyalties?"

Chad shook his head. "Nay," he replied. "I believe it is Henry's paranoia more than anything. He sees everyone as suspect these days, regardless of who they are or how long they have served him."

"Mayhap," Gallus said. Then, he cocked his head thoughtfully. "But it is also possible that de Serreaux is misleading us with this missive. It would not be like one of Henry's personal guards to betray him like that."

Chad shook his head. "For what purpose?" he asked. "It would serve no purpose for Torran to mislead us. Moreover, he is a man of honor. He knows right from wrong. If he senses that Henry is about to do something underhanded or immoral, I feel confident that he would warn us as he is doing now. I do not see trickery in this."

"But it still does not explain how he knew you were at Isenhall."

Chad threw up his hands. "It would not take a genius to determine where I had taken a member of the House of de Shera," he said. "He knew that I had taken Alessandria somewhere, and Isenhall is the logical choice. She would find protection here."

"You do not believe your father told him?"

"Never."

That was good enough for Gallus. "If you believe it, then I believe it," he said. Then, his manner sobered further. "You know that I have sent word to Curtis de Lohr, asking for reinforcements against any aggression from Henry. When I asked for the assistance, however, it never occurred to me that Henry would be sending de Winter troops to attack us. I assumed it would be crown troops only."

Maximus grunted, unhappy. "That means allies will be squaring off against each other," he said. "*If* de Lohr even sends troops, that is. Gallus sent the missive some time ago but we've not heard back."

"He will respond," Gallus said steadily. "Even if it is to decline our request, Curtis will respond."

Chad was thinking on the situation. He believed implicitly that what Maximus said was true; this had ceased to be about the House of de Shera and was more about the loyalty of Henry's supporters. Would they support their family in the House of de Shera? Or would they support the crown, to whom they were all sworn? It was a difficult situation, confusing at best.

But one thing was for certain; Chad's loyalty was to his friends and family. If he had to make a choice, that was what it would be. He was certain his father would feel the same way.

"Should I send word to my father?" he asked Gallus. "He cannot arrive before Henry and Davyss do, but I can at least send him word."

Gallus nodded. "He should know," he said. "Especially if you intend to lift a sword against Henry."

He stated the fact like there was no question to it, which there wasn't. Chad may have saved Henry's life at Evesham but that didn't mean he would support the man in every circumstance, and especially in a circumstance involving his aggression against family. Thinking on the situation they would soon be facing, Chad shook his head in disbelief.

"Against Henry," he muttered as if he had to hear it with his own voice to believe it. "Against Davyss. I cannot believe Davyss would lift a sword against you, Gallus. You are his best friend."

Gallus' features took on a serious cast as he thought of a man who was as close to him as a brother. "And he is mine," he said quietly. "He will not fight against me. He will turn on Henry if he has not already and if Henry is coming to Isenhall without any troops of his own, we could find ourselves in an interesting position. Henry could become our hostage again, for clearly, if Davyss turns against him, Henry will have no military support behind him."

The thought never occurred to Chad. It could be a curious as well as potentially devastating situation for the monarchy, as Henry had spent a year in captivity with de Montfort. For the king to end up a prisoner again was definitely a potential, but not one that Chad would be inclined to support.

"Prince Edward would take up Henry's cause again," Chad said. "We do not want that situation. Edward is as competent a military commander as any of us. More so, in fact. He would bring crown troops to raze Isenhall if you take his father hostage again, and we are trying to avoid the destruction of your home and the displacement of your wives and children."

Now that the information of Henry's movements was settling, the subject drifted to the families Chad had just mentioned. *Women and children.* No one wanted their wives or children involved in a battle. Gallus and Maximus looked at each other, silently dealing with that very fact. It was Tiberius who finally shook his head.

"De Moray wants to take my wife with him to Ravendark," he said. "I told him that she is heavy with child and cannot travel, but given this missive from de Serreaux, I may have to re-think that decision. I do not want her giving birth in a castle under siege."

Gallus sighed heavily. "Either they all go or no one does," he said. "Do you think that de Moray will escort all of them back to Ravendark? My wife will not want Douglass to go alone."

Tiberius turned his attention to the keep as if seeing his pregnant wife through the dark stone walls. He didn't want to be separated from her; none of them wanted to be separated from their wives and children. But it would be better to have the women safe should Henry unleash hell. Evesham was only the beginning; now, the war was coming to Isenhall.

They could all feel it.

"I will go inform de Moray of the missive," Tiberius finally said, "and I will ask him if his offer still stands to take my wife to safety."

"Do it," Gallus said. "Get him out of here. I do not want de Moray within these walls if Henry unleashes hell against us. Moving the women to safety will give him a reason to leave."

There was a distinct sense of foreboding in the air now, uncertainty for what was to come. The situation was growing more complex and dangerous by the day, now with Henry evidently determined to test the loyalty of those close to the House of de Shera. It was a situation that, when finally faced, would determine the course of the future for all of them.

As Tiberius turned for the keep, with Maximus behind him, Gallus and Chad faced one another.

"Lioncross is very close to Isenhall," Chad said quietly. "I will ride personally and seek Curtis' support. I cannot believe he would refuse you, especially in light of the information from de Serreaux."

Gallus nodded, weakly. It was as if the man were lost in thought, perhaps pondering the far-reaching implications his confrontation with Henry would bring. After a moment, he put a hand on Chad's wrist.

"If I asked you to take Lady Alessandria to The Paladin, would you do it?" he asked.

Chad was caught off guard by the question. "Why?"

Gallus squeezed his wrist. "I have told you this before," he said. "I know you would risk your life by taking up arms for me, but this will affect you and your family for years to come. This is my fight, Chad, and…."

Chad reached out and grabbed the man by both arms. "Are you attempting to be rid of me just as you are trying to rid yourself of de Moray?"

Gallus shook his head but something in his eyes told Chad that he was, indeed, trying to remove him from the coming storm. He was trying to do something noble for those who would support him.

Leave Isenhall!

"Alessandria should go home," Gallus said. "Aurelius can protect her better there. It is unfair to the woman to be in a castle under siege."

Although Chad knew that wasn't the reason Gallus had asked him to take the woman north, he, too, was unhappy with the thought of her remaining at Isenhall with Henry on the approach.

"If that is what you are truly worried about, then she can go with de Moray, also," he said. "I do not need to take her north."

"But…."

Chad cut him off. "We have been through this before, Gallus," he said. "I stand with you, as does my father. You cannot get rid of me so easily by telling me to take Lady Alessandria to The Paladin. In fact… mayhap you will consider allowing me to marry her before… well, before the situation turns dire. I intend to send her with the other women to safety and I would like to send her as Lady de Lohr. It will give me something to live for, to look forward to, if I know she is my reward through the tribulation."

Gallus could see that there was no way he could remove Chad from Isenhall, and he was touched and saddened at the same time. Chad was a loyal friend to the end, now intending to stand against the madness of Henry. Gallus wondered if he could live with the guilt if something happened to his loyal friends who were taking up arms on his behalf, but as Maximus had said, it was a much bigger situation than simply the House of de Shera remaining loyal to de Montfort's ideals. An entire world was wrapped up in family loyalties and bloodlines.

And Henry was coming to destroy it all.

"Then take her into Coventry to St. Mary's Cathedral and marry her," Gallus said hoarsely. "It is the very least I can do for you considering the risk you are about to take on my behalf. You have my blessing."

Chad's eyes glimmered with the first bit of joy and relief that Gallus had seen since the missive from Henry arrived. "Thank you, Gallus," he said sincerely, his hand on the man's arm. "I will make her a fine husband, I swear it."

Gallus simply nodded, patting Chad on the cheek as the man flashed him a grin before breaking to the keep. Alessandria was in there, somewhere, and he wanted to give her the good news. Gallus watched him go, the smile fading from his lips, feeling as guilty as he possibly could. He loved Chad; he loved all of them – de Moray, de Winter, and the de Lohrs. They were family, they were brothers, they were comrades-in-arms. But most of all, they were friends.

Was his stubborn pride worth all their lives?

He wondered.

☙

"BUT MY FATHER says that Arthur is the greatest Briton of all," a young lad with dark hair and dark eyes was saying to Alessandria. Bhrodi de Shera, Jeniver and Gallus' eldest son, was quite serious at nearly eight years of age. "My father says there is no one greater in all of history."

Alessandria was seated in the small hall of Isenhall, a larger feasting room that was directly across the entry from the small, low-ceilinged feasting hall where so much of Isenhall's business was conducted. The larger feasting room had a floor covered with straw, not rushes, and it was where the children of the de Shera brothers usually played when the weather outside wasn't mild enough for them to enjoy it. It had become something of a large playroom, in fact, complete with an old black dog that slept by the fire.

Even now, Maximus' two eldest sons played near the dog with their wooden soldiers and cart, and Tiberius' pregnant wife, the tall and elegant Lady Douglass, sat on a soft chair near the fire with a young girl sleeping on her lap while another girl, a little older, played at her feet. Lady Courtly, Maximus' wife, was trying to pick a sliver out of a two year old's finger, and Lady Jeniver sat at the table, sewing on some tiny breeches, while her son listened to Alessandria recite Biblical stories.

As the women and children of Isenhall had quickly come to realize, Alessandria had a talent for telling stories and this particular tale had been about Samson, the strongest man in all the land, but young Bhrodi wasn't having any of it. His father had told him that Arthur was the greatest and strongest man in the land and he wanted to make that clear to Alessandria.

Alessandria, to her credit, was very patient with the lad. She smiled to his assertion that Samson wasn't, in fact, the strongest man of all.

"God made many strong men, Bhrodi," Alessandria said to the lad. "These men lived in different times. Samson lived in the time of the Bible, when men of God walked the earth. Arthur lived much later than that, and he was a very strong and great man himself."

Bhrodi cocked his head curiously; he was a handsome lad, very sharp, the pride and joy of his parents. "But Arthur was the king of all Britons long ago," he said. "Did God not make him king?"

"He did."

"Was Samson a king?"

"Nay, he was not."

"Then Arthur was greater because he was a king!"

It was young boy's logic and Alessandria was trying very hard not to laugh at his insistence. She did the only thing she could do; she surrendered. "Aye, that must be true," she said. Out of the corner of her eye, she was watching Jeniver snicker. "Kings are the greatest in all the land."

Bhrodi shook his head. "Not always," he said seriously. "Not Henry. He is *no*t a great man."

Jeniver's head came up. "Bhrodi," she admonished softly. "We do not speak so of the king. You have been listening to your father too much."

Bhrodi turned his innocent face to her. "But Papa does not like the king," he said. "He will not fight for him. I heard him say so."

Jeniver sighed in exasperation. She didn't want her young son growing up with such an attitude of rebellion towards the English crown. Even though she was Welsh, and Bhrodi was half-Welsh, rebellion, in her mind, only led to problems. It wasn't that she had disagreed with her husband's stance all of these years, for she supported him whatever he decided, but she didn't want her son thinking it was normal and right to choose rebellion over obedience to a king.

It was a difficult subject in the de Shera household, especially since Evesham. The wives, all of them, sincerely wished their husbands would simply swear fealty to a king that was now clearly in control of the country, but the de Shera brothers didn't seem inclined to do it, so the women kept their mouths shut, at least to their husbands. To each other, however, it was much different. There was fear in their manner every time they whispered words to each other, fearful for the men they loved, men who were trying to take a stand for what they believed in.

It was a difficult situation, indeed.

"Bhrodi," Jeniver said as she set her sewing to the table. "You must understand that your father makes decisions he feels are right and true for all of us. That does not mean the king is a bad man. It simply means your father is trying to do the right thing for his family and for your legacy."

Bhrodi went to his mother, leaning against the table as she ran her fingers through his dark hair. "When I am the earl, I will not fight for Henry, either," he said boldly.

"You may not have a choice if you want to keep your lands."

Bhrodi frowned, puzzled by his mother's attitude. It was different from his father's. Jeniver watched her son's expression as the child turned for Alessandria, who was watching the boy with some curiosity. He would be the Earl of Coventry someday and it was clear that he was a strong-willed child. That would serve him well when the time came, especially with the de Shera name. He would need that fortitude.

"Were there great kings in the Bible?" he asked Alessandria. "Were there great warriors?"

Alessandria nodded. "Indeed, there were," she said. "There were many."

She was precluded from saying more as Tiberius and Maximus suddenly entered the keep and their respective children, seeing their fathers, began to squeal.

The two little boys playing in front of the hearth made a run for Maximus, plowing into his groin area. He grunted in pain, picking up the children, as Tiberius made his way to his very pregnant wife and inquired about the location of her father. Douglass thought he might be in his chamber and Tiberius smiled sweetly at the woman, taking the toddler from her and then pulling her up to stand. He left the room with his wife and two children as Maximus went to see to his own wife, who had just managed to remove the sliver from the screaming two-year-old child. Maximus comforted the baby, the gruff brother turning soft in the presence of his children.

Alessandria watched the interaction of her cousins with their families, hoping that she and Chad would one day be blessed with children. The past two weeks at Isenhall had been a lesson in family love and devotion; as fierce as the Lords of Thunder were, they were kind and gentle fathers. There was much family warmth within the old stone walls of the ancient fortress.

Alessandria couldn't help but hope for her own warmth someday as she watched the men with their wives, seeing the devotion between them all. To have Chad look at her the way Maximus was looking at Courtly, or the way Tiberius looked at Douglass, was almost more than she could hope for.

"I suppose my husband will be coming in from the ward soon enough," Jeniver said, breaking Alessandria from her thoughts. The woman stood up, collecting both her sewing and her son. "I will go now and see to the nooning meal. Thank you for entertaining my son today. He enjoyed your stories very much."

Alessandria smiled at Jeniver, at Bhrodi. "I enjoyed telling them," she said, looking at the boy. "Tomorrow, I will tell you about Noah and the boat he built at God's command. He put many animals on the boat to save them when God punished the evils of man."

That had Bhrodi's interest. "I have a pony," he said eagerly. "His name is Henry. My father named him that so that I could ride Henry and force him to my wishes."

Alessandria bit off a smile, seeing Jeniver shake her head reproachfully from the corner of her eye. "I am sure he is a very fine animal," Alessandria said.

"Would you like to see him?"

"Indeed, I would."

"Later," Jeniver said, steering her son away from Alessandria. "We have tasks to accomplish first."

Alessandria stood up. "May I help you, my lady?" she asked. "I would be more than happy to help you oversee the meal."

Jeniver smiled. "Of course you may," she said. "I am always happy to have your company."

Pleased that she wouldn't be left behind and bored without anything to do, Alessandria scurried after Jeniver and Bhrodi as they left the feasting room. She and Jeniver had become good friends, in fact, and she enjoyed the woman's company. They were just to the entry door leading out into the ward when the door jerked open again on its heavy iron hinges, spilling forth Chad into the keep.

A steady breeze blew in behind him and he struggled to shut the door, his gaze on Alessandria. He barely acknowledged Jeniver and Bhrodi before speaking to Alessandria. "My lady," he addressed her. "I have a need to speak with you. Will you indulge me?"

Alessandria nodded eagerly, excusing herself from Jeniver, as Chad took her arm and politely led her into the small vaulted feasting room that was just off the entry. Alessandria had become very familiar with that room, as they ate most of their meals there and it seemed to be the favorite gathering place in the keep for its warmth and intimacy.

As Jeniver and Bhrodi went outside and shut the door, and Maximus was in the other room with his wife and children, Alessandria and Chad moved to a corner of the room where they would have more privacy. The stone walls were heavy here and three long, thin lancet windows were situated nearby, providing light and ventilation for the chamber. Certain that Maximus wasn't anywhere close to see his movements, Chad took Alessandria's hand in his own and brought it to his soft lips.

"I have missed you today," he murmured as he kissed her flesh. "How long has it been since I have last seen you?"

Alessandria grinned, her heart fluttering wildly as he nibbled her fingers. "Not long," she said. "You were with me when you were summoned to the gatehouse not a half-hour ago. Do you not recall?"

He made a face. "We were surrounded by chaperones, as we always are."

She laughed softly. "They are simply protecting my virtue," she said. "Evidently you are a devil that I need protecting from."

He grinned. "I would agree with that statement," he replied. But soon, his expression softened. "I do not like being away from you, no matter if it is a few minutes or a few hours. Any time away from you is too long."

Alessandria flushed at his flattery. "I feel the same," she said softly. "Did you finish your business at the gatehouse, then?"

Chad's warm expression faded; he couldn't help it. "I did," he said. "That is what I must speak to you about."

"Oh?" she cocked her head curiously. "What can it be?"

He grew serious, caressing her hand as he thought of how he would approach the subject. He didn't want to frighten her but she needed to know how serious the situation was. Something very bad was coming, a mighty storm of swords and men and loyalties. Chad was coming to think that she was so much better off in the convent; he struggled not to let guilt consume him, yet again, for having brought her into this terrible situation.

"When we were at Canterbury, you will recall that Henry sent men to take you," he said quietly. "Did I ever mention the name of the knight in command?"

Alessandria looked at him, curiously. "I do not believe so," she said. "Why?"

He lifted his eyebrows at the irony of that question. *Why, indeed.*

"The knight in command is a man named de Serreaux," he said. "I have known him for many years. We have fought side by side on occasion. In this instance at Canterbury, we were, briefly, on opposing sides because of you. I am not blaming you nor is this something you should feel badly about. It was simply the circumstances."

In spite of his words, Alessandria couldn't help but feel somewhat guilty over that. "I understand," she said. "But why do you mention him now?"

Chad sighed heavily and kissed her hand once more before continuing. "Because, in spite of the incident at Canterbury, de Serreaux still seems to have some feelings of friendship or loyalty towards me," he said. "I went to the gatehouse earlier because a missive had arrived for me. The messenger who delivered it was wearing Henry's colors, so we all assumed it was Henry who had sent me the missive. It was not Henry, however; it turned out to be de Serreaux."

Her eyes widened. "The same man we fled from?" she asked. "Did your father tell him where you had taken me, then? He knows where I am?"

Chad shook his head. "My father did not tell him, of that I am sure," he replied. "Aless, it would not take a genius to determine where I had taken you. You are a de Shera; one could only assume I took you to be with your kin at Isenhall. De Serreaux is not a fool – he knew where we had gone."

Her fear grew. "And he is demanding that you turn me over to him?"

Again, Chad shook his head. He could see she was growing distressed and he hastened to soothe her. "He is not," he said quietly. "You were not part of the missive he sent to me. It would seem that Henry is coming to Isenhall, coming with an army no less, and de Serreaux sought to warn me."

Her mouth formed a shocked "O" and she put a hand over her lips as if to attempt to contain her astonishment. "Sweet Mary…," she gasped. "Henry is coming for me!"

Chad grasped her by both arms, gently but firmly. "This has nothing to do with you," he stressed again. "Henry was out to seek vengeance against your cousins long before you came to his attention. Henry is coming to demand loyalty once and for all. That being said, it is imperative that you leave Isenhall. I do not want you in a castle under siege, so I plan to marry you today and send you along with the other de Shera women when de Moray takes them to his home of Ravendark Castle and to safety."

Alessandria was having difficulty processing what he was telling her. *Henry was coming... I will marry you today... you will leave Isenhall before the army arrives...* all of it was spinning around in her head, so much so that her knees gave way and she plopped onto the seat behind her, unable to stand any longer.

War was coming. Henry was coming, and in spite of what Chad had told her, she knew he was only trying to make her feel better. Henry was coming for her and Chad was making it seem like he wasn't.

But she knew the truth. She didn't understand enough about wars and politics to realize that she was the last thing on the king's mind. To her, this entire situation started because Henry had wanted her as a hostage and Chad had prevented that. She was the cause of everything terrible happening to people she had come to love.

Alessandria had never had a sense of family. A careless father, a foolish brother… that was all she had ever known, which was why the nuns at Newington had become her family. Then, she'd come to Isenhall with people who were kind to her, family who cared about her. She had Chad, too, a man who wanted to marry her. Such a wonderful sense of family, fulfilling her like nothing she'd ever known.

And now, this.

Henry wanted her, still, and he was going to tear down Isenhall to get to her. No matter what Chad said, she knew that was the truth. This was her fault, all of it.

"I do not want to leave, Chad," she said, feeling a lump in her throat as her emotions got the better of her. "Please do not make me leave."

He forced a smile, kissing her on the forehead. "It will only be for a short time," he assured her. "I will go now to St. Mary's in Coventry and make the arrangements for our wedding. Mayhap Jeniver or Courtly will let you borrow a lovely dress for the occasion. They are more your size."

He was trying to make light of the situation, to have her focus on the joy of their wedding rather than the impending arrival of Henry's army. But Alessandria wouldn't let him change the subject.

"Chad, you must listen," she insisted. "I know that Henry is coming for me. You need not pretend otherwise. It is only right that you should give me over to him right away. Mayhap then he will not attack Isenhall."

Chad frowned at her. "Sweetheart, I assure you that Henry is not coming for you," he said. "He is coming because he wants Gallus and Maximus and Tiberius to swear fealty to him."

"That is what he wanted me for!"

He shook her gently. "But he does not have you, nor shall he ever," he said. "I do not know how much plainer I can make this – you are not at issue. This has nothing to do with you any longer."

He is only trying to spare me, Alessandria thought. She knew he was doing it to be kind and she didn't believe one word of his denial. The entire reason behind her presence at Isenhall was to keep her from Henry. Now, the king knew where she was and he was coming for her. That made the most sense to her. She both loved and hated Chad for not being truthful with her, for trying to make it easy on her, but the thought of Henry coming to destroy this beautiful place of family and warmth was something she could hardly stomach.

Jeniver... Courtly... Douglass... the children... they would know hardship and strife because of her, because Chad could not be honest and tell her why Henry was really coming. It was more than she could bear and the tears began to come.

Chad saw the tears and he pulled her into his powerful embrace, holding her close, trying to comfort her. He was very sorry he had upset her but it was necessary that she know the truth of what was coming. He, too, was saddened to know that Henry would soon rattle a place he had come to see as a sanctuary, spending time with Alessandria, coming to know the woman who had a heart as big as the ocean.

She was fun to taunt, and made an easy target with her guileless manner, but it was all in good fun. He loved her for it. She was also not beyond returning his taunts and, more than once, getting the better of him. He loved that about her, too. Lady du Bexley's dinner had come up more than once over the past two weeks. They had been so happy here, now to see it all change drastically. It was heartbreaking.

But he couldn't give in to the sorrow of it. They had to make the best of it, to do what was necessary in order to survive. He let her cry a few moments longer in his arms before giving her a squeeze and releasing her. He wiped at the tears on her face as he spoke.

"Everything will be well in the end, I promise," he assured her. "I do not want you to worry overly about it. We will marry tonight and then you will go with de Moray and the other women on a short journey to Ravendark. I will come for you when I can."

So he was going to maintain that she had nothing to do with Henry's approach. Alessandria was nearly mad with his denial.

"Please, Chad," she begged. "The king is coming. He will destroy Isenhall because you brought me here. I cannot let that happen."

He sighed heavily, shaking his head at her refusal to believe him. He had already told her the truth so he chose to push past the fact that she still believed Henry was coming for her. He couldn't let her dwell on it.

"Come along," he said, taking her by the hand and pulling her from the chamber. "We shall find Jeniver and ask her to provide you with a lovely garment for our wedding. I should like to have it tonight, at sunset. We can return to Isenhall afterwards and you can pack for your journey to Ravendark. I've never been there, actually, but I hear it is a very big place. And de Moray's wife raises goats, so you will have your fill of cute little animals and children."

Distraught, Alessandria allowed him to pull her along but the entire time she was planning her escape. She wasn't going to let Henry raze Isenhall all because of her. Everything had been fine before she had come. Perhaps if she left, everything would be fine again. She loved these people, and this life, enough to make that sacrifice.

And Chad... he would go into battle because of her. She couldn't stand the thought of losing the man she had come to love very much. All of the dreams of hope and love she'd had were only that – dreams. Perhaps they were never meant to be. It had been happiness she had never expected, a vision of heaven unlike anything she'd ever known. But like most dreams, they were not meant to last. This dream was over before it truly got started, but at least she'd had a taste of it. That would have to sustain her for the rest of her life because if Henry wanted her, then he could have her if it would only spare Chad's life.

She couldn't let this all end because of her.

She couldn't let *Chad* end.

CHAPTER FIFTEEN

Just outside of Northampton, England

TOMORROW, THEY WOULD be upon Isenhall.

As Davyss de Winter sat in his tent with his brother, contemplating what tomorrow would bring, all he could think of was the fact that tomorrow would see them at the walls of Isenhall. Those dark-stoned walls of that oddly-shaped, rounded fortress had a very special place in his heart, for he remembered the days of his youth when he would play within those walls, running and chasing Gallus and Maximus, and laughing at Tiberius because he was younger and unable to keep up with the bigger boys. Hugh, his own brother, was even younger than Tiberius and would run after the big boys, wailing because they didn't want to play with him. Aye, he remembered those days well.

And now, here they were, preparing to raze those very walls.

"Henry wants to discuss tomorrow's strategy, you know," Hugh said, seated near the brazier and using a pumice stone to sharpen his sword. "He wanted to meet with us after sup. If we do not go to his tent, he will come here."

Davyss grunted at the mere thought of Henry invading their tent. His mind was still wandering the days of his youth.

"Do you remember playing with Gallus and Max and Ty as children?" he asked. "I remember hiding from you. You would wail in distress, trying to find us, and then you'd run to tell Mother that we were not being kind to you. Do you remember that?"

Hugh grinned. "I do," he said. "You were bullies, all of you."

Davyss laughed. "And you were unbearable and spoilt," he countered. "I remember hiding in the loft of the stables at Isenhall, dropping horse dung on your head when you would come inside to look for us."

Hugh snorted. "I seem to remember Mother beating you for that," he said. "Or was it Father?"

Davyss conceded the point. "It was both," he said. "Father was laughing at what I did, but it was Mother who forced him to punish me. He did not hit me very hard, however."

Hugh reflected back to those days. "That is because you were his favorite," he said. "And I was Mother's."

"You were a terrible child."

"I know."

Davyss continued chuckling at the recollection. "I have so many good memories of Isenhall and of Gallus and the pranks we would play," he said. But soon, his smile faded as pain began to glaze his expression. "And now Henry expects me to lay siege to my best friend. He expects me to bring him to his knees. Surely he knows that…."

Hugh looked up from his sword, cutting him off. "You do not have to say it, Davyss."

"I know."

"When the time comes, I will stand with you, whatever your decision."

"You have known since the beginning what my decision will be."

Hugh nodded reluctantly. "I know," he said. "We have made the necessary preparations for it. Our properties are fortified against any… aggressions."

"Aye, they are."

"Then I will ask something I've not asked since we left Wintercroft Castle – why did we agree to come to Isenhall in the first place?"

Davyss turned to look at him, then. "Do you not know?"

"I think I do."

"Someone must protect Gallus from Henry."

The truth of the situation was spoken and Hugh drew in a long, deep breath and returned to his sword. His work with the pumice stone slowed.

"I wish Father was here," he muttered. "I wish I knew that we had his approval in this."

Davyss stood up, cup of wine in hand. It was his third cup, trying to ease the guilt and angst he felt over Henry's orders. He knew, and had known since receiving Henry's orders to march on Isenhall, that he was only going through the motions of obeying the king. When it came down to the command to launch an attack against Gallus' home, that was when Henry would discover that Davyss, for all of his loyalty to the crown, would refuse him. The man simply couldn't move against his best friend, only Henry didn't know it yet. But he would soon enough, Davyss suspected.

Maybe he already knew.

"Father would have tried to reason with Henry," Davyss finally said. "He would have tried to talk the man out of this, but I do not have Father's sense of diplomacy. I am a warrior and *Lespada* does the talking for me, but in this case, my weapon shall remain silent. I will not lift it."

Hugh glanced up at the man. Big, powerful, and cunning, Davyss was the type of knight that all men hoped to be. Even Hugh. As good as Hugh was, and he was excellent, even he admired his brother's skill and sense of honor. This situation with Henry and the House of de Shera was weighing heavily upon Davyss, threatening to topple him, but the man wouldn't waver. He knew what was right and what was wrong. He knew that family and blood was stronger than any king or country. Still, it was a terribly difficult situation for them all.

"Henry wishes to discuss tomorrow's strategy," he said again, quietly. "What will you tell him?"

Davyss lifted his big shoulders. "Nothing for the moment," he said.

"We will ride to Isenhall and see if Gallus can convince Henry not to move against him. Gallus is a far better diplomat than I am. If Henry refuses, then he shall know my stance at that time. Meanwhile, you will ensure that our men are not to respond to Henry's commands of battle. Pass the word through the ranks that all commands to be obeyed will come from me or from you. Will you do that?"

Hugh nodded. "I will do it tonight," he said. Then, he stopped rubbing at his sword and looked at his brother. "We have two thousand men with us, Davyss. Henry has only brought about five hundred, including his Six. We will have to fight off de Serreaux and the others, you know. When our army balks, Henry's army will move against us."

Davyss knew that. He thought on Torran de Serreaux and the other knights with him, men called Henry's Guard of Six. He knew them all very well, as they were all interwoven into Henry's command structure.

"I know," he said. "I do not even know why they brought de Garr, however – the man is in terrible shape after the de Lohr beating. Did you hear the story behind it?"

"I did."

Davyss shook his head, now grinning. "I wish I could have seen it," he said. "Those six against the de Lohr knights would have been a battle to see."

Hugh lifted his eyebrows. "I, for one, would have run at the sight of Jorden de Russe or Rhun du Bois coming after me. Those men are enormous. De Garr is lucky he still has his head after all of that."

Davyss laughed. "De Serreaux is nothing to trifle with, either," he pointed out. "It would have been a battle of epic proportions and I am sorry I missed it. But Chad had what Henry wanted, the de Shera girl, and de Serreaux was determined to gain the woman for Henry's purposes, so a clash of that magnitude was inevitable."

Hugh set his sword and stone down. "De Serreaux told me that he believes Chad is at Isenhall," he said, sobering. "You know that Chad will stand with Gallus."

"I know."

"If Chad stands with him, then his father will stand with Chad," Hugh pointed out. "If Daniel stands with Chad, so will Curtis de Lohr. The entire House of de Lohr will stand against Henry."

Davyss sobered as well, thinking on the greater implications of what was about to happen. "And de Moray will stand with Gallus because his daughter is married to Ty," he said. "Is Henry a fool not to realize all of this?"

They were prevented from further conversation by a soft hail at the tent flap. Davyss went to push back the fabric panel to reveal de Serreaux standing there. Davyss wasn't surprised to see the man but he wondered if he'd heard any of their conversation.

"Torran," he greeted evenly. "Will you come in? My brother and I were just having some wine."

De Serreaux shook his head. "Thank you, no," he replied. "Henry has sent me to retrieve you. He wishes to discuss tomorrow's approach on Isenhall."

The time had finally come to face what they did not want to face. Davyss simply motioned to his brother, who stood up from the stool and stretched the kinks out of his big body as he made his way to the tent flap. Once outside, beneath the carpet of stars against the black sky on a breezy and cold night, the three men headed for Henry's tent several dozen yards away.

As they walked, de Serreaux sniffed the air. "It smells like rot," he said casually. "I smell moldering leaves."

Davyss pointed off to the west. "There is a bog not far from here," he said. "It always smells of compost, worse when the wind shifts."

De Serreaux gazed off into the night towards the west. "You are familiar with this area, are you not?"

"I am."

"And you are familiar with Isenhall."

"Verily."

De Serreaux looked at him. "You and Gallus are childhood friends."

"Everyone knows that."

De Serreaux came to a halt, facing Davyss in the dark. "Henry wants to glean your knowledge of Isenhall's weaknesses to plan this siege," he said. "I'm assuming you already know that as well."

Davyss' dark eyes glittered in the starlight. "What would you have me say?" he asked. "Of course I know. I have known from the start. Why would you ask such a question?"

De Serreaux shrugged. "I simply want to make sure you are aware," he said. "I can only imagine that this is a very difficult situation for you."

Davyss was immediately suspicious of the line of conversation. "That would go without saying," he said, his gaze lingering on the man. "What will you run back and tell Henry of this conversation, Torran?"

De Serreaux could see the defensiveness in Davyss' expression. Not that he blamed the man. It was difficult to let on to the fact that he was sympathetic to Davyss' position. He didn't like what Henry was doing, either, and hadn't since he sent that missive to Isenhall himself. Still, there was a line between him and Davyss; he could see it. It was the line of mistrust.

"Nothing," he finally said. "You and I have not had much opportunity to speak privately on this battle march."

Davyss glanced at Hugh, who was less adept at hiding his wariness of what seemed to be a probe from de Serreaux.

"What could we possibly have in common to speak privately about?" Hugh demanded. "There is nothing to say, de Serreaux. We are doing our duty just as you are. We do not have to be happy about it. What else did you want to know?"

De Serreaux shook his head calmly. "Nothing, Hugh."

Hugh didn't believe him in the least. "Did you want to ask us of our loyalties?" he said. "Come out with it, then. Do not make foolish conversation about bogs. Ask us who we are to support in this battle. In fact, ask us about what men have been whispering of since Evesham – ask us if we have finally regained de Montfort's head from Roger Mortimer. Don't you want to know?"

De Serreaux cocked an eyebrow at the belligerent tone. "Not particularly."

Hugh threw up his hands, exasperated. "The man is my wife's father," he said. "I have personally asked him to give it to us. He is considering it. You can tell Henry that if it pleases you."

De Serreaux's gaze lingered on Hugh, the fiery brother. "I have no intention of telling Henry anything," he said, looking back to Davyss. "I thought we had trust between us. We have fought in a number of battles together, de Winter. I thought trust had been established. I see that mayhap I was wrong."

Davyss shook his head, stepping in to the conversation before his brother's heated manner began to fire up de Serreaux. "I trust you with my life in battle," he said. "But this is a difficult situation. Surely you know that. I have been asked to march against my best friend and I am understandably unhappy about it. There is no secret in that, nothing that requires trust. Henry is aware of it. Now, he is waiting for us, so let us proceed."

Hugh and Davyss continued on but de Serreaux did not; he remained standing where they'd left him. "There is something you should know," he said.

The de Winter brothers came to a halt, turning to face de Serreaux, who moved to catch up with them when he saw that he had their attention. He moved in very close to the brothers, his dark eyes serious.

"I sent word to Chad at Isenhall to inform him of Henry's movements," he said quietly. "Isenhall knows we are coming."

Hugh's eyes widened but Davyss was more controlled in his reaction. He was suddenly quite interested in what de Serreaux had to say and the defensiveness that he and his brother had exhibited eased accordingly.

"You did *what*?" he hissed. "You sent a missive to Chad at Isenhall? He knows we are coming?"

"Aye."

"*All* of us?"

"Aye."

Davyss' jaw dropped; he couldn't help it. "But why did you do it?" he demanded, although his voice was no more than a harsh whisper. "Does Henry know? Did he tell you to do it?"

De Serreaux shook his head. "Henry knows nothing," he said. "I did it because of Henry's mindset right now… he's not right, Davyss. Surely you have sensed it. There is some kind of madness that has infected him ever since Evesham, a madness that has him suspicious of everyone's loyalties, including yours. Don't you know that is why you have been asked to march on Isenhall? Henry wants to see who you will be loyal to – to him or to Gallus. Have you not realized that?"

It took Davyss a moment to understand that de Serreaux didn't like what was happening any more than he did. In fact, he was coming to see that de Serreaux had tipped off Isenhall about Henry's approach, which meant that Gallus and his brothers would be prepared. When the full realization hit him, Davyss nearly collapsed with relief.

"Sweet Jesus," Davyss hissed, a hand to his head in shock. "Of course I know why my army was summoned to march on Isenhall. I know it will come down to a choice between Gallus and Henry. I am prepared to make that choice."

No matter that they were speaking more freely now, Davyss stopped short of giving de Serreaux an answer, still holding the slightest bit of suspicion that all of this might be a trap. De Serreaux could easily run back to Henry and tell the man that de Winter was disloyal, so it was that fear that kept him silent. It was better to be prudent than completely trusting of a man as close to the king as de Serreaux was.

But De Serreaux must have sensed Davyss' reluctance to make a declaration of loyalty one way or the other but he didn't push him. It really didn't matter in the long run; they would all know soon enough. Still, there was more he had to say.

"This isn't only about you," de Serreaux said, his voice low. "Henry wants to see if de Lohr is there to support Gallus as well, and if de Moray has finally been pushed onto the side of his daughter's husband.

He wants to see just who is against him and this is how he intends to do it. Be prepared for this, Davyss. Henry is suspicious of all of you and if he determines that you all support de Shera and not him, the consequences could be very bad, indeed."

Davyss' jaw ticked. "Then Henry is a fool if he believes he can defeat the House of de Shera, the House of de Lohr, and the House of de Winter," he hissed. "Think on the holdings we collectively have and the manpower. We can bring Henry to his knees if he is not careful. I am not declaring my loyalties one way or the other but I am emphasizing to you that if Henry insults our honor and doubts our loyalties with some foolish test of wills, then he will lose. Make no mistake; he cannot defeat us all. We will destroy him."

De Serreaux knew that. He sighed, long and heavy. "Let us hope it does not come to that," he replied. "I simply wanted you to be aware of what is really at stake, Davyss. I see much. I know much. And Henry is out to punish everyone with any association to those who allied themselves with de Montfort. The House of de Shera is his biggest target and along with it, so are all of you."

Davyss sensed the man's sympathy at that point but he still couldn't give in to it and trust him completely. It was better if he didn't. "I understand," he said. "But what I do not understand is why you would betray Henry by sending word to Isenhall of his approach."

De Serreaux shrugged. "Because above all else, I am a man of honor," he said simply. "What Henry is doing is not honorable. It is fed by madness and I do not want to see good and noble men consumed by it. That is the best way I can explain it. As I said, Henry does not know of the missive to Isenhall so I would be appreciative if you did not tell him."

In that small request, Davyss began to understand something; de Serreaux had risked himself for the opposition. For men he considered honorable even if they were on the opposing side. He was asking Davyss to keep that confidence, and Davyss intended to. More than that, it was enough to cause Davyss to finally believe that de Serreaux might actually be telling the truth. He had known de Serreaux for years and he was a man of his word. It was enough to lower Davyss' guard somewhat.

"You have my oath that I will not mention it," he muttered, "but I hope it does not come down to me fighting against you in battle. I should not look forward to that."

De Serreaux's gaze lingered on him. "It is quite possible that I would not let that happen," he said, turning for Henry's tent in the distance. "It is quite possible that I would rather stand by men of honor than by a king of madness."

With that, he walked off, leaving Davyss and Hugh staring at each other in surprise. Was it possible that de Serreaux, leader of Henry's Six, would turn on his king? Or was the man simply saying such things to gain their confidence only to betray them? Perhaps Davyss didn't have as much trust in the man as he thought he had.

In this world, anything was possible.

CHAPTER SIXTEEN

The outskirts of Coventry

HENRY IS HERE.

At least, that's what Curtis' breathless scouts had told him. The king, escorted by the de Winter army, had been seen north of Northampton, camping peacefully in the night, but it was clear that they would be at Isenhall on the morrow.

That fact made Curtis move his army when they should be sleeping.

Up until that point, his pace from Lioncross had been relatively leisurely. But that was no more. He wasn't going to wait until morning to get to Isenhall, given that Henry was already extremely close. He had to make it to the fortress before Henry did, so his sons and knights pushed the army through the darkness, through the last few miles under a silver moon and a brilliant blanket of stars tossed across the cold night sky. The men weren't particularly weary, as it had only been a few days of travel from Lioncross Abbey, so no one particularly minded traveling on a pleasant night. Some of the men had even taken up singing to pass the time, trudging down the road, catching whiffs of the stinky bog to the southwest.

Curtis traveled towards the middle of the fifteen-hundred-man army, allowing Chris and Arthur and William command of the men for the most part. He could hear Chris up ahead, bellowing orders, and Curtis had to smile at a son who reminded him so much of his own father. Over the years, men had come to call him Christopher the Lesser, so that he would not be so confused with his grandfather, a title that Chris didn't much like. He felt that it implied that he was less of a man than his grandfather was, which he surely was not. He was every bit the man his grandfather had been.

It was comforting to hear the voice, to see the man move among the army with such confidence. Somehow, it made Curtis miss his father less when he saw his son moving and acting like him. Curtis still remembered the fresh sorrow from the day his father passed away, a very old man, so his death had not been completely unexpected. It had simply been unwanted.

But it was a tender sense of reflection that Curtis had even now as he watched his sons, typical de Lohr men in the sense of command and size and sheer presence. Men that were all, to varying degrees, like his father. Curtis had continued the de Lohr legacy with his large stable of children and grandchildren, and he knew that when the time came that Chris would make an excellent Earl of Worcester. He was confident in the legacy he would leave behind.

He knew his father would have been pleased.

But this march to Isenhall was something of a threat to that legacy. With Henry's behavior unsteady in the wake of Evesham, there was no telling how the man would react to seeing the de Lohr army spread around Isenhall like a shield, but Curtis had to make that statement to the crown. He fully intended to speak with Henry about the situation and make it clear to the man that if push came to shove, the House of de Lohr would support the House of de Shera.

Yet, in accordance with his conversation with Avrielle, he would also speak to Gallus to try to convince the man to swallow his pride and swear fealty to the king. For the survival of the House of de Shera, and essentially the survival of them all, Gallus had to understand the necessity of it. Curtis could only pray Gallus would. Having descended from the House of de Lohr on his mother's side, Gallus had that stubborn streak in him that all de Lohr males had.

The knowledge that they knew they were right, no matter what the circumstance.

Lost in thought, he was startled when the cry went up through the ranks that Isenhall had been sighted. Driving his spurs into the flanks of his great red steed, he charged forward, through the ranks of men, to the front of the column where his sons were gathered. They were pointing at something in the distance, having come around a bend in the road where a great flat expanse of land was set before them.

Even in the darkness they could see Isenhall in the distance, with her dark walls and flickering points of light as men with torches manned the battlements. Chris immediately sent two messengers ahead to announce their arrival so that Gallus and his brothers wouldn't panic and launch an offensive against them in the darkness. Hearing the thunder of a horse's movement beside him, he turned to his father just as the man rode up.

"I will make sure Gallus knows it is us who approach," Chris said, indicating the messengers that were riding on ahead. "I do not want to have a rain of arrows greet us as we approach."

Curtis nodded, trying to peer through the darkness to see what was ahead. His eyesight had been failing as of late, attributed to age, and it was particularly difficult for him to see in the darkness. With the messengers heading into the distance, he motioned to Chris to come closer. The man did and Curtis pulled him aside, reining their horses off the road as the army passed them by.

They came to a pause in the heavy grass, watching the army lumber by. Curtis turned his horse so that his words would not be heard by the men.

"I have been thinking," he said to his son. "As much as I want Gallus and Max and Ty to know that we have arrived, I also want Henry to know it. The scouts tell us that Henry is camping just outside of Northampton."

"I heard."

"Henry will be here on the morrow."

"Aye, he will."

Curtis shook his head. "You will send a messenger to Henry this night with a message from me," he said firmly. "I want to see Henry before this gets out of hand. I want to talk to the man to see what his mindset is. I have been hearing rumors and hearsay about his state of mind and his objectives, but I want to hear it from him. Furthermore, if he is truly determined to attack Isenhall, then he must know we will not stand by and watch this happen. I have told you this before, Chris, on the day we departed from Lioncross; Henry must know we will not stand by while he attacks our kin. I certainly will not support him in such a move. So if he decides to attack, he must know that I will do everything I can to defend Isenhall."

Chris nodded in understanding. "I know, Papa," he said. "Rather than send a messenger, however, let me send Arthur or William. He will take the message more seriously if a de Lohr delivers it."

Curtis thought on that. "It is a good suggestion," he said. "Tell Henry I will meet him before dawn at St. Mary's Cathedral. We can pray for a solution to this problem. We can pray that we will all remain friends when it is over."

Chris nodded sharply to the command. "Aye," he said. "I will send Arthur. He has a more pleasing manner than William does. Willie can be a bit intimidating at times."

"We do not want to intimidate Henry."

"Nay, we do not. He would not take kindly to it and I do not want to be attacking Henry's army to wrest my hostage brother away from him."

Curtis snorted at the thought. "Willie in chains," he said. "What an image that would be."

Chris was smiling because his father was. "Willie would not think so."

Curtis roared with laughter. "Then send Arthur," he said. "Tell the man to use his best diplomacy. He has more of my father's ability to negotiate."

"And Willie inherited Grandmother's demeanor."

Curtis was back to snorting. "My mother was a fierce and passionate woman," he said. "But her idea of diplomacy was a fist to the eye."

"That is Willie's idea as well."

Curtis' chortling lingered. "I know," he said, sobering. "Therefore, send Arthur on his way. Meanwhile, I am going to speak with Gallus about this and see if we cannot come to a solution that does not involve men dying and a castle being razed. You know I love your cousin, Chris, but Gallus has that de Lohr stubborn streak in him. I hope I can convince him otherwise because, quite honestly, I do not want to have to go the rest of my life protecting him and his brothers from the crown. That will put us in a very bad position, not to mention it will be most tiresome."

Chris understood. "Agreed," he said. "I will go find Arthur and tell him of his mission. Will you ride ahead now to Isenhall?"

Curtis nodded. "I am on my way."

With that, he spurred his fat beast back onto the road, pushing men aside as he moved through the troops, heading for the distant bastion. He had a great task ahead of him this night and he would waste no time getting it done.

For the old knight from a very old and distinguished family, he was being called into action one last time to try to prevent a situation that could have far-reaching implications for many people – the Houses of de Lohr, de Winter, de Shera, and de Moray. The great houses who were also great friends, blood and friendship intertwined until it was all one big family. There were no more divisions except one – Henry.

He could destroy it all. Or he could destroy himself if he tried.

Curtis had to do all he could to ensure that didn't happen.

☙

EVEN THOUGH ISENHALL'S keep was a large place with four floors and an abundance of chambers, it still wasn't difficult to hear others when they spoke, especially if voices were raised. As Alessandria sat in her small borrowed chamber on the top floor of the keep where most of the children slept, she could hear Jeniver's voice on the floor below as it wafted up the stairwell. Something very bad was happening and Alessandria could hear nearly all of it.

She had no idea where Lady Courtly or Lady Douglass were. She never did hear their voices in all of this. At this late hour, everyone should have been asleep and would have been had Chad's cousin, Curtis de Lohr, not arrived in the early evening with his army in tow. A very large army that, even now, was making camp all around the walls of Isenhall, encircling it like a protective web. With Henry approaching, it was clear that Curtis was taking a stand on behalf of Isenhall but he made sure Gallus and Maximus and Tiberius knew his opinion on the matter first.

It was an arrival that had prevented Chad from taking Alessandria into Coventry to marry her. Those plans had been pushed aside for the moment. As the women had listened from the stairwell near the small feasting chamber on the entry level where most of the business of Isenhall was conducted, Curtis had made it very clear to the brothers, as well as to Chad and Bose, that he felt Gallus' continued resistance to Henry was a lost cause. De Montfort was dead and so was the man's rebellion, and Curtis implored Gallus and his brothers to reconsider their collective stance. There were families at stake here, families that could not survive if the de Shera brothers perished in a foolish stance for a man who had been brutally killed at Evesham.

Gallus and Maximus and Tiberius loved and respected Curtis, and they were deeply grateful for the man's show of force against Henry's approaching army, yet they were polite but firm in their argument against him. They believed in greater things for their children and if their deaths would further the cause, they saw no issue with it. At least, that was what Gallus and Maximus said, but Tiberius seemed to be wavering. His voice was not as loud as his two older brothers, and the discussion, soon to be a heated argument, went on well into the night.

Finally, Curtis retired to his army outside of the walls of Isenhall, frustrated and disillusioned at Gallus' stance on the matter. Once Curtis departed, Jeniver stepped into the man's shoes. Even now, she was pleading with her husband to stop his rebellious ways and swear fealty to Henry because she did not want to lose her husband. She did not want her son to lose his father. Gallus was trying to hold his position against her but he was becoming frustrated. When Jeniver began weeping, loudly at times, his responses to her were heartbreaking. The man was willing to die for a cause and his wife couldn't understand why.

So the children cowered on the upper floor, listening to the weeping and begging, and Alessandria listened right along with them, sick to the bone. She knew this was her fault, all of it. She still firmly believed that Chad wasn't telling her the truth about Henry's approach and she was convinced it was because the man knew she was at Isenhall and he wanted her. She couldn't grasp anything else because the entire reason for her being taken from Newington was because Henry had wanted to take her as a hostage. He wanted her badly enough to come to Isenhall to get her and the Lords of Thunder were preparing to defend her.

Still, she knew there was more to the situation than that. She could hear that from the argument between Jeniver and Gallus. She knew her cousins were in support of de Montfort, who was now dead, and it was clear that Gallus didn't want to surrender the ideals that he had fought long and hard for. But, surely with de Montfort dead, those ideals must have died with him. Alessandria, therefore, knew that Henry was coming to Isenhall for her, not because Gallus fought a losing battle.

Henry was determined to have her.

Sickened and confused, she stood up from where she had been seated on her bed, moving to the small window that overlooked the eastern portion of Isenhall's compact fortress. The night was cool and windy, and gazing up at the sky, she could imagine the stars blowing about in the breeze.

It was very late and she knew she should be asleep but she wasn't tired in the least. She wondered where Chad was and how he felt about the entire circumstance. Perhaps he was with his cousin even now, discussing what was to come. The battle that would soon take place because Henry wanted a woman Chad had snatched away from him.

How many men had to die because Henry was determined to have her?

There was a soft knock at her door and she turned to see Lady Courtly entering. With long, blond hair secured in a bun at the nape of her neck, Lady Courtly had a sweet oval face, lush lips, and big eyes the color of a hot summer sky. She was a very hard worker, and very kind, and Alessandria liked her a great deal. When their eyes met, Courtly smiled.

"You are not sleeping, either," Courtly said quietly. "I came to check on the children and saw the glow from your taper."

Alessandria smiled weakly. "I am not tired," she said. "Even if I were, I doubt I could sleep. So much has happened today."

Courtly nodded, coming into the room and quietly closing the door behind her. "Aye, it has," she said, resignation in her tone. She sighed. "I was foolish enough to believe that when Max returned from Evesham, we might finally know some peace. It was an idiotic hope."

Alessandria thought she might have meant her. No one wanted to harbor a woman the king was after. Feeling guilty, she eyed the woman.

"Is… is Maximus in the keep?" she asked. "I would think he would be helping defend his brother against Jeniver."

Courtly shook her head, rubbing her arms as the chill night breeze blew in from the windows. "I have given my husband my opinion," she said quietly. "After hearing Lord Curtis plead for my husband and his brothers to surrender to Henry, I told my husband what I think of the entire situation. It is as we have discussed, Aless – Jeniver and Douglass and I would rather have our husbands alive. We have seen them go off to war many times, always for de Montfort, but since the man's death, we would like to live in peace. Surely, Henry is not a great king; he is not even a great man. But the fact remains that until our husbands swear fealty to him, we will never know peace. I would rather have my husband alive and submissive to Henry than dead for supporting an idea that will never come to fruition."

She said it very sadly and Alessandria went to her, putting a timid hand of comfort on the woman's shoulder. "I am sure that Maximus will do the right thing," she said. In truth, she wasn't sure what she could say, considering how guilty she felt at the moment. "I have been watching all of you for the past two weeks and it is clear that your husband adores you. I am sure he would not want to jeopardize his family."

Courtly forced a smile. "My husband will do what is best," she said. "He always has. Max is a man of deep thought and feeling. He is with Ty at the moment and they are discussing the situation. I have a feeling that the two of them feel differently than Gallus. I am coming to think that in this matter of conviction, Gallus is standing alone."

Alessandria was puzzled by the statement. "Do you believe they will surrender to Henry?"

Courtly shrugged. "Mayhap," she said. "I heard Lord Curtis speak of a meeting with Henry at St. Mary's Cathedral at dawn, but it is possible that it was only talk. However, it seemed that Lord Curtis wished to speak with Henry to avoid any hostilities. Mayhap he will even try to send the man away."

"You heard him say that?"

Courtly nodded. "That, and other things," she said. "You were there. Did you not hear him also?"

Alessandria shook her head. "I was not as close to them as you were," she admitted. "I did not hear much. I could only hear Chad's voice when he spoke."

She said it so dreamily that Courtly's forced smile turned real. "Of course you did," she said, touched by the young woman in love. "But you needn't worry about anything, Aless. You and Chad shall be married very soon and you will go to live at Canterbury, away from this madness."

"I have not seen Chad since Lord Curtis arrived," Alessandria said.

"I assume he is still with his cousin."

Courtly nodded. "I believe he went with Lord Curtis back to his camp," she said. "Bose went with them as well. I am sure they are discussing the situation with Henry and I am equally sure that Chad will come to see you when they are finished. Have no fear, Aless; Chad has not left you. All will be well again very soon."

Alessandria thought the woman was sounding very much as if she were trying to pretend nothing was really amiss. From the weeping and arguing still happening on the floor below them, it sounded just like something was very much amiss. As Courtly patted her on the cheek and left the room, Alessandria continued to stand by the small window, feeling the cold breeze, wondering what Chad was discussing with his cousin.

Were they discussing the real reason behind Henry's approach? The truth that Henry was really coming for Alessandria and the Lords of Thunder happened to be standing in the way? Perhaps Henry truly thought he could force them into submission if he held her hostage; peace was often made in such ways.

Hostages weren't an unusual thing. Some were actually treated quite well from what she had heard. Had Alessandria known what trouble would come to her and those she loved by not allowing Henry to take her hostage, she would have gladly gone with Henry's men when they followed her to Canterbury.

Perhaps that is what she needed to do, after all. Much of this problem started with her and it should end with her, or so she naively thought. She still didn't particularly grasp that the Lords of Thunder had a long and turbulent history with Henry long before the king wanted to take her as a hostage. But in thinking on the situation, Alessandria was coming to think that it was up to her to save the entire family and end this situation. Perhaps if she turned herself over to the king, he wouldn't be so apt to destroy her cousins.

Lord Curtis is meeting Henry in St. Mary's Cathedral at dawn…

In recalling that bit of information, Alessandria knew what she had to do. There was no doubt. Perhaps if she went willingly to Henry, showing him that at least one de Shera was willing to submit to him, then it would save her cousins as well as countless other people who were being sucked into the situation, including Chad.

Chad....

He was ready and willing to fight for her. He had been ready and willing since the beginning, whisking her from Newington and making sure to keep her safe every moment. He'd fought off Henry's knights for her. His father had lied to Henry's men for her. Everyone had done something for her to keep her safe, but the truth was that she needed to return the favor. So many people were facing death and destruction while she remained safely locked away.

Perhaps it was time for her to stop being selfish.

With a heavy heart, Alessandria turned her face towards the small window, feeling the cold breeze on her skin, knowing what she needed to do for all of their sakes. If Henry was going to be in St. Mary's Cathedral at dawn, then so would she. Chad had shown her St. Mary's once, on that lovely stolen trip to Coventry those weeks ago, so she knew where to go. Perhaps her sacrifice would save them all. It would mean never becoming Lady de Lohr, and perhaps never seeing Chad again, but if it would save the man's life, she was willing to do it.

Tears sprang to her eyes as she thought of a marriage that would never be, of a love that would never know its full potential. It was foolish, really – as a ward of Newington, she never expected to find love or marriage.

It had been her desire to become a nun, to serve God, so the insertion of Chad in her life had been completely unexpected. Perhaps like a dream, it wasn't meant to last. It was only meant to give her a taste of a world so beautiful that it was beyond belief. She had known love and she had known a man's touch, his body melding into hers. They were intimate memories she would have to live on for the rest of her life, for now, she could no longer be selfish.

God, she loved him. She loved him so much that it hurt. But her desire to save him was stronger than her desire to stay with him.

Farewell, Chad....

CHAPTER SEVENTEEN

St. Mary's Cathedral
Coventry

"IT IS AT least an hour or two before dawn," Chad muttered. "Are you sure he will be here?'

A group of men were gathered inside of St. Mary's Cathedral, back near the entry door. Bose and Curtis were standing together, listening to Chad stir around, seemingly restless, while Chris and William stood back in the shadows, watching. It was a tense and weary gathering, lingering in the dead of night.

"He shall be here," Curtis said steadily. "Arthur went to fetch him and you know that your cousin is very persuasive. Henry will come."

Chad was wringing his hands through his big leather gloves, pacing around on the packed earth floor. It was very dark and still at this hour, with only a few acolytes moving around near the front of the church to prepare for Matins. Chad could see the skinny, ill-dressed boys setting up for the priests.

"I wonder what happened with Gallus and his wife," Chad turned about and continued pacing. "When we left, she was begging him to surrender. I wonder if she has convinced him to do it."

Curtis shrugged as Bose spoke. "I have spent the better part of eight years trying to convince them to see reason," he said. "Ty, for a time, did serve me under Henry but that ended long ago. Ty seems to be the one most pliable to the suggestion of swearing fealty to Henry but it is Gallus who rules that family. He is passionate in his beliefs."

Chad looked at the big, dark knight. "What of Max?"

"He seems to be more inclined to side with Ty."

Next to Bose, Curtis sighed faintly. "It may not matter in the end," he said. "I received the distinct impression that Max and Ty were coming to see my point but Gallus was simply being stubborn. If the brothers turn against him, he may not have a choice."

Chad kicked at the earth. "Gallus is very proud," he said. "It will hurt him deeply if his brothers go against him."

"It may force him to see reason," Chris said, standing back in the shadows along with his brother, William. "We cannot all be wrong in our conviction that Gallus should at least pretend to swear fealty to Henry."

Chad looked over his shoulder at his cousin. "I hope you are right."

Chris simply nodded, glancing at big William, who was standing in the shadows with his muscular arms folded across his chest. When William caught his brother's expression, he grunted unhappily.

"That so many honorable and reasonable men should swear fealty to a fool is beyond me," he muttered. "If I had half of Gallus' courage, I would stand with him."

"Quiet," Curtis hissed at his son. "You will not speak so foolishly. We must all do as we must to maintain our lands and money and legacy. Sometimes those duties are unsavory, but they are necessary."

William simply rolled his eyes at his father's assessment. Then, he watched Chad pace around, pulling and grinding at his hands. "What are you so nervous about?" he asked the man. "Could it be because your wedding did not happen as planned?"

Chad came to a halt, turning to see William grinning at him. Chris was grinning, too, but trying not to. "Who told you that?" Chad demanded.

Chris spoke. "Ty mentioned something about marrying Lady Alessandria," he said. "Is it true? Have you finally fallen for a woman,

Chadwick?"

No one called him Chadwick unless they wanted a black eye. He hated that name with a passion. Chad advanced on his cousin, but Curtis threw out an arm, preventing him from throwing a punch, as Chris and William giggled like children.

"No violence," Curtis said, frowning at his snorting sons. "We are simply very happy for you, 'tis all. Ty made it sound as if you love the girl. Is this true?"

Chad's initial reaction was to be embarrassed, to deny it, but he found that he couldn't. It wasn't as if the entire de Shera household didn't already know it and they would surely tell the truth, so Chad did the only thing he could do. He admitted it.

"I am not sure how it happened, but it did," he confirmed. "We were hoping to be wed last evening but your unexpected appearance postponed those plans. Now I am not sure when I will be able to wed her."

Curtis grinned, patting Chad on the cheek. "Sooner than you think, I hope," he said. "If we can convince Henry to leave Isenhall intact, then mayhap you can marry your lady later today. I will make sure of it."

Chad reluctantly returned Curtis' smile, pleased that the man was in full support of his actions. "My father does not know yet," he said. "But he knows Aless and I am sure he will approve of her. Our marriage will be one more link to bind the houses of de Lohr and de Shera together."

"I hope that is not the only reason you are marrying her."

"Of course not. I am marrying her because I love her."

Curtis' smile faded. "Then this coming confrontation with Henry means a great deal to you," he said. "It was Henry who wanted to take your intended as a hostage."

Chad nodded. "Either a hostage or, according to Torran de Serreaux, to marry her off. Either way, I have a personal stake in all of this."

Curtis understood, but the conversation immediately was cut off when movement was heard near the entry to the cathedral. The arched Norman doorway was suddenly full of men with weapons, spilling into the darkness of the cathedral, spreading out. Chad and the other men knew instantly that Henry had made his arrival and he had come with several armed men as escort, as befitting the king.

Still, the armed incursion didn't sit well with Curtis or with Bose for that matter; they were armed, of course, as were Chad and Chris and William, but it was only the five of them against at least twenty of Henry's men. Struggling not to sound unhappy about it, Curtis moved towards the entry just as Henry and Arthur came forth.

"I see this is going to be an intimate little discussion, Your Grace," Curtis said wryly. "Had I known you were bringing half of your army, I would have brought half of mine. The odds would have been somewhat even."

Henry, dressed in mail and a pristine crimson tunic, headed straight for Curtis, a half-smile on his face. He liked the fact that he had caught the man off-guard; that gave him the upper hand. He noticed Bose standing next the earl and his focus moved between the two men.

"Worcester," he greeted Curtis. Then he looked at Bose. "I am glad to see you here, de Moray. I had hoped you would come."

Bose stepped forward. "Your Grace," he greeted formally. "I trust your travel has been pleasant."

Henry nodded. "Pleasant enough," he said. "I had great company in the de Winter brothers."

Davyss and Hugh were somewhere behind Henry, coming forward when they heard their names mentioned. De Serreaux and the other Six were spread out around Henry as bodyguards. As Henry faced Curtis and Bose, Chad, standing far back behind the men, happened to notice Torran as the man stood somewhat in the shadows.

He was the man who had sent them the warning of Henry's arrival, but Chad still wondered whose side Torran was really on. He served Henry, after all, but his message to Chad had been contrary to that loyalty. At least, Chad thought so. When their eyes met, Chad didn't acknowledge him, fearful that Henry might pick up on some kind of subliminal gratitude. For all Henry knew, they were still enemies after what had happened at Canterbury, and Chad thought it should remain that way. But he did silently acknowledge Davyss and Hugh.

It was an odd standoff already and the tension in the cathedral was brittle. Men were facing each other across a divisive line, men who were supposed to be allies. Henry saw it, and felt it, and it displeased him greatly.

"Look at us," he said. "We stand here as if we are on opposing sides. Since when did this happen, Curtis? Why do you not embrace me?"

Curtis did. Henry clapped him on the back and shoulders, trying to pretend as if they weren't here for something terribly critical. "That is much better," he said. "Now I feel as if we are family again. So, do tell me – why have you called me here? I would presume you wish to speak about those rebels."

It was the first volley of words in what would hopefully not become a battle. Already, Henry was establishing his position but Curtis maintained his even manner. It would not do to become frustrated this early on.

"I have asked you here to discuss the de Shera brothers," he said steadily. "I spent a good deal last night speaking to them about their loyalties, Your Grace. You know that I do not want to see them harmed; they are good and true men. They are the Lords of Thunder, men to be admired and feared. I asked you to meet me here this morning because I want you to understand something – they did not support de Montfort out of a hatred of you. They supported de Montfort because they agreed with the man's ideals. They, too, want a fair and just England for their children. There is nothing wrong with that."

Henry wasn't keen on accepting Curtis' gentle explanation of the de Shera brothers. "Hmpf," he grunted. "They have been a thorn in my side for nine years, Curtis. Nine years of their subversion and rebellion. Call it what you will, but that is what it boils down to – they are rebels and now their rebel leader is dead. I will have their fealty or I will wipe them from this earth."

He was very plain about his position, without any kindness or tact leading up to his statement. He presented it clearly, for all to hear. There was no doubt he meant what he said and Curtis was careful in his reply.

"It is difficult to change a man's ideals overnight, Your Grace," he said. "Gallus and his brothers still believe in de Montfort's principles. You cannot erase that with a wave of your hand. It will take time."

Henry shook his head, now growing agitated. "Meanwhile, they openly rebel against me?" he demanded. "I will not have it, Curtis. You know I will not. They are powerful enough to pick up where Simon has left off and I cannot have that manner of threat against me. If you were in my position, would *you* tolerate it?"

Curtis was clear. "I would not," he said firmly. "But I would also want to open a dialogue with them to understand what it is they want and what I can do to exist peacefully with them. They are strong men with good ideals, Your Grace. You need men like them. They have great hopes for the future of your country."

Henry hissed. "It is *my* country," he said. "They either serve me and my needs or they do not. There is no negotiation. Is that what you are trying to do? Negotiate for them?"

Curtis was coming to see that the king would not be swayed. He didn't want to discuss a kinder, gentler rule and he was quite sure the de Shera brothers were rebels and nothing more. They were a threat, pure and simple, and that was how Henry would forever see them. They were so intertwined with Simon, and had been for years, that Henry couldn't see them as anything else.

And that was a problem.

"I am not negotiating for them," Curtis replied evenly. "I am simply telling you that men's ideals do not change so swiftly. If you want these men to swear fealty, then you must give them something in return."

"Like what?"

"Perhaps all they need is your assurance that you will listen to them in matters that affect them. Perhaps all they want is to know that you will consider their advice."

Henry sighed heavily with frustration. He was glaring at Curtis but happened to catch sight of de Moray. He pointed at the man.

"You," he said to Bose. "I sent you to relay my terms of their surrender. Did you do that?"

Bose stepped forward. "I did, Your Grace."

"And?"

Bose glanced at Curtis before speaking; it wasn't an easy answer he was about to deliver. "And they are men of strong ideals and convictions," he said. "I believe that Lord Curtis' suggestion is a good one – if you will only speak with them and give them assurances that you will listen to their advice and concerns, they may be willing to swear fealty."

Henry's jaw ticked. "You mean to tell me that you were unsuccessful in securing their surrender."

"Aye, Your Grace."

Henry grunted with further displeasure. He turned away from Curtis and Bose, pacing the floor just as Chad had been doing minutes earlier. In fact, he caught sight of Chad, standing back with his cousins in the shadows, and jabbed a finger at him.

"Where is the de Shera heiress you took from Newington?" he demanded. "De Serreaux told me that you were able to remove her before he could get to her. Why did you do that?"

Chad was strong in the face of an angry king. He came forward, preparing to address his liege.

"Because it needed to be done, Your Grace," he said.

"*Who* told you of my desire for the girl?"

"I heard rumor, Your Grace."

"From whom?"

Chad would not reveal his source. "I cannot recall, Your Grace," he replied. "I was half-drunk in a tavern in London when I heard the information. I do not recall who I heard it from."

Henry scowled at him. "Do you think to lie to me?"

Chad shook his head. "Nay, my lord."

"Was it de Moray who told you?"

"Was de Moray at that tavern? I do not recall, Your Grace."

Henry was growing increasingly frustrated at Chad's evasiveness. He jabbed a finger at him again. "*Where* is the girl?"

"Here, Your Grace."

A soft, female voice came from the entryway and every man there turned to see a small, wrapped figure standing in the arched doorway. When she noticed the attention on her, she swiftly came forward into the light.

Chad, who had been stunned by the sound of the familiar voice, could hardly believe what he was seeing. *What in God's name is she doing here?* He thought wildly. But when Alessandria began to move, he moved as well, bolting forward to intercept her before she could reach Henry.

"Aless!" he hissed, reeling with shock. "Why are you here?"

Alessandria gazed up into the face of the man she loved so well, feeling a lump form in her throat at the sight of him. It was a surprise. Thinking he'd been occupied elsewhere, she had congratulated herself on being able to flee Isenhall without running into him. She'd stolen a horse from the stables and slipped from the gates, losing herself in the chaos of the de Lohr army outside of the walls before taking the road north into Coventry.

Alessandria had spent those few short miles to Coventry telling herself that this was the right thing to do, that turning herself over to Henry would solve all of their problems and that he would no longer be inclined to attack Isenhall. But seeing the armed men in the cathedral, and the unexpected appearance of Chad, had her shaken.

She was doing the right thing… *wasn't she?*

"I did not know you would be here," she whispered tightly.

Chad looked at her in confusion and disbelief, reaching out to grab her arms. "What do you mean?" he demanded softly, urgently. "Answer my question; *what are you doing here*?"

Alessandria put her hands to his face, touching the stubble. He was upset and her resolve to do the right thing was weakening the longer she looked at him.

"Please let me go," she whispered. "You must let me go."

Chad had no idea what she was talking about. "Let you go?" he repeated, aghast. "What does this mean? Why must I let you go?"

Gently but firmly, Alessandria managed to pull herself from his grasp, dodging him when he made another swipe for her. She rushed forward, towards the king and his men.

"My name is Alessandria de Shera," she said. "I am the lady you wanted as a hostage. You sent your men for me at Newington Priory but Sir Chad took me instead."

Henry was looking at the lady with great curiosity. "My lady," he greeted. "This is unexpected, to say the least."

Before he could say anything more, Chad came up behind Alessandria, quickly, and Henry was forced into action. Swiftly, he reached out and grabbed her, pulling her into the group of his men, and when Chad tried to push through, de Serreaux and d'Vant were there to stop him with their swords drawn. Steel flashed in the weak morning light and the message was clear.

Finally, they had their hostage.

Immediately, the mood of the meeting plummeted as the *silver sword* was unsheathed. More swords were coming forth, including *Lespada* in the hand of Davyss. That singing of steel against leather echoed against the walls and men began shuffling around as Chad tried to push forward to get to Alessandria, who cried out when she saw all of the weapons coming forth. She was immediately terrified.

"Nay!" she cried. "No fighting! Please, no fighting! I have come to turn myself over to the king so that he will no longer attack Isenhall. Now you have what you wanted, Your Grace; you have me. I will willingly surrender to you if you will now please leave my friends and family in peace."

So her silly, naïve plan was shouted for all to hear. Henry still had a grip on her and she also had a grip on him, beseechingly. He could see his Six preparing for a battle, with weapons out, and the soldiers he had brought also had weapons drawn. Curtis de Lohr, his sons, as well as Bose and Chad had their swords out and the battle promised to be quite epic.

But as Henry looked around, he also noticed something else, something very odd – Davyss and Hugh were standing with de Lohr and de Moray. He could see the wicked gleam of *Lespada* in Davyss' hand and it took him a moment to realize that, for once, the weapon was not lifted in his defense. It was lifted against *him*. Suddenly, it all came quite clear to Henry and, still gripping Alessandria, he waved an arm at the group.

"Cease!" he roared, shoving through his armed men, dragging Alessandria with him. There was an expression of incredible disbelief on his features as he looked at Davyss and Hugh. "What are you two doing? Do you actually think to stand with de Lohr?"

Davyss didn't lower his weapon. "Aye, Your Grace," he said evenly. "I had hoped it would not come to this but given the choice between defending you and standing with my brothers and friends, I am sorry to say that I will stand with them. You ordered me to march on Isenhall to test my loyalties, Your Grace, and I did. If you did not want to know the answer to that question, then mayhap you should not have asked it."

Henry was astounded. "You would stand *against* me?" he was clearly shocked. "How can you do this, Davyss? You belong to me, do you hear? *You are mine!*"

Davyss remained in position. "I support you in every endeavor, Your Grace," he said. "I will fight and kill and die for you. But if you force me to make a choice between you and the House of de Lohr and, ultimately, the House of de Shera, then you must understand I will choose to stand with my brothers. It is as simple as that."

Henry stared at him, his face growing red. "I *knew* it," he hissed. "I have always known you were a de Montfort at heart, simply waiting for the moment to take a stand against me. Don't you know that? Everyone knows you are the bastard son of Simon de Montfort, because the man seduced your mother those years ago. I was waiting for you to show your true loyalties and now you have. It is bred into you to hate me."

Davyss didn't flinch at the mention of the rumor that had long been about, a rumor that he had known, from his mother's own lips, to be truth. But he would not confirm or deny such a thing. It was, in fact, of little matter. Perhaps he was of de Montfort's loins but he was a de Winter by name, and that gave him all of the power behind it. Before he could answer the king, Curtis spoke quietly.

"I was hoping it would not come to this, Your Grace, but it seems as if it has," he said. "In your hatred and determination to eliminate the House of de Shera, you are, in fact, attacking a family that is kin to the House of de Lohr. I cannot and will not let you raze Isenhall and destroy the Lords of Thunder, not while there is breath left in my body. Therefore, know this; if you choose to follow this path, to destroy the House of de Shera because you feel they are a threat to you, in doing so you are forcing me to take sides. Since I will not see you destroy my nephews, you should know that I intend to stand with them. I will defend them to the death, as will my cousin, Daniel. Canterbury will also join the fight. Is this in any way unclear, Your Grace? Do you understand the path you are choosing and the warlords you will turn against you?"

Henry still had a grip on Alessandria, his face turning red with rage. "Then you would betray me also?" he said through clenched teeth. "The House of de Lohr has always stood with the crown. Will you throw that allegiance to the wind to protect rebels?"

Curtis shook his head faintly. "Nay," he said. "But I would do it to protect family. That is the only thing that matters, Henry. Protecting one's family from a threat and you are, indeed, a threat. I am not sure what paranoia and hatred has brought you to this moment in time, but if we all band against you, you will not win. You will be lucky to survive. I can raise such an army against you that you would be destroyed before you realized what had happened. It is a very dangerous and very foolish stance you are taking against the House of de Shera. I would strongly suggest you gather your men and leave and simply forget about them for now. If you leave them in peace, then I will let you leave without any further action and my loyalty to you will remain intact. But if you choose to be the aggressor, then know I will act in kind. And I have a bigger army than you do. You will not walk away from this a free man, I promise you."

It was as deadly a threat as any of them had ever heard, coming from a man who, indeed, had the power to make it so. Chad, Bose, Davyss, Hugh, Chris, William, and, finally, Curtis were ready to make good on that threat – that much was clear. They were ready, willing, and able to meet Henry in a battle that would constitute one of the greatest battles in the annals of Henry's rule. Once-allies of the king were now facing off against him.

The moment of truth was at hand.

The air in the cathedral was as brittle as ice, ready to crack at any moment. One move, by any of them, and the battle for their lives would begin. Therefore, no one moved. It was a staring game, and a waiting game, waiting to see what Henry would do next. It was all up to him now. Would he concede?

Would he fight?

"Please," Alessandria's soft voice filtered up through the tension. "Your Grace, you have me now. You do not need to fight them. You may use me for a hostage to ensure my cousins' good behavior. I am prepared for a life of confinement."

Henry looked at Alessandria as if suddenly remembering that he had hold of her. It was clear that a thought was occurring to him, for his brow rippled, but it was a thought that none of them were prepared for. Swiftly, Henry snatched a dagger from de Serreaux's belt and immediately put it to Alessandria's neck. He looked straight at Chad.

"Drop your sword or the woman you want to marry dies," he said flatly. "All of you, drop your swords or she dies. Is that clear?"

It was a horrific turn of events, one that had the de Lohr allies uncertain and sickened. Certainly, they couldn't let Henry kill the girl in cold blood but they couldn't drop their weapons, either. But they weren't in love with the girl.

Chad was.

His sword clattered to the floor.

"Please, Your Grace," Chad pleaded. "Do not hurt her. I will stand with you if that is what you wish, but do not hurt her. I beg you."

Curtis, seeing that his cousin was willingly conceding, put out a hand to try and stop him. "Chad, nay," he hissed. Then, he looked at Henry. "Is that what you have become, Your Grace? A murderer of weak women? And this is the man I am expected to swear my fealty to? It is a disgusting prospect."

It was a terrible insult to Henry, who only gripped the dagger tighter. Alessandria yelped when the tip poked her tender skin, sending a bright red stream of blood down her neck.

"I am your king," Henry hissed. "You de Lohrs have sworn fealty to me in theory but the truth is that you have twisted that fealty to suit your whims over the years. You have all disobeyed me at one time or another, but I will not stand for that any longer. Worcester, if you believe standing against me is what you must do, then I say again that I am your king and for that reason alone, you will support my wishes at all times or I will strip you of everything. I will strip all of you of whatever lands or titles or possessions you have, and that includes de Winter and de Moray as well. Is defending the Lords of Thunder worth losing everything?"

Curtis cocked his head. "Ask yourself that same question," he said. "Is your quest to destroy the Lords of Thunder worth losing your most powerful warlords? Because that is what will happen, Henry. You will be the loser in this far more than we will and you know it."

He was correct. Henry knew it; they all knew it, but Henry's sense of pride had him unable to concede the point. His sense of vengeance seemed to reign above all else, even in this instance, and it was difficult for him to realize that what Curtis was saying was true. But with his last wispy shreds of common sense, he began to understand the severity of what was about to happen. He didn't want to lose de Winter and de Lohr and de Moray; God help him, he didn't. Was having their loyalty worth more than seeing the House of de Shera destroyed?

The choice was his.

"I cannot have open rebellion against me," Henry finally said. "If you were in my position, you would not have a threat against you, a threat to your rule, and that is what the House of de Shera represents. They are a threat to me and my rule. How can I simply ignore that?"

"If we promise not to participate in any action against you, will you leave us in peace?"

The booming voice was not Curtis'. It came from the doorway and, once again, everyone turned with surprise to see three big men standing in the entry. The day was beginning to dawn outside, shades of purple and blue illuminating the silhouettes of three unarmed knights.

Their appearance was unexpected. Perhaps it was even unwanted. But there was no turning them away, not now.

The Lords of Thunder had arrived.

CHAPTER EIGHTEEN

GALLUS, MAXIMUS, AND Tiberius entered the cathedral, without mail and without weapons. They were in simple clothing, tunics and leather breeches, clearly making a statement. In fact, they were attempting to convey that they were not a threat. They were easing into a group of men with weapons, indicating they would not fight. It was a symbolic stance as well as a necessary one.

They were making a clear statement to Henry.

However, they were not foolish; entering the cavernous hall and into two groups of heavily-armed men, they paused far enough away so that if the swords began to fly, they wouldn't get caught in the melee.

Gallus' gaze moved over the men standing for him; Curtis, Bose, Davyss and Hugh, Chris, William, and even Chad, although Chad was standing halfway between Curtis and Henry. Then his gaze fell upon Alessandria, in Henry's grasp with a dagger at her neck and blood on her skin. He sighed faintly.

"Let her go," he told Henry. "Let her go and we will speak."

Henry was shocked to the bone to see Gallus and Maximus and Tiberius standing not far from him, weaponless. He immediately let go of Alessandria and thrust her towards Chad, who caught her easily. Chad picked her up, sweeping her away from the men with weapons, as Henry turned to de Serreaux.

"Take them," he ordered. "They have no weapons. You can easily take them now and we can be done with this."

Curtis, Bose, and the others moved swiftly to surround Gallus and Maximus and Tiberius, preparing for the fight to come, but de Serreaux didn't move a muscle. He simply looked at Henry.

"I think not, Your Grace," he said. "They have come under the guise of peace and without weapons. I will not attack men without weapons."

Henry's eyes widened. "What's this?" he demanded. "Insubordination from you, too?"

"If being honorable in this situation means insubordination, Your Grace, then I suppose it is the truth."

"You have gone mad!"

De Serreaux's gaze lingered on him. Then, he moved away from the king and took up station directly in front of Gallus in a completely shocking move. The leader of Henry's Six was making it clear that he did not agree with the king's order or even his stance, and there wasn't one man in the cathedral that wasn't astonished by the move.

Henry's Six were loyal to the death, so in de Serreaux's move, the obvious statement was there – de Serreaux had spoken of Henry's madness, of the man's lust for vengeance, and he had lamented it. He was a man who valued honor above all else and in this case, he'd been given an order that he saw as completely dishonorable. There was nothing more he could do than follow his own heart in the matter.

He would not obey the command.

"These are ethical men, Your Grace, and they are attempting to negotiate with you," de Serreaux said. "I have served you flawlessly for years, Your Grace, and I can honestly say that this is the first time I have seen you forget your honor. Your madness to punish those associated with de Montfort has made you question those around you. You insult all of us with your lack of faith. De Lohr and de Winter have tried to tell you that. They have tried to tell you that this mad vengeance against the House of de Shera is not only unnecessary, it is unhealthy. Look, now; the Earl of Coventry and his brothers have come to discuss peace with you and still you seek to harm them. Is it not better to have their strength behind you rather than destroy it? These are men of great honor, Your Grace; treat them as such and they will treat you with the same. At some point, you must stop the vengeance and begin to trust again."

De Serreaux's words rang out in the cathedral, filling every man there with a sense of truth and justice. Even Chad and Alessandria, standing back in the shadows, were filled with pride for the words spoken and, in Alessandria's case, a sense of understanding. She was coming to see that Henry, as great as he was, perhaps simply didn't have a grasp of what normal and good men feel.

Years of war, of betrayal, had taken their toll on the man. While she should have been angry with him for trying to hurt her, she found that she pitied him. Henry had been a king his entire life; survival, in any form, was all he knew.

"You are still the captive of de Montfort, still being betrayed and hunted," Alessandria said, her soft voice causing the men to turn and look at her as she stood back in the shadows. Chad tried to stop her but she waved him off, gently, and stepped forward to address the king. "I thought I could help the situation by surrendering myself to you, Your Grace, but I see that I was wrong. I did not understand that the situation was much more than you simply needing a hostage. Your Grace, I have spent the past two weeks at Isenhall Castle with Gallus and Maximus and Tiberius and their families. These are true and good men, men that only want to love their wives and children, and live in an England that knows peace and prosperity. I believe we all want to live that way. Can you not see that the men around you do not want to betray you? They understand something you do not, something I did not until only recently – some things are worth fighting and dying for. Love and family are worth fighting and dying for. I have never known that kind of love before. Will you not at least listen to Gallus and Maximus and Tiberius? They are here because they are trying to protect their world, just as you are. You need not fear them. You must listen to them and understand them. Will you not do this, Your Grace?"

Such true and noble words, spoken by a young lady who had a rather naïve view of the world. But it was a true view. She spoke not from the point of politics or loyalties, but from the heart. Chad, who had initially tried to prevent her from speaking, was very proud of what she had said. He reached out to take her hand, gently pulling her into his embrace, as Henry's gaze lingered on her dark red head. Something she had said resonated with him…

You are still a captive of de Montfort.

Perhaps she was correct. Perhaps he was still being hunted and betrayed, enough to see that kind of fault in the men around him, men who had proven their loyalty to him over the years. It wasn't a feeling he could easily be rid of, he knew that. But he also knew that men he was viewing as betrayers were not, in fact, turning against him. He had caused that with his own bitterness and paranoia.

Perhaps there was truth in what the lady said, after all.

Henry's focus moved to Gallus.

"Someone once told me that men cannot change overnight," he said, glancing at Curtis. "Did you not just tell me that?"

Curtis nodded vaguely. "I did, Your Grace."

Henry's gaze lingered on Curtis a moment longer before turning to the group, to Alessandria as Chad held her protectively. He was coming to feel foolish and struggled not to. He didn't want to lose his warlords, his friends, but his need for vengeance was great. Yet, perhaps his need for peace was greater. There was that possibility. He took a long, deep breath before turning to Gallus.

"You said that you promise to lay down your arms against me," he said. "Do you mean that?"

Gallus, who had been looking at his rather astute little cousin, returned his attention to the king. "I do," he agreed. "My brothers and I have had a long discussion. We all agree that we cannot keep going as we are. Something must change. We are willing to lay down our arms for the time being if you will simply leave us in peace."

"And your loyalties?"

"Give us time, Your Grace. We all want to see a better and stronger England, much as you do."

Henry folded his arms, wrinkling his fine tunic. He eyed Curtis, Bose, and the others before speaking. He even eyed de Serreaux. "I must trust you and you must trust me," he said to Gallus. "How are we to do this when all we have ever done is fight one another?"

Gallus sensed that, perhaps, he actually had the man's attention. It was a surprising realization. "I am a man of my word, Your Grace," he said. Then, he looked to the men around him. *His friends.* "Men I trust have sworn loyalty to you. That means they must trust you. If they can trust you, then mayhap I can as well."

Henry sighed, looking at the collection of men that was no longer poised to fight. He had to admit that he liked them better this way. It was a struggle to force that anger away, to subdue the vengeance that he'd been feeding off of. But he knew that if he didn't, he would lose everything.

"If you promise to no longer fight against me, I believe we can come to an equitable arrangement," he finally said. Then he spoke with irony. "If I do not agree with you, then I can see it will only cause trouble. You have many friends who are willing to defy me in order to support you."

Gallus looked to the men around him, men who still had their swords drawn. A wry grin creased his lips. "They are good men, Your Grace," he said. "They are men I would willingly die for."

"As they would evidently die for you."

Gallus eyed the king, his men, and the crown soldiers who were now standing around looking rather confused. From the threat of a fight one minute to the discussion of peace the next, they weren't sure whether to wield a sword or sheathe it. The mood of the conversation was ebbing and flowing, with the king no longer entirely agitated over what was transpiring. In fact, he seemed to be calming a great deal, but a measure of confusion in his expression lingered.

Truth be told, Gallus was still confused, too. He wasn't entirely sure this was what he wanted to do or even if it was the right thing to do. He still had his convictions. But his wife, as well as his brothers, has asked that he at least try. For their sakes, he was willing to. He still couldn't stand the sight of the fair-haired, gangly man several feet away who ruled England, but that didn't much matter. He had family and friends to think about. Much like Henry, it would be a mess if he didn't agree to least try.

"Would you accept Isenhall's hospitality, then?" he finally asked Henry. "I have some very fine wine from Spain that should keep the conversation flowing nicely."

Henry shrugged. "I do not believe I have much of a choice," he said. Then he pointed at de Serreaux. "Come back to me where you belong. We are going to Isenhall to feast."

De Serreaux immediately lowered his sword and went back to Henry's side, but his dark eyes were glittering with mirth. They all saw it. That caused Curtis to grin, followed by de Moray, as the older men ordered the youngers to lower their swords.

They were grins of relief and of understanding; understanding a stubborn king who had a difficult time compromising. But he had. Davyss and Hugh, weapons now placed back in sheathes, moved to Henry's side once more but the king looked at them both with disapproval.

Still, he didn't say anything. He was simply glad to have a de Winter by his side again and didn't much consider Davyss' recent stance against him a failure of loyalties. Deep down, in the jumble of his convoluted mind, he understood.

He wished for such loyalty from his friends and men, too. All men did.

It was an oddly peaceful and quite conclusion to what could have been a battle for the ages. It was better than any of them could have hoped for. As the group began to filter out of the cathedral into the dawn of a new day, Chad and Alessandria remained behind.

For them, the conclusion had greater meaning. Even though it was a situation that had consumed them for weeks now, in the case of the Lords of Thunder, it was a situation that had been a part of their daily lives for the past several years. Now it was over and there were no dead bodies on the ground. That very fact still had Chad reeling.

"I would not have believed this entire happening had I not seen it with my own eyes," he said. "Did you have any idea that Gallus and Max and Ty were coming in behind you like that?"

Alessandria, still looking a bit shocked, shook her head. "I rode all the way from Isenhall and never saw them," she said. "If they saw me, they certainly made no attempt to contact me."

Chad shook his head, baffled. "Amazing," he muttered. Then, he squeezed her, still in his grip. "And you; what you did today… were you truly going to turn yourself over to Henry as a hostage? Why would you do such a thing when I worked so hard to keep you from him?'

She struggled not to feel foolish. "When you said that Henry was coming to Isenhall, I thought you were trying to spare me the real reason," she said. "I knew he was most assuredly upset because you had taken me away so I thought… I hoped… that if I turned myself over to him, he would no longer be angry and try to raze Isenhall. I was trying to save the lives of the people that I loved, including you."

His smile turned gentle. "You love me?"

She flushed deeply, averting her gaze. "Did you not know that, Chad?" she asked. "You are a brilliant man. Surely you knew."

He shook his head, grinning. "Tell me," he murmured in that deep, raspy tone she loved so well. He pulled her closer. "Let me hear it in your own voice."

Gazing up into his handsome face, Alessandria realized this was the moment she had been waiting for her entire life. Up until a few minutes ago, she was fairly certain she would never have the opportunity to tell him what was in her heart. Since that drunken night they'd spent together when the two of them became one, and she had realized her love for him, she'd never had the opportunity to tell him. Perhaps this was the moment as it was meant to be, telling her of her love for him even as she had just attempted to prove it.

"I could not let you face Henry if there was any chance I could save you," she whispered, feeling warm and giddy. "You – and all of your friends and family – have been so very kind to me, Chad. Your father and mother and sister were very kind. Even your knights were kind. Gallus and Tiberius and Maximus and their wives have been gracious and generous. They are my family, Chad – I have never known family in my life, ever. Not with my father or my brother, yet with these strangers – and with you – I have known more love and happiness than I have ever experienced in my life. Of course I love you. I cannot remember when I have not loved you."

He stroked her cheek gently, deeply touched by her words. "And you loved enough, and were unselfish enough, to give yourself over to a man who would hold you hostage."

She nodded. "If it would save you, I would do it a thousand times over."

His smile deepened and he bent down, slanting his lips over hers. It was a kiss of pure magic, of pure joy, and as the sun continued to rise and the sky turned from blues to pinks, Chad held Alessandria against him, cherishing the feel of her in his arms. He would never be without it.

"Even if you did not tell me that you loved me, your actions have told me so," he told her, kissing her forehead. "I love you, Aless. I will love you for always and forever, until the sun ceases to rise and the stars fall from the sky. Even then, I will continue to love you. There will be no end to what I feel for you."

His words warmed her soul. "Then you are not angry that I came?"

He shook his head. "Nay," he admitted. "Your motives were pure, as is your heart and your soul. I am a fortunate man, indeed."

She smiled, vastly relieved. It was a tender moment between them but it was interrupted by people entering the cathedral as Matins approached, and the priests were beginning to filter in as well. They were up by the altar, preparing for the coming mass. It was no longer just their private moment.

"Mayhap we should leave now," Alessandria said, indicating the incoming throng of worshippers. "Mayhap we should return to Isenhall."

Chad looked around, noting the people, but he was mostly interested in the priests. An idea occurred to him and a faint smile creased his lips.

"Not so fast," he said. He nodded his head in the direction of the altar, far across the hard-packed floor of the cathedral. "We were denied a marriage last night. Mayhap we should speak to the priest while we are here."

"Why?"

"So he can marry us now, of course."

Alessandria's eyes widened. "Now?" she asked. "Will you ask him to marry us this morning?"

Chad's answer was to wink at her. Taking her by the hand, he led her to the front of the church where two brown-robed priests were preparing to intone the mass. The priests shied away from Chad somewhat, considering they had seen the entire confrontation with Henry and several other knights. They recognized Chad as having been part of that group but when Chad explained his wants, the priests didn't seem so wary of him. At least he had a genuine purpose for being there. Then, a generous donation of coinage made the men of the cloth plainly eager to do Chad's bidding.

Finally, Chad would have the wedding he wanted.

Therefore, as the sun crested the horizon in the east, shining its great and golden glow across the land, Chad and Alessandria stood at the great Norman entry to St. Mary's Cathedral while the canon, a man who knew the de Shera family well, intoned the wedding mass as another priest, several other acolytes, and about half of the town of Coventry watched. The questions were asked of the intended couple, the responses given, and once that part of the ceremony was completed, Chad and Alessandria followed the priests into the cathedral to finish the mass.

Theirs was a relationship that had started in a priory and now came full circle in a cathedral, and Alessandria thought it was all quite perfect. Nothing could have been more heavenly or more appropriate. When she finally left the cathedral later that morning, it was as Lady Thorndon, wife of Lord Thorndon. Her husband, a worthy man from a fine family, collected his steed from the livery across the street and returned his new wife to Isenhall Castle. The lady's extended family, upon hearing the news, threw a grand feast for the occasion in which the King of England, a man who had once been their mortal enemy, was an honored guest.

All things happen as they should, Alessandria thought as she watched Henry and Gallus and her husband, as well as a host of other knights, drink fine Spanish wine long into the night. It was a surreal experience, to be truthful, and a glorious feast, an unexpected ending to a most unexpected day.

The one thing that was expected, however, was her new husband's behavior when he'd had too much wine. With all of that rich red wine flowing, it was only a matter of time before the breeches came off and strains of *Tilly Nodden* could be heard.

Unfortunately for Henry and the others, Chad and his love of good wine had him flashing his buttocks repeatedly, cheered on by Tiberius, Chris, Arthur, and William. De Serreaux, fairly drunk himself after a most strenuous day that nearly saw him lose his position as the leader of Henry's Guard of Six, took great offense to Chad's bare buttocks and took to throwing pieces of ember at him, trying to hit the pale white backside with something that was on fire.

Twice, he'd made contact, causing Chad to smack the man on the side of the head with a piece of kindling, much to the amusement of the others. De Serreaux thought it was humorous as well, but his Guard of Six cohorts saw it as a challenge. Soon enough, Chad and his cousins were locked in games of chance against de Serreaux and his comrades while Henry and Gallus found themselves trying to keep the peace between the drunken knights. It was a complete turn of events, with Henry and Gallus as peacemakers now, that went on long into the night. As odd as it sounded, it was something of a bonding experience for Henry and Gallus. After that, they understood each other much better.

Alessandria was tolerant of her husband's drunken antics. She rather liked watching him behave like a fool because he was really very funny. The man who would one day be the Earl of Canterbury deserved the chance to relax and laugh with friends, she thought. She certainly wouldn't begrudge him that, as the path to this moment in time had been a difficult one for them both.

But Jeniver and Courtly soon closed ranks around Alessandria, removing her from the loud and drunken men, and escorted her to her small borrowed chamber on the top of Isenhall's keep to prepare for her coming wedding night.

Alessandria made no hint, of course, of the fact that this would not be her first sexual encounter with Chad, as Jeniver and Courtly helped her to dress in a fine dressing gown made from silk that belonged to Jeniver. Douglass didn't participate because, being heavily pregnant, she had retired early for the night, so it was Gallus and Maximus' wives assisting their cousin with her toilette in preparation for her new husband.

Alessandria appreciated their efforts, loving the women as she would sisters. The days of Lady Orford and her terrible daughter were long gone as she finally found acceptance with her cousins' wives. The whole world had come full circle for her and she swore that she would never again take life, or love, for granted. It was to be treated with the greatest of care, something to be treasured, always.

Alessandria tried to stay awake that night, waiting for her husband's return, but her exhaustion had the better of her and she ended up falling asleep on the small bed she was expected to share with him. She happened to awake at one point when she felt the bed give, having no idea what time it was, and she opened her eyes to Chad's naked buttocks perched on the side of the bed as he drunkenly tried to remove his breeches and boots at the same time.

Your husband has a bread-dough arse and I want to sink my teeth into it!

Old Lady du Bexley's words suddenly popped into her head. Of all the times to remember such a thing, that time was now, but it was actually quite appropriate. His buttocks *did* look like two unbaked bread loaves. As Chad struggled to remove his clothing, Alessandria would have the last laugh. She did exactly as Lady du Bexley wanted to.

She sank her teeth straight-away into his taut, delicious buttocks.

After that, Chad seemed to lose his penchant for flashing his arse when drunk and no one could seem to figure out why. But Alessandria knew… and so did Chad. Having discovered a wife who liked to bite him, Chad was less apt to give her the opportunity, at least in public. But in private, he rather liked her gnashing little teeth. Now, she was the only one who saw his arse. He had promised her that much.

Love, laughter, and family. Those were the things that made life worth living.

The de Lohr dynasty lived on.

EPILOGUE

Canterbury Castle, early May
1267 A.D.

IF NOTHING ELSE, Chad had always been entertaining.

Daniel knew this because he'd watched his son grow from a very active, somewhat devilish boy into a man who hadn't left much of the boy behind when he'd become an adult. There was still a great deal of boy left in Chad, as Daniel was witnessing now, as the man celebrated the birth of his first child.

Katrine, they had named her, in honor of Liselotte's mother and also in honor of Chad's twin sister who had died at birth. A little girl that Daniel could still see, even now, with her perfectly formed features and sweet little face. His heart still ached for his baby girl, just a little, but holding Chad's daughter had helped ease that pain. He hoped, through Katrine, that his long-dead daughter might perhaps live again, just a little.

And she was a big baby, too. It had taken Alessandria nearly two days to give birth to the child, struggling to bring forth a fat baby with downy-red hair who screamed the moment she was born until the moment her mother put a nipple in her mouth to feed her. Daniel had been given the pleasure of holding the baby well after her birth, when she had been fed and swaddled and was snug as a pea in a pod. But his joy in holding her had been brief because Liselotte wanted to hold the baby, and then Chad wanted to hold her again, so Daniel had been forced to admire the baby in someone else's arms, mostly.

But he truly hadn't minded in the least.

That had been a week ago. Chad had sent word to Gallus and Maximus and Tiberius on the birth as well as everyone else he could think of, including the king. He wanted everyone to know he had a healthy, beautiful daughter. It never even crossed his mind to be disappointed that it wasn't a son. To Chad, it didn't matter in the least. He couldn't have been more thrilled.

His joy was evidenced in the fact that he'd celebrated the birth, nightly, since it had occurred. His wife was still bed-bound and couldn't join him in the hall, but Chad celebrated enough for the both of them. He'd given up excessive drink at the request of his wife and Daniel hadn't seen the man drunk or even tipsy since their marriage, but the birth of little Lady Katrine seemed to weaken her father's resolve to behave himself. Therefore, every night since Katrine's birth had been something of a party with Chad front and center.

Even now in the great hall of Canterbury, the big hall they rarely used, Daniel watched the man as he sang a very noisy chorus of *Tilly Nodden* with his brothers and fellow knights. Rhun du Bois had a terrible singing voice and his tone-deaf baritone could be heard throughout the hall of Canterbury, causing Stefan and Perrin to throw things at him to force him to be quiet. It was quite hilarious to watch but Rhun would not be deterred. He sang bravely as bread crusts and even utensils were flung in his direction.

So Daniel sipped his sweet Spanish wine, listening to the terrible singing, and laughing at the antics of his sons and his knights. These days at Canterbury, there was much to be joyful for as well as grateful for. He was reflecting on that gratitude when he was joined by Liselotte.

Into the noise and smoke of the hall, she emerged from one of the smaller doors that led to the kitchen yard. It was dark outside, as night had fallen, but the kitchen was cooking full-force for the men in the hall. Daniel could smell the freshly baked bread as the scents wafted in behind his wife. He smiled at her as she came to the table.

"Has Chad dropped his breeches yet?" Liselotte asked as she sat beside her husband.

Daniel poured his wife a cup of wine, handing it to her. "Nay," he said, grinning. "But I am sure that will come at some point."

Liselotte accepted the wine. "He has not flashed his buttocks this entire week, has he?"

Daniel was silently laughing. "He has not," he said. "He has threatened once or twice, but he has yet to complete the deed."

Liselotte sipped the strong, sweet wine. "Let us hope that he does not," she said. "Aless has asked me several times if he has taken to flashing his buttocks and I have told her every time that he has not. In fact, she has sent me down here to tell Chad to go attend her. She wants him up in the chamber with her, not down here with the men."

Daniel simply lifted his shoulders. "He is having more fun down here," he said. "Let him enjoy himself a little while longer."

"And he cannot enjoy himself with his wife and child?"

Daniel took her free hand, kissing it. "Of course he can," he said. "But the man cannot belt out a chorus of *Tilly Nodden*, can he? It will wake the baby."

Liselotte fought off a grin, watching her eldest son as he stomped around on a tabletop nearby, singing the song of the cross-dresser, Tilly. "He reminds me a good deal of you at this age," she said. "You were so very lively, Daniel."

"I still am."

Liselotte laughed softly, patting his cheek. "Aye, you are," she said. "Forgive me, sweetheart."

Daniel turned to his wife, grinning. They sat there for some time in comfortable silence, enjoying their wine and enjoying the entertainment that the drunken knights provided. It was good to see such joy with men who faced life and death on a daily basis. Daniel was growing weary as the hour grew late, thinking on retiring, when the door to the hall suddenly lurched open, spilling forth a collection of knights.

Since all of the knights at Canterbury were already in the hall, the sight was a curious one. Still, it didn't take long to figure out who they were; Daniel and Liselotte turned to see three familiar faces entering the hall, bundled up against the cold May weather. Emerging from the shadowed doorway and into the light and warmth of the room, Gallus, Maximus, and Tiberius made their presence known.

"Gallus!" Daniel, surprised, called over to them as he rose to his feet. "Maximus! Welcome to my humble home!"

Gallus and Maximus headed in his direction but Tiberius, lured by the song and dance and drunken revelry, headed over to Chad and the others. Daniel hugged Gallus, and then Maximus, as the brothers sat heavily, with exhaustion, across the table from him.

"You did not tell us you were coming," Liselotte said. "I would have ordered a great feast prepared in your honor. As it is, we have venison and rabbit, for my sons went hunting today. It is plentiful but not elaborate."

Gallus, his face sporting a few days' growth of stubble, waved her off. "You are always the consummate hostess, Lady de Lohr," he said. "Your hospitality is well known. We will be quite happy with whatever you can provide."

Another loud voice joined in the chorus of Tilly Nodden and those at the table looked over to see Tiberius with a cup of wine in hand, already singing loudly with Chad and the other men. Daniel shook his head, snorting.

"Tiberius has that revelry streak in him," he said. "I am not sure who it comes from, but someone in the de Lohr bloodlines loved a good party. I have that streak, as does Chad, as does Tiberius. My wife was just commenting on how lively I used to be."

"You still are," Maximus said, accepting a cup from the nearest servant. "You are as lively as a man half your age."

Daniel dipped his head in gratitude. "You have my thanks," he said. He took a deep drink of his wine, smacking his lips. "So you have come to help celebrate the birth of Chad and Alessandria's daughter, have you? That is well and good. She is a fat, healthy baby and we are very blessed."

Gallus scratched his cheek as Maximus cast him a glance. Daniel and Liselotte should have suspected there was more behind their visit than simply to help celebrate, but neither one of them noticed that, between the de Shera brothers, there was something on their minds. Their expressions spoke volumes.

"Aye, you are," Gallus replied. "My best wishes and congratulations on the next generation of de Lohr offspring. She is healthy, you say?"

Liselotte was the one who answered. "Very healthy," she said proudly. "And big, too. She was a very big girl when born. It took poor Aless two days to bring her forth, but have no fear – Aless is well and so is the child. Some babies simply take longer than others to be born, 'tis all."

Gallus focused on the woman. "She was big, you say?"

"Aye, verily."

"Then she was not… born early?"

Liselotte shook her head. "Nay," she said. "She was right on time. Why do you ask?"

Gallus sighed heavily, looking at Maximus, before hanging his head and shaking it. Maximus eyed his brother a moment before replying. "Because Chad and Alessandria were only married in September," he said. "That would mean this child was conceived *before* they were married if, in fact, she was not born early, as you say. I will be truthful, my lady – we have come because it seems that Chad *had* to marry our cousin, if you get my meaning."

Liselotte's eyes widened and she looked at Daniel, who remained calm. Suddenly, the mood of the conversation took an odd and sobering turn. Daniel was not only surprised by it, but he was offended as well.

"I get your meaning," he said steadily, some of the joy out of his expression. "Do you not think that has crossed our minds, also? We can count, too."

Maximus didn't waver. "I realize that," he said quietly. "But we came to ask Chad the truth of the situation. It has occurred to us that Chad may have forced himself upon our cousin given that he was her escort, alone, for several days, and therefore behaved not as an escort should."

Daniel was becoming annoyed. "Are you serious?" he demanded. "You have not spent the past several months around them, Max. You have not seen how they adore each other, so even if Chad did something unseemly, as you say, it matters not now. They love one another and they have a beautiful child as a result. Did you wait until you were married to bed your wife?"

Gallus and Maximus nodded emphatically. "I can truthfully say that I did," Maximus said. "So did Gallus and Ty. We *all* did."

Daniel pursed his lips wryly. "Then you think you are a better man than my son, who may or may not have demonstrated his love for Aless before they were properly wed?" He shook his head reproachfully. "Mayhap you waited until you were married to bed your wife, but you, Maximus, have a bastard from another woman and we all know that Tiberius was no saint, either. Many women and their angry fathers will attest to that. And you have the gall to come to my home accusing my son of forcing himself upon a woman before he properly wed her? I am shocked to say the least."

Maximus backed down, ashamed, as he lowered his gaze, but Gallus spoke up. "We are not accusing him of anything, Daniel," he said quietly. "We simply want to know the truth."

Daniel was becoming angry. "Why?" he wanted to know. "Will it change how you feel about him? Will you punish him for touching her? How dare you come to my home acting as if neither you nor your brothers have sampled the flesh of a woman you were not married to. You were not virgins when you met your wives, any of you."

He was rightfully heated and Liselotte finally entered the conversation, putting her hand on her husband's, trying to calm him down. An irate Daniel was never a good thing.

"If what you say is true, then it really is of little matter," she said calmly. "He and Aless love each other a great deal. They always have. What has you so perturbed that you would ride all the way from Coventry to ask Chad such a personal question?"

Gallus was trying not to feel like a fool. He looked at Maximus, who simply lifted his big shoulders. It had been their intention on coming to Canterbury to champion their young cousin, but perhaps they were really being foolish, after all. Perhaps it really didn't matter in the grand scheme of things. Gallus kept looking a Maximus for support, who finally lifted his shoulders again, this time with irritation, and refused to say anything. He kept his gaze on his wine. Gallus sighed heavily.

"Because she is our family and we look at her as we do any other female member of the family," he said. "If a man did this to my daughter, I would kill him. If a man did this to *your* daughter, you would do the very same thing. Aless' brother is an idiot, her father cared nothing for her, so Max and Ty and I had appointed ourselves her protectors in a sense. Can you not understand, Daniel? Someone in the family should care for the girl and we have made it our business to do so."

Daniel understood, somewhat. His manner softened. "So you have appointed yourselves the defenders of her honor."

"Something like that."

Daniel's gaze lingered on Gallus for a moment, looking to Maximus who kept his gaze averted. He sighed. "That is noble, but unnecessary," he said. "Chad is her defender now. What are you going to do if he tells you that your concern is none of your affair? Will you demand satisfaction?"

Gallus was coming to feel even more foolish now. "I will not put myself between a husband and a wife, of course," he said, eyeing Lady de Lohr, who was still gazing at him anxiously. "I know Chad loves her and that she loves him. Hell, *I* love Chad. We all do. But an early baby… he took liberties that he should not have."

Daniel moved to pour Gallus more wine. He had cooled down a bit now that he understood their motives. "It happens," he said simply. "He married her. He did the right thing. Fortunately, he loves her. You should be satisfied with that."

As Gallus stewed on the situation, wondering if he'd made an arse out of himself with foolish concerns, Chad broke away from the group of singing and drinking knights and made his way over to the feasting table where his parents were sitting with Gallus and Maximus. The first thing he did was throw himself on Maximus' back where the man was sitting, bear-hugging his head and practically smothering him.

"I love you, Max," he said, drunkenly and exaggeratedly. "I love you dearly, my hairy friend. When are you going to shave your beard?"

Maximus was trying to pull himself out from underneath Chad's arms. "I will shave my beard when you cut your hair," he said, finally pushing Chad away. "Go embrace Gallus. He has been waiting for you to do so."

Chad happily focused on Gallus, who put up a hand just as Chad threw his arms around his head and shoulders. Gallus found himself blinded as Chad hugged his face.

"Gallus," Chad muttered, kissing the man loudly on the cheek. "Thank you for coming. I have a new daughter. She is beautiful. Have you seen her yet?"

Gallus wiped the slobbery kiss off his cheek. "I have not," he said, eyeing Daniel, who was shaking his head in resignation at Chad's drunken behavior. "I should like to congratulate you, Papa. I bring my wife's best wishes as well."

Chad grinned broadly. "I *am* a papa now," he said, looking to his father. "Do you hear? I am a papa just likc you."

Daniel fought off a grin. "Aye, just like me," he said. "Sit down before you fall down."

Chad pushed himself in between Gallus and Maximus, shoving the brothers apart. "She is a beautiful lass," he said. "She has red hair like her mother. I think she is going to look like my Aless. I have the most beautiful wife in all the land. Don't you agree?"

Gallus looked at Chad, finding it very difficult to be angry with the man. Chad was a man with a true and noble heart; he knew that. They all did. And if he bedded the woman he loved before he married her, was it really Gallus' concern? Of course it wasn't. But in his defense, Gallus' only concern had truly been for Alessandria. Knowing how his uncle and cousin had treated her, he felt compelled to stand up for her.

But it was a ridiculous stance. He knew that. Now that he sat with Chad and saw the man's joy, he knew it was ridiculous. He, therefore, sighed heavily to Chad's question and lifted his cup.

"She is a de Shera," he said, forcing a smile. "Of course she is beautiful. And I am pleased that she has found the love of her life in you. I could ask for nothing more."

Chad was back to kissing him again and Gallus fended him off. "She is my heart and soul," Chad said, putting his hand over his chest as Gallus stood up and went around the other side of the table to sit next to Daniel. "My Aless… she is the most wonderful woman in the world. I was so fortunate to have found her. Thank God for Henry's terrible determination to hold her hostage. I would have never met her had I not been told to go to Newington Priory. It was destiny!"

"Aye, it was destiny," Gallus agreed from across the table. "Had it not been for you, Henry surely would have taken her. She would have found herself married to someone else, more than likely."

That brought Chad's ire. "I would have found her and killed the man!"

"How would you have known?"

That brought Chad to a halt. He cocked his head, trying to reason through his alcohol-hazed mind. "You have a point, dear Gallus," he said. "I would have never known. I would have been forced to marry someone else and my beautiful daughter would not have been born. It would have been tragic."

Maximus, still sitting next to Chad, put his hand on the man's shoulder. "You needn't fear," he said. "You found her and she is yours."

Chad nodded, stealing Maximus' cup and taking a long drink from it. "She is mine," he declared. "She has been mine since the beginning. Since the moment I took her from Newington, she was mine. I knew she was mine the moment I saw her sitting in the tub in the knight quarters, trying to keep that silk dress over her body to protect her modesty. She was hiding all of that beauty from me."

Gallus and Maximus looked at him in shock. Daniel, given what they had only recently discussed, could see what they were thinking. He put out a hand to catch their attention.

"It is not as he makes it sound," he said, his voice low. "Henry's men were in the keep so I had Chad take her to the knight quarters to hide her from the Six. Unfortunately, there was a fire whilst Aless was taking a bath and Chad and the other knights were forced to put it out. She was caught in a less than desirable position but my wife was there the entire time. Nothing unseemly happened. It was simply… unfortunate."

Gallus and Maximus understood somewhat but Chad was smacking his hands on the table. "Nothing unseemly happened," he repeated his father's words rather exaggeratedly. "But she was mine even back then. I knew it. We fled to Lady du Bexley's home and I told Lady du Bexley that she was my wife. I did not want Lady du Bexley to think ill of my Aless."

Gallus was looking at him from across the table, his gaze intense. "If you told Lady du Bexley that Aless was your wife, then I am assuming the two of you shared a room."

Chad nodded before he even had time to think about the implications of his answer. "It was that night that I realized I loved my Aless," he said sweetly, putting his hand over his heart. "I loved her then and my love for her has only grown. Are all men so fortunate, Gallus?"

Chad didn't realize that, around him, his father and Gallus and Maximus were adding up the situation, coming to suspect what may have happened at Lady du Bexley's manor. The timing on the birth of the child was perfect and Daniel cast a long look at Gallus, wondering how the man was going to react. His answer wasn't long in coming.

"Not all men," Gallus said. He decided to simply come to the point because Chad's tantalizing hints were making him mad. He'd come all the way from Coventry to discover the truth, even if the truth really didn't matter at this point. "Since you shared a room with my cousin, can I assume that you behaved properly, Chad?"

Chad looked at him. He may have been drunk but he wasn't a complete fool, at least not yet. Through the veil of drunkenness, it now began to occur to him what Gallus was asking and it further occurred to him that his parents were listening, too. It was a very personal answer Gallus was seeking but one that, Chad suspected, he already knew the answer to.

There was no use in denying it.

Chad and Alessandria had figured out fairly late in her pregnancy that the child had been conceived on that momentous night at Lady du Bexley's manor. The baby grew big, very fast, and even the midwife had commented on it. But it didn't occur to Chad that others might wonder about the timing of the baby as well. After all, his beautiful baby girl was born less than nine months after their marriage. Therefore, he supposed there was no use in denying the obvious. Men could count the months, after all.

"I behaved like a man in love," he finally said. "And Aless behaved like a woman in love. She loved me, then, too. Draw your own conclusions, Gallus, but whatever you think, and whatever outrage you may feel, know that my daughter was conceived in love. Not many children can make that claim. Not many parents can, either."

With that, he stood up and staggered back over to the drinking, singing knights, leaving a subdued table in his wake. Daniel, knowing that Gallus and Maximus had their answer regarding the child conceived before marriage, looked to the brothers.

"Well?" he said. "He did not lie to you. He was honest. Are you satisfied?"

Maximus looked at Gallus; it all depended on him. Gallus was the one with the strong will, the powerful sense of right and wrong, at times, sometimes ridiculously so. Certainly, Maximus had his own opinions and if he really disagreed with Gallus, the man would listen to him. Most of the time, he agreed with him. But in this case, Maximus would defer to Gallus. He had seemed to be the one, from the beginning, most willing to take up the defense of Alessandria. As the Earl of Coventry, that was his duty as well as his right.

But Gallus was looking at Daniel, not oblivious to Maximus' gaze. His expression was one of resignation, of acceptance.

"He loves her," he said. "If anyone understands that, I do. Love is the most powerful force of all, over kings and loyalties and even escort duties. You can read his love for the woman all over his face. Everything about him screams it. Aye, I am satisfied, Daniel. I apologize for ever questioning him."

The men were friends again and Daniel put his arm around Gallus, hugging him, as he went to pour them all more wine. All was well in their world, now with a new generation of de Lohr having been born. Liselotte, having watched the entire exchange, was full of relief and joy for her son as well as for her husband and the de Shera brothers. She knew that their motives had been true. Alessandria was very fortunate to have so many noble men to watch out for her.

More than that, she had a fiercely protective mother-in-law. As Daniel and Gallus and Maximus drank to baby Katrine's health, Liselotte caught a flash of something she'd not seen in some time.

Bare buttocks were flashing again.

As fast as lightning, Liselotte leapt up from her seat and swiftly made her way over to the collection of knights where Chad was exposing his bare buttocks for all to see. She happened to pass by the hearth as she went and, quickly, snatched a fire poker that was leaning against the stone. With the iron rod in hand, she made her way over to the men who were now singing another bawdy tavern song about an old whore named Rose. Chad still had his breeches down but at the sight of his mother's approach, the breeches quickly came up.

Still, that didn't stop Liselotte. She pushed through the group of singing, happy men, rod in hand, and Chad bolted away from the woman, begging her to spare the rod. But Liselotte didn't listen; she chased him all around the room and out into the ward, where Chad finally made a break for the keep where his wife and daughter were lodged. It seemed like the safest place for him to go. Once Liselotte saw him head into the keep, she lowered the rod and headed back into the hall. But she couldn't hide the grin on her face.

When Alessandria heard, from her husband's own lips, what had driven him out of the hall and back into her waiting arms, she laughed until she cried.

And so did Chad.

☙ THE END ❧

The de Lohr Dynasty:

While Angels Slept (Lords of East Anglia)

Rise of the Defender

Steelheart

Spectre of the Sword

Archangel

Unending Love

Shadowmoor

Silversword

About Kathryn Le Veque

Medieval Just Got Real.

KATHRYN LE VEQUE is a USA TODAY Bestselling author, an Amazon All-Star author, and a #1 bestselling, award-winning, multi-published author in Medieval Historical Romance and Historical Fiction. She has been featured in the NEW YORK TIMES and on USA TODAY's HEA blog. In March 2015, Kathryn was the featured cover story for the March issue of InD'Tale Magazine, the premier Indie author magazine. She was also a quadruple nominee (a record!) for the prestigious RONE awards for 2015.

Kathryn's Medieval Romance novels have been called 'detailed', 'highly romantic', and 'character-rich'. She crafts great adventures of love, battles, passion, and romance in the High Middle Ages. More than that, she writes for both women AND men – an unusual crossover for a romance author – and Kathryn has many male readers who enjoy her stories because of the male perspective, the action, and the adventure.

On October 29, 2015, Amazon launched Kathryn's Kindle Worlds Fan Fiction site WORLD OF DE WOLFE PACK. Please visit Kindle Worlds for Kathryn Le Veque's World of de Wolfe Pack and find many action-packed adventures written by some of the top authors in their genre using Kathryn's characters from the de Wolfe Pack series. As Kindle World's FIRST Historical Romance fan fiction world, Kathryn Le Veque's World of de Wolfe Pack will contain all of the great story-telling you have come to expect.

Kathryn loves to hear from her readers. Please find Kathryn on Facebook at Kathryn Le Veque, Author, or join her on Twitter @kathrynleveque, and don't forget to visit her website at www.kathrynleveque.com.

Made in the USA
Las Vegas, NV
19 November 2020

11148910R00157